Praise for *The Bookshop of Secrets*

"Book love, buried treasure, and a family mystery combine in a story of redemption, faith, friendship, and new beginnings. Where old pain once separated a wounded young woman from all she had hoped for, seeds fall like summer rain and broken places become the growing ground for new love in Mollie Rushmeyer's warmhearted and bookish literary debut."

—Lisa Wingate, #1 *New York Times* bestselling author of *Before We Were Yours*

"Rich with believable, dimensional characters, an appealing setting, action, romance, and even delicious literary references."

—Julie Klassen, bestselling author

"*The Bookshop of Secrets* has it all—mystery, history, romance, and more than a little literary magic."

—Laura Frantz, Christy Award–winning author of *A Heart Adrift*

"Rushmeyer has created complex, layered characters who tug at the heartstrings. Readers will be rooting for Hope as she overcomes her horrific past and learns to trust again with the help of faith, a caring new community and the love of a good man. A tender, emotional story."

—Lee Tobin McClain, bestselling author

"*The Bookshop of Secrets* will charm the hearts of bibliophiles and romantics alike. A story of light shining in dark places, of healing, and of the complex nature of relationships, the reader will delight in unraveling both the secrets of the town and the secrets of the protagonists."

—Erica Vetsch, author of the Serendipity & Secrets series

The BOOKSHOP of SECRETS

MOLLIE RUSHMEYER

LOVE INSPIRED

Stories to uplift and inspire

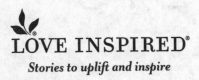

LOVE INSPIRED®

Stories to uplift and inspire

Recycling programs
for this product may
not exist in your area.

ISBN-13: 978-1-335-42621-5

The Bookshop of Secrets

Love Inspired
22 Adelaide St. West, 41st Floor
Toronto, Ontario M5H 4E3, Canada
www.LoveInspired.com

Printed in U.S.A.

For my grandpa, Chuck McMurray, for sharing your soul-deep love of stories and showing me the magic living within each page. Until we meet again.

Acknowledgments

This is, without a doubt, the most difficult thing I've ever written.
How does one sum up a lifelong dream and an ocean of prayers, tears and joy?
And thereafter acknowledge all of the many hands
who have touched it and blessed it on its way to fulfillment?

Because this book was dead and buried (or so I thought), I give the first glory to the One who's in the business of resurrection and redemption. Thank You, Father, for holding my dreams in Your capable hands and never giving up on me. I'm so grateful. Thank you to my grandparents, Chuck and Alice McMurray, for praying over me and encouraging me throughout my life and in the pursuit of publication. To my mom, for believing in me, for your unceasing support and love, and for never laughing at these big impossible dreams of mine. I could honestly say the same about my aunt, Denise Westerberg. Thank you for the power of your prayers, the use of Westerberg Inn (the best little B and B around) so I could attend jam-packed writers' conference weekends, and for your listening ear and open heart.

My husband, Mark Rushmeyer, deserves a huge shout-out for putting up with all of my quirky writerly habits—not the least of which is picking apart every movie for its plot holes and character arcs. But also for his support and bravely caring for our two children on his own at times while I immerse myself in made-up worlds, attend writing meetings/conferences and brainstorm with like-minded souls. For my daughters, may this remind you both dreams are worth fighting for. I love you all.

Thank you, Michelle Aleckson, for being the most caring, encouraging friend in the writing world and in life I could've ever asked for. I didn't know I needed a friend like you until God placed you right in my path at our local ACFW meeting. I couldn't do this without you! Speaking of which, I must acknowledge our amazing ACFW Minnesota N.I.C.E. writing group—thank you all. The hope, help and inspiration you give to writers are immeasurable.

To the Love Inspired Trade team and, specifically, Emily Rodmell, thank you for taking a chance on this story I love so much and on me. Last but certainly not least (you may interpret the saying "save the best for last" however you wish), thank you to my incredible literary agent, Cynthia Ruchti. How can I say thank you enough to the person who is so much more than someone who represents me in the publishing world? Friend. Confidante. Prayer warrior. Shrewd businesswoman. Whatever you call the person who talks you down off the literary cliff on occasion. These descriptions don't do you justice. Love you and thank you! Your belief in me means more than you will ever know.

Strength and honour are her clothing;
and she shall rejoice in time to come.
—*Proverbs* 31:25

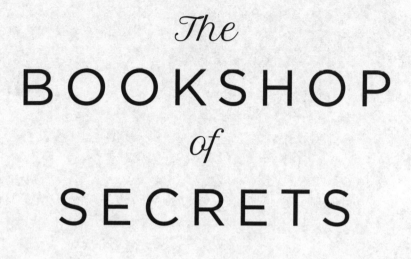

The
BOOKSHOP
of
SECRETS

Chapter One

Only the sharp clang of a bell above the door and lopsided towers of books greeted Hope Sparrow as she entered Dusty Jackets bookshop.

She breathed in their ancient paper dust, their gentle decay. Between pages like these, she'd always found her refuge.

Her Lucy Maud, Jane, the sisters Brontë, dear Louisa—all whispered the words she'd pored over in the dead of night and now fortified her strength for what she hoped was the last leg in a long journey.

"Hello? Anyone here?" She strode to the empty wooden sales counter, blew out a slow, steadying breath and set her tattered cloth suitcase containing all of her worldly possessions at her feet. The coach bus that had dropped her a block from the shop rumbled away in the distance.

If this worked out the way she'd planned, she'd retrieve what she'd come for, find a place to stay for the night and catch the next bus back to Chicago. So close to fulfilling her dreams now.

In a rounded alcove, a silky black cat snoozed atop a pre-carious sun-drenched stack of tomes. Nothing stirred in the transformed Victorian home, where every available space held piles of books resembling mini–Leaning Towers of Pisa.

Her nose wrinkled. This was no joyful celebration of liter-ature. This was where books came to die. A book graveyard.

"Austenite." A voice creaked in the still air like a window groaning open after winter.

She whirled around. How had she not noticed the small round room to her left, a long-ago sitting room, perhaps? A tuft of white hair bobbed between the book pillars.

She moved closer. "Excuse me?"

"I said, Austenite." A small elderly man, all eyebrows and shining forehead with a lone patch of hair on top, popped out from behind a pile of now-obsolete—or so many assumed—encyclopedias. "I'd know one anywhere. It's the buttoned-up self-satisfaction." His wink rang more jovial than his words.

She put a hand to the tidy bun at the nape of her neck, and her lips tugged at the corners. "Guilty. Though I prefer the melancholy beauty of Charlotte Brontë's moors or Lucy Montgomery's charming Prince Edward Island." She clutched a hand over her heart. "But give me a book aged to perfec-tion in one hand, a cup of hot oolong tea in the other, and I'll be there till the sun turns cold. A bit like C. S. Lewis that way, I guess."

A tingle of heat swept across her cheeks. This is what she got for living and traveling alone for three years. Spouting weird things at strangers. She needed to quickly adopt people skills for her plan to work. Or at least learn how not to act awkward around them. The thought twisted her gut. How could she gain expertise in something never in her wheelhouse, even if the opportunity to hone her social etiquette hadn't been sto-len from her for ten years?

But the older man beamed and stuck out his hand. She shook it, trying to hide the anxiety human touch brought on. "I couldn't agree more. I'm Ulysses Barrick. I co-own Dusty Jackets with my wife, Margaret. Welcome to Wanishin Falls. I hope Lake Superior and her steely gray wiles are treating you well. And, love, you are…?"

She cringed at the word *love*, not only for the meaning—so foreign a concept—but for the memories threatening to bring her under their churning undertow. "I'm…"

Ulysses poked a finger into the air. "Fear not: for I have redeemed thee, I have called thee by thy name; thou art mine. When thou passest through the waters, I will be with thee; and through the rivers, they shall not overflow thee: when thou walkest through the fire, thou shalt not be burned; neither shall the flame kindle upon thee."

The words "thou art mine" clenched her stomach in a tight fist while the rest pulled at a little-used place in her chest.

"That's lovely. Paul Laurence Dunbar?"

"Isaiah. Old Testament. Beauty and truth, I think." He dipped his chin in a precise nod.

She couldn't help but smile at this eccentric, seemingly kindred spirit.

"I'm Hope Sparrow. I've been trying to call, Mr. Barrick. I understand you're—were—the brother of Agatha O'Brien. She was a good friend of mine, and I think she sent some very special books for you to hang on to until I was able to collect them."

"Oh?"

She squeezed her nails into her palms. "She spoke so highly of you and your love of books. She said you loved them as much as she did. And being a librarian herself, that says a lot…" She was rambling again. "Anyway, I hadn't seen her for a long time. When I arrived at the library where she worked to tell her I had come for my books, she'd already passed. And the books were gone. They weren't with her personal collection. I checked."

"That's unfortunate." His tone bright but not uncaring.

"She told me that if anything happened to her, I should contact you. It wasn't in the context of my books, directly, but I have nowhere else to look."

His eyes, unfocused, gazed over her shoulder but seemed to travel farther than the wall-to-wall bookcases behind her. "Oh, yes, Aggie. She'll be along any moment now. She's to take me to my piano lessons. We always stop at the library afterward if I sit nicely for my scales."

"Mr. Barrick? Are you all right?"

With generous brows gathering behind silver-framed glasses, Ulysses brought his eyes back to rest on her face as if just noticing her for the first time.

The bell above the door clanged, making Hope jump. She'd meant to keep her exits in her line of sight.

In breezed a compact woman with a silver bob and a sharp chin. She stopped short, eyes appraising Ulysses, then Hope. "How is he today?" She beelined to Ulysses, placing a light hand to his shoulder. "I had errands to run. He insisted on covering the shop alone. But we can't keep doing this."

The woman spoke as if she knew Hope, but only one person, her one friend in the world, Dee, knew her or her real name. And it was best kept that way.

Hope shifted from one foot to the other. "Well, I was talking to Mr. Barrick about some books I'm looking for. I believe his sister may have sent them. She was a good friend of mine. I'm not sure, but he seems to think Agatha is still alive."

On cue, Ulysses wandered away. "Aggie, we'd better put supper on. Mama will be home soon. Make sure her book and reading glasses are by her chair." His voice trailed behind him as he disappeared to the back of the house.

A soft, somber expression changed the sharp lines of the woman's face. She sniffed, turned back to Hope and extended a hand.

So much physical contact in one day. It made Hope's stomach squirm like a bowl of worms, but she shook the woman's small but strong hand.

"I'm Margaret Barrick. Everyone calls me Mags. Ulysses is my husband." She hung her head. "He was diagnosed with dementia not long ago, as you may have gathered."

Hope had no clue what to say to that, especially to a perfect stranger. She chose, "I'm Hope Sparrow, and I'm so sorry to hear that."

Judging from the small smile from Mags, this was a good choice. "Thank you. I really can't leave him alone anymore. It's just hard. We own a small greenhouse farm to help supplement our income. And this place—" she gestured to the shop "—well, this has always been Ulysses's dream. I'm losing him a little bit each day, and I'm not sure how to keep both places going. It has become a literary jungle in here." Mags let out a mirthless laugh.

Again, lost for words. "Mmm-hmm." She infused as much empathy into the sound as she could and hoped she didn't come off as dismissive.

"Tell me about the books you're looking for. Would Aggie have sent them here all at once?"

"Yes, I think so. There was a copy of *Anne of Green Gables*, the first volume of *Little Women*, and the three-volume set of *Jane Eyre*. All first editions. All with inscriptions." Saying the names brought back the bittersweet memories—her mom, her gentle voice, the way she smelled of lavender when Hope curled into her lap and listened to her read.

Mags's lips pursed. "You know, that does sound familiar, but I'm afraid Ulysses was more into the day-to-day goings-on around here than me. And I don't think he's going to be able to help you." Her words weighed heavy. Sadness?

This couldn't be happening. She'd searched for too long, had scraped together what money she could to travel to Minnesota and move on to her dream of opening a combination food truck and bookshop. Hope bit the inside of her lip, blinking back the prickle of impending tears. "Would you mind if I looked around? I've come a long way to get my books back."

"Of course." Mags stepped past a chalkboard Help Wanted sign on the sales counter, gesturing to the back of the shop. "But you must be exhausted and ready for a warm-up. We're having a chilly late April. Let me fix you something."

Hope held up a hand, already shaking her head, but Mags beckoned her forward. "It's the least I can do. You've come all this way from...?"

Swallowing hard, Hope finally said, "Illinois."

"Right, where Agatha lived."

Mags bustled through what Hope guessed used to be a dining room, now filled to the ceiling with books, and then a large swinging door, into a U-shaped kitchen with an eat-in dining nook in the corner. Light and bright with windows on three sides. Views to one side showed the shops and charming little houses along the main street of Wanishin Falls and to the other, the great lake, down the hill behind Dusty Jackets.

"Do you like oolong tea?" Mags, on tiptoe, stuck her nose into the cupboard.

Hope couldn't suppress the ironic laugh. "Yes. I do." She laid her suitcase and old wool coat on the long window alcove seat in the eating nook.

"Thatta girl. We'll get along just fine, won't we?" Winking, the smaller woman busied herself with preparing the modern electric teakettle and two very antique-looking china teacups with delicate roses and silver rims.

"So, you and Aggie, God rest her soul, were from the same place—near Chicago?"

"I was. I've been…bouncing around a little. Haven't taken root anywhere."

"Searching?" A thin eyebrow rose.

Hope's fingernails bit into her palm. This was what she didn't want. People knowing too much. "Yes. Constantly searching, never really landing, I guess."

"Those books must mean a lot to you. To come all this way." Mags's eyes seemed to study Hope's over the hot water she poured into the cups.

Backing into one of the seats that offered the best escape route at the rectangle farmhouse table, Hope took in a slow breath, not sure how to answer. "Yes, the books mean just about everything to me. There's no plan B. I need to find them."

Swallowing what felt like a jagged stone, she added, "They belonged to my mother. She left them to me. Well, she left them in Aggie's care until I was old enough. Now, I'd like to find them and be on my way." *The sooner the better.*

Mags handed her a cup. Hope took a gulp, letting the sweet and bitter wash over her tongue, carrying with it all the words she could not say.

Mags's angular features warmed as she brought a tray of accompaniments and a teapot to the table. "Well, if you entrusted them to Aggie, I'm sure she sent them here. The question is where are they now? I'm sorry I don't have an immediate answer for you."

Shuffled footsteps creaked the old wooden floor. The kitchen door swung open, and Ulysses stumbled in. From where Hope had no idea. The sound met her ears before her eyes registered it, a book lover's worst nightmare, the harsh rip of Ulysses tearing pages away from a book's binding. His hair had grown wild, as had his eyes.

Mags gasped, hand over her mouth. Tears already pooling on her lashes. Frozen.

He muttered as he strode into the room, oblivious to their presence. "This is all wrong. I must get to the end. I must get to the end! This isn't right!" Faster and faster he tore the pages.

Something so sharp, so keen, it took her by surprise—concern for this man—clawed around Hope's chest. She stood and took slow steps toward Ulysses.

"Mr. Barrick? May I get you some tea?" She placed a light hand to his arm, which stopped tearing. He looked up from the book, but his gaze held no recognition for her.

"Who are you? What are you doing…here?" His forehead wrinkled as though he fished for the word *kitchen*.

"I'm Hope Sparrow. I was friends with your sister, Aggie. I came to look for some books she sent here."

A spark lit up his face. "I get it. Hope Sparrow. Like the poem, 'Hope is the thing with feathers that perches in the soul, and sings the tune without the words, and never stops at all…'"

How could he know, this man losing himself? Yet, it had been her wishful thinking that had chosen the name Hope Sparrow for herself three years ago after reading the Emily Dickinson poem. She wanted more than believed hope could still exist for people like her.

Hope cleared her throat. "That's right, Ulysses. Like the poem. Now, why don't we set this book down? That's not a very good one anyway. I'll get you some tea." With gentle movements, she removed the book from his frail hands and guided him to a seat.

Mags wiped her eyes, mouthing, "Thank you."

When the awkward silence morphed into pleasant enough

conversation about the shop and Wanishin Falls, with Ulysses popping in and out with varying degrees of cognizance, the air in the kitchen seemed to lighten.

Hope traced the rim of her teacup with her thumb. "So, do you mind if I look around for the books? I'll try to stay out of your way."

"I don't mind at all. It's just…" Mags gestured toward the kitchen door that led to the shop front. "I truly have no idea if we have your books or where they would be. It may take considerable time to find them. The question is, how much time do you have to devote to searching?"

Her bottom lip tucked in as she considered the question and the implication that her "quick enter, quick exit" strategy had crumbled before her eyes.

"A couple weeks? Maybe a little longer. I don't know. I'm trying to work toward opening a food truck and I had hoped to secure what I need in the next couple of months so that when it cools down here in the north, I can make my way south this fall. But I *did* plan to have my mother's books before I moved on."

"You have anywhere to stay?" Mags lifted a brow.

A simple question, but it cornered Hope. Maybe she didn't have this plan so airtight after all. "Uh, no. I guess I thought I'd find my books right away and head to a cheap motel for the night."

The thought of a dingy motel sent a chill racing down her spine. Too many memories. Hope bit the inside of her cheek, willing them away.

"If you don't find the books in the next day or two, would you consider staying?"

Hope's forehead pinched. "What do you mean?"

Suddenly, a grin pushed Mags's rosy cheeks toward her eyes. Teeth too perfect to not be dentures gleamed at Hope. "Well, now that you're here, is there any chance you'd agree to work for me and help straighten out this overrun book disaster and keep an eye on Ulysses while you hunt for your books?"

Hope skidded her chair back, almost toppling it in her hurry to bring her cup to the sink. "I... I don't know."

"It may not take long. Who knows? Maybe you'll find them right away." Mags's shoulder lifted, though the prospect seemed to sag her features.

Panic wrung Hope's throat, making it hard to breathe. She leaned on the counter for support. This was the last thing she wanted. To stop. To be confined. And yet, she had always known, in order to move forward with her dream of a mobile café-bookstore, she needed to go back. To find her mother's books. To find herself. She also needed more of that pesky little thing called money.

When Hope made a slow return to the table, Mags chuckled. "You look like I asked you to sign your life away, young lady. It's not imprisonment. I assure you, we're not hard to work with."

The word *imprisonment* reverberated in her mind, echoing in the empty caverns of her heart.

Mags must've noticed her words had the opposite effect than she'd intended. She stood, taking in Hope's shabby suitcase and her fraying wool coat.

"Listen, you're welcome to just look around if you want. But you might as well do a little tidying up and get paid for it while you're at it, right? If you do decide to work for me though, I would love it if you'd commit to a couple of months of employment, regardless if you find your books. We could really use the help and that still gives you time to get going south before cold weather sets in here."

A couple of months? Could she do that? Stop moving so

long? To stay still was to allow the memories of her past and the monster-filled nightmares to catch up with her.

Studying her scuffed black boots, Hope clutched her hands together. "Why would you trust me? You don't even know me."

Mags shrugged. "If you were a friend of Aggie's, then I know you're all right. Plus, I've always had a nose for a good soul. And I could tell the minute I met you."

Little did Mags know how wrong she was. A stained, broken soul. A wandering soul. But not a good soul.

Despite Hope's reservations, Mags had a point. Hope needed to make money for her dream fund and look for her books. She might as well do both at once.

Hope found herself extending her hand—three times in one day.

The words "Okay, I'll do it. I'll work for you while I look for my books. Two months. I can promise no more though," spilled from her mouth before she could change her mind.

Chapter Two

Jane Austen once wrote, "Know your own happiness. You want nothing but patience—or give it a more fascinating name, call it hope."

For her, the books, the very pages her mother touched, told her own story and she'd anxiously awaited the day she would hold them in her hands. Her patience may've been lacking. But the hope—of finding them and the joy that would follow—she clung to.

She sighed and pushed herself up from the window seat under one of the tall upstairs windows at Dusty Jackets, giving Fitzwilliam, the cat from downstairs, one last scratch under the chin. The lazy black-and-white cat was a permanent fixture of the store, Mags said, and a favorite among the children who visited. She loved the nod to Jane Austen with his name and guessed Ulysses must've chosen it.

Mags told her a room came with the job the day before. Hope couldn't tell if the older woman had made up that detail because she felt sorry for her after Hope's confession she hadn't booked lodging. Of course, she hadn't thought she'd be staying longer than a night, let alone two months. But either way, the little powerhouse of a woman convinced Hope to take a look. Once Hope saw the well-preserved, round, turreted room with soft feminine decor and a four-poster bed with the fluffiest down comforter she'd ever seen, she accepted.

She hadn't bothered unpacking her belongings though. Most of them were books anyway.

Weak early-morning sun turned the great expanse of Lake Superior from dull gray to liquid silver. Slivers of light filtered through the gossamer curtains. It turned the steep, lifeless cliffs edging the water into rich russet laced with white, like an intricate veil. The spring snow still dusted the trees and rocks, turning the scene into something she imagined as she'd read C. S. Lewis's *The Lion, the Witch and the Wardrobe*.

"This is only temporary. Not forever." Her whisper made Fitzwilliam blink one eye at her before settling into a purring snore once again.

As she stood in the middle of the room, the beauty of Wanishin Falls seeping through the windows—the place her mom was born—her mom's words seemed to nudge against Hope's heart. She dug the letter her mom had left her out of her fabric suitcase. She'd found the precious words of her mother at the library in Chicago in her and Aggie's special hiding spot.

Aggie, a sweet friend to her mom and then to Hope, in her mother's absence. The library where Aggie worked had become the solace she'd needed over the years. The one place she could escape to when the rest of her life, filled with one foster home after another, was like shifting sands beneath her feet. Until she'd tried to find acceptance and love somewhere she shouldn't have…

The worn paper of her mom's letter brushed her fingertips feather soft as she opened it for the millionth time. The faded stationery, a picture of a lady's slipper flower with a circle around it—the Minnesota state flower—and her mother's feminine, looping handwriting greeted her like an old friend.

My Dearest Emily,
As I sit and write this, I'm watching seven-year-old you sleep. And I'm overcome with a grateful but grieving heart. I've prayed so hard that I might stay a little longer, to see you grow. I want more than anything to see your still-baby curls and soft round cheeks mature into the beautiful and intelligent woman I know you'll become. I guess that sums it up. I want more. More time. More memories with you. God has chosen otherwise. I don't understand why. But I will face this with trust in my heart as I hope you will.

In this moment, I am thankful. So very thankful He made me your mama, no matter how short a time. I read once that when a mother carries a child, she is changed forever, down to the very cells in her body. Each will carry the DNA of the other all their days. You will always be a part of me, just as I will always be a part of you. I hope you see me in your smile. That you'll feel my love wrap around you when life gets rough. I pray you will put your faith in your Heavenly Father Who loves you so well. You were His precious child long before you were mine.

I'm entrusting this letter and these books to Aggie. She will give them to you when you're old enough to know what to do with them. Our history lies in Wanishin Falls, Minnesota. I want you to learn about who we are as a family. Find us. Find yourself. Take back what is rightfully yours. There is something so much more valuable in these books than words.
Forever and always my love goes with you,
Mom

Her mom had included a list of the books her daughter was to find with the cryptic last words, "The family stories aren't just fables."

Family stories. Fables.

Memories kept prodding the back of her mind. Her mom, after reading to her, would often rock her and talk about their family. She could still hear her mother's sweet voice say, "It's our family treasure, my love. Our legacy. Someday, it'll be yours. All that you will ever need to be free, to answer to no one."

Freedom. It beckoned her.

To a child's mind, the treasure had been a fairy tale. Like gold at the end of a rainbow. As a young girl, she conjured images of lost family heirlooms and becoming like one of the strong heroines she read of in her beloved books. She'd been eager to create a fantasy for herself, knowing she'd soon lose her mom to ovarian cancer, leaving her an orphan.

As she grew up, all thoughts of family treasure went to the wayside against the stark, grisly nature of her reality. But after reading her mom's letter a couple of months ago, the seed was planted and sprouted—the treasure might be real. After all, her mom wouldn't have lied to her.

The question was, where was it? The books must be the key. Wherever they were.

Her prepaid phone chirped from the pocket of the shoulder bag she used as a purse.

She fished out the phone. "Hello?"

"Oh, honey, are you okay? I've been worried about you." A familiar tone, worried with a hint of sass, greeted Hope. "I thought you were going to call when you got to Minnesota. You're traveling all over, Lord knows where. Would it kill you to let me know you're alive once in a while?"

Hope could almost see the scowl on the large woman's face, her hand on her hip.

She sucked air through her teeth. "Hi, Dee. I'm sorry. It was a long trip. I—"

"Yeah, I know, missy. You thought maybe I'd stop checking in. Stop caring. But I won't. On both counts."

Hope crossed to the window again, biting down on her lip. "No, it's not that. Really."

Dee Edmundson had been a mentor to her in one of the darkest times of her life. In complete honesty, even with the outspoken Chicago native's persistent kindness, Hope struggled to stay in contact. Stay connected.

"Well, girl, I'm here for you, all right?"

"Yeah, I know." Her own words warmed.

"So, did you finally track down those books of your mom's? What about the food truck plan? How's that coming? I always told you, you'd give Gordon Ramsay a run for his money."

Dee had imbued her with a love of cooking.

Hope laughed. "And I always told *you* that you should have your own restaurant or teach in one of those fancy culinary schools like you taught me."

It had always been easier to talk to Dee than anyone else. Well, except Aggie. Hope filled Dee in on Dusty Jackets and accepting the job for an opportunity to look through a houseful of volumes in search of her books.

"That does sound like it fell right into place, almost like there was a divine hand moving the parts together." Dee paused, let that hang in silence across the miles between them. "You know, my offer still stands to help you get that business up and running."

She squeezed her fingernails into her palms, a habit she'd need to break one of these days. "I told you, I can't accept that. I have to do this on my own." The words she wouldn't say remained unspoken: *I won't owe anyone anything. I won't be tied down, beholden to anyone again. Even you.*

"I know, I know." Dee tsked. "I keep hoping you'll change your mind. What is a childless widow going to do with her late husband's life insurance money? I don't need much. I still work over at the women's shelter several days a week. It's enough for me."

The shelter—a place for lost souls, broken bodies, shattered hearts as well as dreams to seek refuge and healing after a life of imprisonment and violation at the hands of vile captors and their patrons. The place she'd needed more than she cared to admit five years ago. She'd still been damaged when she decided to leave the safety of the shelter three years ago, change her name for a fresh start, and set out on her own after two years at the shelter.

"Dee?" Her voice came out more strangled than she intended. "I've got to go. New job. First day and all."

The shop didn't open for another hour, and she had already dressed a half hour ago. But, as usual, she kept things on a need-to-know basis.

"I'll be praying for you, Hope. And, honey...?"

"Hmm?" Hope tapped her fingers along her arm, suddenly anxious to get off the phone.

"It's okay to trust again. Don't be afraid to let them in, to see you, all right? We're not meant to live in the shadows, unseen. Everybody needs to know and be known by others."

Her stomach twisted, lungs burning as she held her breath. She would not cry. She would not show what those words, those living, breathing words, did to her insides. Instead, she cleared her throat. "That's why I have you though, right?"

Dee's tone wobbled as she bade Hope farewell, making her promise to do her best at opening up.

Although she agreed to appease her only friend in the world, the ironclad protective wall around her heart held steady. She needed to focus on her two goals, her books and her mobile café. There simply wasn't room for more than the present search in her life, even if she could find a way to trust other people.

And finding the books might be the answer to starting the food truck too. If, that is, they held something of great value like her mom promised. But what form would it take and what value?

She placed her phone back in her bag and stopped for one more check in the mirror above the pedestal sink in her room. The face staring back at her reflected every bit the years, hardships and grief she'd experienced.

A scar along her jaw marred her olive skin. And though her face still had a youthful smoothness, something haunted lived behind her eyes. She made sure to pull up her shirt collar to hide the marks as she silently thanked God for the cold Minnesota early-spring weather so she didn't need to explain her constant long sleeves. Of course, that was as far as her conversations ever progressed with God lately. How could she talk to Someone she didn't trust?

A dark lock of hair had come loose, so she rebraided and twisted it into its usual tight bun, then dipped her chin at her reflection.

She made sure to lock her room with the skeleton key Mags had given her. Fitzwilliam followed on her heels as she wound her way down the large curved staircase and landed at the edge of the bygone sitting room she'd glimpsed the day before.

A hushed reverence lived in the silent room. The kind that made her heart flutter and expand. Wall-to-wall, floor-to-ceiling bookshelves overflowed with books. Even the floating dust motes, caught by rays streaming through the windows, glowed like fairy dust. She inhaled deeply the scent she loved so well and took back her book graveyard assessment from yesterday. This was magic. Disorganized magic, but magic nonetheless.

Creaks and shuffles floated from the back of the house. She followed the sound and stepped into the kitchen.

The fridge door slammed shut and Ulysses popped up from behind it. Hope jumped.

His smile widened, his eyes focused today. "Hello again, lovely Hope."

She waved. Good, he knew who she was. She'd dreaded having to explain why a stranger was in his house.

"Mags is popping over to the general store for farm supplies. She'll be back in a bit. She told me you took the job, and we're on the hunt for your books."

"Yes, indeed."

"Well, I do love a good treasure hunt." His bushy brows waggled.

Interesting choice of words, given what supposedly accompanied her volumes. "Should we start now?"

"Oh, not on an empty stomach, I think." He patted his own small, rounded tummy. "Capers, onions and tomato on rye is my usual breakfast—"

She put up a hand. "Why don't I make breakfast? I've been told I can hold my own in the kitchen."

His silver eyes twinkled. "She can cook, and she knows her way around her classic literature. What a catch you are, Miss... Miss... Lark?" Waving his hand, he cast around for her last name.

"Sparrow," she provided with a wry grin.

"Ah, yes." His index finger poked the air. "I should introduce you to my grandson." He passed her and sat at the table in the windowed alcove.

Hope clamped her jaw and turned to dive into the cupboards and fridge to gather what she needed for breakfast.

She'd ignore the grandson comment. The sweet old man meant no harm. Five short years ago, after a comment like that, she would've been out the back door so fast the windows would've rattled.

Wounds and time. They were funny things. When she read a book, it spoke to her soul in a distinct way. But she could pick up the same book a year later and the words could say something different because of how she'd grown or changed over time or because of her present circumstances. The memories of her past were a little like that.

She needed a new story. A new life. And she determined to write it, one page at a time, as she beat egg yolks, lemon juice and smoked paprika into hollandaise sauce while Ulysses hummed a jaunty tune, reading his namesake, *Ulysses* by James Joyce.

After placing the last of the dishes in the dishwasher from her take on eggs Benedict with pork belly and smoked-paprika hollandaise, she dried her hands and turned to Ulysses.

"Can I start by going through your computer records for inventory and sales?" She loathed the idea of him placing her books in his shop to sell, or worse, actually selling them, but she had to be realistic.

His shining forehead folded.

"You do have everything on a computer system, right?"

He swiped at the air. "Computers? Oh, no. We don't have any of that newfangled stuff here. No, we do it the good old-fashioned way. Receipts, paper. Stuff you can trust."

Any other time, she'd give a resounding "Hear! Hear!" She didn't trust technology or anything that could track her, find her, expose her. But not today. She needed to get those books so she'd be ready to roll in two months. Rotating her shoulders back, she straightened and steeled herself for what could turn into an arduous mission indeed.

"All on paper, huh?"

As if one of the mammoth bookshelves caved in on top of her, she found it hard to breathe. All of those shelves. And God only knew how many boxes of receipts and ledgers they had. But no matter how long it took, she wouldn't leave Wanishin Falls without her books and whatever treasure might lie within them.

"You'll be happy to know that our grandson, Ronan, is planning to drag us into the twenty-first century. But that'll take some time."

That was the understatement of the twenty-first century.

Ulysses didn't seem fazed by the task. He chattered away and led her out of the kitchen toward the front door. He flipped the sign to Open. Then he dug a piece of paper out of the back pocket of his trousers and keyed numbers into a security panel. He turned his head to her and shrugged. "My grandson. He worries. The kids around here sometimes get up to no good. Just bored, that's all."

He unlocked the ancient latch on the door. "And we can't forget to check the basement. Loads of stuff down there. Oh, and the attic."

So close…maybe. Yet so far away.

"All right. Where should we start? Any particular place you think you may have put them?" Hope clapped her hands together.

He cast his gaze about the room and scratched his chin. Not good.

The whoosh and click of the back door announced Mags before she strode into the shop front.

"Well, how'd everything go this morning? I apologize I wasn't here when you woke. As I said, it's getting difficult to juggle both the greenhouse farm and this place. I'm going to have to sell the farm. Just a matter of time." Mags's thin lips pressed together. "You ready to tuck in?"

Hope glanced between Ulysses, who rummaged behind the sales counter, and Mags's bright, sharp eyes. "You mean, you guys are going to help me? Then what are you paying me for?"

Mags let out a warm laugh. "Sometimes you just do things because it's the right thing to do. Helping you is my pleasure." She put out a hand as if to touch Hope's shoulder. But when Hope flinched, the older woman let it drop to her side. "Besides, I want to see you reunited with those books. They mean a lot to you. My own mother died when I was young, and I know I'd go to the ends of the earth to find something, anything, she left to me."

"Thank you." She fidgeted under the kind words like they would somehow fetter her to this place.

Mags rubbed her slender hands together. "All right. Let's get cracking."

Three hours later, Hope and Mags had nothing to show for their efforts but paper cuts, filthy, dust-covered sleeves, a love note probably never sent, a pile of dirty socks, grocery lists, unreadable receipts, and bubble gum wrappers, all left in the used books. And, so far, seventeen versions of *To Kill a Mockingbird*. Sure, there had been the occasional *Anne of Green Gables* or *Jane Eyre*, but not *her* copy.

Ulysses wandered and muttered to himself. His presence of mind had dwindled after breakfast.

"Phew!" Mags sat back from the stack she'd been working on and rubbed the back of her forearm across her forehead. "Find anything?"

Hope stood from her perch on a tufted stool where she studied an inventory logbook from the last year and stretched her aching neck. She bit back the irritable response burning at the back of her throat. "Nope. You?"

"Nah. I think we should get some sustenance. Build up our strength for another search later." Even Mags's tone came out ragged and dusty.

Discomfort wiggled around Hope's belly. Why was Mags so insistent on helping?

Bangs and clatters from the kitchen had Hope exchanging a raised-brow glance with Mags.

"Oh, Daisy May, how does your garden grow? I'm making lunch, dear!" Ulysses's singsong words drifted to the women near the front of the shop.

Hope frowned at Mags.

Mags's smile didn't reach her eyes in return. "Daisy was his first wife. She passed away many years ago. He forgets sometimes now. I better go make sure everything is okay in there. I've tried telling him not to go in the kitchen alone anymore, but..."

The sharp, acrid scent of smoke met her nostrils. "Oh, no!" Mags yelped. They sprinted to the kitchen. Despite only ten minutes left to his own devices, total chaos awaited them—pots and pans everywhere, flames reaching up from the range cooktop from what used to be a kitchen towel, broken eggs, flour on the floor and a whole giant ham thawing in the sink.

Mags screamed, legs bolted in place. Frozen like she'd been the day before.

Hope's instincts kicked into superchef survival mode. She led Ulysses away from the fire to stand by Mags. Then she grabbed a large stockpot lid and slammed it over the flames, which instantly died. Fishing out some tongs from a utensil drawer she'd seen that morning, she grabbed the burnt kitchen towel and threw it in the non-ham side of the dual sink and ran water over it.

She blew out a breath. "There. That should do it. No harm done."

Both Ulysses and Mags stared at her, slack-jawed. Ulysses in bewilderment, as if he couldn't figure out why he stood in the kitchen, and Mags with sheepish gratitude.

After she and Mags ensured Ulysses hadn't hurt himself, they began cleaning up the mess.

Mags stopped her. "Thank you. I was in shock, I think. See, I told you, you're a good soul." She dug in her purse. "Will you run down the street to Kat's Corner Café and get some sandwiches for lunch? I'll finish cleaning this up."

When she tried to hand Hope the rolled-up bills, Hope shook her head. "No, I—"

"I insist." Mags pressed them into her hand. "My treat for not letting our house burn down while I stood there like a deer in headlights."

Both let out a shaky chuckle.

"All right." Hope grabbed her coat from the hook by the door.

"Hey." Mags stopped her. "Let's plan the rest of the afternoon off after lunch. You can still look around, but I think Ulysses and I are going to need a nap after this." Her hand swept out, indicating the rest of the mess.

"But don't you want me to keep it open for you?"

"Nah, that's okay. You've done enough work for one day. Besides, the great thing about a small town? We all know each other. The old bookstore owners don't have to explain themselves if they need an afternoon siesta." She winked, waving Hope out the door.

Hope kept her shoulders hunched against the unforgiving wind swooping off the lake as she emerged from Dusty Jackets. She'd seen the little café with a wraparound deck bigger than the restaurant itself as the bus had dropped her at the station a block from the bookshop.

Leaves swirled around her feet, slow dancing in the breeze before their final resting place on the frosty ground. The old was making room for the new life coming, even if the crisp air said otherwise. She grew up in Chicago's outskirts and knew the signs of an impending Great Lakes spring just like she knew what it was like to change foster homes as many times as the Midwest changed seasons.

Tall Victorian houses sandwiched between craftsman and ranch-style homes. A city park down the quiet, tree-lined street. The word *quaint* came to mind. A twenty-first-century Minnesota version of Avonlea.

Cars bordered the block ahead outside Kat's Corner Café. All 408 residents from the posted sign outside town seemed to have crammed themselves inside.

The din of laughter, boisterous talking, dishes clattering and sizzling from the see-through kitchen charged her senses the minute Hope opened the door. But though most customers wore smiles, some checked their watches. A thread of discontent murmured its way through the crowd.

Hope raised a hand to signal a harried waitress who called, "Just a minute, hon. I'll be right with ya."

Another woman, in a sharp business suit and equally sharp angled pixie cut, stepped up to the cash register in her red Chucks to ring up customers who had finished their meals. Her smile warmed her confident stance, her "Thank you for coming in" genuine to each person.

When the woman, probably around Hope's age, spotted her, she waved Hope over like an old friend.

"Hey, new girl. What can I do for you?" She lifted a defined brow.

"How'd you know? That I'm new, I mean." Suddenly it

seemed like every eye zeroed in on her even though the place was so loud, no one could have caught the words.

"Oh, honey. It's a small town. Surely you've heard of the danger of a small town."

Hope held her breath. Danger? Heart thudding, she checked her exits.

The woman let out a rich feminine laugh that must've made men drool. "Don't look so scared, honey. I just mean that everyone knows everyone. And in Wanishin, I do mean everyone." Her tone dried out, brushed with irritation. She sighed. "Anyway, what can I get you? We don't have any free seating. But you could do takeaway or wait—"

A growling shout ripped right through the woman's words.

The waitress she'd seen earlier stomped out of the kitchen, throwing off her apron. Something choking and burnt wafted into the air.

The waitress glared at the business suit woman behind the register. "I'm done, boss. I told you, I'm not a chef!" She didn't give a backward glance as she pushed through the front door.

The woman waved it off. "That's my cousin. She'll be back. Told you everyone knows everyone."

"Wait, do you own this place? Are you having trouble in the kitchen?" She regretted her unrelated questions and general curiosity the minute the words tumbled from her mouth.

"Yeah, name's Kat Sinclair, as in Kat's Corner Café. This is my family's restaurant, or was. It was left to me by my dad. Nice to meet you...?" She extended her hand.

Hope shook it. This was becoming easier. "Hope. Hope Sparrow. I'm staying over at Dusty Jackets with the Barricks. Helping them in the shop. We actually had some trouble of our own in the kitchen. That's why I'm here."

Kat filled her in that the regular cook and his wife, the

sous-chef, were home sick and couldn't make it. A twinge in her gut. No, she didn't need to involve herself.

"I could help." She fidgeted with her shirt's hem. "I'm not a professionally trained chef or anything, but I've been told I'm pretty good and I've worked at a few restaurants. I love to cook." It was way more than she'd meant to say, but the part of her that wanted to share her love of food overruled the part of her that desired to stay anonymous.

"But I just started over at Dusty Jackets. I'm supposed to bring Mags and Ulysses lunch. I don't want them to wonder where I am."

Kat's smile widened, dimpling her cheeks like a grown-up Tinker Bell. She called to one of the line cooks in the kitchen and ordered him to make and box up a couple of sandwiches and soup to take over to Mags and Ulysses. Pulling out her cell phone, Kat tapped on it and explained the situation to who Hope assumed was Mags on the other end. She then whipped back around to Hope, hands clasped together. "Oh, new girl. We are going to be the best of friends, you and I."

No, they wouldn't, because she wouldn't be there long enough for that to happen.

But on the outside, Hope made herself return the smile before diving into one of the only things on the planet— other than delving into a fictional world—that could soften the razored edge of her memories and make them bearable for a while.

Chapter Three

"Are you sure you want to do this?" Brock Barrick, Ronan Barrick's father, spoke from the shadows of Wanishin Falls City Hall.

Ronan stepped onto the sidewalk from his pickup truck, giving his German shepherd, Charlotte, one last pat on the head.

Brock stood straight and every bit as tall and broad shouldered as Ronan himself. But his father's hair had gone gray, and something harder and more unyielding lived behind his silver-blue eyes. Unlike Ronan, he was a whole man. Not three-quarters.

"What are you doing here, Dad?" A ragged breath shook Ronan's chest. He couldn't tolerate this same argument again. Not now.

"I don't understand why you want to put yourself through this. Nobody is going to allow you to do this." His father followed as Ronan strode with his hitched step toward the city hall double doors.

"You mean do something good for the town?" Ronan's knuckles cracked, gripping the folder he carried.

His dad put a hand on Ronan's shoulder to stop him. "That's not it." His father seemed to assess Ronan's face, then leg and with it, his abilities as a man. Ronan must've come up wanting. "You know all of Kyle's family is in there, right? And, Harold, he's never going to—"

At the names, Ronan halted. All the cool spring air was sucked out of his lungs.

His father shook his head. "You can't bring him back."

What his father wouldn't say out loud was, *And it won't put you back together.*

Ronan let a humorless laugh slip between his teeth. "If only the old stories of family treasure were true. But this is the messy reality of life. No hidden treasure. No sudden rain of providence. I have to do this myself."

His father's gaze darkened like gathering thunderclouds. "Just be sure you're doing it for the right reasons."

He pushed past his father, who didn't stop him.

"You're going to go broke or get yourself hurt. Or both." His father's words carried on the crisp wind.

Ronan limped forward. Inside the large whitewashed space, the seats overflowed. Even for their sometimes overly involved citizens, this was an incredible turnout for a random Tuesday-afternoon city council meeting. And when many glances rushed his way as he stepped to the front, where the council sat behind a long C-shaped table, Ronan knew it wasn't a coincidence.

He'd called the people filling the seats neighbors and family all his life, even if there were always going to be those who held the Barrick name in contempt over a one-hundred-year-old tragedy at the hands of his ancestors. Some faces in the crowd held encouraging smiles, but others boasted scowls or distrustful frowns. No matter their feelings toward him or his family in the past, they had most certainly changed three years ago. Everything, his whole world, had changed three years ago.

The head of the historical society, Lois Lewandowski, there to plead the same case as his, beamed at him. She gave him a thumbs-up in her neon-pink pantsuit. Enthusiastic, yes. But he'd have to carry the business side of the conversation.

He took his seat near the front, facing the man whose son was dead because of Ronan. The man who just happened to be the mayor. Harold Gunderson. His cold expression cut through the sudden hush.

Harold shook his head, his jowls shaking along with it. "Well, I don't know where you'd even start to sort out that mess…"

The uproar in the council chambers drowned out Ronan Barrick's groan. *Here we go again.* If it were anyone else with the same request, there wouldn't be such a to-do over it. His plan to work with the Wanishin Falls Historical Society to renovate part of the building as an educational historical center was the only reason they agreed to hear him out at all.

"Order!" Harold's booming tone rebounded over the raised voices. He brought down his gavel, wielding it like he did the measure of power afforded him as town mayor.

When the room quieted, his bristled mustache dipped, making the large man walrus-like as he evaluated Ronan from his seat behind the curved table.

Shifting, Ronan's right leg began shaking after standing before the city council for almost an hour. He met Harold's gaze. "I understand that you can't give it to us with no compensation. But it's just sitting there. You're receiving no tax benefits or payment at all right now. As is, it's a draw for litter and a too-convenient abandoned spot for the kids to party. I've talked to law enforcement. They've been called over there by concerned neighbors three times in the last month alone."

Poppy McGoven flailed her willow-thin arm. "Excuse me! Excuse me, Mr. Mayor, but I've offered to purchase the property numerous times. It's what's best for the community. Why not let me use the space to prosper the town? I'll bulldoze it and build you twenty-first-century condominiums."

Harold's forehead folded. "Yes, so you've said. But I'm not convinced that someone who breezed into town a couple of years ago would know what's best for this community nor that you have the capital to undertake such a project."

If there was something Harold disliked more than Ronan, it was busy-body outsiders.

Her thin hands clenched. "And you think these two do?"

Harold raised a hand to stop her. "We are not here to discuss your proposal, which we already denied. Please take your seat, Ms. McGoven."

She sat with a huff, folding her arms over her chest.

Leaning forward, Harold steepled his hands, pinning Ronan once again with a glare. "Tell me again what you're suggesting, Mr. Barrick." The words ruffled his mustache.

The other members nodded and murmured their agreement. Lois bobbed her head in encouragement.

Ronan straightened, trying to hide his surprise that they seemed to be considering his and the historical society's proposal, especially Harold. "We want to clean up the lot and convert the building into a gymnasium and hangout center for youth in the community on the main level. Upstairs would be an educational space for the historical society. Partly museum and the rest can be used by the community to host education courses and small business events. They will charge modest fees and admission for the museum. We've both worked hard to obtain grants for youth programs, restoring historic build-ings and educational programs since the staff want to educate the youth and community about Wanishin Falls's history."

Once again, Harold's near-unibrow lifted as he smirked at his fellow councilmen and women. "And...you believe you have what it takes to do all of this, do you?"

Ronan didn't miss the way Harold's eyes skimmed over his right leg.

Jaw tightening, hands clamped tight with the passion in-side his gut, he strode closer to the council table, his limp ever so slight.

"Yes, I believe we do, but I'd appreciate volunteers from the community as well." He indicated the crowd. "Anyone who cares about the youth and wants to see them have a place to go where they can learn, have good clean fun and be safe as well as preserve the history of this town."

The townspeople in the crowd were split in reaction: some dipped their chins in agreement, while others muttered and grumbled behind their hands to the person beside them.

Ronan avoided their scrutiny, pushing away the nagging thoughts of his own mistakes, from the past he couldn't change. The way he needed to redeem himself. No, he couldn't make this about himself. This was about the kids. Only the kids. He said a quick silent prayer for the right outcome, whatever that might be.

Harold leaned farther out of his chair. "My proposal back to you, Mr. Barrick and Ms. Lewandowski, is this—I will give you until the end of June to get your youth and history cen-ter running, permits and all. Otherwise I'll entertain more profitable endeavors." His chin jutted in Poppy's direction.

"But that only gives me two months. That's hardly enough time to—"

"Take it or leave it. Those are my terms." Harold shook his

great big head, the fluorescent light overhead bouncing off it like strobe lights.

Ronan knew it was as good an offer as he'd likely get and only because his father was a well-known retired navy officer and ship captain and construction business owner in the community, and Harold was nothing if not proud of the Wanishin Falls heritage.

Ronan leaned down to Lois, her wrinkled smile bright as ever. "I think we can do it, Ronan. We have to trust God will provide all we need." Her voice sparkled with optimism.

Finally, Ronan straightened. "Okay, agreed."

Harold called for the vote. Ronan held his breath, reaching down to swat at an itch he couldn't scratch on his nonexistent leg.

To his great surprise, all members voted yea. Though Harold looked like he'd swallowed some bad lutefisk as he did so. They discussed the payment of taxes, but wouldn't be required to make any further payments until after the first six months. He hoped they could get all of their grant funding in line by then.

"Thank you." It was all he could manage. He'd jump and whoop if he could. Lois leaped up and squeezed him around the middle, nearly knocking him over.

He barely registered the hitch in his step nor the soreness of standing for so long as he made his way back through the crowd.

"Oh, Mr. Barrick." Harold's voice stopped him. "The next item on the docket concerns you too. I'd stick around."

Ronan returned to the front.

"We have the fate of a young juvenile delinquent in our hands, and for whatever reason, the judge made the uninformed decision to allow you the final say." Harold zeroed in on Ronan in that frigid, calculating way again.

"What do you mean?"

"It's Tate Morgan. He's gotten himself in trouble again. He spray-painted some lockers at the high school and damaged the property inside as well." Hissed whispers from the back told Ronan the troubled kid's family was probably present.

Harold continued. "Tate can either serve 160 hours of community service with our city maintenance department or go to a juvenile rehabilitation facility for four weeks. Those are the options. If our sole city maintenance employee—" his pudgy finger jabbed toward Ronan "—refuses to host his community service, the boy will automatically go to rehab."

The whole place quieted, waiting for Ronan's answer. Before he knew what was happening, he found himself agreeing to host Tate—a boy he'd tried to impact in the church youth group for a while. How could he not? After all, that was his goal with the youth center, right? To help the youth in this town.

The city maintenance department—i.e. him—or the role of glorified town handyman in a place as small as Wanishin Falls didn't keep him all that busy. He'd be able to keep up with his part-time work, since he received some benefits from the accident that took half of his leg from the knee down, *and* the youth center *and* Tate community service, right?

"Sure, I'll supervise him."

In a daze, he took the information Harold handed him and stepped once again into the swirl of late-April air outside.

"So, you got the approval." It was a statement, and from his father's tone, not a proud or happy one.

"I'm not a child. I'm a grown man. I can handle it." He tossed his words over his shoulder, striding to his truck where his ever-faithful dog, Charlotte or "Charlie," waited for him in the truck bed.

His father let him go, which was just as well. It wasn't like his dad had ever been able to talk Ronan out of something he'd set his mind to anyway.

Ronan whistled for Charlotte and opened the door, where she jumped into her regular shotgun spot.

"Come on, Charlie." The only girl he had time for in his life wagged her tail and turned a toothy dog grin at him as he pulled away.

He knew two people who'd be proud of what he'd done and couldn't wait to share the news. But for now, he'd celebrate with takeout from the only pizzeria in town and some catch on the beach with Charlie.

If Grandpa Ulysses was having a good day, Ronan would be able to talk to him. *Really* talk to him. A flicker of hope lit in his chest. He missed the easy conversations about everything from their favorite books to the weather. Mostly he missed the way his grandpa knew him like no one else. Now, there were days his grandpa's dementia took Ronan's name from his mind.

What an incredibly selfish thought, one Ronan pushed away as he drove the short distance from his converted lighthouse home on the point at the edge of town to Dusty Jackets, where his grandpa and step-grandma—though she was the only grandma he'd ever known—lived.

He'd run home after work, daylight already slipping away. The sky had turned from blue to amber as he parked outside the shop, the place of many boyhood memories. The water out back, smooth liquid glass, the kind of evening he'd relished during his days as a captain aboard a thousand-foot cargo ship, or "laker," as they were called by locals.

Charlie followed him to the door. The light in the shop area still cast its homey glow. Normally, after 5:00 p.m., his grandparents turned it off and turned the sign to Closed. He tried the front door—open. The familiar bell announced his arrival.

"Hello? Anyone here?" Charlie scampered off, probably to do her favorite thing—irritate the resident cat, Fitzwilliam.

"We're closed." An unfamiliar voice sailed in from the former sitting room. "I just haven't locked up yet. Sorry."

A lithe figure stepped out from one of the book pillars. If he had to describe her, he'd say she looked like the stereotype of a buttoned-up librarian. Except for a tidy fringe of eyebrow-grazing bangs on her forehead, the rest of her dark hair was pulled tight against the back of her neck into a bun. The pair of glasses she wore looked like dollar-store readers that belonged to someone twice her age.

He glanced around for his grandparents, to keep from staring. "I was looking for Mags and Ulysses. Are they around?"

Instead of answering, she bobbed her petite chin, gesturing behind him. "I don't think you're supposed to have your dog in here, sir. Please take him outside." Though she pulled her shoulders up, businesslike, her voice quavered.

"Her." Ronan stepped over to the counter and leaned against it, crossing his still-there foot over the prosthetic one. It had taken a long time to master any sort of smoothness like that.

"Excuse me?" She set down a stack of books.

"The dog. She's female, and her name is Charlotte."

Her nose scrunched, making her glasses slide down its narrow bridge. "Sir, I do need to close up. So, is there something I can help you find?" She eyed him, then the door, as if checking her exits.

He should probably tell her. But how often did he meet someone who didn't know who the messed-up Ronan Barrick was?

"Well—"

She fidgeted with the hem of her turtleneck sweater. "You know, maybe you should come back tomorrow and I can spend more time helping you find what you need. I'm kind of new here and still trying to get my bearings."

That was a nice way of saying his grandpa's mountainous book terrain overwhelmed the senses.

"Aren't the best bookstores supposed to be like this? Sort of a treasure hunt?"

Warmth flooded her expression. "You're right." Her delicate fingers brushed lightly, almost lovingly, against a gilded leather book cover on one of the tables beside her. "I don't think there's anywhere else in the world you could find original late-eighteenth-century poetry and bare-chested Fabio mass-market romance on the same table. Nor this."

She held up a handsome yet unassuming tan hardcover volume. "A limited-edition, 1926 T. E. Lawrence, *Seven Pillars of Wisdom*. It's easily three thousand dollars, and if it's inscribed, probably worth as much as this shop. I can't imagine what I'll find next. Every stack is indeed a treasure waiting to be discovered."

Her cheeks pinked, as though she hadn't meant to say so much.

Ronan let out a whistle. "Wow, you sure do know your literature. I can see why Gramps and Grandma hired you."

Light dawned in her strange, luminescent amber eyes. "Wait, what?"

Right on cue, Grandma Mags and Grandpa Ulysses walked in from the dining room.

Mags hugged him and stood on her tiptoes to kiss his cheek. "Oh, I see you've met Hope. She's helping us with the shop." She turned to the girl. "This is Ronan, our grandson."

Shock registered across her face. The rosy color in her cheeks drained away.

A twinge of guilt pulled at his gut as he extended his hand. "Nice to meet you."

Her handshake lasted all of one second and she fairly ran for the stairs afterward, excusing herself to the room his grandma said she was staying in.

He listened politely to his grandma's explanation of the woman's presence in their shop and then told them about the youth center.

"Well done, Brock. I knew you could do it." Grandpa took Ronan's hands between his own wrinkled ones, squeezing.

They weren't supposed to correct or argue with Grandpa's mistakes or lapses in memory, but he wouldn't have anyway. The older man's eyes filled with joy.

Despite the festive tone of the evening, his thoughts kept drifting upstairs to the mystery woman. He'd have to keep a closer eye on his grandparents with her around, as much as she may seem a good fit. He wouldn't stand for someone taking advantage of his kind, trusting grandpa and grandma.

People could say they were anyone nowadays. Hope might not even be her real name.

Chapter Four

After she survived the first week getting into the swing of things around the shop, Hope's attempts to avoid Ronan Barrick were demolished on Monday afternoon.

Giving Ronan a quick nod as he entered the shop, she busied herself with reshelving a stack of books she'd sorted by genre and author. Her process of methodically combing through the books and organizing them for the Barricks as she went hadn't yielded even one of her own volumes. But her brain did crave the order. Something about the precision, the knowing what came next, soothed her nerves.

The search had produced more than a few handwritten notes in a shaky hand. They said things like "It's real," and "You have to remember. For them." And one ominous scribbled note read, "She's coming."

Did Ulysses write them? It seemed possible. Perhaps he'd tried to remind himself of something before he forgot again. And "she"? Was he referring to Hope, knowing she'd come for her books someday?

Mags and Ulysses visited at the back of the store area with their grandson—a man handsome enough to turn heads on the street but rugged enough to make her believe he'd hold his own in the wilderness.

Today, Ronan wore a flat tweed cap. His wild hair peeked from underneath. An oversize wool coat would have seemed comical on anyone but him. It gave him a rustic, European edge.

Ronan and Mags chatted about youth center plans for the community.

Ulysses plopped onto a chaise longue in the rounded alcove where Hope continued shelving books. Fitzwilliam followed—he seemed to trail the older man everywhere—and jumped into Ulysses's lap with a great rumbling purr. She'd enjoyed Ulysses's company throughout the last several days. Sometimes it proved difficult to help a customer and keep an eye on him, but they made it work.

He leaned in with a conspiratorial hand cupped around his mouth. "You know, I own this whole place." The lack of recognition in his expression said he had no idea who she was at the moment.

"It's pretty great. You should be proud."

His chin dipped in a solemn nod. "Try not to judge a book by its cover around here."

"Hope is looking for some books that Agatha sent here before she passed." Mags's voice carried, still at the back.

"Really? What are they?" Ronan turned raised brows toward Hope, where she tried her best to blend into the books. It wasn't too difficult with her own worn, muted attire.

She told him the titles. Who wasn't going to eventually know her business in this town? Kat's words about small towns played back in her mind.

"Did you say a first-edition *Jane Eyre*?" Ronan let out a long whistle. "Those are incredibly rare. Only five hundred were printed in the first go around."

"You're a fan of *Jane Eyre*?" She slipped her reading glasses off her nose and into her pocket. She would have taken him for more of a Louis L'Amour enthusiast. Hemingway, maybe. Or John Grisham. *Jane Eyre?* But who was she to judge? Especially when it came to men.

Ignoring the pressure at her temples, her shortness of breath, the dull ringing in her ears—her anxiety's calling cards—she stepped closer to Ronan and Mags.

Mags, beaming like the proud grandma, reached up to pat Ronan's straight shoulder. "Oh, this boy is sharp as they come. And he knows his literature, don't you?"

Ronan scraped at his jaw, as though uncomfortable with his grandmother's gushing. "Does your copy have the original board binding? Those early copies were often re-covered in leather or cloth."

And she considered *herself* a book nerd. "I'm not sure. I haven't seen the volumes since I was a child."

His gait tilted to the right as he moved to the front counter and leaned an elbow on it.

"You know about bookbinding too?" She tried but failed to keep her voice even, neutral.

He chuckled, as did Mags.

"I guess being around these two and this shop as long as I have sort of rubs off on a person. And I've always loved the craftsmanship of artistic bookbinding. The detail and the work they did both by hand and with their binding machines. They don't make them like they used to."

He cleared his throat. "Anyway, how long will you be in town?"

"Two months at the most."

"Well, that was decisive." His gaze passed between his

grandparents and her. Assessing her? Maybe deciding if he should trust her with his grandparents or not. She didn't blame him.

Mags stepped to her side. "She's been a tremendous help to us already. She's cleaning and organizing. I've never seen anyone so orderly. And she's helping with your grandfather while looking for her books." The smile she turned to Hope was warm.

"By the way—" Mags clamped her hands together and pointed them at Ronan "—that's why I brought up Hope's books. I was wondering if you've seen the titles she's talking about. Do you know if they were sold by accident or stored somewhere?"

A crease formed in the middle of his forehead. "I don't remember seeing them. I think if I had, especially the *Jane Eyre*, I would remember."

A twinkle sparked in Mags's eyes. "You know this place inside and out. You should've seen him when he was a boy. If he couldn't be found, his nose was buried in a book in some corner of this house. Or if the weather was nice, he was out by the water, either fishing or reading or both."

His square jaw flexed. "That's great. Thank you for that, Grandma. What, again, was your point?"

Hope scratched her nose to cover the smile pulling at the corners of her lips. The "man's man" had *blushed*.

Mags pinned him with a scowl. "My *point* is that you should help her. You know every square inch of this place."

Hope's sputtered words mixed with Ronan's. "No… I can't… I don't need help… I have so much to do…"

Hope took a step back, raising her hands as if the Barrick family were in attack mode.

Ulysses grunted, trying to get his legs underneath him.

Mags helped Ulysses from his spot to the grumbled disappointment of Fitzwilliam.

"Well, it was just a thought. I'll go fix supper." Mags lifted a shoulder, but Hope didn't appreciate the gleam remaining in her eyes as she led Ulysses to the kitchen.

An awkward silence settled. Hope assumed Ronan would get the hint and follow his grandparents while she continued sorting and stacking. Instead, he hung around, browsed the shelves. His mouth opened twice as if he tried to coax words past his lips. But the only sound to break into the quiet was the whisper of pages turning, the *shoosh* of books sliding into place and the creak of the wood floor beneath Ronan's boots.

The front door opened with its usual tinkling bell. The air from outside gusted in while relief burst out from Hope's lungs.

Kat bounced in, still wearing her ruby red Converse Chucks, this time with a denim skirt, bright orange tights and some band shirt with a message Hope couldn't fully read beneath a leather jacket. "Hey, chica. Oh, hey, Ronan."

After a round of greetings, Kat paced around the other side of the front counter. "So, I'm looking for something to help me with Matthew."

"What's wrong?" A vein pulsed in Ronan's neck.

Kat bit her thumbnail before jamming her hand into her jacket pocket. "I'm not sure, but I feel like I'm doing something wrong."

When Hope cooked for Kat's Café the week before, Kat had jabbered her ear off about anything and everything. Kat shared she had an older brother with special needs. He'd suffered a traumatic brain and spinal cord injury in high school and would need caregiving for the rest of his life.

"He's been agitated lately. More than usual." Kat paced to the other side of the room and back. "I think it's tough on him with Mom and Dad gone more and too many hours in the café waiting for me. It's getting to us both, I guess." She stopped her march.

Why would this woman she hardly knew share so much with her? Hope didn't trust herself with her *own* secrets.

Both Kat and Ronan stared at her. Kat asked for a book suggestion, and Ronan waited for Hope to do her job. It clicked into place. She could do that.

"Okay, follow me."

Waving Kat over to the large space to the right of the checkout counter, once a sitting room, Hope called over her shoulder, "I'm putting together a nonfiction section in this room."

She ran the tips of her fingers along the book spines until she found the one she sought. "I came across this earlier, hiding among young adult science fiction in the castle room."

"The castle room?" Ronan stood propped against the doorway, arms crossed.

"The round room, right? It's like we're in a castle made of books here, Rone. Keep up." Kat's expression said, *Obviously.* Kat gestured to Hope. "You were saying?"

"It's a book about caring for a loved one, and it looks like it has some excellent information included about caring for yourself too, the caregiver." She handed Kat the medium-sized volume, which started with a handful of endorsements before the foreword by a well-known author.

Paging through it, Kat nodded. "Thank you, this looks perfect. I gotta do something. We're both struggling."

"It caught my eye. I thought maybe Mags would like to read it someday." She remembered her audience and cast a quick glance at Ronan. Other than a tightening around his eyes, he didn't show emotion over her statement.

Ronan cleared his throat. "You know, I really do think Matt would benefit from some equine-assisted therapy like I did. It helps with all sorts of things, not just physical disabilities. The guy who runs the rehabilitation center knows his stuff."

Kat was already shaking her head with a heavy sigh. "You know I can't bring him. Mom and Dad would never go for it." Her eyes misted over.

Kat wrapped Hope in a one-armed hug before Hope even knew what happened. "This is great. It's exactly what I was looking for. If your plan to open a food truck falls through, you'd make a killer librarian. I always thought it would be so cool to have a mobile library."

Hope didn't remind her that her dream was actually to have food *and* books, but rang up her purchase at the counter. Maybe the "Have a good day" she usually said was not sensitive enough. Instead, she opted for, "I hope this helps."

Kat wished them both a good evening and added that she'd bring it back to lend to Mags when she was done with it.

The uncomfortable silence returned. Unspoken words hung in the air like invisible balloons. But they didn't belong to her. If Ronan waited for her to lasso those words down, he'd wait forever.

As soon as was polite to do so, Hope excused herself. Dee would be so proud of the girl who once acted like she was raised by wolves.

She grabbed something quick from the kitchen and planned to eat in her room to give Ronan, Ulysses and Mags time as a family. She'd told Mags right away she didn't expect to be included in their family meals. She was their employee, after all. Mags tried to argue, but Hope changed the subject and left it at that.

From the little market down the street, Hope had simple sandwich fixings, apples because they were cheap and a few breakfast staples. So, she made herself a sandwich and plucked an apple from her stash before ducking out of the kitchen and Ronan's watchful eye.

Fitzwilliam, who had done figure eights between her ankles when he wasn't sitting with Ulysses, followed her. Once she had locked the door behind them, she sank to the plush-carpeted floor and devoured her food. Something caught in her throat. It wasn't her half-chewed sandwich.

She closed her eyes, squeezing a tear beneath her lashes. She didn't belong here. This was so much harder than she'd thought it would be—the proximity of all these "normal" people. She was pretending. Living someone else's life. She wasn't the sweet bookstore clerk, Hope Sparrow. She could move, change her name, but she would always be the stained orphan, Emily Carrington. The girl cast aside by every foster home, hated by the other foster kids, betrayed and abducted by the first guy to tell her he loved her, and her heart permanently a mangled mess after years of captivity and physical exploitation.

Drawing up her knees, she buried her face into her palms, trying not to feel the hands that clawed at her, inside and out. The memories so real, she could almost believe her flesh tore open, blood flowing as fast as her tears.

Her captor, or "trafficker," sold her body to anyone willing to pay for it. But often, it felt like bits of her soul were the true purchase price of the violation she endured.

Fitzwilliam nudged her arm, purring. She crossed her legs and let him curl up on her lap.

She needed to get on her way with her plans for a mobile café-bookshop. The enormity of the task still before her to make that happen made her muscles buzz with anxious energy. She made a quick decision to expend it on her search.

The clock read 8:30 p.m. The Barricks went to bed early and arose before the sun showed its brilliant head every day.

Fitzwilliam, who slept and snored, grumbled as she set him on the floor and stood. He followed her as she tiptoed out of her bedroom toward the attic at the end of the hall. She wanted to look somewhere she wasn't able to during the day when she needed to operate the shop and watch over Ulysses downstairs.

The floor let out a long, low groan. She stopped, her breath huffing in the quiet that followed. It wasn't like Mags had forbidden her from searching in the attic. In fact, the older woman told her to take free rein in any room she wanted. But for some reason, it felt strange rummaging through their house at night.

She crept up the narrow stairs to the attic. Cool drafts prickled her arms, and the scent of mothballs made her throat constrict. Pulling a cord turned on an old bare light bulb overhead. A maze of banker's boxes, more books—how could the house possibly hold any more books?—abandoned sewing machines, dress forms, a wooden rocking horse and boxes marked with things like Christmas Decorations and Family Photos sprawled before her.

Hands on hips, she did a 360 turn. Where to start? But when she turned, Fitzwilliam weaved through her feet, tripping her. Feline and legs entangled. He mewled. She cried out and fell hard on top of a box. It did nothing to break her fall. Her bottom and elbow screamed in pain, where she'd tried to catch herself.

She sat up, not surprised to hear footsteps on the stairs after the racket. So much for not waking anyone.

"I'm okay," she called to who she guessed must be Mags. "I tripped over Fitzwilliam. I'm sure I got the worse end of the ordeal."

"Well, I don't know about that. He looked pretty shook up when he flew past me." The deep voice took her by surprise.

Ronan emerged through the doorway. He offered a hand

where she was still stranded, legs slung over the crumpled box. She hesitated but took it. Being downstairs with Ronan, with Ulysses and Mags near, was one thing. But when she stood, Ronan's height towered over her, and she wasn't a short woman. The low ceilings and clutter closed in, suffocating her. It didn't matter that he smelled of pine, fresh air and lake water. She hadn't been alone with a man, this close to one since...

She stepped back, but again, the infernal box stopped her progress. She wobbled, but his arm reached out to steady her. His hand was gentle, but she flinched as he righted her and let go. This time *he* trod backward.

She straightened her sweater and smoothed her slick bun. "I thought you'd gone home."

"I was just cleaning up and setting the alarm system for them before taking off. Half the time they forget. I heard a crash. What are you doing up here?" An accusation sharpened the edges of his tone.

She answered the question he hadn't asked instead. "You're probably worried I'm some kind of con artist who's going to take advantage of your grandparents and then take off. Well, I'm not."

The space between his lips disappeared. His eyes met hers down the straight line of his nose without flinching. Seeming to study her again. So that *was* what he thought.

She crossed her arms. "Trust me, if I didn't have to be in this little town, I wouldn't be. But I have to find my books and I promised your grandma I'd stay for a couple of months to help out. Then I'll be out of everyone's hair. I promise."

He cut across the small space and sank into an abandoned wingback chair with torn upholstery. "And until then?"

"I'll take good care of this place and your grandpa. You have my word." Though her heart thrummed in her ears, she managed a stable tone.

His shoulders lowered as if letting out a held breath. "Okay, then." He reached for the nearest box and opened the lid.

"Okay, then, what?"

"Okay, I'm going to help you look." He already sifted through the contents of the box.

Her lips pinched together. Should she take that as *I'm going to help you to be rid of you*?

"Fine." She settled cross-legged on the floor a safe distance away from him to begin her own search. She kept herself closest to the door.

They worked in silence with only the rustle of papers and scratch of cardboard.

"Hey." Ronan's hands stopped leafing through a ledger. "I'm sorry about the day we met. I should've told you who I was right away. It's, well, it's complicated. But it was kind of nice having someone not know who I was. Even if it was for a few minutes."

She swallowed. No one knew *her* real name. How could she condemn him? "Why would someone like you not want people to know who you are?" The muttered statement slipped through her teeth.

"Like me?" One brow lifted.

She couldn't say "normal" or "not broken" out loud.

When she kept her mouth clamped shut, he cocked his head to the side as though debating a reply. "There's a century-old grudge this town has with the Barricks. Not bad enough for our family to be driven from our homes, but enough to make me wish my name didn't still bring a sense of distrust at worst or become the back end of people's jokes at best."

Ronan stood, moving with his slight limp to a freestanding bookcase in the corner with rows of what looked like ledgers for the shop.

She couldn't imagine anyone being mad at sweet Ulysses or Mags.

"This grudge, does it extend to your grandparents?"

He stopped, ledger in hand. A faint smile curving his lips. "Somehow the 'Barrick Curse' doesn't seem to touch them. My grandpa used to say people would make comments about our family to his face when he was younger. But now, it's like everyone has forgotten their connection to the name and what it means to the history of Wanishin Falls. I think all of that distrust has passed to me." His broad shoulders lifted once then fell. "But who can blame them? Who could dislike Gramps and Grandma?"

While there was relief in his tone, there was something else? Sadness? Bitterness? Regret, perhaps?

"Really? So, the town is still mad about something that happened a hundred years ago? That's kind of harsh." She leaned in, another box lid stilled in her hands.

He brushed his hands free of dust, hesitated again. "Little towns have long memories. Great short-term memory too, so it would seem." The last words almost a whisper.

Secrets. It seemed he had them too.

"What was it your ancestors did, if you don't mind me asking?"

He scratched his jaw. "My great-grandfather-to-the-fourth-power caused two shipwrecks in one night."

Before she could ask more, he rushed ahead. "Why these books? What makes them so important?" He traced the years labeled on the side of the ledgers with his finger as he spoke.

She dropped a stack of papers inside the box in front of her and jammed the lid back in place.

His words hung in the air for a minute, then she surprised herself by saying, "You're right. It's personal. They were my mom's. She left them to me when she died."

He stopped his hands on the ledger. "I'm sorry. I lost my mom a few years ago. That's rough. If those books were important to her, I can see why they'd be important to you."

They resumed their search, but her curiosity got the better of her again. "Why that abandoned lot and building? Why a youth center?" She shrugged at his openmouthed gaze. "I heard you talking about it with Mags the night we met. Sorry, I wasn't trying to eavesdrop."

He ran a hand over the back of his neck. "My plan is to turn it into a youth community center. Where the kids can come and hang out, play games, instead of getting into trouble or staying home alone. Many kids around here have hardworking parents. Some are gone a lot, working on the big ships on the lake." His shoulders slumped. "They're so lonely, you know? I want to give the kids a safe place to belong."

She knew loneliness, so consuming it threatened to drown her, all too well. After a childhood of hopping foster care homes, all she'd longed for was to belong and be loved. Then she found it, or so she thought, in the wrong place. She'd trusted the wrong person.

Hope gulped down the gnawing at her throat. The town wasn't the only one with a long, persistent memory. "That's great. I hope it works out." The words scraped from her throat as though dragged from someone dying of dehydration. Maybe she was too. But her thirst ran deeper.

She ignored the odd expression on his face.

"Aggie's stuff…" His gaze shifted to the box she'd crushed in her fall.

"Hmm?"

He pointed to the box.

Though distorted now, it read Aggie's Stuff on the side.

"I wonder…" She bent to lift the lid and set it aside. Ronan stood over her.

She struggled to lift the heavy box from the floor.

"Here, let me help you."

An argument rose to her lips, but she let him take the box, which he placed on a small spindle-legged table. She pulled out several pictures of a young Agatha and Ulysses. Their smiles so similar. How did she not notice before? She lifted out a gigantic tome, as big as the family Bible she'd seen at Dee's house.

Hope read the title aloud: "*The Histories of Women: Unraveling the Mysteries of the Female Life and Mind.*" No author listed, but it appeared to be from the late 1800s, judging by the book design and binding.

He laughed. "I can see why it's so long."

She bit her cheek to hide her smile at the same time his nearness caused a zing of panic to course through her chest. *It's okay. You're okay.* Now to believe herself.

Ronan touched the gilded leather rectangle on the cover. "I haven't seen a paneled calf cover in this kind of shape for a long time. They didn't usually make books this large unless they were important. Too expensive. Whoever crafted this was a master in his trade."

"Or hers." She threw him a pointed look.

He bobbed his head and kept quiet, but she knew men typically ran the trades in that era.

She set the strange book aside, sifting through letters and papers, ready to call it another dead end. But there, at the very bottom—she gasped—one of her books. It had to be. The dear face of *Little Women* stared up at her.

"Is that—" Ronan shuffled closer but didn't touch her. Maybe he sensed her inner discomfort.

She opened the cover. Could it be? Her grandma's name—Dottie McDonnell—was scrawled in elegant handwriting on the first page. "Yes. This is it." Her words more like breaths.

She clutched it to her chest and blinked away the tingle

beneath her eyelids. At the moment, she didn't care who was there with her. She had the first piece of this complicated puzzle. Anything seemed possible now.

"Do you mind if I look at it?"

Reluctantly, she handed it over. His hands traced the green cloth cover. "So, you were left the first volume?"

"Yes." She knew the original *Little Women* came in a part one and part two, much like *Jane Eyre* came in a three-volume set. So did he, it seemed.

"And it's supposedly a first edition?" His face creased, inspecting the spine and the first few pages.

"What is it?" She leaned in, but couldn't see whatever he saw.

"Well, not that it makes it any less meaningful personally, but this is a forged first edition. Lots of them were made in 1869 instead of 1868, the year of the first printing. It's still pretty valuable, but not first-edition valuable." He handed it back.

"That's okay. My grandma still touched these pages and read these words." Her cheeks warmed, but Ronan's sharp chin softened.

She was pretty sure her mom knew it wasn't a true first edition. She was the literary and history buff studying to become a history professor before she died. The value lay beyond these pages anyway—both in the emotional ties to her family and the literal treasure these books would hopefully lead her to.

They put the contents back in the box, but when they came to the big, strange book, Hope paused. "Do you mind if I take this to my room and look at it?"

"Not in the least. No offense to women everywhere—" his hands flew up in a defensive gesture, as though the women of the world would overhear him and bust in the doorway "—but I don't think I'm ready to sit down and read that mas-

sive thing anytime soon. I'm sure my grandparents would say
you should keep it, if it makes you happy." He shifted and
winced as if in pain.

"Thanks." She stacked both books and hiked them onto
her hip like a mother would a child.

"I mean, not that I couldn't stand to learn a few things."
His fingers raked through his unruly hair. "You know, about
the female mind and all." The words tumbled over each other,
his face changing color with each one.

They stood close now. She inched toward the door. "Well,
thank you for your help."

He grabbed another box of the ledgers. "I'll keep looking
through the sales and inventory around the time my grandfather started losing his memory. Maybe I'll see your other
books in there."

They bade each other good-night.

As she locked her bedroom door, for the first time in a long
time, she knew she needed to trust someone other than herself
for help. With Dee, she had only let the woman in so far. She
certainly would never have let Dee assist her on this journey.

But that night, Ronan proved he knew his stuff and eventually, his knowledge of the town where her family once re-
sided would come in handy. It was likely not all of the books
remained in the shop. They'd been fortunate with this one.

Though she didn't want to attach herself to a place she'd
soon leave, she couldn't ignore the compulsion to see the town
her family loved. To walk where her mother, her grandmother
and others of her family tree once walked.

The real question was whether it was worth allowing
someone—especially a man—closer in order to find her books.
Dee's words about letting people in haunted her as she plopped
onto the bed with the two volumes, ready to discover what
secrets they held.

Chapter Five

The strangest thing about *The Histories of Women: Unraveling the Mysteries of the Female Life and Mind* was that it wasn't a book at all. When Hope had opened it last night, handwritten words greeted her inside. A woman named Grace Holloway seemed to have had the book created to use as her journal. Hope became taken with the woman's writing and the woman herself. The journal was a fascinating glimpse into her 1895 life.

On the inside cover, Grace had inscribed in slanting, elegant script:

This shall be written for the generation to come: and the people which shall be created shall praise the LORD. Psalm 102:18.

The birds welcomed Saturday morning with their songs despite the cold, as though willing the weather to match the date on the calendar. Tomorrow would be May. Mags had given Hope the day off since she'd be home with Ulysses. Plus, Hope had worked the full week through.

In celebration of finding her grandma's book and her first week of work, she told them she'd make a special dinner that night. She'd already gone to the grocery store and couldn't wait to test some literary-themed dishes on them—some potential menu items for the mobile café she dreamed of. But the meal prep could wait.

The chill of the ice-cold boulder beneath her seeped into her skin, her bones. A shiver disturbed the gigantic diary balanced on her lap. From her spot on the lakeshore, Dusty Jackets was behind her and up the hill, and the whole of Arrowhead Bay was spread out to either side.

She'd found the bay mesmerizing yet disconcerting at times, with the hollowed rock "face" of Lost Lover's Island sneering back at her. And with the water always doing as it pleased. Sometimes fierce, pummeling the rocks so hard it sounded like a thunderstorm. Sometimes gentle with barely a whisper against the pebbled shore. It took orders from no one. Today, the waves lapped quietly at her feet, white foam gathering at the edges like the world's largest bathtub.

Tendrils from the braid she'd twisted into a bun tickled her cheeks as she read in Grace's journal:

...to say that I am a stranger in a strange land is quite the understatement. Or, as the locals would say, I'm a fish out of water. I know my father has done his best to do right by us since Mother passed. He sees the untapped potential for industry in this rugged, wild land known as Wanishin Falls, Minnesota. But I admit, I am grievously homesick for London. I've taken my comfort from the company of my sisters, the warmth of the people, despite the cold of their landscape, and the beauty here in spite of its inherent harshness.

The lighthouse on the point of Arrowhead Bay lights the way for the fishermen on the saltless sea known as the Great Lake Superior, and I feel in my heart a reminder. Through every storm, the deepest of nights, darkest of hours, through the loneliness or feeling lost, there always has been and ever shall be a Beacon to lead me home.

The very lighthouse Grace referenced still perched atop a point at the northern tip of the bay. But now it sat dark.

"It's freezing out here!" a voice called from behind her. "What are you doing down there?"

Hope turned to find Kat waving and smiling from the top of the hill. She waved back, closed the journal and hiked it and her book-laden shoulder bag up the hill, hoping it wouldn't bust.

Her breath puffed white fog into the cold air. "Hey, Kat. I was just reading."

Kat's head tilted to the side, eyeing the big book. "The history of the universe?" She had a stocking cap over her pixie coif and wore the Chucks with slim dress pants.

"The history of women, actually, but it turned out to be a woman's diary. I think she was trying to be ironic with the cover title." She handed it to Kat, who inspected it.

Kat quirked a dimpled side grin and passed it back. "Or ensure that her brothers or dad would never go near it with a ten-foot fishing pole."

They both chuckled. How tongue-tied the confident Ronan became about the book came to mind.

"I'm on my way back to the café. Why don't you come with me, and I'll get you something hot to drink?"

She stashed the diary in her bag and followed Kat.

Hope needn't have worried about adding much to the conversation. Kat chattered away about the town and its residents as they made their way along the main street.

"...and that's Mrs. Baranski's house. She's, like, two hundred years old. But she's sharp as a tack, that one. See how her entire yard is like a Christmas explosion?"

Hope nodded. The whole exterior of the house and every inch of her front lawn held strands of lights and Christmas decorations—from big waving Santas and his elves, to the sacred. Even a life-size nativity scene.

"She wins the Christmas display contest every year, but Dad always said that's sort of cheating since she never takes them down all year long." Kat's dimples deepened as she laughed.

Hope wrangled a rogue piece of hair back into her bun, debating whether she should get to know this woman better or not. "So, your dad... You said he gave you the restaurant. Is he retired?"

"Him? Sit still? No way." An impish grin added sparkle to her eyes. "He and my mom have taken on extra responsibilities at church, and they say they're feeling called to ministry. They just don't know what area yet."

"What about you? Do you like running the café?" Hope adjusted her shoulder bag, which grew heavier with each step.

Kat took the bag from Hope. "I guess... I've never thought about it. No one's ever asked me that." A wrinkle—the only wrinkle—formed on her forehead. "I like talking to customers. It's sort of a family in there. I love seeing what's going on in everybody's lives. I like matching employees to the tasks that bring out their strengths. But, unlike you, I don't have a real knack for the culinary arts."

Hope had asked but remained unprepared to respond. But they had arrived at the café's front door. If she kept questions directed at the other person, they were less likely to ask her any. A little social trick she'd learned in her reentry into the "normal" world.

A burst of warmth embraced Hope as they stepped into the café. Kat swept her hand out, saying Hope could pick whichever seat she wanted and Kat would bring her an extra big mug of hot tea. Hope picked her way through the booths and tables, about half-full with late-breakfast or brunch patrons. She skirted past a boisterous table of gray-haired men playing cribbage and settled into a corner booth by a line of windows. Facing the door, of course.

Kat brought her the tea, but then the early-lunch crowd filed in, whisking her away. Hope pulled her grandma's book from the shoulder bag and traced the signature on the first page. She had read *Little Women* as an adult a couple of years ago, barely remembering the story her mom had read to her as a child. As much as she loved holding this book in her hands, she didn't care to read it again yet.

Something had ached in her chest when she'd read about the close-knit family. Sisters—something she'd never know anything about. The thought pulled at an unseen thread hemmed around Hope's heart. The late-night talks, the lifelong confidantes, the laughter, even the fighting.

She closed *Little Women*, and as she'd done every chance she'd gotten lately, opened the diary. Grace wrote about meeting the man who kept the lighthouse and his son. Grace's father had launched a logging business on the outskirts of Wanishin Falls. Her father found it difficult to work with the proud shipyard master to export the wood. Her older sister, Clara, had met a promising prospect for a husband, whose father worked with their father. So engrossed was Hope that when Ronan sank into the seat across from her, she jumped and hit her knee on the table leg.

A ledger dropped onto the table with a loud thump. Ronan

pointed to its cover. "I think I've found something." He grimaced. "Sorry, I didn't mean to startle you."

She swallowed, her heart racing from the shock of being pulled from her fictional world into the present—a frequent liability for a bookworm like herself. Worse for someone who also lived with the fear she did. "Found what?"

"An entry." He opened the large book of figures, pointing with his worn, calloused finger. "There was a sale for a *Jane Eyre* three-volume set, first edition. Look at the date."

Hope stood, leaning in closer. Her head a mere inch from Ronan's. She pulled back. "Is this when you said your grandpa started to show signs of dementia?"

He sighed, taking off his flat cap. Today he was looking like a mix between an old sea captain and a 1920s newsboy, but not in an unattractive way. "I'd say that's when we finally admitted he was more than just forgetful. But yes, that was around the time of his official diagnosis. You can see the sale was signed by Grandpa. Grandma was probably with him, but she would have had no idea what they'd sold."

"So, do you think Ulysses wandered up to the attic where he'd kept my books with Aggie's stuff and decided to bring my *Jane Eyre* down to the shop?"

"I do." His fingers folded together over the ledger. "I know Gramps would never sell them intentionally—especially since I'm sure Aggie told him what they were and that you'd come for them one day. He probably brought them downstairs to look at them but had a hazy day and forgot all about them and who they belonged to."

"Ulysses is the sweetest. I certainly don't think he tried to do it. Now the question will be, where did my other books go?" After spending the week keeping Ulysses from hurting himself or damaging anything, as well as witnessing him forget time, place, even himself, who knew where the others ended up...

Ronan's finger traced along the lined paper. "Look here. The guy who bought the set got an incredible deal. This, uh—" he squinted at his grandpa's minuscule, sharp handwriting, much like the notes she'd found "—Mr. Richard Allen."

"$5,000" was marked next to the title of the book.

Hope slumped back into her seat. "Yeah, not enough zeroes there. Even so, I doubt he's going to part with it for anything less. I have some money saved, but..."

It would be most of her savings. Her nest egg of every little penny she'd scrimped and saved over the last several years. Working whatever low-paying jobs she could get for a person with no reputable work history. She'd pulled double and triple shifts as a line cook and bussing tables to save what she needed to buy a bus or van to turn into her dream mobile café and bookshop. It wasn't like she could sleep in those early years after she escaped from her captor anyway, for fear of nightmares.

After several years of hard labor, she'd felt emotionally ready to go back to her childhood town and track down the kind librarian, Aggie, who'd been her ally as a forgotten foster kid. Instead, she found Aggie had died and her mom had left her the books with a promise of treasure. She just hadn't thought she would need to *buy* the books her mom had left her as a gift.

"You could sell this or trade it. I already asked my grandparents about the book, and they said you can have it." He tapped the edge of Grace's diary, bringing Hope back to the present. "I looked up this Richard Allen. He's an antiquarian bookseller and antiques dealer in Duluth. He might give you a good trade to bring down the price on your books. Collectors love stuff like this. I looked up the title too. Can't find it anywhere. It's one of a kind."

She pulled the journal closer, not wanting to admit how

much it had dug its yellow-paged claws into her heart. She'd sooner part with her growing collection of *North and South* copies by Elizabeth Gaskell, one of her favorite stories of all time.

"No, I couldn't. This isn't actually a book at all. That's why you can't find any record of it."

His prominent brow puckered. "What is it, then?"

Opening the first couple of pages, she turned it so he could see the handwritten words. She filled him in on Grace and her personal writings about her life in the late nineteenth century.

His dark features contrasted with pale eyes lit up. "That's fascinating. I don't blame you for wanting to keep it. We'll find a different way to barter your book back."

She didn't miss the way he said "we." The word stuck like hot coals in the back of her throat.

He ran a finger along the journal's spine, accidentally brushing warmth against her wrist. She pulled back her hand in haste, but he didn't seem to notice. "Look at that craftsmanship on the binding. The question is, who made it for her? And where? You know, there used to be a bindery here in Wanishin."

"Really?" Her excitement meshed with his over the little piece of history before them.

"Yes. It's the building we're turning into the youth center and history museum. I wonder if someone there made it for her." He rubbed the back of his neck. "You should come out there sometime. I'd love to show you around."

A throb started at her temples, but she was saved a response when Kat skipped over to the table and scooted into the booth seat beside her.

"What are you two up to over here? The conversation looks scintillating." Her fingers clutched under her chin, her dimples on full, adorable display.

Even though Hope and Kat were close to the same age, no doubt Kat was often mistaken for much younger.

When Ronan filled Kat in, she dropped her hands to the table. "Ugh, bookworms. Here I thought it was something juicy. This town is so boring!"

Her petite features scrunched up like a teenager asked to take out the garbage.

"I've seen lots of cities, Kit Kat." Ronan tilted a smile at her. "Trust me when I say that it's a good thing to have a hometown where people know and care about you." His eyes darkened as he muttered under his breath, "Or at least they used to."

Kat put a hand over Ronan's across the table, and Hope tried to look anywhere but at the display of...affection? Friendship? Or more?

All at once, the moment was gone and Kat removed her hand to slap the table. "Well, this gal could use some excitement. I'll drive you to that Richard guy's antiques shop in Duluth to get your book back, Hope."

Even as Hope started to say, "Oh, thank you, but—" Ronan protested, hand up. "But I was—"

"What? You think a couple of girls can't handle it?" Kat's hand slid to her sitting hip.

Eyes widening, Ronan let his gaze roam from the diary's title to Hope and then Kat. "No. I... You know I'm not... Of course not."

With a triumphant nod, Kat grinned like her feline namesake. "It's settled, then."

To Hope, that truly was a win. She thanked Kat. There was no way she'd take a solo trip in the car with Ronan, no matter how polite and helpful he seemed so far. She knew more than anyone how first impressions could be deceiving.

"You're sure your car is up to it?" Ronan's expression held genuine concern.

Kat stood from her seat. "What's that supposed to mean?"

"Well, your car is usually on its last wheel."

"Red Betty? Nah, she's like a cat. Nine lives."

He quirked a lopsided grin. "Aren't you on the twentieth life now?"

While they bantered about her history of car mishaps, Hope was the odd person out. They'd clearly known each other a long time, probably grown up together.

For the first time since she'd arrived, the fact that her family was from here, had grown up here too, took root in her mind. She'd been too preoccupied with acquiring what she'd come for so she could leave as soon as possible. She hadn't given her family's connections to the area much thought since the night she'd reread her mom's letter. What if some of the people here knew her family? Maybe someone would remember, if not her mom because she'd moved away pretty young, perhaps her grandma or great-grandparents.

It was an unsettling notion she quickly shoved behind the door where all of her forbidden thoughts and memories lived.

After she and Kat made arrangements to go to Duluth on the following Friday, the soonest Kat could manage time away from the café and her brother—who would hang out with Ronan and the kid he was supervising for his community service for the day—her spirits lifted.

Now she would have to come up with some sort of plan to pay for the set of books or trade for them. Hope paid her bill, waving away Ronan's money as he offered to get the check for her "brown water" as he called it.

Ronan blew out a breath, wishing it'd blow away the frustration building in his chest at this woman beside him. She was so buttoned up, so secretive and mysterious. How could he trust her? Yet the pain living in those eyes…

He'd only glimpsed it here and there when she seemed to

let her guard slip. But there it was. And it made him want to understand what haunted her.

"You know I'm not trying to insult you, right? Or hurt you." He opened the door for her as they left the café.

Her eyes stared off in the distance, unfocused as she clutched her bag. He'd known better than to ask if she needed help with it. She mumbled an absent "Hmm?"

"By offering to pay for your tea. Or opening the door. Helping you with your search…"

Her full lips flattened into a thin line.

He adjusted his cap back in place over his too-long waves and tucked the ledger under his arm and fell into step beside her. "I'm not… I mean, I was raised with old-fashioned values, *small-town* values."

"What do you mean?" Her forehead creased.

"I was taught the golden rule, and that if you can help, you should."

Even with Hope's height, he still had to bend his neck to meet her eye. He scrubbed at his stubbled cheek as they stepped onto the sidewalk. He'd parked at his grandparents' and walked to the little diner—about the only restaurant, other than the pizzeria and the new Thai place at the edge of town—eager to tell Hope the news about the ledger. But he also needed to keep up with his exercise. Though he'd completed physical therapy a while ago, it was ingrained in him now.

He jammed a hand into his jacket pocket. "I'm no good at this. I don't mean to, but I seem to keep upsetting you at every turn."

"How do you know you're upsetting me?"

"So I am?"

Her lips pressed so tight together this time they disappeared.

"Look, I don't know what kind of people or *men* you're

used to, but I'm not helping you in hopes of anything in return. You don't owe me anything."

Ronan turned back, now several paces ahead. She'd stopped
dead, feet planted, her bag dropped to the ground. Her already
pale cheeks blanched white.

He retraced his steps to where she stood but shook the notion to reach out in reassurance, sensing it wouldn't be welcomed. Instead, he grabbed her bag and handed it back to her.
"I'm not sure what you've been through—"

Her eyes fluttered closed, dark lashes brushing against her
high cheeks before she opened them to gaze over his shoulder.

"—and you don't have to tell me. I just want you to know
that you're safe with me, okay?"

She drew a shuddering breath, head turning away.

He mustered his gentlest voice, the one he had only ever
used with Matthew and his mom during her illness before she
died. "All right? I promise I won't hurt you."

"Where have I heard that before?" The words were so quiet,
the wind had almost whisked them away. But in the end, her
chin dipped. "Okay."

The mood needed lightening. "You know, my dad is a gruff
guy. Tough love and all that, but he taught me that chivalry
should never go out of style. He treated my mom like roy-
alty." *Me, not so much.*

He shoved his hands into his pockets. "Dad said that no man
should sit if a woman is standing, to open doors for others,
take my hat off in the presence of a lady—guess I'm breaking
that rule." He ran a finger over the rim of his hat.

"Because he—you—assume we're the weaker gender?"

This was the most emotion he'd seen out of her, her chin
set high, one hand grasping for her hip, bag in her white-
knuckled fist.

"No, not weaker. The opposite. Most of the women I've

known, especially my mom, were braver and stronger where it counts than anyone I've ever met. And they deserve respect."

Her eyes, glowing like molten gold in a ray of sunlight, seemed to study him. To search for a lie in his words.

Finding his opening, he continued, "But above all, my father taught me that I should give a woman no reason to ever be fearful in my presence." He glanced down at her again. "Honor and trust are so important in our family. I take that seriously. You will never have anything to fear from me."

How could honor and trust not be important to the Barrick family when the legacy prowling after them had everything to do with both?

For the first time in his company, her shoulders lowered as if the muscles had finally relaxed. "Thank you. Modern chivalry isn't something I've ever experienced, but I'll try to get used to it. If it's as innocent as you say." Her chin lifted once more.

She reminded him of a composed librarian again. He shot her a smile. He wasn't foolish enough to think they were friends now. She was still too much a stranger. But maybe she wouldn't act like a frightened, cornered animal around him anymore.

They continued their walk to Dusty Jackets in silence, but not the tight, tense kind. Companionable, like the kind between two people who had finally burst the uncomfortable bubble between them.

When they arrived, Hope scuffed her worn sneakers against the sidewalk. "So, I'm making a nice meal for your grandparents to celebrate my first book find and a week of work." She pulled her lips between her teeth, then rushed forward. "You should stay…and celebrate. I mean, I couldn't have gotten this far without your help."

He chuckled. The invitation seemed to cause her a fair amount of distress. He almost offered her an out and told her no. But before he knew what his mouth was doing, the words "Sure. That sounds great. I'd love to try some of this cooking everyone has been talking about" popped out.

Everyone except Hope, who bustled with professional efficiency around his grandparents' kitchen, settled around the corner table to play Five Hundred, a family favorite.

"And that's how you win!" His grandpa, the old twinkle back in his eye, slapped the table. It was a good night for him and it not only lifted his own spirits but Grandma Mags's as well. He hadn't seen her laugh this much in a long time.

"Take it easy on us, Gramps." Ronan laid down his cards, stretching back in his chair.

"Not on your life." Grandpa's bushy brows twitched with humor.

"Dear?" his grandma called over to Hope, where taste-bud-prickling aromas wafted from whatever she was doing. "Is there anything I can help with? I feel like a lazy stump sitting here while you're doing all the work."

Hope laughed, a sweet, musical sound. "Absolutely nothing, Mags. I told you. This is my treat."

"This girl can cook!" His grandpa's face turned earnest as he thumped his stomach with his palm. "You just wait, Brock..." His lips compressed as if searching. "Ronan, I mean."

"So I hear." Ronan frowned at the memory glitch but quickly shuffled the cards and his attention away.

"You're too sweet, Ulysses. Never have I had such an enthusiastic fan of my cooking."

Despite how unsure Ronan had been about letting this stranger into his grandparents' lives, he couldn't deny how well they seemed to be getting along.

His grandpa put a forefinger in the air. "'One cannot think well, love well, sleep well, if—'"

Hope stopped stirring in the large mixing bowl under one arm. They both finished, "'—one has not dined well.'" Grinning ear-to-ear, they said together, "Virginia Woolf!"

"You two are a pair matched in literary paradise." Grandma Mags clasped her hands together, glowing. "I don't know if you believe in such things, Hope, but I do. God had a reason for you to come to Wanishin Falls, and it wasn't solely for your books."

Hope ducked her head, back to stirring. "Maybe. He's a bit hard to hear lately."

"Sometimes we have to stop moving around and quiet down to realize He's been there all along." Grandma Mags smiled at Hope but then turned it on Ronan and squeezed his hand across the table.

Oh, how he'd waited to hear the voice of God in the last three years since the accident on the lake that took his leg and the young crewmate under his watch. Kyle, Harold Gunderson's son. He didn't blame the man for his bitterness toward him. Ronan had been the ship's captain, after all. It was his job to ensure his crew's safety and bring them home in one piece.

Often he'd look up and find himself asking, "What now?" And he didn't like the answer, which seemed to be, "Wait. Trust." Not encouraging words for a doer.

Grandma Mags patted his hand once more and sat back. "How are things coming at the old bindery lot? What about that boy, Tate?"

He stood to refill his grandparents' iced teas and his soda, skirting around Hope. "It's going okay. Tate has been quite a bit of help. He remembers me from my volunteering with the church youth group, so that helps. And when he's done sulking for the day, he seems to genuinely want to see this youth center get going. The ladies upstairs from the historical society think he's a riot. His snarky attitude doesn't put them off at all."

He didn't mention how hopeless the whole venture felt and how much he could use some serious divine intervention to get the manpower and finances to complete this thing. He didn't want them to worry.

Instead, he peered over Hope's shoulder, careful not to get too close. "Can I ask what you're making? It smells awesome, especially to a man living off microwave dinners and anything I can catch with a hook."

Her cheeks rosied. "I'll give you credit for cooking fish. That's not easy. But if my other competition is frozen microwave meals, I should be okay." She pulled on oven mitts and retrieved something sizzling from the oven. "I'm making a *Little Women*–themed dinner, inspired by their Christmas meal. Why not have Christmas on the verge of May, right?"

His grandpa pounded on the table with a "Hear, hear!"

"It's warm beet greens with sour cream dressing, rosemary roast beef—because the grocery store didn't have duck—sweet potatoes Anna, and cranberry-molasses pudding with vanilla hard sauce." A palpable passion had risen in her voice.

He let out a long whistle. "That sounds amazing."

He hadn't noticed because they'd been enjoying themselves, but it was getting close to 7:00 p.m. She'd been cooking for hours.

"Tell Ronan about your café on wheels, Hope." Grandma Mags gestured to Hope, who seemed ready to crawl into the nearest hole. "Come on, it's a great idea."

"Well…" Her voice quavered. "My dream is to open a literary-themed food truck café where the food is inspired by the books I'll sell. Like cucumber-and-shallot white gazpacho instead of the 'white soup' mentioned in *Pride and Prejudice*, Turkish delight trifle from *The Lion, the Witch, and the*

Wardrobe, crab-stuffed avocado from *The Bell Jar*...menu items like that. Maybe some fun things for children, like the cakes from *Alice in Wonderland*."

She moved her hands as she spoke. "I enjoy unique foods that tell a story of their own. I want to give people more of a fine dining experience but on the go, if that makes sense. I'm just trying to figure out how to do that on a budget." Her words rushed over one another and at the end, she stopped, face flushed.

How could this enigma of a woman seem so confident, so serious and secretive one minute, and so vulnerable and shy the next?

He leaned an elbow on the counter. "Did you always like to cook?"

She paused as if choosing her words carefully. "I didn't always have the opportunity to cook. My mom used to let me help her in the kitchen—kid stuff, like adding the chocolate chips to the cookie dough or mixing the pancake batter." Her smile warmed her expression. "It wasn't until a few years ago, when a good friend and excellent cook took me under her wing and taught me all she knew, that I realized how much I loved being in the kitchen and creating food."

Hope retrieved the roast and sweet potatoes from the oven, setting them on hot pads beside the pudding already cooling on the counter.

When she faced him again, he tried to give her his best encouraging smile. "That does sound like a great idea. Really. I think people will respond to the connection between a good meal and a good book, especially if they can find both in the same place."

Hope bent her head, but this time with a grin. "The taste is for a moment, but the memory is forever. Just like the way you remember how a book made you feel years afterward. That's what I'm trying to do with food as well."

This was the most he'd seen her smile or talk since arriving.

Wiping her hands on a towel, then flinging it over her shoulder, she turned back to him. "I'm not trying to compete with your grandparents though, truly."

Grandma Mags swatted the idea away with her hand. "We're well aware there will be more than one place to find books in this world, dear. Don't you worry."

Hope retrieved the carving knife for the roast beef. "Besides, I'll probably buy half my stock for the little-bookshop-on-wheels side of the truck from here. And I'll be heading out of town soon, after I find my books anyway. Chasing warmer weather—that's what people in the food truck business do, I guess."

Tightness formed around his grandma's eyes. "Where will you go first?"

Hope kept her focus on her work, slicing the roast. "Well, if I find the books and can find the bus or van I need this summer, I'll probably stay close to Duluth with it being tourist season. They have a peddlers, or mobile food vehicle, license so I can go from park to park."

Her delicate fingers arranged the meat on a platter. "As it gets colder, I'll head south as I mentioned. I was thinking possibly South Carolina or maybe Orlando, Florida. I've read that it's the least expensive place in the US to get a food truck license and easiest to maintain with operating fees."

He would never be the one to discourage a dream—look at him with this youth shelter—but had she *really* thought through how she would do this on her own? But he didn't doubt the determination written into the lines of her face.

His fix-it brain whirred to life—all of the ways she might need help, connections, equipment, et cetera.

"It may be helpful to talk to a bank about a small business loan or maybe Abe and Sophia, the cooks at Kat's café. They owned a food truck before coming to Wanishin Falls. I could—"

"No, that's okay. I'll manage." A small smile hitched up her lips, but there was no argument in her words.

Perhaps she'd do more prep, not with his help though, and he tried to stuff the tug in his gut away. The one that said he needed to be the one to be there for her. It wasn't his gig. He had enough going on and he didn't need to get any more involved in Hope's life than he was already.

Ronan grabbed the plates, utensils, and filled a cup with iced tea for Hope.

They ate and laughed—even Hope—over the best meal he was sure he'd ever had. *Sorry, Mom. May God rest your soul.*

After they cleaned up from dinner, he stretched his arms to the sides as though it would find another nook or cranny for the food expanding his stomach. "Well, who's up for a little evening outing to walk off the meal? I'd love to take you over to the old bindery lot and show you around, Hope, if you'll join us."

Grandma Mags agreed. Gramps stared at Hope with his head cocked to the side. Before Hope could answer, he stood from his chair so fast it fell over.

His grandpa's eyes were focused, but Ronan suspected whatever was about to come out of his mouth would be the dementia talking. He didn't want to be right.

"Dottie, dear. I told you the stories are true. They're all true. I'm close, I can feel it. The treasure is real." Gramps strode around the table, standing before Hope.

Instead of the usual kind smile lighting her face, Hope's skin paled as though she'd seen a ghost.

Chapter Six

The days crawled from the night Ulysses randomly called her by her grandma's name until Friday. Hope and Kat planned to travel to retrieve her book from the antiquities and bookseller in Duluth that afternoon. With bated breath, she'd waited to make a move toward her next challenge, another book to cross off her list.

In the meantime, every muscle in her body tensed whenever Ulysses looked at her for more than a few seconds. Would he mix her up with her grandma again? And why would he?

No one had noticed anything amiss with her when Ulysses had called her Dottie. They seemed intent on not embarrassing Ulysses. They'd left for their stroll to the youth shelter site. She'd feigned a headache and stayed behind.

The old rotary phone at the checkout counter rang, the sound so jarring in the quiet space. "Dusty Jackets Bookshop. How can I help you?"

"Is a Miss Sparrow there? This is Richard Allen of the Antiquities and Oddities in Duluth." His voice barked out so she had to hold the phone away to save her eardrum.

"Yes, this is Hope. Thank you for calling me back. I'm coming out to Duluth today and I'm looking for—"

"I'm aware of what you're looking for and like I told my assistant to tell you, I prefer to handle my business *in person*, especially with one such as yourself…"

What did he mean by that? The hairs stood at attention on the back of her neck.

She rushed forward. "And as *I* told your assistant, I wanted to be sure the volumes were still at your shop and talk about what you'd be willing to sell them back to me for."

"All in good time, my dear. Maybe we can grab a drink once business is settled. I'll see you soon." His words leaked through the phone like an oil spill. Viscous. Toxic. She'd heard this tone before.

Before she could argue, he'd hung up.

She returned the receiver. At least she wouldn't go alone.

Ulysses sat in one of his tufted wingback chairs while he sorted through a pile of books for her at a little table. He'd begged to do something useful. The wit sparkling in his eyes told her he was himself that afternoon. Hope absently thumbed her way to the back of the book she held.

What had he meant by treasure the other night? Was it a story made up in his fading mind or a true memory, something shared with her grandma, perhaps? The questions burned her tongue. Despite her brain screaming *No!* she approached the older man.

"Ulysses?"

He adjusted his glasses, eyes still searching the titles in front of him. "Hmm, my dear Austenite? What can I do for you?"

She pulled an antique Queen Anne chair closer, opposite

Ulysses, and laid down the book she carried. "May I ask you something?"

"I think you already did, dear." He met her gaze and winked. "That's what you'd call a dad joke, only in this case perhaps more of a granddad joke." A chuckle floated from his belly. Something warmed in her own at the sound.

"The other night after we had dinner and before you, Mags and Ronan visited the youth shelter lot, you said something in passing I wanted to ask you about."

His shoulders drooped. "I'm afraid you can't put much stock in what I say these days, my dear. But what was it?"

"You looked straight at me and called me Dottie. And then you said something about treasure. Is there anything you can tell me about that?"

A gentle smile curved his lips. "Ah, yes. Dottie. She was a childhood friend of mine and Aggie's. She…" And then it happened again. His head cocked to the side as if seeing her for the first time. Mouth moving, no sound.

His bushy brows gathered, then rose high on his forehead. "She looked— You look just like her." His words, slow and shaky. "Hope, is there anything you'd like to tell *me*?"

This was why she should have kept her big mouth shut. She'd already said too much about her plans for after she left Wanishin Falls, unintentionally inviting Ronan to offer her even more help, more involvement, the night she'd made them dinner. Not that he didn't have a point.

She sighed, glancing heavenward. This was all much more than she'd planned to share, but Ulysses deserved the truth. "Dottie was my grandmother. The *Little Women* I found was originally hers. I know she used to live in Wanishin Falls, along with most of my family. All dead now, I've heard."

He nodded, pushing his hand forward to squeeze hers. She let him. "Yes, we were good friends growing up. She was a little buttoned-up, like you." He winked again. "I was the one looking for adventures and following rumors of treasure."

Rumors. "About that... My mom used to say there was a family legacy, something of value. Do you know if that's true?" Fitzwilliam nudged her leg beneath the table. She bent to pat his head.

Ulysses stood slowly, grabbing a small stack of the books he'd organized by topic and author at her instruction. "That's the fuzzy part, I'm afraid. I know Dottie and I speculated, based on stories from both of our families."

"Wait. You have a family story of treasure too?"

"It's one and the same story, my dear. One treasure for our two families. Or so the tales go." He laughed at her slack jaw and set the books on a nearby shelf. "Our families go way back in history. About a hundred and twenty years, to be more precise. We were once leaders of this town, and our families were close."

She sensed a *but* in there, though she didn't press the matter. Too many questions and random thoughts grappled with one another, each clamoring to be the first to break free of her mouth.

"Did you ever look for it? My mom told me about the treasure. At first, I believed because I was a kid and that's what they do. As I got older, I didn't, but then I read the letter she left me and I thought maybe...hoped it was true. Do you know what the treasure was supposed to be? Why did it sit there instead of our ancestors using it? Does Ronan—"

"Does Ronan what?" The man himself popped around the corner.

A jolt, like lightning hitting her chest. Her heart stuttered, then pummeled against her rib cage. A high whine in her eardrums blocked out Ronan's next words. His mouth moved, no sound. She clutched her chest where air should fill her lungs, but only quick, shallow wisps wheezed in and out. A clammy sweat slicked her brow and upper lip. Stomach churned.

Panic attacks, and what Dee had helped her name a complex form of PTSD, born of her years of repeated abuse. A small startle could trigger the devouring beasts. They held no sympathy for time, place or inconvenience. Gave no quarter and were brutal in their ability to rob her of what little joy her life held and replace it with the purest sort of terror.

Hands. Kingston—her once-boyfriend-turned-trafficker—reached out his hands and grabbed her. Shook her. Squeezed around her throat. Pulled her hair. Left her without choices. Took everything that made her, her. Snatched every hope she ever had. His weren't the only ones. So many hands.

She threw her own palms in front of her face to ward him off.

"Stop!" Her eyes squeezed shut. "Leave me alone."

The ringing faded but her own labored breaths remained loud, ragged.

Hands—not Kingston's—laid gentle pressure on her shoulders. She blinked, lowered her finger shields.

Ronan knelt in front of her. When had she fallen to the floor and pulled her knees to her chest like an animal protecting its soft, vulnerable organs? Like the heart.

His voice cut through the haze of fear and anxiety. "Hope, can you hear me? Are you all right?"

She pulled back farther until his arms fell from her shoulders. Ulysses had gone back to stacking books so his mind must have shut the door to the present again. Ronan remained at eye level and studied her. As her breathing slowed, heat crept up her neck and face. What would he think of this woman who'd come to stay with his grandparents now?

"I'm... I'm okay. I just..." What could she say?

"Have panic attacks?" There was no mocking, only concern in his stormy silver-blue eyes and his tone.

"How did you know?" Her words croaked out of a dry throat and her body shook. An episode always zapped her of strength and hydration.

"Because I had them too, after my accident." He sat across from her and slung his forearm over a raised knee. "Nightmares too."

She focused on slow streams of air, in then out. "Accident?"

He knocked a hand against his straightened leg. A metallic sound rang back beneath his jeans. "I used to captain one of the laker ships…until a crane line snapped and a shipping container fell on my leg."

The pain of it, inside and out, still evident on his face.

"I'm sorry." Her heart thumped, almost back to its regular rhythm. At least this time it didn't seem like the symptoms would last hours. "The memories, the panic. They can blindside you out of nowhere. Creeping monsters, always watching and waiting."

But she couldn't bring herself to share the source of her own monsters.

"Mmm-hmm." His answer was short, but the understanding gaze lingering over her face, long.

He maneuvered himself to standing, with a little difficulty and a wince. "At least my costume is more believable for the Founders' Day Festival now. You know, with the Lake Superior pirates and all. I can go as a peg-legged crewmate."

"Lake Superior pirates?" Her lips twitched. He must be joking. "Or maybe Captain Ahab and dress Charlotte up as the white whale?"

"If she'd sit still long enough to wrangle into a costume." He chuckled.

When her legs shook, pushing up from the ground, he

frowned. "I'm going to get you some water. Why don't you sit by Gramps."

She slumped onto the chaise longue across from Ulysses, who whistled while he worked.

Ronan returned and handed her a glass of ice water. "Thank you." As she sipped, the cold trickling down her throat worked to revive and refresh her. She placed the now-empty cup on a side table.

Ulysses's head lifted, eyes rounding as though just noticing his grandson. "Ah, Ronan, my boy. Do you have a favorite classic? That's what you asked, right, Hope?"

She turned her palm over to say, "Not sure what he's talking about," but they both went along with it.

Ronan sat in the chair next to Ulysses. "I love a good wilderness story like *Call of the Wild*. Anything by Dickens, Gramps, like you. I like his commentary on social classes and the plight of the working class and poor."

Not exactly what she thought he'd say. Hope picked up the copy of *North and South* she'd found while organizing and looking for her books from a stack beside her on the longue. She placed a featherlight touch to the humorous last words on the last page. "That's why I love this book." She held up the lush leather-bound edition she had half a mind to purchase and add to her collection.

"And I'm sure it has nothing to do with the brooding Mr. Thornton." Ronan's grin turned boyish.

She rolled her eyes. "If you must know, I also like that she gets to be the hero in the story. Margaret Hale's no damsel in distress, and she saves John Thornton in the end. It's not just love—it's mutual respect." Words flowed like a tap straight from her heart when confronted with cooking or books. Why couldn't she shush? Hadn't she already revealed too much about herself, especially to Ronan?

"Do you make it a habit to read books backward?" Ronan gestured to the *North and South* in her hands.

"She does indeed," Ulysses chimed in, back to his sorting. "I've seen her perusing the last page of just about every book here."

Ronan cocked his head.

Hope shrugged. "In my case, I don't judge a book by its cover. I judge it by its last line. I've never been wrong. Plus, I like to know what's coming."

Ronan stepped closer, examining the volume in her hands. "I can understand that. But some of the best things in life come as a surprise. Things we may not see coming but end up being the best thing for us. You know?"

Hope's chest tightened. She opened her mouth, not that she knew what to say. The front door dinged, rescuing her.

A spindly middle-aged woman with flaming red hair walked in. A shiver shook her little body as she pushed the door shut against the blustering wind outside. The forecast showed the weather was about to turn. Hope prayed they were right.

"Hello, Poppy. And how are you this fine day?" Ulysses ambled over, tipping his head toward the woman.

She stood, hoping her legs would cooperate now.

"Hope Sparrow, this is Poppy McGoven. Poppy is… Well, I'm not exactly sure. She wants to pave paradise and put up a parking lot, in this case, in Wanishin Falls. Poppy, Hope is helping out at the shop and…" He trailed off as the woman's eyes grew wide.

Poppy thrust out her hand, bone wrapped in skin. "Ulysses, please. I'm trying to bring at least some of the town into the twenty-first century." Hope reluctantly shook her hand. The woman had a cold, strong handshake. "Pleased to meet you, Hope." Her gaze remained sharp, studying Hope's face.

Hope attempted to release herself from the woman's intense scrutiny by slipping into business mode. "What can we help you with?"

Poppy let go of Hope's hand and rubbed hers together. "Since I'm no longer working toward attaining the old bindery property—" she cast a scowl toward Ronan, which he returned with a smirk "—I've decided, along with my business partners, to create an adventure tour company in Wanishin Falls. And I need to do some research to make the experience as authentic as possible. A real immersive up-north feel." She spoke like she was already filming the commercial.

"What kind of information will you need?" Ronan asked.

"We need books on the town's history, the best natural sites in the area and, of course, the Lake Superior pirates."

Hope couldn't help the giggle that escaped over the idea. "I thought Ronan was kidding. Swashbuckling pirates in the Midwest's Northwoods?"

But Poppy's face stayed sober, her angular face sharpening further. "Oh, you better believe they were a real thing. They don't call this the saltless sea for nothing."

Hope cleared her throat. The phrase reminded her of Grace's words.

Ulysses rubbed his bristly chin. "Yes, the stories of pirates terrorizing, plundering and smuggling weren't only in the Caribbean like Hollywood would have you believe. They stole from merchant and cargo ships, sometimes commandeering the vessel for themselves. Illegal liquor, goods and even coins and valuables like we usually think of when we hear 'pirate treasure.' The Lake Superior pirates were just as cutthroat as any on the ocean and maybe tougher too. They had to endure these harsh winters, after all."

Poppy bobbed on the tips of her narrow feet, cheeks flushed. "I still get the heebie-jeebies from the portrait of Captain

'Cold Hands' Robert Bartholomew, one of the most famous pirates from this area, at the history museum. His eyes seem to follow me. No wonder there is no end to the old wives' tales about him." Her shoulders quivered.

Hope's fingers tightened around *North and South.*

Ronan's arm brushed against Hope's as he sidled up beside her. "And yet you would've closed down our history museum... People need something to whisper about."

Poppy's thin nose lifted, pinning him with a pointed glare. "Hmm, seems they have plenty."

"What old wives' tales?" Hope's words came out a whisper.

Ronan's arms crossed over his expansive chest. "Oh, there are local legends about Captain Cold Hands still sailing a ghost ship on stormy nights and such."

The tingle of goose bumps crept up the back of her neck.

Hope glanced between the other three. "Why? What makes people say that?"

Ulysses held a finger in the air. "Ah, now that's the question, isn't it? Because no one ever found him or his ship. It was as though he vanished into the fog 120 years ago. Some say he sails the lake looking for his hidden treasure."

Her ears perked up. "Treasure?"

All of them smiled, but Poppy answered. "Many people have looked. No one's found a thing. More than likely, it sank with him and his ship. But you know how people can be about that kind of thing."

Ulysses and Ronan moved to the back holding area to find the books Poppy requested. Hope had no choice but to endure the odd woman's scrutiny. Hope placed the book in her hands back on the chaise and busied herself by dusting the front counter.

Poppy tapped her foot and let out something between a sigh and a groan. "You remind me of someone. I can't put my finger, or rather, my brain, on it, but you do. I'm afraid I'm going to lose sleep over it."

Hope stopped polishing the worn wood, heart drumming in her ears. Oh, no. This was it. Someone else recognized her. For a moment, the notion to flee yanked at her feet. Grab whatever she could from her room and run. It was what she was good at.

Anytime someone asked too many questions or she whiffed that they recognized her as Emily Carrington, she ran. Emily Carrington was an orphan, a foster kid, unwanted, abused, trafficked and had a record. Granted, Dee and a women's advocate from the shelter had worked with a public defender to have her charges of theft, forgery and misdemeanor drug possession—done under Kingston's coercion—dropped. But the bookings, fingerprints, mugshot and the record of her arrests and original charges would always be there waiting to shame her should anyone dig into her real name.

Hope Sparrow was none of those things. A blank slate with dreams for a better life.

She didn't run. Instead, she froze under Poppy's razor-sharp glare like a deer caught in headlights, as though standing still could hide her presence.

Ulysses and Ronan returned, arms loaded with volumes of various sizes to satisfy Poppy's request. Poppy shook her head as if she gave up trying to place Hope.

She blew out a breath she didn't remember holding.

Kat burst in with her signature bright smile and artfully messy pixie.

"Hey, new girl. Are you ready for our little road trip?"

Hope silently thanked God for His timing and nodded with a little too much enthusiasm.

Mags had already insisted Hope leave a little early for the trip. Ronan would close the shop for her.

Ronan's smile warmed as he said goodbye and hoped it went well in Duluth.

The conversation with Ulysses drifted back to her. She'd been so distracted with her panic attack and everything else afterward. *Oh, please don't let Ulysses say anything to Ronan.* Who was she asking? God surely didn't answer prayers built on deceit. She still had no idea how to or *if* she should tell Ronan about their family's connection. And how could she possibly do that without telling him who she really was?

She didn't like the narrow gaze Poppy leveled at her, so she didn't mind when Kat grabbed her elbow and ushered her out the door with hardly a wave goodbye and thanks to Ronan.

Kat pointed to a woman, an older version of Kat, sitting in the driver's seat of the delivery van parked outside. "Do you mind if my mom drives us? Don't tell Ronan he was right."

What could Hope say except "Sure, that's fine"?

Kat offered the front but Hope declined and slid open the back van door and slipped inside.

Kat turned as soon as she hopped into the front passenger seat. She gestured to the stylish woman, maybe in her late fifties. "Hope, this is my mom, Marian. I hope you don't mind her tagging along." Kat's impish grin earned her a tsk from her mom.

"No, not at all. The more the merrier." She hoped her voice didn't sound as contradictory as it did to her own ears.

Meeting another new person wasn't good. She'd shared too much with the Barricks as it was. If people found out who she was and all of the baggage that went with it, would they understand why she'd lied about her name, her past? Would they trust her around Ulysses and the bookshop after seeing her arrests? Could a reputation follow her as she tried to start her small business?

Her record coming to light would only open up questions. Questions she didn't want to answer. And if the Barricks found out and made her leave before she found her books, she would never have the longed-for connection with her mom and family, nor would she have the promised treasure to help her achieve her dream. Though, now, after talking to Ulysses, she realized the treasure may not be hers alone, which was fine. But she'd have to tell the Barricks. Which led her back to why she didn't want them to know who she was in the first place. Roadblocks, U-turns and detours—those were the paths before her.

"Nice to meet you, Hope. I've heard all about you." Marian's dimples, youthful like her daughter's, deepened as she smiled at Hope in the rearview mirror, snapping Hope back to the present. Her face had a little more roundness and her short hair was softer and less spiky than Kat's.

She managed a smile.

It wasn't like Hope hated people. But with each person she met, a little thread spun out from her heart like a spider's silk attaching her to this place. What if it imprisoned her? What if she couldn't cut herself loose when it was time? The rising panic clutched at her throat again.

She tried grounding for five—counting five things she could smell, see, touch, hear and/or taste. A coping skill from the trained trauma counselor she used to see at the women's shelter. She focused on sight. A man walking his dog, a jogger, Kat fiddling with the radio station, a large oak tree sprouting spring-green leaves, her hands in her lap. She did the same with her sense of touch. Faux leather seat, spongy wool hem of her sweater, fingernails pressed into her palm, rough canvas of her shoulder bag, the cool window on her temple as they pulled away from the curb.

Her breathing slowed.

Marian turned out of downtown Wanishin Falls, exiting onto Highway 61, headed south toward Duluth. "If Kat would ever get her oil changed on her car like her dad keeps telling her, she could've driven you herself."

Kat tapped her fingers on the window's ledge. "Yeah, it's in the shop. Sorry." She gave her mom a playful tap on the shoulder. "I know the real reason you're helping us out is that you can't pass up an opportunity to bargain shop or go to Duluth."

"I certainly don't mind if I do. Love it there. Plus, I might be able to help Hope get the best deal on buying her book back. I'm persuasive when I need to be."

Hope could see where Kat inherited her confidence.

Hope fiddled with the money in her purse. Counting. Recounting. All the money she could use from her savings and selling the books she could part with—five thousand dollars. Even so, it may not be enough. A mix of phantom food smells permeating the café van's interior made her stomach turn.

Or maybe it was the idea of haggling with Richard Allen, the antiquities dealer. She shivered. He'd certainly given her the creep vibe on the phone, but her radar tended to stay on overdrive.

"So, Hope, Kat tells me you're thinking of opening up a food truck. Maybe you should come hang out at the café and see how the business end works. Kat told me you already have the cooking side down."

"I would love to if Kat doesn't mind a shadow for the day."

"Not at all. I'd love to show you the ropes of the business side of owning a restaurant sometime." Kat's tone was bright.

But it grew uncomfortable when Marian tiptoed on the nosy side about Hope's upbringing.

Kat turned in her seat. "You'll have to excuse my mother. She's got small-town-itis. It's where you think everyone's whole life story is fair game for conversation."

Marian clucked her tongue. "Oh, now." But then she shot Hope an apologetic grimace in the rearview mirror. "Sorry. I do forget sometimes that not everyone wants to talk about, you know, everything."

"That's okay."

"Oh!" Kat threw her hand out, making her mom yelp. "I forgot to tell you, Hope. Our chef, Abe, didn't realize you helped out the other day. He says thank you for stepping in."

"It was no problem. It was nice to work in a big kitchen and practice cooking for a crowd."

Marian drummed her fingers on the wheel. "You know, he and his wife, Sophia, owned a food truck for a few years before moving here."

"I've heard."

Kat directed a brilliant grin at Hope. "Yes, that's what I was going to say. He said he'd love to talk with you about it sometime. Said he and Sophia could even help you create a business plan if you want."

See, she didn't need to involve Ronan in any more of her life or plans than he was already. The idea held excitement and apprehension. "That's so nice of them. I might take them up on it."

As the van hugged yet another curve in the road an hour and fifty minutes later, the rugged wildness gave way to a bustling city and panoramic views out the driver's side windows. The Aerial Lift Bridge, dual lighthouses, and shipping harbor appeared in the distance.

The closer they drove to the downtown antiques shop, the faster her heart pumped.

"Richard Allen—I've heard of his shop." Marian turned down a street headed for the heart of Duluth's city center. The old architecture mixed with the new gave off an eclectic, urban vibe. "I think his Antiquities and Oddities is over on West First Street."

They pulled up to a rich redbrick building marked Trading Post with the year 1858. Hope clutched her purse and took a steadying breath as they piled out of the car.

Kat squeezed Hope's shoulder. "We've got this. Don't worry, okay?"

Hope tried to smile.

The door played a short melody to announce their entrance.

"What can I do for you?" A slick-haired, roundish man stepped from behind a gleaming counter. His voice matched the man she'd spoken to on the phone.

The shine of his hair rivaled that of his trinkets perched on glass tables and in display cases. It was certainly nothing like Dusty Jackets. Not a speck of dust anywhere. But it also didn't have the heart of the shop she had come to enjoy.

"I'm Hope. We spoke on the phone about the *Jane Eyre* volumes you have." The short but unsettling phone call they'd had made her itch to run in the other direction.

Kat and Marian wandered the store and stopped, enthralled by a display of Victorian mourning jewelry with bits of hair preserved inside.

"You are even more beautiful in person, Hope." He leaned back onto the counter, a snide smile playing beneath his mustache. "Maybe dinner could be the purchase price." Swill edged his tone.

She stumbled back a step.

"I'm only kidding. No need to panic. People these days." But something hardened in his beady eyes as he returned behind the sales counter.

Her already fraying nerves brought back memories of another man she'd made the mistake of trusting. Someone who she never guessed had the darkest of intentions for her. The panic attack from earlier left her emotions too close to the surface with just an eggshell-thin layer between her "socially acceptable" facade and the "cowering on the floor" self inside.

This wasn't her captor or any of his cronies. She repeated it silently to herself and straightened her shoulders. "Of course." Her laugh quavered. "May I see the volumes?"

"Why don't you step into my office and we can discuss this further." He gestured toward a curtained door behind him.

Her fingers tightened around her purse. She turned to find Kat and Marian perusing fine porcelain teacups behind smudge-free glass. They caught her eye.

Kat called over, "Do you need any help, Hope?"

She swallowed, shaking her head. "That's okay. Enjoy looking around. This won't take long." *I hope.*

They both nodded, but each wore an identical wrinkle between their brows.

Richard tapped his meaty fingers on the pristine checkout surface. "Well? I don't have all day, even for an exquisite beauty like you."

Her cheeks heated, but, she noted, not with a spark of pleasure…like under Ronan's gaze. Wait, where had that thought come from? No, that couldn't be true.

"I believe we can do our business right here." Her words tremored, but she held her chin high.

Something ticked in his jaw, and it set her teeth on edge.

"As you wish. I'll be right back."

He disappeared behind the curtain and within a minute returned holding a special protective plastic sleeve with a cloth-bound bundle inside.

As the curtain whooshed back into place behind him, a gust of stale cigarettes and whiskey—or was it brandy; she never could tell the difference—assailed her senses. Throat closing, lungs burning, she pressed her bag to her chest and told herself not to hyperventilate. Those smells, mixed with the hardness in this man's eyes and his arrogant demeanor, worked together with her recollections of the man who she thought she loved fifteen years ago. The man who would, for the next decade, become her trafficker and living, breathing terror.

Kingston Brasher. If that had even been his real name. Probably not. To the girls he "owned" he insisted on King, and the alternative was a gruesome beating. But it didn't start that way. To a lonely foster kid of fifteen, he'd appeared as a handsome, mature older guy who paid attention to her. For a kindness-starved girl, he'd laid an irresistible trap.

He'd found her at the library one afternoon—hiding out with Aggie from her latest foster home where the other kids picked on her mercilessly. She'd been unpopular even among the other orphaned and abandoned children. King started asking her to sneak out at night, right under the noses of her foster parents. She and King would sit on the dew-damp grass at the empty park down the road, watch the stars, talking about the future. Their future. He'd told her he'd get her away from there, take care of her, even how much he loved her.

He bought her expensive gifts. She was so naive, she never questioned any of it. Just ate it up. She ignored the red flags, the possessive and aggressive tendencies, the way he isolated her further. Even from Aggie, her one confidante. She excused him, telling herself he was passionate because of his love for her.

She hadn't felt loved since her mom died. So it didn't take much for her to fall hard for him. She would've followed him anywhere.

But it was all a sham. The lies—everything—shattered when he revealed his true nature the minute he'd lured her away from her foster home and imprisoned her with two dozen other girls. She'd believed she was running away with the love of her life, her dreams finally becoming reality. Instead, it was the beginning of a ten-year waking nightmare.

Richard Allen cleared his throat, startling her. He pulled the books out of the sleeve and unwrapped the cloth, laying the books side by side. "Well, Miss Sparrow, are these the books you're looking for?"

The man in front of her wasn't Kingston Brasher. No more than Ronan had been earlier. This was Richard, a bookseller. She was safe. Kat and Marian stood just feet away, but she couldn't stop her legs wobbling as she inched toward the counter. The calm didn't come back as quickly as it had with Ronan.

She had no memory of picking up one of the volumes, but suddenly her fingernails bit into the leather. Richard's mouth moved, talking. She tried to tune in. He showed her different features to determine if they were her *Jane Eyre*. She caught her mother's handwriting, but all she could do was say "Mmm-hmm" where it seemed appropriate. The room faded to a faint whisper, far away.

Sometimes she couldn't explain why one thing conjured another. The stale cigarettes and the sharp, astringent smell of brown liquor crowded her senses until the walls closed in and her world spun on its axis.

Richard was saying something, but Hope grabbed her temples and words burst from her mouth. "I need to go. I... I can't be here."

The air moved as Kat and Marian encircled her.

"What's wrong?" His rounded face tightened, not so much with concern but wary with either alarm or suspicion.

Marian put a hand on her shoulder. Hope jerked away.

"Hope, what is it?" Kat leaned closer, inspecting her face for some outward illness or injury.

Not again. Not again, you stupid PTSD! "I'm... I'm not feeling well. I need to go." She turned to Richard and forced out, "Will you take five thousand dollars? Please? These books be- longed to my family. They should've never been sold."

Never been sold.

He chuckled. "Miss, you cannot expect me to agree to that offer. You must understand how much this set is worth. No matter how much of a bargain the old man gave me and who they belonged to, they are mine now."

Mine now.

Her teeth scraped together. "Can I trade you for other books of value?" The floor seemed to sink beneath her. This was nosediving, and fast.

Kat whispered, "Should we leave? We can always come back."

She waved off Kat's kindness. "I have other antique books in my collection, Mr. Allen. What do you want—*Pride and Preju- dice*? Ten copies of *North and South*?" A horrid notion erupted. She allowed herself to be whisked away with it. "What about a copy of *Seven Pillars of Wisdom*? It's worth more than most books in this place put together."

His narrow, calculating eyes widened as he leaned over the desk, fingers intertwined in front of him. "How important is this to you?"

"Very."

"Don't let him take too much from you, Hope," Marian whispered in her other ear.

What had Kingston and all the men after him taken from her?

"Well, this set is important to me too. I've waited to get ahold of a first-edition *Jane Eyre* for quite some time. I re- ceived the volumes back from the appraiser and now they'll be the crowning glory of my rare-and-collectible books sec- tion. They're worth at least ten times what I paid for them."

He crooked a smile that reminded her of a fox who'd invited a pig over for dinner. "Of course, I *might* be willing to part with it, provided you bring in that copy of *Pillars* to show me you're not bluffing *and...*"

She leaned away from the counter. "And what?" But her stomach already roiled, suspecting the answer.

"And what?" Marian repeated, a glower darkening her features.

The glint. Hope had seen it a thousand times in countless sets of eyes. "Maybe we could work out a more friendly form of payment..." He scowled back at Marian, his gaze swept over Kat.

A loud thump ripped through the air before she realized she'd tripped over her own feet jumping back.

Kat and Marian had her upright in seconds. Richard stood still with a calm, smug smile. Mother and daughter wasted no time escorting Hope out of the building.

"Hope, are you okay?" Kat brushed Hope's damp fringe of bangs away from her forehead. "Are you sick? That guy was a piece of work, huh?"

How could Kat possibly understand it was so much more than that?

"I just want to get out of here."

"But without your books?" Marian patted Hope's arm. "Let me at him with my negotiating skills." She drew herself up, but her smile faltered as she lingered on Hope's dogged resolve.

"We're leaving," Hope said. "He won't take the price I offered and I will never—" The words grated over clenched teeth, her fists cracking around her purse straps. "I'll never *ever* pay the price he's asking." In her mind, she added *again*.

Kat and Marian exchanged looks.

How could they not have felt what she did? Was Hope the only one who sensed what that slimy man was after? Maybe she'd imagined it. No. That was a lie. She knew the difference between oversensitive and discerning. Didn't she?

"I can't believe the nerve of that guy." Kat's expression had never looked so menacing. Her small hands curled into fists. "I think we should call the police."

Maybe it hadn't been just her.

Kat and Marian spoke in terse low tones until Hope put out a hand.

"No, let's get out of here."

When Hope reached the car, she leaned over it, covering her face with her hands.

What if she couldn't become this new person, Hope Sparrow? She gripped her head tighter, while Kat rubbed her back and said, "It's okay," as if that would erase anything.

She had believed she could learn coping mechanisms, change her name, deny who she was and become someone else. She'd thought the years she spent in the shelter for extrafficked women would equip her to forget. Move on with her life. Yet all it took was one startle and one jerk to put her right back in King's clutches, in her mind anyway.

She hadn't really moved on. Her life had been empty since she'd set out on her own. Moving from one job to the next. She hadn't let anyone close, except maybe Dee. That was arm's length at best. She'd told herself she didn't need anybody, and more importantly, she couldn't trust anybody. But the crashing tides of loneliness pushed and pulled, squeezed around her lungs, and told her she might be wrong.

Know and be known, as Dee had said. But that part of her had broken and scattered before violent gales long ago. Never to return.

Blowing out a long breath, she finally turned to face Kat and Marian, who still watched and waited. She hadn't noticed she'd been crying until the wind cooled the tears on her cheeks. The women strode forward then, wrapping her into a tender embrace.

"It's all right, Hope." Kat's words landed softly on Hope's ears. "We'll get your books back somehow."

"You'll see," Marian added, her voice both gruff and tender. "That brute will regret not giving them back."

Hope didn't stop them. The *Little Women* images of what she'd thought it would be like to have a family played out in the flesh this time. It was an indulgence she couldn't afford. Nonetheless, she let the warmth reach beyond the distrust, the pain, the isolation. Something lived there. Something she hadn't believed possible. A tiny spark of hope.

But, for her, hope was always followed by the bleak truth of her life. Ironically, her chosen name seemed a winged creature after all. One she could never seem to catch.

Chapter Seven

Throwing what felt like the thousandth bag of garbage into the dumpster behind the old bookbindery building, Ronan wiped the sweat from his brow with the back of his gloved hand. The air was like spring. About time. Warm, actually. Like summer wouldn't be far behind.

He and Tate spent their Saturday clearing out the junk and evidence of parties past, but concentration came hard. Hope kept swimming to the forefront of his mind and how strangely she'd acted when she'd returned from Duluth yesterday.

Something had gone down, but Kat wouldn't say anything, especially in front of Hope. Kat and Marian stayed long enough to ensure Hope was safely inside, then left. Hope's eyes, red and swollen, avoided his. When he asked if she'd gotten her books, she shook her head and claimed she didn't feel well and needed to get to bed early.

He limped over to his truck and pulled down the tailgate. With a grunt, he backed up to it and jumped to sit on the ledge, pulling off his gloves.

Why had he felt such a strong desire to go after her and hold her against his chest the night before? He wasn't sure they knew each other well enough—he certainly didn't know many things about her—to feel much of anything toward her. And yet, from the night they'd spent looking through the attic together, he'd had a keen interest in helping her. Maybe it was the vulnerability and loneliness he detected behind her sometimes dry humor and quiet distance.

Was it helping her that kept his thoughts wandering throughout the day? While he made his maintenance rounds for the city—changing light bulbs at city hall and the city offices, checking smoke detectors, raking the leftover dead leaves from fall and winter, and readying the lawn for spring planting and mowing—her rare, hard-won smile passed through his mind again and again. The kind of smile he wanted to keep putting there, no matter how difficult it was, because the moment it appeared it was like the sun had finally broken through a dismal gray sky. Brilliant and breathtaking.

He gave himself a good mental shake before reaching for his water bottle next and guzzling down most of it within seconds. He groaned as he massaged the area below his knee, where the stump of his leg met the prosthetic. Painful and stiff after a full day of work. Weekends no longer existed for relaxation.

Tate brushed his sweaty mop of hair back, revealing the shaved sides, or undercut, as the kids called it. He'd put away the tools in a storage garage detached from the main building in the back.

Ronan checked his cell phone for messages. The time read 7:00 p.m. "Sorry you're missing youth group for this. If you want, I'll take you late."

"I think I'd rather clean out that ancient bathroom again about seven times." Tate grabbed his water bottle from Ronan's truck bed and emptied it in four impressive swallows. "You stopped helping with youth group." It wasn't a question.

Leave it to a kid not to mince words.

"Yeah, I guess I did." It was all he could say. Anything else would sound like excuses.

Guilt churned in his gut. Lately, sitting in his same pew on Sunday mornings, the one he'd sat in all his life, felt…off. He'd experienced the shame of stepping back from volunteer work within the church, the judgment, but couldn't bring himself to help the church kids when he couldn't seem to help himself. God stayed quiet while his every failure and inadequacy roared louder and louder.

Ronan tapped the side of his truck. "Are you still going to youth group?" Attending church wasn't the definition of being a Christian. But the times in his life he least wanted to be around other believers were the times he most needed to be.

Tate did a shrug-arm-flop combination. "Nah. I'm not loving the hot seat of judgment right now."

"I get it." He didn't say how much. "They're worried about you."

"More like they want me to straighten up my act."

Ronan couldn't help his chuckle. "Yeah, that too." Tate's mom struggled to manage life and the kids while his dad worked on the lakers, gone for weeks at a time.

Tate kicked a rock across the parking lot and used the neck of his vintage Frodo Lives T-shirt to wipe the sweat from his face.

"Hey, maybe we should go together to church tomorrow. Safety in numbers?"

Tate's brow creased. "All right. Fine." The words sounded pulled out kicking and screaming. "Whatever. You can pick me up."

"Wow, can I? Thanks." His tone dry.

A reluctant grin spread over Tate's face.

"Hey, hard workers, coming up for air?" Kat strode across the lot.

"Yeah, I think we're done for today. What are you up to?" Ronan scooted to the side of the tailgate, giving the spot next to him a tap.

She hopped up, swinging her Chucks back and forth. "Ah, nothing. Just thought I'd see how the youth center is coming along."

"Nothing elaborate plans and a lot of prayer and elbow grease can't handle."

She stayed quiet.

He'd known Kat for a long time. They'd met in kindergarten and had every class together through school. And the slight pull at the corners of her lips, the usual mischief in her eyes dampened, meant she had something serious to talk about. She'd chewed him out enough times on the playground for pestering her for him to know he didn't dare press her. He waited before he broke the ice.

"So, I take it the trip to Duluth didn't go well yesterday?" But maybe he could get her started.

Before Kat could answer, Tate waved to get his attention. "Um, can I go? Or is there some other grueling manual labor you have planned to torture me with?"

Ronan rolled his eyes at *him* for once. "I guess I'm done tormenting you…for now. Aren't you fortunate I had the judge approve help with the youth center as part of your hours? I have so many fun things planned for us."

He'd hated it when his dad said things like that to him as a teenager. But his dad hadn't been teasing.

"Great. Can't wait." Tate's words dripped with sarcasm. He handed Ronan the folder from the truck's front seat with the community service papers. Ronan signed the hours for that day, and Tate started to walk away.

Ronan hopped down from the truck. "Oh, hey! After church tomorrow, we're going over to the beach." He gestured for Kat to wait as she mouthed, "We are?" Ronan continued, "With my family and Hope. Why don't you come with us?"

One brow tilted. "Why? You assume I don't have plans?"

Teenagers. So touchy. "No. I didn't say—"

"Because I don't." He shrugged. "Sure. That's fine."

"Okay, go take a shower...please." He smirked. "I'll pick you up at nine for service."

Tate flipped his skateboard into his hand. "Don't make me regret agreeing to this." With a salute, he dropped his skateboard on the pavement and pushed himself away toward home.

"What?" Ronan lifted a shoulder in response to Kat's stare when the kid was a block away. "I want to get out and enjoy this weather tomorrow with the cold finally gone for now. You can never tell in Minnesota. We could have a snowstorm next week."

He didn't voice his desire to restore the smile on Hope's face and get her mind off whatever happened on their road trip. "So, why did you really come here?" He took another swig from his water bottle.

Her legs stopped swinging. "Something happened in Duluth. I'm not exactly sure what. Mom and I were shopping in the front of the store while Hope spoke with the owner at the counter. All of a sudden Hope seemed upset. Panicked."

His grip tightened on the water bottle until it crumpled in his hand.

Kat's fingers twisted together in knots. "And what I saw on her face, I've only seen one other place."

"Where?"

"On the faces of the women I used to work with in college when I volunteered at the domestic violence shelter in Duluth. Fear, anger, pain. Like someone had taken anything resembling safe footing in her life, and yanked it right out from under her."

He paced a few feet away. "Are you saying you think she has a history of abuse or something?"

Kat opened her palms. "All I know is what I saw. At first, I thought she was just upset about not getting her books back. But the more I thought about her reaction..."

"Not to sound like I don't care, because I do, but why did you tell me this?"

She followed suit, jumping down from the truck. Her eyes seemed to study his. "Because I know you well enough by now. I know the way you look at her holds at least some interest. If you didn't have any attachment, you wouldn't be so devoted to helping her—into the wee hours of the night, I hear."

"Hey, now. They need a lot of help with Gramps, so I go over there every chance I get."

Her perceptive smile made his teeth clamp together.

"I mean it." He strode a few feet away from her prying eyes. "I'm not sure I know what to make of her, honestly. I hardly know anything about her." But maybe this was why. Maybe she had something hard in her past that made her hide from people.

"Mmm-hmm. Which is why I came here to tell you to be careful, Ronan."

He turned back, grinning. "Aw, you're trying to protect your old friend?" He nudged her shoulder, but in a more serious tone, added, "Don't worry about me."

She elbowed him right back. "I'm not worried about you, you big lug. I meant be careful because I don't want *her* to get hurt."

"Barrick men are nothing if not gentlemen." His back straightened. "You should know that."

"I do, but I'm making sure you're extrasensitive with her. She's been hurt. Bad. One wrong thing and she'll bolt. I can feel it. I saw it a hundred times at the shelter."

But he couldn't help a twinge of unease at the memory of his ex-fiancée leaving him after his accident, when he'd become less than a whole man. She'd run. From him. As fast and as far as she could. He could do nothing to stop it. But Hope wasn't Mackenzie.

He drew a slow breath. Why hadn't he pieced this all together sooner? Hope shuddered anytime they touched in passing. She hardly ever looked him in the eye even if he was talking to her. She jumped at the slightest sound, and the first thing she did when they entered a room was look at the exits. Not to mention the panic attack he'd witnessed before Kat arrived the day before.

The list went on. He raked a hand through his hair. He'd sensed something was amiss, but not what. Maybe that was why he'd felt compelled to tell her she didn't need to fear him that night he'd brought the ledger to the café.

"Well, what should I do, then? If I wanted her to feel safe around me. As a friend." He rushed to add the last part.

"Go slow. Prove to her over and over you can be trusted. That she can count on you. Every day. And be the man of your word I know you are."

"Oh, is that all?" He lifted a brow, but the words dived right into his chest. "All right."

She patted his shoulder. "I'll be praying for you. And Hope. Maybe if she sees she has true friends here, she can let us in."

With that, she left him to himself. He packed up his equipment and threw the last of the collected garbage away. He stumbled over his prayers where Hope was concerned. He couldn't help the jumble of thoughts mixed with prayers he threw into the Almighty's lap, for which he apologized, already knowing he didn't need to.

Was it best he didn't show he cared? She would leave soon. Her life didn't need any more complications, especially since she'd made it clear she had no plans to stick around. Maybe he should leave her alone. But he immediately struck the idea down.

He had already involved and invested himself. Plus, he had the sense she was alone in the world. His desire to help her, to show her she was cared for in any way he could, seemed to line up with what he knew to be right. Ronan prayed for a way to do what Kat suggested—be trustworthy, kind and dependable. But not only with words. That wasn't going to work with someone like Hope. With his actions.

He turned the big old key in the bindery door to lock up. A small crew of volunteers from the historical society had worked on their space upstairs earlier, but they'd left over an hour ago.

Gravel crunched behind him. He turned to find the bony features of Poppy McGoven appraising him.

"Hello, Mr. Barrick." He'd told her to call him Ronan, but she insisted on formalities. "I was wondering if you've found anything of historical significance that might help the tour company I'm starting." Her natural scowl moved to the building and his hand, where he still clutched the key.

"No. I don't think so. Just lots of garbage and junk so far." He rubbed the back of his aching neck under her uncomfortable glare. "But I can find you if I do."

She flipped a business card unnecessarily from her jacket pocket—like he didn't know who she was—and handed it to him. "Call me directly. My cell number is on there."

"Okay, sure. No problem." He shifted, sore muscles groaning for a hot shower, his stomach for food.

"Would you mind if I took a look around for myself?"

"I'm sorry, but I have to get going. Maybe another time." His gut twinged. Perhaps his to-be-found dinner called to him.

"Another time, then." She turned on her heel.

But within a few steps, she spun back. The corners of her lips quivered as though filled to the brim with secrets. "Oh, and I'd be careful if I were you. I don't think Hope Sparrow is who she says she is."

"What do you mean?" His fingers cracked as he flexed them.

"Let's just say, this little birdie is hiding something. The question is, what." With a smirk, she stomped off, leaving him with his mouth still open.

What on earth could Poppy mean?

Great, two people in one day telling him to be careful because of Hope, but for two very different reasons. What was it about this girl that created such strong reactions, one way or another? He couldn't help the seed of doubt sprouting from Poppy's words. He had, after all, told Kat he didn't know much about her. Not really.

As peaceful as his grandparents' bookshop had always been to Ronan, something about the last couple of days since the Duluth debacle had changed the quiet to a morose silence. It wasn't like Hope was moping exactly, but the blazing drive he'd seen in her to locate her books had dimmed to a small flicker. And, if possible, she was quieter than usual.

After he attended the early church service with his grandparents and Tate—Hope had declined the invitation—he strode with purpose under a calm blue sky and a warm late-morning sun into Dusty Jackets. He'd dropped Tate at home to change before picking him up for the beachside picnic Ronan had planned. He let Charlotte in behind him.

The pastor had talked about forgiveness that morning. It seemed to prod a sore spot in his chest. He didn't blame people for not forgiving him for what happened to his young crew-mate. After all, he couldn't forgive himself. But maybe the thing he'd never considered was whether *he* had forgiven God for allowing it in the first place. Not for his leg, but Kyle's death. Despite his uncomfortable thoughts, it was good to be in church again. Tate had looked even more uneasy than Ronan felt, but the kid made it through the service with an audible sigh when it concluded.

His ears rang with the absence of sound. It was funny how in such a short time he'd become accustomed to the chatter between his grandpa, Hope and sometimes Grandma Mags. Of course, Sundays were naturally quiet since the shop was always closed on "the day of rest," as his grandpa used to say.

Hope had nestled herself into the window seat in the rounded parlor, or castle room, as Hope and Kat referred to it, a book open in her lap. Fitzwilliam curled into a furry doughnut shape at her drawn-up feet while she gazed out the window. She jumped. "Oh, hi." She put a hand to her heart but avoided his eyes.

Undeterred, he pulled up a chair. "So, what trouble did you get into while we were at church?" He flinched. Everything about the question was wrong, wrong, wrong. Real smooth.

She slipped off her reading glasses and closed her book. It was her copy of *Little Women*. Her delicate fingers traced its cover. "I spent the time trying not to feel guilty about read-ing inside when it's so beautiful outside." Her lips turned up slightly.

"Exactly."

She frowned at his big grin.

He bounced his prosthetic leg and ignored the creaking that had once embarrassed him. "I think you should get out and enjoy the weather. Vitamin D is good for the body *and* soul. That's why I'm here to invite you to a beach picnic."

Her book slid from her lap, but he caught it with one swoop of his palm and handed it back to her. His fingers grazed a white puckered scar on the back of her hand and she sucked a breath through her teeth.

"Thank you." She tapped the book. "Well…" Her eyes kept straying to the stairs that led to her room. She stood.

"I mean, of course, my grandparents will be there and I invited Kat and her family too. Oh, and Tate, the kid I'm working with." Only gentle persistence was going to get him anywhere today.

Her face brightened. "Sure. It does sound nice to get outside for a bit. I feel like I've been cooped up a lot lately. Do I have time to change?"

"Sure."

No matter the doubt Poppy had planted, he'd concluded that even if Hope was hiding something, it didn't mean she was dangerous. If she'd planned to steal something from his grandparents or harm them in any way, she would've done it by now.

He paced and waited, settling in for the long haul. But she strolled down in less than ten minutes, transformed. Her usual buttoned-up, business-casual look had morphed into something more carefree. Even though she wore a less than open expression, the pale blue lightweight sweater, jeans and braid that stretched the length of her back made her look softer and more approachable. Nothing like her tweed and sleek updos. But shadows still hung beneath her eyes.

They picked up Tate and drove to the pebble-strewed

beach below his lighthouse home. Grandma Mags was help-ing Gramps down to the shoreline. Grandma spread a thick quilt on the sand, one she'd sewed herself. Ronan raced as quick as his uneven gait allowed to help Gramps into a camp-ing chair near the blanket.

Grandpa smiled benignly up at him. "The wind's picking up from the west. Be sure you're strict on your times tonight, my boy. Strict on your times. Storm's a-comin'."

Ronan squeezed his hand gently and tried not to let the helpless feeling of losing his grandpa swallow him. The man must've reminisced to nearly fifty years ago when the light-house was still operational and he helped his father run it. But, as things often do, technology and necessity had changed things. The shipping yard in Wanishin Falls wasn't used as much these days, in favor of Duluth and others.

Hope had lifted most of the picnic fare, another blanket and a small cooler from his truck by the time he returned. To his surprise, Tate took Hope's load and carried it for her. Ronan grabbed the small charcoal grill and called for Char-lotte to get out.

Charlotte bounded across the beach, almost knocking Hope over in the process.

"Sorry!" he called. "She still thinks she's a puppy. She doesn't know she's roughly the size of a small horse."

"A small horse?" Matthew, Kat's brother, echoed. His slurred words held laughter. "Maybe I should saddle her up."

Kat had arrived in the family van with the wheelchair lift and she'd lowered Matthew onto the parking lot pavement.

"Whoa there, cowboy. Don't get any ideas." Ronan set the grill and charcoal down and backtracked to where Kat struggled to move Matthew's wheelchair onto the boardwalk that ran up and down the beach. Ronan had successfully petitioned the city council for it so people like Matthew could enjoy the beach up close too.

"Where are your parents?"

Matthew's always-moving arms shrugged. "Where are they always?"

Though on the outside Matthew was a thirty-four-year-old man, his behavior and mental processing was closer to that of a ten- to fifteen-year-old. The latter showed in his slumped shoulders and scowl.

Ronan wrangled his wheelchair onto the path. Matthew took it from there, steering his electric chair with the lever on his armrest.

Kat sighed. "Mom and Dad are at the church helping organize a food drive."

Ronan recalled the pastor saying something about it during the service that morning.

Kat crammed her hands into the pockets of her overalls. "He misses them. But how can you argue with God's work?"

How indeed? He had defended his decision to create the youth center plenty of times—citing all the reasons it was a good thing. As if his good works would stop people from giving him the look of pity mixed with distrust. Maybe Marian and David, Kat and Matthew's parents, were trying to make up for something too. But then, they didn't have anything to prove the way he did.

He took in a lungful of the lake-water air he loved—filled with the tang of seaweed and fish, the sweet decay of driftwood and the surrounding evergreens.

As he prepped to grill their burgers and bratwursts, he soaked in a sense of unexpected joy at the scene of Tate and Hope chattering about Tate's love of all things Tolkien, Kat helping Matthew with his kite, Grandma Mags laughing at something a bright, alert-eyed Gramps said and Charlotte jumping over the small waves sliding up the shore.

The charcoal lit and he slapped his hands together. "Okay, who's hungry?"

That missing piece, the thing he'd lost along with his leg—self-respect? Purpose? Peace?—always nagged at him. He shoved it away. Not today. He didn't have anything to prove today.

Chapter Eight

Lying back on the blanket after eating her fill of cheeseburgers, fresh raspberries, strawberries and potato chips, Hope sighed. A mingling of contentment and overstretched stomach. "That was delicious. You guys will have to roll me back up the hill. I bow to the chef here."

Ronan saluted her with two-fingers. "To be fair, Grandma Mags had to save most of the burgers from being charred, and I pretty much can only make things over an open flame."

"Such a wilderness man." Kat's tone was teasing.

Ronan retrieved a Frisbee from his truck. Kat, Matthew and Charlotte played Frisbee. Charlotte tried to take over everyone's turn. The big overgrown German shepherd puppy seemed to love it when the Frisbee made it to the water, leaping into the waves with a big, tongue-lolling doggie grin. Ronan, clothes and all, splashed in after her up to his knees.

Tate had gone down the beach in the other direction, saying he wanted to chill on his own for a while.

Hope stretched out on the blanket, staring up at the puffed clouds' lazy trail across the sky.

The seagulls called from overhead, hoping for leftovers. Ulysses dozed in his camping chair. Mags and Hope soaked in the sunshine on the picnic blanket. Rays, steady and strong, told her summer was finally on its way, nearly mid-May.

Hope watched the Frisbee group, absently wondering if the water was very good for Ronan's prosthetic leg.

Soon Kat made preparations to leave. Matthew seemed tired and agitated.

Hope helped carry their stuff to the wheelchair-accessible van Kat drove. Kat leaned in. "Too much social time for him causes outbursts. I want to get him some peace and quiet before that happens."

Hope prayed her expression conveyed the empathy she felt. She marveled at Kat's compassion and patience with her brother.

Before they drove away, Kat made Hope promise to help with a special project at the café that week. Other than a couple of worried glances from Kat, she seemed to respect Hope's wish to pretend her emotional breakdown at the antiques store in Duluth hadn't happened. Ronan had given her the same space.

Hope settled back on the blanket next to Mags. Ronan threw a tennis ball now for Charlotte, and a reluctant Tate joined in. The smile Tate tried to hide peeked out.

"Ronan has always loved the water. It runs in his veins, I guess." Mags smiled, her pleasant wrinkles deepening, arms over her bent knees. "He was always a good swimmer."

"Oh?"

"Mmm-hmm. He won state in high school on the swim team. Said he felt like he could fly in the water. Things have changed a little in the last few years…" Her eyes misted, gazing out at her grandson. "But not his love of the water."

Hope stayed quiet, studying Ronan's broad smile on his often brooding face. But she'd come to see he might be more introspective and passionate about the things important to him than he was serious in the traditional sense. And she'd started to see a bit of his sense of humor now and then too.

"You know, he's not my blood-related grandson."

Mags brought Hope out of her scrutiny of Ronan, and her cheeks warmed as she turned to the older woman who'd caught her. She swallowed. "I didn't realize that."

It explained why Mags with her sharp wit and memory didn't recognize Hope's family resemblance.

"Yes, yes," Mags continued, either ignoring or not noticing her embarrassment. "I married Ulysses several years after his first wife, Daisy, died. You've heard him talk about her."

"Yes, sometimes."

How hard it must be to have her husband not recognize her at times.

Mags brushed sand from the edge of the quilt. "I married Ulysses when Ronan was just a little boy. And that grin—" she pointed at the still-boyish twinkle ignited in Ronan's silver-blue eyes as he scratched Charlotte behind the ears "—was what melted my heart. I was a goner. I was honored and forever grateful the moment he called me, *me*, Grandma. A woman unable to bear children of her own."

Hope swallowed. "I know he loves you. You're a wonderful grandma to him. He's blessed to have you and Ulysses, all of you. If I had— Well, sometimes I wish…" The words stayed locked inside. But the meaning was clear and reflected in the understanding on Mags's face. The ache in her throat expanded, making her gulp for a breath.

"He's been through a lot." Mags, with casual but careful,

measured movements, picked up one of the food containers and set it in the picnic basket. Eyes on her hands. "He may have told you some—you may have guessed at others. But the last handful of years has tried Ronan's faith, his relationships—" She didn't mention Ronan's father, but it seemed he must be on that list from what Hope could gather. "His career, his physical abilities, everything he's envisioned for himself since he was a boy. I have no business telling you about the nitty-gritty of each of those things and what that looked like for him. If he chooses to tell you, that's up to him."

"Absolutely…" She tipped her head, waiting for the point of this little statement.

When Mags drew a breath to go on, her expression was kindness itself but something steely clung to its edges, like a mama bear poised to protect her precious young. "I have come to care for you, Hope. I want you to know how much." She grasped Hope's hand tight. It felt right. Hope relaxed into another human's touch, and it didn't go unnoticed.

"You've become part of our family already," Mags continued. "In our family, we don't have to tell each other everything. We all have things we prefer to leave unsaid. The door is always open to share if we choose. But what's shared in the Barrick family, stays in the Barrick family."

Mags let go of her hand and leaned back. "That's a choice we each have to make. No one else can do it for us. But we also don't allow what's unsaid to hurt someone else. Do you understand, my dear?"

The message was clear: *Don't hurt Ronan with your secrets. He's been through enough. But your secrets are safe with me, should you choose to share them.*

"Yes, I understand." The words croaked out of Hope's throat.

"Hmm. Good." Mags seemed content, leaning back onto

her elbows. The serene smile in place again, she watched her grandson and Tate. "I imagine this is very different than where you grew up near Chicago."

"You're right." She took off her beat-up tennis shoes and socks and dug her toes into the sun-warmed sand and added what seemed safe. "There's certainly more fresh air in Wanishin Falls. And it's so quiet. I've never lived anywhere I couldn't hear police or ambulance sirens at least a couple of times a night. There's something about the lake though…"

She sifted the sand through her toes, watching the ceaseless waves tumble onto the shore, recede, the splash and the hiss, over and over again. Beyond which lay the great expanse of water.

"Do you like water?"

"I've always been scared of it. Even the little I could see of Lake Michigan in Chicago. I guess the thought of the waves pushing and pulling me, being out of control, frightens me. And the not knowing what's under there, watching, waiting. I don't know…" The hairs on her arms stood on end with a dark memory trying to push its way to the surface. "It's sort of terrifying. At the same time, I can't seem to look away." She let out a self-conscious chuckle.

Mags's face softened. She patted Hope's hand. "Well, we're all scared of something."

Or *everything.*

"Sometimes I look out at that water, especially when the waves are rough," Mags said, gathering the rest of the picnic plates and containers, "and I think, Lord, if it had been me You called out on the water, would I have come?"

Mags's hands stilled on the basket, a little V forming between her brows. "Jesus called Peter to walk out to Him on the water. Have you ever heard that story?"

"Yes, I have." Hope smiled. Dee had shared many Bible

stories during Hope's time at the shelter. She'd given Hope a leather-bound Bible of her own too. Her chest tightened. It was the one book she owned she rarely opened.

Mags went on, "Trust. Faith. It's a difficult thing when we have our eyes on the waves instead of on the One who commands them. We can get so lost in the depths of our circumstances, we forget to look up."

This had turned serious. Hope had no escape. Something squirmed in the pit of her stomach, but she managed a grimacing smile.

Mags straightened, her angled jawline sharpened. "There was a time when I felt I'd lost everything. My first husband left me after we'd lost baby after baby in miscarriage. I was in the deepest pit of my life. And then I found Ulysses. His kindness and this place seemed to soothe something in me."

Hope rubbed her forehead and glanced skyward where the gulls dipped and soared.

"That's like something Grace said in her diary." Hope had shared the diary with Mags, who had no memory of the book and assured Hope she was welcome to it. "Grace said when she first arrived in Wanishin Falls she felt lost and in despair, but she would watch the water every day. Day after day. The constant tumble and rush of the waves lapping on the shore reminded her of the unchanging nature of God's love. She'd come out here—" Hope gestured to the beach "—breathe this air, feel this same sun and know He was in control of it all."

Mags turned her face to the great golden giant in the sky, eyes closed. "She was a wise young woman. Right too. He is constant. We are never lost from His sight."

A glimmer of something deep in Hope's chest warmed her, but she couldn't admit out loud how much Grace's and Mags's words still confused and pained her.

Mags squeezed Hope's hand again, brushed off a spot of

sand on her leg and stood. She threw a shell out into the water, smiling over her shoulder at Hope.

"That's what it means, you know."

Hope stood too, sifting through the sand to stand at her side. "What *what* means?"

A sparkle lit in the older woman's eyes. "Wanishin Falls. *Wanishin* means 'she is lost' in Ojibwa. But I've always rather thought of this as a perfect place to find oneself. I know I did." With a wink, she ambled over to Ronan.

"I think that's it for us old folks," she called to her grandson. She and Ronan woke Ulysses and helped him to his feet. "We need to recharge our batteries."

Hope, along with Ronan and Mags, helped bring Ulysses back to their car. She and Ronan waved off Mags's offers to help haul back the picnic stuff. Mags told the now-bored-looking Tate she'd give him a ride home.

And just like that, Hope found herself unintentionally alone with Ronan again. She could've insisted on going back with Mags and Ulysses, but she didn't. Maybe it was the gorgeous sunshine. Maybe it was the company of someone who, for the first time in a long time, felt safe. Whatever the reason, she stayed right where she was. Toes dug into the sand.

The Frisbee flew over Hope's head, and suddenly there was Charlotte bounding into her chest, knocking her backward with an "Oomph!"

She'd lounged in the vacated camping chair, leafing through her copy of *Little Women* again while Ronan frolicked on the beach with Charlotte.

"Hey!" She wiped sand and water from her eyes, trying to untangle herself from the folding chair.

Ronan moved as fast as the shifting beach and his leg allowed, sand flying out behind him. "Sorry! Are you all right?" He dropped to his knees, wincing.

He helped her sit.

"Yeah, I guess so." She wiped off her book and put it back into its plastic sheath.

Ronan grabbed a small towel Mags had thrown in with the picnic fare and dabbed her face. The twitch in his chin gave away the laugh trying to escape. "Charlie's kind of a bull in a china shop no matter where we are."

His face close, his breath whispered against her cheek. The smell she'd come to associate with him—fresh pine, the warmth of sunshine and a hint of mint mingled with the faintly fishy breeze coming off the lake.

She swallowed the fear of being close and the fear of *wanting* to be close. The thought at once had her pulse jittering and her stomach flipping. "I'm fine, really."

But as she brushed the sand from her palms, a sharp pain made her suck air through her teeth. She stared at a gash where she'd tried to catch herself. The metal legs of the chair must've sliced her hand.

Ronan had removed his prosthetic leg to clean out the sand. He left the leg on the blanket and scooted closer to take her hand in his, inspecting the wound. "It isn't too deep, but we should get it cleaned up and bandaged so it doesn't get infected." His brows drew together, emphasizing his prominent brow bone and straight nose.

He was exactly what she'd picture in a long line of seafaring folk, perhaps Scandinavian in descent. Except for his dark, ruffled hair.

While Hope sat with her mouth slightly open an awkward moment too long, Charlotte snatched his prosthetic leg and bounded across the beach with it. The dog's tail wagged like she thought herself the funniest animal in the world.

Pulling himself to a kneeling position, he yelled after her. "Charlotte! Get back here!"

Hope jumped up, hastily wrapping the small towel he'd used on her face around her hand. "I'll go get her." She bolted after Charlotte, which the dog took as an invitation to play keep-away.

Ronan's deep rolling laughter trailed her as she and Charlotte zigzagged across the beach. Into the frigid water up to her ankles and then out. Finally, they arrived at an impasse as Charlotte swam out twenty feet from shore, Ronan's leg still clenched in her jaw.

"Charlotte, get back here this instant." Hope stood, hands on her hips, water now up to the knees of her pants, legs numb from cold. She was covered in sand and her hair fell from its braid.

Charlotte swam back to shore, giving Hope a wide berth, and bounded toward Ronan. He lunged for her on his good knee at the same time Hope grabbed the dog's big, sopping wet body. Hope tripped over Ronan and they both fell, but he managed to get his arms under her to cushion her fall.

Charlotte dropped the leg and with a doggie smile as if they'd played the best game of fetch, swiped up the forgotten Frisbee and sprinted away.

Hope's pulse pumped in her ears as Ronan held her against his chest. She forgot about the pain of their impact and her hand.

"That's why I prefer cats." She'd meant to be funny, but her voice lowered to a whisper.

His smile stretched wide a couple of inches from her face. He was warm against her frozen limbs, his arms gentle yet strong, but the feeling didn't remain a welcome one. Although his touch wasn't forced, the memories it conjured made her insides scream for air. Had she yelled out loud? Since he didn't look alarmed, maybe not. On the contrary, his eyes held something else entirely—heat, yes, but a tenderness she'd never seen before. Certainly never from a man.

Clearing her throat, as quickly but gently as she could, she plopped down beside him instead.

"Maybe it's the right time to confess something."

"What?" She frowned.

He scratched the back of his neck. "My real name isn't Ronan."

Her lips parted. Was this a ploy? Did he know she was keeping her real name from him?

"Remember the stories about pirates on the Great Lakes? Cold Hands, and all that? Well, my name is actually Peg Leg Pauly, and I moonlight as a singing pirate on Fish Fridays at Kat's Café."

She pushed off the ground and stood with a growl, but couldn't hide the spread of a grin. "You say Charlotte forgets she's not a puppy. I'd say that's a bit ironic." She handed him his leg.

He took it, chuckling, wiped it off and strapped it below his knee.

"Argh! We best be gittin' ye a bandage lest it turns gangrenous." He growled the words, rolling every *r* with a wink.

She allowed him to lead her back to the truck, both with an armful of picnic gear. Charlotte hopped into the back with a reluctant glance back at the beach.

Ronan pulled up to his lighthouse home, above the beach access, Hope quiet beside him.

The way he'd cradled her warmth against his chest still sent jolts of electricity through his body. Despite her height, she fit perfectly in his arms. But he'd revolted her, no doubt. After all, he was only part of a man. She'd tensed and removed herself from him the moment she could. But the words Kat said pricked at the back of his mind.

"We're here." He turned off the truck, which seemed to bring Hope out of her daze.

She blinked, full lips turned up. "When your grandparents said you lived in the lighthouse, I thought what an amazing place to call home. So, it has been in your family awhile?"

"Yup. My family ran it for generations. When it was de-commissioned, Gramps bought it."

Her round eyes rounded further.

He jumped out of the truck, calling Charlotte to go play in the front yard, and strode around to Hope's side to open her door, where she still sat. "Wait, so your family ran the light-house? For how long?" She finally got out but didn't take his offered hand to assist her. Instead, she clutched her wounded hand with the other.

"For almost two hundred years a Barrick has operated and/or lived in this lighthouse."

"Are there any other lighthouses in Wanishin?" Her gaze still seemed an intense study of him and his home. Her eyes darted to the structure, then back to him.

"Nope. This lighthouse was one of the busiest beacon light-ers between Split Rock Lighthouse and the various lighthouses concentrated around Duluth and their big shipping yards."

He led her into the ground-floor rounded living room with lake views off the jagged cliff on which the lighthouse perched. He'd worked hard to renovate the lighthouse, which was once a workplace first and a living space second.

"Did Ulysses ever live here?" She stepped slowly through his living room and into the open dining room and kitchen. The long fingers of her uninjured hand traced the lines of the bay window facing the water in the added-on rooms.

"When Gramps was a boy, but then the lighthouse became

unnecessary. My great-grandfather rented it for a time, and then Grandpa Ulysses bought it from the government to keep it in the family when he was in his early twenties. He wanted a Barrick to have it, but my father never desired to live here. When I more or less inherited it, it was in pretty bad shape. But as you've noticed, I like a challenge. So, I've restored it and added on a little bit at a time."

She sighed. "Well, I think the lighthouse is beautiful. You did an amazing job. You really are a jack-of-all-trades, aren't you?"

"Thank you."

She seemed to take in the tall stone fireplace rising in the middle of the rounded living room, the added-on light and bright kitchen and combined dining area, and the spiral staircase with twisting bookshelves all the way to the next floor. Her eyes lingered there the longest. He collected books like his grandpa, but Ronan kept his in neat order.

Something about her smiling approval made him straighten and stand a little taller. His own father couldn't stand to be associated with any of their family's legacy, especially the lighthouse.

She turned back to him. "That night we looked in the attic for my books, you mentioned the town having a long memory of an accident. The two shipwrecks in one night. Did it have something to do with this lighthouse?"

"It did—does, yes. My ancestor was supposed to light the beacons one night. There was a terrible storm. It was a job the Barricks and the town took very seriously, so when he didn't light the way for the ships and they crashed, it was about the deepest shame a lighthouse keeper family could face."

A sour taste rose in his throat as he moved his gaze out to the deep cerulean and the rocky islands that spelled disaster for the two ships over one hundred years ago. "I guess it passed down through the generations. Sometimes it seems like I've continued that legacy of disgrace, you know, after my own ship accident."

Her mouth moved without sound. He cleared his throat into the thick silence.

Turning, he gestured to the kitchen sink. "Here, you can rinse your hand and take a seat wherever. I'll get the first aid kit." His leg ached, and errant grains of sand in his leg sock chafed against his skin, but he kept moving.

When he returned with the kit, she had taken up a lounging spot in his leather recliner, paging through *Little Women*, her lips pressed into a line.

"Looking at it again?" How many times could she read one book?

Her expression turned rueful when he pulled a stool in front of her. "Yeah, I was just thinking I wish I'd gotten the volumes of *Jane Eyre*. I'm not sure what to do now."

"I know you want it for different reasons, but I never really liked that book. The story, I mean." He dabbed at the two-inch cut across her palm with an antiseptic pad. She winced. "Sorry."

She laughed, musical and rare. "All this time, we could've been comparing notes on the Brontë sisters."

"Let's not get carried away." He smirked, running a hand through the sand-covered, unruly waves on top of his head.

Finishing with the bandages and dressing, he wrapped and then tied the loose ends, reluctantly relinquishing her hand. "I can't justify Jane Eyre's choice in going back to that weasel, Edward Rochester."

Her nose scrunched, making her look like an adorable little mouse. "What do you mean? She loved him."

He stood, gathering the waste from the bandages. "But she could've done better than his lying self. He was dishonest, and with his secrets, he put Jane in danger as well as everyone in that house. He also tried to marry her under false pretenses. A man with any integrity would never do that. I mean, how could they build a relationship when it was founded on deceit and selfishness?"

Did he imagine the green tinge to her complexion?

"Even though I normally could argue for days on the merits of Jane Eyre's decision, I'm kind of tired." Lifting her bandaged hand, she tried a little flex. "Thank you."

"I should know better than to come between a girl and her book."

"No, it's not that…" She stood, shifting her feet. A stray lock had come loose from her braid. His hand itched to brush it back from her face.

"Where did you learn first aid?" She seemed to fish for a change of topic.

Unfortunately, the innocent question wandered into a painful part of his past. But maybe that was exactly what he needed to do with her. Dive into the deep end of his past. He'd vowed to make himself trustworthy in her eyes. She didn't seem able to open up to him about whatever had hurt her on her own. So, maybe he needed to go first and share the uncomfortable parts of his own life.

"Can I show you something special about this lighthouse? I promise you're going to like it."

Her eyes strayed to the door. Finally, she nodded. "All right."

He grabbed a glass of iced tea for her and a soda for himself from the fridge before nodding to the stairs. Indecision raced across her face but she followed him, giving plenty of room between them. She kept her book clutched to her chest like a shield.

He told her about the lighthouse building as they wound their way to the top, suddenly nervous about what he planned to do.

They emerged on the deck at the very top of the tower where the now-out-of-commission lamp lens was housed. He set their drinks on a small table and pulled up two padded outdoor lounge chairs. She sat in the offered chair, shoulders lowering, as though relaxing as she took in the view of water, sky, rocks and trees below. The wind whipped the stray lock of hair, and a small smile played at the edge of her lips.

"This is what you wanted to show me?" She sipped the iced tea, eyeing him over the rim.

"Yes, and to tell you something."

She set the glass on the table between them and absently ran her fingers along her book's edge. "Okay…"

His hands gripped the arms of his chair, knuckles white and visible beneath the weather-roughened skin. "I haven't told you everything about the day I lost my leg. You may have gathered there was more to the story, especially since I never returned to working on the ship."

"I suppose I didn't think it was any of my business." Her words were careful, polite, as though plucked from one of her beloved books. But he heard the faint edge of curiosity.

"Well, I'd like to think we're becoming friends." Her jaw tightened, but he pushed ahead. "I'll tell you what happened. If you want to know."

Whatever her secrets, it had become clear they were the wall she put between herself and everyone else who might come to care for her. Maybe he could help her break down her wall by lowering his.

He was rewarded with warmth in her voice as she said, "Yes, I would like that."

"I was captain of the *C. M. Spence*, a Lake Superior laker, for three years. From age eighteen, I'd worked my way up, first as a deckhand then to the kitchen crew. Anything I could get my hands on. Then I went back to school for mechanical engineering. But I couldn't wait to get back on the water. When I returned, the captain I'd sailed under previously secured me a position in engineering. When he retired, he put in the good word to promote me to captain."

Ronan couldn't help the memories that filled his gut with bittersweet mire. Hope sat, quiet, her amber eyes studying him.

"The water was a balm for some rough stuff going on in my life."

He straightened his shoulders, drawing strength for the next part. "By the time I took on the role of captain, my mom had become ill and my relationship with my father was strained, to say the least. He told me not to take off to the ship when I did. When she lay dying."

"Is that why...?"

She didn't have to finish the thought. "Yes, he seems bitter toward me because he is. He blames me for her death and we haven't been the same since. I had to escape. It was selfish and wrong. But I had to distance myself. And the quiet of the water, the rigid schedule of ship life and the isolation became a sort of a refuge for me. I wanted—no, I *needed*—to be by myself. I even distanced myself from my crew as much as possible."

He chanced a glance at her face, expecting loathing and disgust, but instead found understanding and compassion.

"When we were in port at Duluth, dropping off a shipment and picking up another, I received word that Mom had passed the day before. I had a cell phone, but I didn't always have coverage in the middle of the lake."

He ran a hand down his now-stubbly jaw.

"I should've gone ashore to seek a replacement and returned home. I was in no right mind to captain the ship that day."

Breath coming faster, he anticipated the end of the tale he already knew. "That night one of the new recruits, a nineteen-year-old kid from Wanishin, Kyle Gunderson, who'd wanted to be on my crew, was helping with the crane, moving the shipping containers. I was on deck when I saw the crane line snap. I ran to push him out of the way but didn't land how I meant to. The freight container crushed him and my leg. He died before we could even call the Coast Guard or an ambulance."

"That must've been horrible. I'm so sorry." Her expression faraway, she reached around the table to grab his hand. Though he hadn't told her to gain sympathy or her touch, the warmth and tingle of both couldn't be denied.

She stared at their hands intertwined and let go.

"I will never begrudge God this leg. I should've been the one. The one to die. He was so young. I can't understand why he lost his life and I didn't. After that—" should he tell the rest? "—the Barrick name had more than one stain upon it."

Tears pooled along her lower lashes. She blinked them away, turning again to the view of the lake. "I can't understand why such horrible things happen when we're supposed to have a loving God. That's something I struggle with."

He nodded. "I do too. But I keep coming back to—okay, mostly dragging myself back to—the knowledge that if He made me, not to mention the whole universe, He must know what He's doing with my life." Did it sound like he believed himself? Did he?

Her thumb, again and again, riffled the pages of her book. Suddenly a picture appeared on the edge of the pages.

"Hope!"

Her back went rigid. Terror flashed across her face. "What?"

"Do that again." He tried to lower his voice so as not to frighten her this time.

"Do what again?"

"Fan the pages like you were." He stood and leaned closer.

She did as he requested until the image appeared again. She gasped.

He grinned. "It's a fore-edge painting."

Her return smile told him he needn't explain to a literary enthusiast like her about the hidden paintings—most popular in the late eighteenth and nineteenth centuries—artisans created on the edges of book pages.

The painting, only visible when she held the edges of the pages at a certain slant, showed a rock formation dipping into the water, a natural archway in the shape of fingers steepled together with a space between the two wrists.

He chuckled. "I know that place."

She rose now too, examining the picture. "This is a real place?"

His chin dipped as he ran his fingers along the pages. "It's not far down the shoreline. It's called Praying Hands Arch." What could this mean?

He moved to the railing of the deck and pointed down and to the left where the natural wonder had formed over many years of erosion. He watched as she followed his finger with her gaze, mouth slightly open.

Together, they observed the sun start its dive into the horizon. The light reached through the rock hands, setting the water ablaze in orange and crimson.

For the second time in less than two minutes, she clasped his hand, ignoring her bandage, fervor now in her touch. "Will you take me there?"

He wasn't sure if there was anything she could request just then that he'd say no to. Instead of asking why it was so important, he found himself saying, "Yes, of course. Someday soon, when we have lots of daylight left."

At least the fire he thought had left her had returned. It seemed now more of an inferno.

Chapter Nine

Like a beacon of light to a ship tossed on the waves of a storm, so too is my dearest friend, Edward Barrick, to me in this sometimes tumultuous and often lonely life. Fitting, as he and his family have the immensely important responsibility of keeping the Wanishin Falls Lighthouse. Edward brings to my mind our Lord, both in compassion and in his kindly spirit, reflecting His light and hope to us all.

The words in Grace's diary played and replayed in Hope's mind like Ulysses's record player did on occasion at the shop when it hit a scratch in a record. Curious how the one damaged record that skipped the needle backward played Billie Holiday's "All of Me" over and over. Could she show anyone all of herself?

So, Ronan's ancestor was the friend Grace continually spoke of in her writings? She had started to expect as much, especially after Ronan showed her his lighthouse-turned-home and talked about his family as the lighthouse keepers for many years. Was it time to tell Ronan who she was and the connection between their families?

She mulled this over while she helped Kat unpack food in Mrs. Baranski's 1950s-style kitchen. The elderly woman was the proud owner of the front-yard year-round Christmas extravaganza.

"Thank you for helping me with my food deliveries." Kat grabbed one of the bags, full of take-out cartons, from Hope's hand.

"No problem. I've enjoyed it." And she meant it.

When Hope had shown up at Kat's Café on Friday of the following week, ready to help her with a mystery task, Kat told her she needed help making and delivering meals to those in need around town. Hope wasn't sure she was the right person for the job. The extreme introvert, book nerd, woman of hidden truths that she was.

But as she planned the meal and prepared it, her excitement grew. She'd used the café's kitchen to make shepherd's pies topped with fluffy mashed potatoes and shredded parmesan-romano, which she turned golden brown with a brûlée torch—warm comfort food. She'd also portioned out lettuce salads into plastic containers, and homemade buttered dinner rolls.

As she made her way around Wanishin Falls with Kat, she was greeted with kindness by the people on the receiving end of Kat's generous spirit. Hope found the smiles contagious. They prodded at the wall around her heart, finding the cracks and crevices like the planks of a worn wooden floor. Sneaking through, threads of warmth and light.

"Girls, now you must stay to eat with me. I couldn't possibly finish all of this." Mrs. Baranski shuffled into the kitchen as fast as her walker allowed. With her wisps of white hair swept into an elegant knot on top of her head and her sagging cheeks pulled into a rosy grin, Ethel Baranski had the air of a woman who was once a ballet dancer.

"Oh, you know I can hardly pass up food, Mrs. B., but Hope has to get back to the bookshop." She winked at Hope. "She has a date with Ronan."

Hope could only imagine how many shades of crimson and violet she turned with her cheeks tingling and hot. "I... I... No, hardly. I mean, he's just helping me with the books I—"

Ethel's pink lips quirked. "Such a handsome boy. Always has been. And such a gentleman too. You don't see that much nowadays."

Since it had rained the full week through, she and Ronan hadn't checked out the Praying Hands Arch yet. He'd promised to bring her today, and the weather had obliged.

Kat angled her head and winked. "Indeed. He's a good egg, that one."

"Never did buy into that Barrick Curse nonsense like the rest of the folks in town. Sometimes, for reasons only the good Lord knows, bad things happen to good people."

Ethel scooted toward the large patio door off the dining area.

Mrs. Baranski didn't wait for them but slid the door open. "Well, then, if I can't feed you, let me send you home with some bounty from my garden."

Hope and Kat helped her down the small step onto the paving stone patio.

If the front yard was a museum to all things Christmas, then the backyard was an homage to all things forgotten. The sweet perfume of lily of the valley sprang from a row of old rain boots along the bright blue painted fence marking the edge of Mrs. Baranski's spacious backyard. All manner of things—an antique clawfoot tub, the front half of a rusted-out 1960s Ford truck with its hood open, a red wagon, a chipped

antique teapot and cups on a wrought-iron table, even an
out-of-commission commode—served as planters, sprouting everything from tulips and columbine to lush greens and
rhubarb.

Ethel spoke into Hope's shocked silence. "I don't wait to
plant by seed anymore. Not at my age. My son buys the first
starter plants from the greenhouses. We get some from Mags's
organic farm. Then we fertilize like crazy to get them going
this early in the season, but then they don't need much maintenance. I start them in pots on my kitchen counter, then
bring them out after the last freeze of spring. I get the feeling
they're grateful."

The beginnings of tomato plants sprouted, as did peppers,
carrots and the apple tree buds preparing to birth their fruits
later in the fall.

Kat had grabbed a vacant basket as though she'd done this
a thousand times. Perhaps she had. She headed straight to the
rhubarb climbing out of the old commode. She plucked three
stalks and added them to the basket, then turned with a dimpled grin. "Who knew a toilet could grow the best produce
you ever tasted?"

Hope laughed. "That's something you don't hear every day."

Pride lit the old woman's face. "I don't let anything go to
waste." Ethel thrust her chin, indicating her yard, answering
the unasked question. "What others would say is no longer
useful, broken and ugly, I see as capable of producing something beautiful." She grunted a laugh. "It used to embarrass
my kids. They called me a pack rat."

"You were right. This is amazing." Hope breathed in the
sweet, pungent scent of growing things and sighed.

Hope helped Ethel sit in a lawn chair. Ethel's lined but
sharp eyes pinned her. "I always thought that's rather how
God sees us."

Kat gathered big leafy lettuce and radishes at Ethel's insistence that she couldn't manage to pick or eat them all before they rotted. Hope sat beside Ethel. "What do you mean?"

"We might think we're too damaged to come to Him. That we're forgotten, cast aside. But He can make something beautiful out of the broken places of our lives. Even the most desperate places inside of us just need light in order to heal and grow."

She knew better than to assume everyone in Wanishin Falls had some kind of special connection with God. But here was another version of Mags talking about God to her. Coincidence? Hope put the brakes on her jaded musings. She couldn't help the tears suddenly stinging her eyes, the pressure at the back of her throat. Her whispered words "But some places are too deep, too dark…" floated away on the breeze.

As though waking from her own intense thoughts, Ethel blinked at Hope. "What was that, dear?"

Swallowing, Hope put on her best grin. "Nothing. I said we should probably get going. Thank you so much for the produce."

As Hope stood, Ethel put her hand out but didn't touch Hope. "Say, has anyone ever told you you look like someone who used to live here a long time ago? Spitting image."

Kat returned, basket laden with produce and a small bunch of cut tulips. "Who's that, Mrs. B.?"

"Her name was Dottie. A great friend of Ulysses, in fact. Surprised he didn't mention her to you since you look so much alike." She rubbed her sagging cheek. "Though I suppose he doesn't recognize people the way he used to."

Ethel paused. "You look like someone else too. I can't figure it out."

Kat eyed Hope, one brow raised as Hope made her thanks and bustled them out of the woman's home as quickly as she could without sounding rude. That speculative look on Kat's face remained as she started the drive back to Dusty Jackets.

Before Kat could question her, Hope brought up something she'd thought since she found out how much opening the youth center meant to Ronan.

"Mags said that the Wanishin Falls Founders' Day Festival is coming up the first weekend of June."

"And you want to see what it's like to wear a corset and dress up with the historical society ladies?"

Hope chuckled, her chest lightening after the conversation with Ethel. "Definitely not. I was thinking maybe you could help me with something. I'd like to set up a food stand to raise money for the youth center project. The historical society already has a booth arranged. Mags said that lots of places around town set up booths to sell things and raise money for different organizations."

Hope had never seen Kat's dimples so deep. "Oh! That's a fabulous idea! I love it!"

It didn't take long for Kat's excitement to bubble over with a barrage of ideas. "My mom and dad would be happy to help. Matthew could hand out pamphlets. We'll set up a stand and you can pick the recipes. I'm sure Abe and Sophia would help with the prep. Show off your skills, girl. Wanishin has never seen cooking like yours. We'll make a boatload for the youth center."

Kat's hands squeezed together over her chest. "Just wait until Ronan hears about this. He'll be his usual stoic self, but he's gonna be floored."

Hope clutched the edge of the car seat to steady herself. Kat had said what Hope was thinking. She couldn't wait to tell him.

They'd arrived at Dusty Jackets, both rushing out, still chatting away about Hope's ideas for the menu—which ultimately would be a little preview advertisement for her mobile café— when they bumped, literally, into Poppy descending the front porch stairs from Dusty Jackets. A stack of books she'd balanced against her sharp chin flew down the steps.

"Oh, excuse us!" both Kat and Hope gasped.

Poppy smoothed and preened the front of her immaculate red blazer as if they'd thrown dust on her, looking much like the skinny crane she resembled.

Kat bent, retrieving the books Poppy had dropped, leaving Hope to avoid the older woman's strange gaze. Hope fidgeted until Kat stood once more, handing over the books. The topmost caught Hope's eye—*Lost Treasures of Lake Superior.*

Poppy seemed to take note of Hope's questioning gaze, and shot Hope a shrewd grin. "Oh, yes. This place holds many secrets." She patted the book's cover. "This is for that research I'm doing on the Lake Superior pirates like I told you. For the tour business."

Kat pointed at the book. "Does that one have the local legend about Captain Cold Hands's treasure?"

"It's not legend if it's fact." Her slim, sharp nose rose into the air. "Cold Hands's ship did sink offshore, I've found out from my research, the very night the irresponsible Barrick family ancestor failed to light the beacon."

Hope's fingernails poked into the tender skin of her palms. She winced at the sudden sting of her still-healing wound. Poppy's mention of Ronan's ancestor, Edward, made Hope's teeth grind together. She had come to know and like this man of integrity in Grace's journal.

Whatever reason Edward had had for not lighting the beacon, it must've been important. Her gut confirmed it. So did the integrity he passed down to his great-grandson-to-the-fourth-power, Ronan.

"Yeah, I heard of that treasure too." Kat crossed her arms, a half grin making one dimple pop into existence. "We used to go tromping around in the woods looking for it when we were kids. I believe the ship sank, but I don't think there was any treasure. Or if there ever was, it's long gone. Too many people have dived in these waters only to come back empty-handed. It's silly to believe these treasure-hunter stories. They're just old wives' tales."

Poppy straightened. "Well, I'm no one's wife nor am I very old, thank you very much. And I'm not some silly schoolgirl either. Good day." With that, she stomped down the steps, the *clip-clap* of her heels echoing down the street.

Kat shrugged. "Sensitive."

Hope opened the door for them both. Mags had pushed the old wood-frame windows up to let in the warm summer-like air. The lace curtains were sucked in against the screens as they entered. Mags had covered the shop, giving Hope a day off.

She called to wherever Mags was, "It's just us!"

"Okay, dear! I'm cleaning something up in the kitchen!"

Hope knew what that meant—Ulysses had wandered off while Mags had helped Poppy at the register and must have made a mess. He seemed to do that quite often.

Setting her purse on the checkout counter, Hope turned and leaned against it.

Poppy was quite possibly more socially awkward than she was. She couldn't help her curiosity. "Has Poppy lived in Wanishin Falls long?"

"Not really." Kat ran an absent hand along a book's edge on a new Charles Dickens display Hope had created. She'd told herself it wasn't because Ronan mentioned Dickens as one of his favorite authors.

Kat rounded the table display. "Poppy showed up one day a few years ago and planted her feet firmly into Wanishin Falls. I don't know much about her. Where she's from or why she moved here. She doesn't say much about her life before Wanishin Falls, but she sure does have opinions about how this town should be run."

Kat's shoulder lifted. "Well, I'll let you get ready for your nondate. Thanks so much for today." Kat reached over and squeezed her in a one-armed hug. Since the little breakdown in Duluth, the physical awkwardness with Kat had all but disappeared.

It was a bittersweet realization that Hope had her first almost friend and yet as soon as she found her books and put in a couple months of work for Mags, she'd be leaving.

Hope bade her goodbye and sprinted upstairs to change.

Warmth filled her soul as she anticipated telling Ronan about the fundraiser, but she needed to stay on her guard. She couldn't let him get too close. For both of their sakes.

Tying her hair in a knot at the top of her head, she scrutinized her reflection. The plaid button-up she wore barely covered the scars on her neck. The scar on her jaw was always visible. What would Ronan think if he could see her? Like, really *see* her. Where had the thought come from? It started a roiling storm in her chest.

And she definitely didn't like the hiccupped beat of her heart when the bell from the front door met her ears. Ronan had arrived.

"Okay, you did realize we were going to have to go into the water if you want to get a closer look at the arch, right?" His hair, free of his iconic cap, twisted in the persistent but soft wind glancing off the water's edge. The large two-person kayak sat at his feet, water lapping gently at its sides.

"Theoretically, yes. I just..." Hope bit down too hard on the inside of her cheek, drawing a salty tang of blood. She winced.

She needed to do this. Why would her book have a picture

of this place if not to send her there? A whisper kept coming back to her—her mother's words, *The family stories aren't just fables.* What if all the stories were true? What if this arch was the first clue?

A twinge of guilt knotted her stomach. She hadn't told him this was, according to Ulysses, probably just as much his treasure hunt as hers. It wasn't that she was unwilling to share. If this actually led to something of monetary value, she certainly would. But how could she tell him without giving other things away she didn't want him to know?

His eyes narrowed as if assessing her. "You're afraid of water." It wasn't a question.

She grimaced. "Well, yeah. You would be too if you didn't know how to swim and all that was going to be between you and two-thousand-nine-hundred cubic miles of water was a thin plastic boat." She tried crossing her arms over the bulky life jacket but didn't succeed. Instead, she settled for tucking them at her sides.

He handed her one of the paddles, which she took reluctantly. "I won't let anything happen to you. I promise."

She kept the *Famous last words* to herself.

Her feet danced from one to the other. Nerves building until she spouted, "Did you know Lake Superior has five hundred and fifty-one billion gallons of water and it's the world's largest freshwater lake by surface area, or that it's roughly the size of Maine? It holds ten percent of the world's surface freshwater and has enough water to cover both North and South America under a foot of water." Oh, wow. Brilliant.

His head angled at the same degree his smile did. Amusement dancing at the corners of his lips. "I love that you know random facts and spill them at will. The only person who knows, well, knew I guess, more useless—" She sent him a sharp glare and he corrected, "I mean, more *fascinating* knowledge is—was—Gramps."

Her heart pounded against the life vest as though adding its own argument against this idea, trying to free itself from the jacket and flee. Ronan's hand inched toward her slowly, but when she flinched, he stopped. For the first time, something coiled around her chest like regret.

Ronan straightened, but she caught the pained expression flash across his face. "You don't have to do this, you know. I told you what's out there. Stone. A bunch of graffiti. It's been a while, but if I remember right, a painted Bible reference. That's it."

Blowing out a slow breath, she lifted her shoulders. Her mom had sent her on this journey. She had to complete it. "Yes, I do have to see it. Up close, like my mom would've wanted."

Ronan carefully climbed into the back seat. She objected, not wanting the vulnerable position in front, seeing nothing but water ahead of her. He explained that the person in front paddled, while the person in the back took the responsibility of steering the kayak. He held the kayak steady with the paddle against the sand and rock bottom. Before her boots could leak too much, she waded into the shallows and scrambled into the front, holding tight to her paddle like a seat belt. Ronan paddled them into the deeper water.

The boat rocked with his movements and hers. She couldn't breathe. One hand gripped the paddle across her lap, her still-healing hand aching with the pressure. Her other hand curled around the boat's side. She turned, the shore already shrinking away with his smooth paddling.

"It's okay—just take slow breaths." Ronan's steady voice cut through her quick, shallow gasps. "Hold the paddle shoulder-length apart. Dip the left blade into the water, scoop, then the same on the right. Slow and measured. I'll do the hard work. You concentrate on finding a rhythm. I'll match yours."

Every time she paddled, she felt the strong, sure movements of his paddle slicing through the water behind her. Somehow reassuring. Soon they were in sync, their movements as one. Only the small splashes of the water against the boat and her heart thudding in her ears disturbed the quiet. Ronan stopped. She turned, swaying the kayak. Letting out a squeak, she froze.

"What are you doing?" She couldn't help the terrified agitation in her tone.

"Stop a second and look."

More slowly this time, she turned her gaze, first at him and then at the small ripples of water. "What?"

"Sometimes you have to stop moving. Crush the fear by standing still."

His words, barely above a whisper, embedded a drop of warmth in her chest. She let it spread. Curling around her ribs. As though a veil had dropped from her senses, she took in the gulls overhead, the lapping of water and the gentle rocking of the boat, a mother loon calling to her two babies, the sun turning the water's surface into glittering gold diamonds, even the strange pockmarked beauty of the Lost Lover's Island off to their right, in the distance. Her terror had strove to silence all those things. Her heart still pumped in her ears but slower now.

"See? It's not so bad out here. Is it?"

She let out a shaky sound, a cross between a whimper and a chuckle. "It is beautiful. I'd still prefer enjoying it with my feet on solid ground though."

Instead of laughing the rich deep laugh she'd come to know, he cleared his throat. "Why are we really out here, Hope?" His words took her by surprise. She was glad he could only see the back of her head.

"What do you mean? My book showed a picture of this arch. I just wanted to see it up close." Her voice quaked more than she'd meant it to.

"Come on. I've never pressured you to share more than you're comfortable with, but you need to know you can trust me with this. It's safe with me."

He was right. He hadn't pressed her about how his great-aunt Aggie had been connected to her mother or her. He hadn't even balked at the task, which she had never asked him to participate in, of finding the books that meant so much to her.

But now? With the fore-edge painting sending them off on a mystery outing for who knew what? She sighed. No wonder he had questions. But the more she said, the more he would know about her. More threads of attachment to this place. To him.

"It's not that I don't love gallivanting down these rabbit trails with a beautiful woman—" his tone jovial now "—but I think I might be more helpful if you tell me why we're looking at an arch instead of for the rest of your books."

Her back stiffened, but her face tingled when he'd called her beautiful. Again, she was glad she didn't have to look him in the eye.

While she decided whether or not to tell him more, the sound of a boat motor on the other side of the arch interrupted the stillness. The wake from the boat spread out, finally hitting their tiny kayak, jostling it from side to side. She gritted her teeth and clutched the side of the boat again.

With a held breath, she put her paddle's blade back in the water. She chose the most truthful answer she could, finding it ever harder to tell the white lies she'd told for so long to survive. The half-truths she'd justified for her own safety stood on shaky ground before this man. "I'm not sure what we're doing here either. But the painting on my book was this arch, and I think my ancestors are trying to tell me something."

He paused.

"Okay," he said. "Let's go figure out what they're saying."

The confident strokes of his paddle once again matched the speed of her softer ones. The terra-cotta-colored arch, as tall as Ronan's lighthouse, loomed above them. An ancient sentinel, created from the wind and rains. Hollowed out in the middle from the storms it survived. Just like her.

Ronan steered them right up next to it. She touched the sandpaper-like surface of the outer side of the arch. Not cold like she'd assumed, but warmed by the sun.

"Can you at least tell me what we're looking for here?" His deep voice reverberated against the rock.

"Hmm, maybe something with a literary reference or the book itself or family ties or..."

She held her paddle in her lap, searching the many "so-and-so plus so-and-so equals love" and "BFFs" scratched into the surface. "I don't see anything on this side."

Ronan paddled them around to the other side, into the middle where someone had spray-painted in black, "Moe was here." His growl resounded in the partially enclosed space. "Would you look at that? No respect for something that's been here since long before Moe."

"You care deeply about the history and nature around here, don't you?"

"I do. I think it comes from living here my whole life. But when I worked and lived on the lake, it was kind of like living in connection with it. I knew what the weather would be based on the sky the night before, what the winds meant and when they changed, the way the water moved. I appreciated the beauty but had a healthy fear of the dangers."

She heard his slow inhale.

"And I guess that's why I want to preserve the history too. I saw the historical society struggling and it hit me. Why not use that big space, if I got the bookbindery building, as not only a place for the kids to hang out but also a way to preserve the history of Wanishin Falls and pass it on to the future generation." Passion filled his voice.

"I think it's a great idea."

Another speedboat passing by disturbed the water further, making them bob up and down. A yelp escaped her throat.

She stretched her gaze to the top of the arch. The wind whistled through their little alcove space. It was majestic, but she didn't like how the restless water churned and splashed against the rock.

Halfway up the inside arch was a painted message:

Between the pages, truth shall bear. One cannot where two must share. A treasure for both in a loathsome lair. Matthew 18:20.

"See, I told you, nothing much here."

Hope pointed to the words. "What's that? Is that a Bible verse? I don't recognize that one."

"No, not that I know of. It's some weird saying. Some kind of riddle, maybe? But it does reference Matthew 18:20 for some reason underneath."

That was when she noticed a rough etch of a flower—a lady's slipper perhaps—with a ring around it above the inscription.

The symbol was familiar—the flower on the stationery on which her mom's letter was written.

"Look! The flower." She whirled around in her excitement, arms waving. The momentum of her movement rocked the kayak violently. Before either could do anything, the whole vessel flipped over. He toppled in, and she followed. Her head dunked below the surface first.

Her nose and mouth filled with icy water, cutting off her scream. For what felt like an eternity, stabbing cold pressed against her body, darkness closed in on all sides…until her life jacket, defying gravity, pulled her right side up.

One lone word broke the surface the same time she did. "Ronan!"

She coughed and gasped in turn. Thrashed at water and air.

He was there, arm securing her around the middle. Her back pressed against his chest. Her nose and lungs burned from the water invasion.

Ronan groaned when her kicking foot connected with his body. But both his touch and his murmured reassurances were calm, even though she didn't stop to hear the words.

Finally, his voice cut through her panic-scrambled brain. "Hope, I'm here. It's okay. You're safe."

Something about those words filled an empty spot she didn't know was there.

"I'm going to turn you around, okay? I won't let you go." Slowly, he turned her body so they were chest to chest with only their life vests between them.

"I… I'm s-so sorr-ry." Her teeth clacked together with such force she was afraid they'd crack. From the cold or the fear, she wasn't sure.

The small lines at the edges of his eyes deepened. Flecks of darker cobalt amid the ice blue—something she'd never noticed because this was the closest she'd ever come to him. "I mean, if you wanted my attention, there were easier ways of getting it. You didn't have to knock me out of a boat." His tone teased.

"C-c-cold."

He held her tighter, and she didn't argue. "I'm going to

get us back in the boat, all right? Then we'll go warm up and laugh about this later. Sound good?"

His confident tone made her panic recede an inch. "M-much l-later."

His chuckle bounced off the rock. "Hang on to me. Tight." She did as she was told, digging her fingers into his life jacket, even though a voice warned her not to. He kept one arm around her, using his other arm to swim them closer to the kayak bumping against the rock wall.

He flipped the boat over after several attempts with her finally helping with one hand while the other kept its death grip on him.

When they had retrieved a paddle within arm's reach, he guided her to hold on to the kayak. "I'll get in first so I can help you up."

Fear strangled her. "N-no. D-don't let go." Her heart pumped hard against her rib cage.

Tenderness filled his expression as he swept back a lock of hair stuck to her cheek. "Hope, listen to me. It's going to be okay. Your life jacket will keep you up and you can hold the side of the boat. You can do this. We can do this. Ready?"

She tried not to dwell on the unfathomable dark depths below her kicking legs. "Okay."

She held tight to the boat while he hoisted himself across the middle of the kayak. Once he was across the center, he swung his legs up, now lying along the length of the kayak on his stomach. He slowly rolled to his side then turned himself to a sitting position.

He panted, his wavy hair plastered to his forehead but he wore a bright smile. "Piece of cake. Your turn." She was glad to see his prosthetic leg was still intact.

The stomach-sinking vulnerable feeling of being alone in the lake with all that water underneath her sent electric jolts of panic coursing through her frozen body. No way she could do what he'd just done, especially without tipping the vessel again.

"I don't th-think I can."

"Of course you can. Put your arms across the kayak first to grip the other side."

She did.

"Great. Now start pulling yourself up. Don't pull the boat. Pull yourself."

A little bit at a time and with his help and guidance, she shimmied herself onto her stomach like she'd seen him do.

"Easy now. Get to your side and very slowly turn and sit up." She was practically in his lap, so she didn't need to be told twice. He braced his hand on the rock wall to stabilize them.

Finally, trembling and huffing, she regained her position. "I did it— I mean, we did it. Thank you."

"Before I get you out of here so you don't shake so much we capsize again, what were you saying before we took that little water adventure?" The humor was back in his voice.

At that moment, in what they had just shared and the trust she'd started to build with Ronan since the day they'd met, she made up her mind. She may not be ready to tell him everything, likely never would be, but she could tell him this. He deserved to know this much.

She glanced at the writing—sure it came from Ronan's and her ancestors—then down to her wet, cold-splotched hands. Her bandage had fallen off her hand and the cut reopened and bled afresh. "Let's go warm up first. There's something I need to tell you. It's about our families…"

Chapter Ten

"Our families, they're connected."

Ronan handed a pale and still-shivering Hope a steaming cup of tea.

He'd brought her back to his house, which was closer than going to Dusty Jackets.

"What do you mean they're connected? How?" He added another blanket to her lap and tucked in the sides, and she didn't argue.

They'd both dried off and he'd sent her to another room with a dry flannel shirt of his and shorts Kat had left once after a day of swimming with her family. Hope had dressed, then returned to the living room and wrapped herself in every available blanket while her clothes tumbled in the dryer.

The way she huddled on his couch staring into the blazing fireplace with blue-tinged lips made him want to sit beside her and take her into his arms. Even though they shared a moment in the lake and she seemed about to open up about something, there was still an invisible wall between them. But he'd take this bit of honesty as the first plank in the draw-bridge he hoped to build to connect with her.

She took a sip, closed her eyes a moment as the hot liquid touched her lips. "Your grandpa told me about a treasure and said our families are linked—that somehow this treasure belongs to both of our families. I know it seems far-fetched, something out of one of the stories I love so much. But I'm starting to believe it's true."

He sank into the leather armchair nearest the side of the couch she occupied and leaned over his knees. Charlie lay at his feet, always wanting to be a part of his conversations.

"Wanishin Falls has lots of old stories about treasure. I wouldn't let some painted-on words in an arch or what my grandpa said let you get carried away." His jaw popped as he gritted his teeth. There was a time when everything his grandpa said was fact. But not anymore.

Hope's shoulders slowed their shivering with each sip of her tea. Her straight line of bangs had dried in wispy waves, and her long locks of damp hair fell past her blanket-covered shoulders. He had an urge to brush it back, to see if it was as soft as it looked, but restrained himself.

She gazed into the depths of her mug. "See, that's the thing. Ulysses isn't the only person who talked about a treasure." Her dark lashes lifted as she met his eye. "My mom did too. She told me to come here."

"What about the books?" He couldn't help the wash of suspicion needling up his spine.

"Yes, for the books. But they are supposed to be the key to the treasure—wherever and whatever it is. And, I think it belongs to us both." She placed the empty cup on the coffee table. "Did you see what it said on the arch wall?"

"Well, I *was* sort of in the middle of being knocked into freezing water." A chuckle escaped his throat at her horrified, sheepish expression. "Just kidding. One of these days you're going to learn when I'm making a joke. Albeit, a bad one."

Her face relaxed, her pale cheeks blooming with rosy color. "You must've seen those words before, right?"

He squinted, recalling the words. "'Between the pages, truth shall bear. One cannot where two must share. A treasure for both in a loathsome lair.' Sure, everyone here has seen the words. They've been there as long as I can remember. But I doubt it's a clue to anything. Probably just a little rhyme written by one of the treasure-obsessed hunters a long time ago."

"I wouldn't be so sure of that."

"Why?"

"Did you see the lady's slipper symbol above it?"

"Yes."

Hope scooted to the edge of her seat, leaning forward. "Before she died, my mom wrote me a letter asking me to find the books and told me the stories about a family treasure weren't just fables. The symbol on the stationery was a lady's slipper with a ring around it."

He stood, taking strides across the room. Patted Charlie on the head, when she followed. "Hmm, that is odd, isn't it? Maybe too much to be a coincidence, especially since the inscription mentions treasure."

Her hands untangled from the blankets. "Here's everything I know." She held up fingers in succession. "My mom told me the books led to something even more valuable than the books themselves, your grandpa and my mom talked about a family treasure, your grandpa said our families are somehow connected to each other and the treasure, the fore-edge painting told us to go to the arch, and when we got there, a message seemingly reiterated two families needed to unite for something. Plus, that lady's slipper symbol."

He scrubbed at the five-o'clock shadow irritating his chin.

Indeed, it was well past 5:00 p.m., and they needed to find supper soon.

"A treasure? A real one? It's hard to believe." He crossed his arms, leaning against the mantel.

"I know. I'm just saying I don't find the idea as absurd as I might have a few years ago. But then, a few years ago, I could never have imagined setting foot inside of a boat either. Water and I don't have a great history." A tremor passed through her body that didn't seem to come from the cold anymore.

"Can I ask…?"

She pulled her lower lip between her teeth as though deciding whether or not to allow the answer past her mouth. Her shoulders squared beneath the blankets.

"You know that my mom passed away when I was still in elementary school. I grew up in foster care homes. Lots of them. I was quiet, read books and tried to keep out of the way, but I had the knack for being the outcast. Even among the other foster kids. Especially in the last home I was in. It seemed like they could find anything to use against me. They loved to pull my hair, hide or break the few possessions I had and blame the bad things they did on me to the foster parents. I'd hide out at the library as much as possible. Aggie was so kind to me."

Her sad smile clamped around his chest. Scared to say anything lest she stop the first real conversation they'd had since she arrived, he dipped his chin to encourage her to go on.

"They didn't know what to do with the anger they felt at being abandoned by their birth parents. I knew. I felt it too. Not that my mom could help it. She had ovarian cancer." Her hands gripped her knees, revealing the white puckered marks of scars on her wrists. She tried to cover them, but they peeked out of her sleeves sometimes.

Her leg bounced under the blanket as she tucked a piece of hair behind her ear. "One night, they told me to come outside and they'd tell me where they hid my necklace—the one piece of jewelry I still had of my mom's. Instead, they thought it would be funny to push me into the pool. I didn't know how to swim. Still don't. Obviously." She picked at her nails. "It was a good thing my foster parents woke up in time."

A million responses swam through his brain. A pill to fix it. Take away the pain. Find the kids who did this to an innocent child, even if they were adults themselves now, and do things a God-fearing man should never contemplate. But when he met her gaze, the fingers he hadn't realized had curled into fists straightened. None of that would help.

"That's horrible. Kids can be so cruel. But sometimes it's the circumstances that cause them to behave badly like that. Just look at Tate. I know things are strained at home. His dad isn't around, and I don't think he takes much interest in the boy when he is." His hand craved to reach out, but he didn't. Instead, he'd reach out with words. "If you ever want to talk, I'm here. Okay? You never have to hide yourself from me."

Her lips upturned. Not a full smile but a start.

"Would it help to know I wasn't exactly the most liked person growing up?" He let out a gruff chuckle, the kind still edged with his own set of hurt and bitterness. "I was never doing enough in my dad's eyes. My mom's illness… I should've been there. Somehow, my dad thinks if I'd been there she wouldn't have died. And maybe he's right. Maybe if I had come home when she… Well, maybe a lot of things wouldn't have happened."

The truth was she'd had a massive heart attack that left her incapacitated and it claimed her life a few days later. She hadn't had good health for the previous several years. He knew the stress of his own estranged relationship with his father hadn't helped her condition. So, when it was all boiled down, maybe he did hold partial blame.

Anguish pumped through his veins. He paced to the other side of the living room. Charlie watched his progress. "Then there's the accident on the ship. No one seems to care that the kid wasn't following the safety procedures for operating the crane. He shouldn't have gotten out and stood where he stood when the line got caught. I tried to save him. I did. And then, not to mention that you can hardly go a day in this town without hearing someone say, 'Don't go and pull a Barrick,' when they're referring to someone blowing it or shirking their responsibilities. Because of my ancestor…"

Stopping midstride, he clamped a hand over the back of his neck. Embarrassment swept through him. He'd sounded like a teenager complaining about his parents. "I apologize. I guess I didn't realize I'd bottled that stuff up."

Her expression held no judgment or, thankfully, pity. He could handle anything but pity. He got enough of that already.

She stood but didn't approach him, kept the coffee table between them. "Don't be sorry. Keeping things in can feel like invisible chains. I would know." Her gaze dropped to the floor before she added, "Same to you. If you ever want to talk, I'm here." Her voice shook but held conviction.

"Thank you. I appreciate that." He excused himself to retrieve their clothes from the dryer. As he pulled out her plaid shirt, letting the warmth soak through his arms then wrap around his chest, he couldn't help but feel her words and understanding had done the same on the inside. He hoped she felt the same about him.

He said a silent prayer for this hurt woman and his friendship with her, asking for God's guidance to help her and never give her another wound like the ones she already carried.

When he returned to the living room, Hope, blankets still around her, studied his bookshelves, mouthing the titles silently.

"I would think you're sick of reading book titles by now."
He stepped to her side.

"Never." She turned a soft smile his way.

He let her know her clothes were in the guest bedroom she'd used before. She plodded slowly, encumbered by the layers around her. He refreshed her tea while she changed, and set out a plate of crackers, smoked and sliced turkey and sharp cheddar cheese, the only snacks in the house. He really needed to grocery shop. But between the renovations on the old bindery building, keeping an eye on Tate and helping Hope, there hadn't been much time.

The prayer he'd said moments ago, that he might help her with the confusing mix of things she was dealing with, suddenly seemed ridiculous. How could he help someone else when he was such a mess himself? His gut twisted but so did something in his chest. He shook his head at the ceiling. He couldn't deny that something—no, correction, *someone*—had taken root inside of him. A little space she now occupied. And there was a tug to let it grow.

All he could do was ask for God's wisdom again as he whispered, "I'm in trouble, aren't I?"

Charlie cocked her head to the side and whined in agreement.

Hope stood before the mirror in Ronan's whitewashed wood-plank guest room, dressed in her regular clothes again. She reluctantly folded the flannel shirt he'd loaned her with one last sniff of the fresh laundry detergent and hint of evergreen before laying it on the bed. She marveled at not running. From him, from this vulnerability, from this level of honesty. Her legs zinged with pent-up adrenaline, ready to sprint at a moment's notice, but she kept them still.

Instead, she took out some energy on detangling her hair with a comb she'd found on the dresser top. After a silent debate, she left it down, cascading over her shoulders in chocolate waves.

The slant of the sun had cast the room in a golden glow. But despite the beauty, surrounded by the windows, she felt exposed. Split open. Or maybe it was the enormous initial relief and subsequent panic of sharing a piece of herself, her real self, with Ronan. And yet, it was okay. All the usual alarms blared inside of her head, telling her to escape like always. But it was like the security system for a house. A stray dog strolling through the backyard could set off the alarms just as much as a burglar. Maybe her mind and heart were set to automatic security mode to keep her safe for so long that they no longer recognized perceived danger from real danger.

She expected this was a little like parachuting out of a plane. Both terrifying and freeing at the same time, hoping all the way to the ground it would turn out all right. The problem was, telling Ronan or anyone the full extent of her past—her horrifying ten years as a captive and trafficked woman—would tear that parachute to shreds. Even these hints at a normal life she'd experienced in Wanishin Falls, with people who seemed to care for her, would whip past her violently on her descent to doom.

How could they love or understand someone who'd seen and done the things she had? Dee and her counselor in Chicago had told her time and again it wasn't her fault, she had nothing to feel ashamed of. But the grime coating her innermost being screamed out that they were wrong. Every single time.

Straightening her sleeves to hide what she could of the scars. If only she could hide both inner *and* outer scars from everyone.

A little tug inside reminded her that she could conceal as much as she wanted to from everyone else, but there was Someone from whom she could never hide. He knew it all.

Witnessed everything she'd ever been through. Her lonely childhood. The bullying by her fellow foster kids. The love she thought she'd finally found in a boy who "saw" her. And every gruesome act that followed.

So why didn't You save me? Her lashes fluttered against her cheeks as she asked God the question she'd asked so many times. Met with silence once again.

Drawing a deep cleansing breath, she grabbed the blankets she'd used and walked back downstairs to the living room. She put the folded blankets on the edge of the couch. Ronan had laid out more tea for her and a can of Coke for himself. The meticulous way he'd arranged the meat, cheese and crackers on the tray made her smile.

"Well, never say I haven't made you anything from the kitchen." He threw his hand out, indicating the food with a self-deprecating smirk. "The good news is that it's incredibly hard to burn a meat-and-cheese platter. I mean, I'm sure, given the time, I could pull it off, but..."

She placed a hand over her heart, working to keep her face solemn. "Little did you know, a good charred meat-and-cheese platter is my favorite. I love that smoky flavor."

His grin spread wide, brows lifting. "Wow, so she does tell jokes, ladies and gentlemen. I knew it was in there somewhere."

An old leather-bound Bible on his side table, next to the couch caught her eye. "Why do you think there was a Bible verse reference with that cryptic message? Do you know that verse?"

He grabbed the Bible and flipped through its worn pages. "It's the verse about where two or more are gathered, there God is also." He handed the Bible to her for inspection.

She read it and handed it back. "Okay, so could that be significant somehow?"

"Maybe. The church isn't the only place people gather to pray, but it would be the most well-known. The stone church up on the hill was started pretty much the same time the town was. I know our family contributed to building it. If—that's a big *if*—our families were trying to tell us something, maybe it's to tell us to go to the old church."

"Well, let's go, then." She couldn't keep the excitement from her voice. "I'll even make you a proper dinner afterward. I want to try out a *Pride and Prejudice* soup recipe I'm concocting for my food truck."

They put away their cups and the snack tray, and he grabbed his keys. He motioned for Charlotte to join them. After the game of keep-away with Ronan's leg, Charlotte seemed to think they were good friends and nudged Hope's hand with her wet nose, asking for a pet.

Charlotte jumped into the back of the truck. Ronan opened Hope's door and stuck a thumb out toward the dog. "She likes you. I can tell."

"Well, if that's how she treats people she likes, I'd love to see what she does to those she doesn't."

"No, you wouldn't. Trust me." She could hear his laughter even after he shut her door and climbed into the driver's side. He pulled onto the road leading back into the heart of Wanishin Falls, heading up the hill to a gray stone church at its peak.

Ronan's smile had dimmed, expression changing to introspective.

"Did Charlotte attack someone or something?"

His fingers tapped on the steering wheel. "Well, no. She gave my dad a scare a few times. But she really didn't like one person in particular."

"Oh?"

He glanced over. "Uh, ex-girlfriend. Ex-fiancée, actually."

"Ex-fiancée? What happened?" She hoped she sounded casual.

His broad shoulders shrugged. "She was ambitious, much more than me. But I think we made it work because we had so much in common, at least we thought we did. We both love the outdoors—kayaking, swimming, diving, fishing…"

Hope caught her stomach doing a flip, comparing her interests, not to mention her bravery, to that list.

"And she was the adrenaline junkie. She loved to cliff jump, parasail. She was even training for her pilot's license."

"Wow, she sounds like quite the woman. So brave." Hope dug her fingernails into her palms. *So brave.* Could she be brave?

Ever since her big brave act of escaping her trafficker by jumping out of a third-story window when one of Kingston's men wasn't looking, she'd put away her courage. Eventually, she'd found help at a church which connected her with the women's shelter. It took every ounce of nerve and planning she could muster.

But now she was hiding again. Like she'd escaped one prison to put herself right back into another. One of her own making. Too scared to step out from her cell into the light of day.

"She was brave." He nodded his acknowledgment. "But also cold, selfish and ultimately, when I lost my leg and couldn't do all of the things she wanted to, she tossed me aside so fast my head spun."

They pulled into the parking lot of the church, which was empty on Friday evening. He put his truck in Park.

Before Hope could ask or even wonder, he continued, "It was the best thing that could've happened though. I've wondered *why* often enough…" He indicated his leg. "But I'm learning that sometimes things have to be broken to be made stronger. I would've soon found out what kind of person she was, but it might have been too late. I was blinded by my own plans and what I thought my life should look like. You know what I mean?"

She wasn't sure she did, but she so wanted him to keep talking. Somehow it became a salve to her own wounds.

His brow wrinkled as he tried to find the right words. "I think in a way I was hiding. Before the accident. I was doing what my dad, a retired ship captain and navy officer, thought I should with my life. My ex-fiancée, Mackenzie, was the daughter of one of my dad's navy friends. She had all these ideas of how I needed to advance my career and join the navy too." His hands opened, palms up. "I never once prayed or asked if that was God's plan for my life. I was following someone else's plans."

His hands wrapped around the steering wheel. "So, I hid and ignored all the promptings to do something meaningful, selfless. Not for my own glory or for someone else's. Until that day when all of my plans and best intentions fell short and there was nothing I could do to save that kid or myself."

"It's amazing you didn't die." Hope's hand inched toward his arm, but the ever-present fears flared and she stopped short.

"You're right. Amazing it was." He smiled. "I have to believe I was saved for a purpose."

She said, "Mmm-hmm," but as much as she believed it for him, she couldn't for herself.

He winked, gesturing toward the side of the church.

"Come on, let's go check out the founders' plaque on the west side of the church. Might be a good place to start."

He opened her door and limped over to the side of the church. She followed.

The metal plaque on the corner of the brick exterior said the church was established in 1891 and the building sponsored by the Holloway and Barrick families, which raised both of their eyebrows.

"I knew my family was on there, but Holloway... Isn't that the last name of the woman who wrote that journal you're reading?"

"Yeah. I think her family must be one of the founding families too."

"Let's check the rest of the outside. Then we can go in and take a peek around. I do some maintenance for the church, so I have a key."

She trailed behind him, not sure what they were looking for, but nothing stood out.

Ronan locked up and they walked back to the truck.

Ronan held her door for her, then hopped in the other side. "Well, as you could see from the plaque, the original church is not what you see here. It went to ruins during the Great Depression, and this building is a replica built in 1953. So, if there was a clue in or on the original building, it would have been lost in the rebuild. I should've guessed that."

"Right. Or maybe that's not what that painted message meant."

They both quieted. She mulled over what they'd found and hadn't. The urge to figure out this riddle churned inside of her, pushing and pulling. She had to get her other books back. There was no doubt now. They must be the key.

"Hey, if you're not too sick of this wild-goose chase yet, I'd like your company for something."

He pulled back onto the road toward Dusty Jackets, shooting her a wide, heart-stopping grin. Warmth traveled from her chest down to her toes. "Oh, yeah? I think I've still got some room for chasing fowl in my schedule. What is it?"

She set her jaw. "I have a book I need to get back. This time I'm not leaving without it."

Chapter Eleven

Growing steady each day is my belief in the power of words. They can cut to the very core, bolster one's confidence, and rally the waning spirit. A true friend, a brother or sister in Christ, as is my dear friend Edward, can be the voice of the Lord to my soul. Truthful, leading me to repentance at times, but always in love. I only pray I may be the same for him.

The swoosh of the leaves on the trees surrounding the back porch at Dusty Jackets was like thousands of tiny books rustling their pages. Tempting her to get lost in the living, breathing story before her. She closed the diary and set it back on the antique wrought-iron patio table before her. For the first time in her life, the world outside of her books didn't seem so dark. Uncertain and confusing, yes, but perhaps not as alien and foreboding as it once did.

The last bite of the Lighter than Clouds gruyere cheese, bacon and morel mushroom soufflé melted in her mouth while thoughts of her future swirled in her brain. Ronan, the wilderness man, had found the morels in the woods by his house. A gift of morels was no small thing. *Cloud Atlas* by David Mitchell inspired the recipe she'd created for her dream café, but today it seemed like a fantasy she would never see come to fruition.

She still needed to talk with Kat's team, Abe and Sophia Ramirez, the husband and wife chef and sous chef. Maybe they could help her create a more realistic plan.

The shop was closed, and she planned to take advantage of the gorgeous warm weather by walking to the youth center building with Kat and her brother, Matthew, and see the progress.

Her phone chirped from her bag on the chair next to her. "Hello?"

"There you are, girl." Dee's voice, sweet and sassy, rang out on the other end. "I wondered if you fell off the side of the earth or into Lake Superior or something." She couldn't know how close she was on the falling into Lake Superior part.

"How are you, Dee?" Remorse pinched her insides, but Dee would *always* say she didn't check in enough. Even if Hope called every day.

"Me? Oh, I'm fine. Don't you worry about this lady. How is your book search going?"

As she told Dee about the hunt, allowing in a few details about Kat and the Barricks, including Ronan, a knowing smile expanded in Dee's tone.

"Honey, I'm so proud of you."

Hope's foot tapped a lively beat under the table. "Why?"

"Because those are the seeds of growth. And it sounds like you've got a great group around you. Don't be afraid to let them care." Dee's words leaked through the cracks in the wall she'd built around her heart. As had Ronan and the rest of her new friends. Had she really used the word *friends*?

"Understood."

"It seems like they already do."

She should've argued. Rationalized. Overanalyzed, like she always did. But all she said was, "Yeah, they do care. Lord knows why, but they do."

"You're right. He does know."

They said their goodbyes, with Hope's usual vow to stay in touch and Dee's promise to never stop praying for Hope.

Hope had asked Mags and Ulysses if they wanted to accompany her to the youth center, but they were exhausted. Another doctor's appointment and change of medication. Ulysses had become less mobile and verbal. Hope swallowed an imaginary egg-sized Lake Superior agate of pain thinking about the sweet old man deteriorating before her eyes. She hadn't wanted to form any attachments in Wanishin Falls. But her plan wasn't working well.

After she put her dishes in the dishwasher, she flew up the stairs to get ready. She stacked the diary next to her other books on a little shelf near the fireplace. She told herself she'd unpacked them for convenience, not to put down roots.

Hot weather had started. She dreaded this time of year, struggling to decide what to wear, to find ways to cover up her scars without dying of heat. She'd gone with Kat to the cute resale shop, Second Chance Boutique. Both Kat and the saleslady told Hope the sunny shade of the lightweight long-sleeve top complemented her eyes and dark hair. She kept most of her hair down, pinning back small sections around her face. She applied a little blush but immediately wiped it off.

Hope grabbed her purse and dashed down the stairs to meet Kat and Matthew on the sidewalk.

A whistle sailed through the air. Her blood froze. She clutched her purse, preparing to run.

"You must have a date." It was Matthew, Kat's brother, in his stilted but jovial voice.

His wheelchair sat between two parked cars. Kat leaned on the hood of one of the cars, her own Red Betty, a beat-up Honda.

"Just with you two," Hope called back.

Matthew's arms trembled and waved, which they did when he was either agitated or happy. But the huge grin told Hope it was the latter.

Kat squeezed Hope into an embrace. "How are you, new girl? What have you been doing all week?"

Hope stiffened. Her brain was so used to telling her that physical touch hurt, even when it didn't. Now she had to tell her brain to stay calm. It was okay.

"Well, you know, taking care of Ulysses, answering lots of awkward questions from Poppy, looking for my books and, oh, a buried treasure. The usual."

"This is certainly an interesting development, between you and Ronan."

Kat pulled back, her petite nose wrinkling as she smiled.

Hope sucked in her cheeks and tipped her head.

Kat put her hands up. "What? I meant this treasure business." Her twinkling smile turned serious. "I appreciate you trusting me with this. Really. So, you guys think it might be real?"

"I'm not sure yet. I think I need to get all of my books back to look for more clues."

"You and Ronan are going to Duluth tomorrow?"

Hope clamped her teeth together. "Mmm-hmm."

Hopefully, she'd get her *Jane Eyre* volumes back once and for all from Richard Allen. Ronan knew the first attempt hadn't gone well, but he didn't know about the suggestive comments the guy had made. Maybe this time would be different and she wouldn't need to worry about that. Maybe— she said a silent plea-prayer—Mr. Allen would relent and sell it back to her for a reasonable price without a fight or another panic attack on her part.

She took in a slow, calming breath. "Please keep the treasure stuff among us and the Barricks, okay?"

Kat put two fingers in the air. "I promise."

Matthew pushed the lever on his wheelchair and sped across the street.

"Hey!" Kat ran after him. Hope followed.

His chair climbed the slope onto the sidewalk. Kat caught up with Hope close behind.

"Hey, buddy, you can't zoom across the street without me. You could've been hit." Kat's tone, usually so patient with her brother, erupted weary and frustrated.

Matthew didn't turn, but the grating sound of his gnashing teeth said he'd heard. "I'm not a baby. I'm still your big brother." His words slurred together. His enunciation seemed to worsen when he was upset or tired. "Even if I am in this stupid chair."

Kat's head hung, shoulders slack. "Sorry about that," she whispered. Her chin jutted toward Matthew, now half a block ahead of them. They followed but let him have his space.

"No need. I'm sure it's tough on both of you. So much time together and life so busy."

A pained expression etched creases around Kat's usually bright eyes. "I'm working so much at the café. With my parents at the café less and less and my taking care of everything plus Matthew, I'm worn-out. I'm not sure I can do this." The pep in her step, gone. Her Converse Chucks scraped the sidewalk.

Hope's chest tightened. "You're a resourceful woman. I've never seen anyone run a business as efficiently as you. And you're such a caring sister. You'll have your days—" Kat gave a good-humored humph "—but you're doing a great job with him. And you love him. That's the most important part. He knows it too."

When Kat shot her a doubtful look, Hope added, "He *does*. He's having himself a good sulk right now, like my mom used to say."

Kat sucked in a long breath and let it out in a slow, measured stream through her mouth. "Thank you." She straightened her shoulders.

They walked a moment, letting the chattering birds fill in the silence as they bounced from tree to tree in front of the picturesque mix of 1950s and nineteenth-century homes lining the street. Someone had baked something apple and cinnamon. Apple pie? Strudel? The cozy scent wafted from an open window.

"What was she like? Where was she from?" Kat interrupted the quiet. When Hope stared blankly, Kat added, "Your mom. You don't talk about her much."

Hope squinted at the clouds overhead. How much should she say? The truth seemed like a good start for once. Since Ronan knew, she couldn't see the sense in keeping it from Kat any longer. There would always be a bit of her story she needed to lock away, but not this.

"Well, she loved to read." Her heart hummed with the disjointed but precious memories. "She constantly read to me too. I remember climbing into her lap on lazy weekends. I'd read my picture books while she read her novels."

Maybe her collection of good memories was larger than she realized. "Mom would wrap us in a big blanket. We lived in an old apartment building in Chicago so it was cold more months out of the year than not. She read the classics to me. I remember loving the way the dusty old paper smelled and how her voice carried all of the emotions of the characters."

Kat slowed her steps. "She sounds like she was an amazing mom."

"She was." Tears stung Hope's eyelids. "She didn't mean for me to end up in foster care. The adoption she had set up for when she was…gone…fell through. I never knew why. She hadn't meant for a lot of things to happen." So much lived between those words. Her mom's heart would've broken had she known all that was in store for Hope after she died.

"Parents absolutely want the best for their kids." Kat sighed. "It may not always work out the way they planned. I think of God kind of like that. He wants the best for us. He's our Heavenly Father. But unfortunately our own or other people's plans sometimes get in the way of the best for our lives."

Hope chewed on that for a moment. Time to redirect the conversation. "You know, my mom was from here. Wanishin Falls."

Kat stopped walking. "Wait, what? And you didn't tell me all this time?"

Matthew called over his shoulder, "Come on, you two slowpokes! Last one there is a stinky old fish!" He squealed and raced ahead.

They started walking again, with Kat casting furtive looks Hope's way.

"I'm sorry I didn't tell you. Honestly, I didn't want to tell anyone. It's just…"

"You didn't trust us. You thought we were murderers out to eliminate you and confiscate your 'family treasure'?" Kat wiggled an eyebrow at her.

The truth felt so vulnerable. New. Raw. Somehow right.

But Kat didn't know all of the details yet. How much did Hope dare share?

"I wanted to leave immediately when I got here. You weren't too far off. Minus the treasure stuff. I didn't know for sure if it was real. I hoped. And I definitely didn't know anything about the Barricks and our connection. I just wanted to keep to myself, get my books and get out of here. But—"

"This little town got its hooks into your heart, didn't it? Not to mention the lovely—" Kat pointed to herself "—and sometimes handsome townsfolk." At this, Kat winked, waving a hand ahead to the back of a familiar wavy-haired gentle giant standing in the parking lot of the youth center.

Hope's face heated. She pursed her lips and bumped Kat's elbow with a gentle nudge.

"Hey, stranger." His greeting echoed Kat's as they neared, his grin bright and genuine. He held out his hand to Kat's brother. They did a series of secret handshake maneuvers. Then both did a whoop. "Hey, bud. Nice to see you." Ronan clapped Matthew on the shoulder.

When Kat reached them and offered her hello too, Ronan waved the three toward the front doors. "I'm taking you guys on the grand tour. We got the elevator fixed, so you're riding first-class today, sir." He saluted Matthew, who waved his arms in jubilation.

It was bittersweet to realize Matthew and Ronan, both two years older than Kat, had been best friends growing up. How it must have crushed them both when Matthew was thrown from a horse in high school and suffered the traumatic brain and spinal cord injury he never fully recovered from.

Inside the first level of the building, Ronan adopted his official guide posture and verbiage.

"This bindery used to be buzzing with binding machines."

Ronan threw his arms wide to indicate the now-empty, large, high-ceilinged space.

There was a perceptible bounce in his step. "This will be a gym and activities room—" he pointed down a hallway on the other side "—and that's a row of offices where we can hold programming as the center grows. Life skills classes, group therapy, support groups and a place for mediators and probation officers to meet with the kids or families too."

"The possibilities are endless." Ronan clasped his hands together with a loud clap that echoed in the empty space. His eyes danced with excitement.

He jogged to the other side of the gym. "Come on, I want to show you guys something."

Along a back wall was a counter with a slide-down cover, like the kind at a mall food court where the sliding gate could shut and lock when the restaurant closed. Ronan pushed the metal gate up. It made a grating screech, setting Hope's teeth on edge and sending Matthew into a rage.

Ronan's proud grin vanished in an instant. Both Ronan and Kat bent at Matthew's side. Ronan apologized profusely. Hope understood just a little what it was like to be hyperaware of her surroundings and sensory details, especially sounds. She'd slept with an eye on the nearest exit when she'd arrived at the women's shelter. Dee had done everything she could to make Hope feel safe, even setting up her room with a sound system that played soothing music. Hope knew it was no accident gospel music typically poured out of the speaker. No matter what noises swirled around the shelter, real or imagined, Hope turned on the music and a cloak of peace fell around her shoulders.

Without thinking, Hope hummed the one she knew best— "Amazing Grace." It carried in the cavernous room like a warm breeze. Kat, who knelt by her screaming and flailing brother, looked up with tears in her eyes. She offered a weak smile. Matthew started to calm. Ronan's expression was unfathomable but piercing.

Kat joined in with the words. She had a beautiful voice, clear with a rich tone.

"I once was lost, but now I am found…
And grace my fears relieved…"

The lines shook Hope to the core. A longing she couldn't put into words. A whisper. An embrace. Deep inside. The part of her, who at seven years old with her dying mama's help, cried out to the Father of the whole universe and asked for Him to be *her* Heavenly Father. The part of her that knew He was the One who once heard her childlike faith-filled prayer, knew He might have been the One who found her, lost in fear and physical bondage, and freed her. What if He was the only One who could save her from her inner prison now?

Once Kat's last note doubled back, Hope drew a shuddering breath, mentally shaking off the uncomfortable notion.

How, God? How can I possibly trust You?

In the moment that followed, as Matthew quieted, everyone stayed motionless. Hope heard it. The still, small voice. Not an audible one. But the little stirrings from her childhood before the cacophony of life took over and drowned it out.

A nudge deep in her soul that said just because her life changed drastically after that prayer, didn't mean God's love for her had. But could she trust Him, after everything? Did He have her best interest at heart and know what He was doing like Ronan said?

Everyone seemed to draw a collective breath, ready to move on. Hope tried to do the same.

Ronan pointed to the kitchen window he'd opened. "Right

here is a kitchen with a window we can open and a counter to serve the kids. We'll set up tables and chairs, maybe some couches and things, on this side and keep games on the other side."

Kat bounced on the balls of her feet. "I heard the church is already taking up a collection, and the pastor put up a notice so people can donate their unwanted but usable furniture."

Ronan walked them through the side door into the kitchen. "The equipment isn't too bad. The building was used as an office space for an insurance company for a while before it sat empty. So, there were still a few appliances. They'd used this as an employee kitchen and hosted some events here. It might need some updating though. Especially this funky-smelling old fridge with no separate freezer."

He explained that they'd need to get it all inspected if they wanted to serve food to the kids. Everything needed a good scrubbing. The kitchen—the whole building actually—had an abandoned feel to it. After the insurance company, it had was turned over to the city and they'd used it for storage only.

Hope walked around the old prep station. "What will you serve the kids?"

Ronan shrugged. "I'm not sure. We could at least have snacks and fruit available. Popcorn, maybe. Pizza? Water and juice, hot chocolate in the winter."

He crossed his arms, leaning back on the serving counter. "These kids don't always have a two-parent home. Or if they do, one is gone on the boats working and the one at home has to work too. So the kids aren't always getting regular meals. It's the least we could do—give them something to fill in the gaps."

Hope bit on her index fingernail, wheels spinning. "I could plan easy snack recipes and light meal options for when I'm—" She was going to say *gone*, but suddenly the idea was harder to say out loud than she'd anticipated. "For when you need them. Could you find funding for something more substantial?"

Kat's fingertips fluttered together, and Matthew did a little arm jig in his chair.

Ronan slid away from the counter, light dancing in his eyes. "That would be awesome. I'll take all the help I can get." He scratched at his jaw. "I came across a grant with the USDA for youth organizations. I wasn't sure I'd be able to use it. You know, with my cooking skills. To receive funding, you have to incorporate all of the food groups for each meal or three food groups for snacks served. But with your direction, I think we could make that work."

Her heart pumped stronger, with more purpose. She'd never thought helping others could start stitching up the gashes in her own heart. But already between helping Kat deliver food, watching over Ulysses, planning the fundraiser for this place and now this...

Something wrapped around her wounded heart. An invisible bandage perhaps. It wasn't permanent. But maybe it was a start.

Warmth poured from every crevice of Ronan's handsome face. He held her gaze until Kat cleared her throat.

Matthew grew a lopsided grin. "If you can't stand the heat, get out of the kitchen." His laugh was that of a boisterous tweenager.

"You said it, bro." Kat fist-bumped Matthew.

Ronan ducked out of the kitchen. If she wasn't mistaken, his cheeks had rounded in a reddened but pleased grin. He hesitated by the back door, muttering to himself, "I'll save the best for last."

They followed him into the hall and toward the elevator.

"All right," he said. "Going up."

* * *

"Come in! Come in!" an excited voice bubbled out of the open door ahead as Hope and the others exited the elevator.

The older woman hurried over and stood on tiptoe to kiss Ronan on the cheek, leaving a ruby-red lipstick mark. Hope suppressed a giggle as the woman rubbed away the heart-shaped imprint. From Ronan's grimace, the woman hadn't been gentle. Kat squeezed Lipstick Lady around the middle and asked after her family.

Ronan gestured to the older woman. "This is Lois Lewandowski, Hope. We're building partners. She's the head of the Wanishin Falls Historical Society. Hope is—"

"Well now, I know who Hope is. You don't live in a small town like ours and not hear about the mysterious woman living and working at Dusty Jackets. Hope Sparrow, right?"

Hope wasn't sure why, but it unnerved her to have someone call her mysterious. It made her sound like she was underhanded. Well, she was still hiding something—her real name and the ten-year period she never talked about.

Lois didn't seem to notice Hope's discomfort, bending to say hello a little too loud and a little too slow to Matthew. He let out an annoyed grunt. But Lois didn't seem to notice that either. The cheerful woman probably didn't mean anything by it, but the inadvertent condescension must get old.

She waved them through the door behind her into a large space, already partially set up as a maze of exhibits and glass displays.

"Hey, Ethel! Our guests have arrived! Where's that nice boy helping you? Have him come here too."

With slow but sure movements, Ethel Baranski slid her walker and herself closer. Tate trailed behind her, hands shoved into his pockets, feet shuffling along, looking like he'd rather be anywhere else. But then, Tate always looked like he'd rather be somewhere else. Tate had been allowed to count time helping the historical society as some of his community service hours. And since Ronan had taken a break to show them around, he said he'd sent Tate upstairs to help the historical society ladies for a while.

Ethel beamed at Hope. "Oh, I'm so glad you could make it over here. I'm still craving that shepherd's pie you made. And those butter rolls were amazing. What's your secret?"

The wariness melted away, as it often did at the prospect of talking about one of her two favorite subjects.

Hope surprised herself by patting the older woman's hand. "That's easy. The secret with any yeast bread is in the proofing. You have to let the dough proof until it's doubled in size. And you want the dough to be really elastic. Make sure you can read a newspaper through it if you stretch it thin."

As Lois led them around what would be the Wanishin Falls History Museum, Ethel and Hope talked of cooking and baking tips and Ethel's life. The two older women had been friends since high school.

"Now the two Mrs. Skis—that's what they used to call us because of our last names—are two old widows. We figured we might as well do our best to preserve the history of our town. We're practically part of the history books ourselves anyway." She chuckled. "And we like the idea of getting the kids excited about history too. It'll be a great partnership."

Hope agreed.

Ethel had been in the historical society longer, but with Lois's exuberance for the job, she was voted the leader. Both seemed content with the arrangement.

"Lois," Ethel called across the room, "didn't I say Hope reminds me of somebody? My memory isn't what it used to be. What do you think?"

All eyes focused on Hope. She shifted under the scrutiny.

Lois's face scrunched in concentration. "I don't know, dear. My memory isn't any better than yours."

Ethel puckered her lips and slung a hand onto her hip. "Well, that's why there's two of us. Put our two half memories together and we should get a whole."

Ethel shrugged. "Live as long as I have, and pretty soon everyone looks like someone you've met." She rubbed her hands on the walker's handles like a motorcyclist revving the engine. "No point waiting for an answer to show up. Usually isn't until three in the morning anyway. Right, Lois?"

"So true. So true."

Ethel continued to lead them through the maze of partially finished exhibits. "Back to the task. We've had so many things in storage for so long. It'll be great to display all of the wonderful artifacts and pictures that haven't seen the light of day for ages."

Lois nodded, her red lips pouting. "Yes, our little downtown space didn't have the room."

She clapped Tate hard on the shoulder, which he endured with a grumble. "Our sweet Tate here—" Hope was fairly certain he hadn't been called that by anyone else, from his bewildered expression "—has helped set up new displays. We're going to have one about the founding families and one over here with local history about the Lake Superior pirates."

Ronan caught Hope's eye with a smirk. She guessed his thoughts.

The visitors split up and wandered while Ethel answered their newly installed phone at the front desk and pay counter. Ronan pulled her aside behind a cubicle-like wall as the others checked out an interactive shipping exhibit, complete with the bow of an old fishing boat attached to the wall.

His hand pulling hers launched a war within her—memories

of pain fought the thrill of his strong, steady fingers enveloping hers in warmth.

"Do you mind if we bring Tate with us to Duluth tomorrow? There's no school for an in-service day." He let go of her hand, and the simultaneous relief and disappointment made her slow to register what he'd said.

"Well, no. I don't mind. But does a fifteen-year-old want to hang out with a couple of old people like us?"

He bumped her arm with his elbow. "Who are you calling old?" He peeked around the corner of the room divider. Apparently satisfied no one could hear them. "I'm telling him this can count toward his hours too. The thing is, I know his dad is leaving on a laker again. He'll be gone for a month. His mom is working all day too. After doing some digging—" his jaw tightened "—I figured out Tate's run-ins with the law and acting out have pretty much all coincided with times when his dad was gone."

"So, you want to make sure someone's keeping an eye on him for the day."

"Right. But without making him feel like he's with a 'babysitter.'"

"I'm a little concerned, not because I don't want to have him hang out with us, but because of what we're doing. Mr. Allen isn't exactly a nice guy and, well…it didn't go well last time." Should she say more?

Ronan rubbed his chin. "Hmm, I see what you're saying. Maybe he can stay in the car while we go into the shop. Hopefully, it won't take long and we can go out for dinner and ice cream after to celebrate getting your book back afterward."

If only it could be that easy tomorrow. *Please let it be that simple.*

"Okay, sounds good." She swallowed. "Yeah, of course. He should come with us."

After all, she'd been grateful when Aggie took an interest in her, even if Hope hadn't spent as much time with the older woman as she would have liked. How could Hope abandon someone like Tate when he needed people to reach into his life with a little compassion?

"Great. Thank you for understanding." He squeezed her hand. A tingle traveled up her arm in the direction of her heart. "I mean, if that antiques guy gives you trouble again about your books, we can always sic an angsty teen on him. I've heard the rolling-eye death stare can be fatal."

They covered their laughs as he led her back to the group. The subject of their discussion appeared thoroughly bored, arms crossed and eyes studying something on the ceiling.

Ronan signaled with his hand to get everyone's attention. "Hey, I have something to show Hope. Please excuse us."

"Huh?"

He didn't answer, just gestured toward the elevator. She stayed close as they entered the elevator and dropped back to the main floor. She marveled, not for the first time, that she wasn't going into panic mode being alone with anyone, let alone a man.

Outside the elevator, he beckoned her to follow him. "This way. I have something for you." His tone full of the excitement of a child on Christmas morning. Not that she'd know much about that. Only snippets with her mom.

Ronan flung the side door near the kitchen wide-open.

Parked in the middle of the back lot, amid the myriad junk waiting to be cleared away, sat a short bus with signs of disuse.

His expression brimmed with delight.

"Uh, okay…"

"It's a bus."

"I can see that." Her forehead tightened. She didn't have

any good memories of her school years. Why would she find a dilapidated bus interesting?

"It's for your mobile café and bookshop."

He'd obviously been bursting to share this bit of information, but his shoulders drooped when she stood silent. "You hate it. It was a stupid—"

It clicked. "Oh, my!" Her hand slid to her throat. "I can't believe this. You got this for *me*?" Tears slipped down her cheeks.

"I did. Well, it was here, and the school district doesn't want it anymore. They've sometimes used this lot as a bus lot and garage. They said it goes with the property. Whatever we decide to do with it. I thought it would be perfect for you, and the historical society ladies agreed. What do you think?"

He didn't wait for an answer but rushed forward to open the bus door. His words spilled out, reminding her of Kat. "We'll repaint, of course. I can take out these windows to create an order counter out here. On the other side exterior, we'll build enclosed shelves for the books. Kat knows some guys with discounted kitchen equipment. The engine needs a little work, but I'm the handyman, remember? I'll get it running for you." He paused, staring at her statue stance.

Suddenly every bit of rust, the half-scratched-off lettering, the obnoxious yellow, everything about it was the most beautiful sight she'd ever seen. It was hers. "I can't believe it. Are you sure? I don't know if I should accept this."

He drew closer, hands encircling her arms. "It's your dream. I saw the bus and knew we could take this old piece of junk and turn it into something amazing. Say you'll take it."

Ethel, with her garbage-turned-garden, would no doubt wholeheartedly agree.

To her own astonishment, she threw her arms around his neck, letting his warmth and kindness seep into her. After a stunned second, his arms wrapped around her back, holding her close. Her cheek fit perfectly against his chest. She clung there for dear life. And it felt like that. A door, opening into a new life. Like she'd found the key to the Secret Garden. A whole beautiful world of friendships and a normal life lay inside the wall. She could glimpse it ahead.

But would she be brave enough to walk through the door?

Chapter Twelve

Hope's long exhale fogged the rain-streaked window of Ronan's truck. The rain had stopped, but the gray sky remained restless, much like her mood. Tate shifted his gangly fifteen-year-old legs in the extended cab behind her. He'd seemed subdued but quite the young gentleman, insisting she sit in the front seat. Either that or he was mad at Ronan for dragging him along on this excursion and didn't want to sit next to him. Ronan cast her an encouraging smile, but she squeezed her nails into her palms harder and couldn't manage to smile back.

She should've been jubilant at finally laying the foundation for her dream with Ronan's gift. Plus, they would hopefully come back from Duluth with her volumes of *Jane Eyre*.

This time, she'd prepared by bringing the copy of her mom's will from the safe-deposit box in Chicago. Dee had been glad to overnight mail it to her. The will stated her mom left all her worldly possessions to her daughter, which amounted to a stack of books, with their names, descriptions and identify-

ing information listed. For some naive reason, Hope had assumed explaining the situation to Richard Allen would be
enough proof last time. After all, the three-volume set of *Jane
Eyre* was sold to him by mistake.

But if Richard studied the will, he'd make the connection
that the name on her ID was Hope Sparrow, not Emily Carrington. The prospect put her stomach in a vise grip. But she
had to keep her focus on the mission—to get her volumes back
and not on the many ways this could go wrong.

She felt the heat of Ronan's glances more than witnessed
them.

"Don't worry. We'll get the book set back. Okay?" His tone
was strong, confident.

Something about the statement bugged her, but she couldn't
put her finger on it. She made a noncommittal sound in her
throat and held tight to the folder containing the will.

The small glimpses of Lake Superior between the thick trees
spread wide-open, and with it, the full, glorious vista of the
historic town of Duluth. It had sped her heart and pulled the
air from her lungs in wisps when she'd driven with Marian
and Kat. The view did the same now. Breathtaking. Literally.

But as Ronan wound his way closer to the antiquities and
curiosity shop, adrenaline pumped for a different reason.

Ronan parked in front of the shop, and Tate squeezed out
of the separate cab door before Hope could put her feet on
the ground.

"I'm starving. Can I go walk around and find something to
eat while you guys do whatever you're doing?" Tate shoved
his hands in his pockets and tossed back his hair, revealing the
shaved sides underneath.

"No. Definitely not." Ronan shook his head. "I'm supposed
to supervise you, remember? I can't let you roam around on
your own."

Tate kicked a stray cigarette butt on the sidewalk. "I'm not a little kid."

Tate's comment seemed to strike Ronan differently. Perhaps Ronan connected it to the strained relationship with his own father.

"I know. But I would get in trouble for letting you walk around a big city unsupervised, okay? I promise we'll get something to eat as soon as we're done with this errand."

The first eye roll of the day served as Tate's reply.

Hope inserted, "Yeah, ice cream will be on me if—I mean, *when*—we get my book back. This guy is kind of holding my book set hostage."

This met with a small gleam in Tate's rich brown eyes. "I could always use some of my persuasive talents."

"Oh?"

"Yeah, I've got what you might call light fingers." He wiggled his fingers. "I could steal them back. If you want."

Both she and Ronan said, "Tate!" at the same time.

He ducked his head but still laughed. "I'm kidding! You should've seen your faces. So scandalized. Relax, wouldja?"

Hope smirked. "All right, Mr. Light Fingers. We're going in to get my book. The right way. Stay here and try to keep your persuasive talents to yourself."

But Tate didn't make a move back to the truck. Instead, he crossed his arms. "I'm going in. So this dude is hard to work with? So what. Maybe I can help. Besides, I thought you needed to be my constant babysitter, Ronan." He quirked a brow at them.

Ronan blew out a loud breath like it would clear away any frustration, and threw his hands up, then locked the truck doors with his key fob. "Fine. Just keep your hands where I can see them." His tone brooked no argument but was tinged with humor.

As she entered the sterile, too-shiny shop once more, she hoped she could hang on to the blossoming bravery she'd felt over the last several days. It was like a new bloom, just emerging. Delicate. Prone to close up or wilt under stress. But when Richard Allen emerged from the back and a catlike twinkle lit his beady eyes, the lunch she'd eaten hours ago did a flip in her stomach.

The smell of stale cigars caught in her throat. Acid rose to meet it.

"Ah, Ms. Sparrow, are you back to take me up on the offer I extended last time?"

The skin on the back of her neck crawled at the implication his suggestive tone implied. She didn't dare glance at Ronan to see if he'd noticed.

"Or maybe you've brought that sweet little copy of the *Seven Pillars of Wisdom* we discussed?" Richard rubbed his meaty hands together, then seemed to notice Ronan was not another customer. He was with her.

Hope's lips numbed. "I, uh…"

Ronan shot her a quizzical look. All she could do was grip her bag with the folder inside.

Richard stepped forward with his hand extended, his face a prime example of sheepish. "I'm Richard Allen, owner of this place." He chuckled nervously as he shook Ronan's hand.

The line from Ronan's jaw to cheekbone sharpened. "I'm Ronan." He ended the handshake quickly and gestured to Tate's lanky form. "This is Tate."

Tate lifted his chin. "S'up? This place is sick, man." He moved to a shelf of strange specimens floating in glass jars.

It was subtle, but Hope caught Ronan's slight shift forward to put himself closer to Richard than she was. "Mr. Allen, I might be careful how you address a lady and a potential customer. In business, reputation is everything, isn't it?" So, he'd caught Richard's tone and innuendo too.

A snaggled tooth protruded when Richard's smile widened, but it held no joy. If a smile could wash over a person like ice water, it'd be this guy's. "Of course, Mr....Sparrow? Hope is your significant other, wife? I apologize. Maybe I'm a little behind in this politically correct world. No intention to offend you." His tone said the opposite.

Significant other? Wife? How was that any of his business? A flame ignited in her veins. Of course, Mr. Allen would assume she was Ronan's "little woman" by his possessive stance and the veins bulging in his neck as he'd told Richard to knock it off, in so many polite words. The boiling beneath her skin dipped and sputtered as she told herself Ronan only wanted to help. But when Ronan put a hand on her shoulder, she jumped like he'd pricked her with a needle.

She stepped around Ronan's protective position. "Look, Mr. Allen. I know you don't *have* to give me my book set back right now. You did buy them after all—"

"You're right, my dear. I did purchase them." Richard leaned back on the pristine counter. "Fair and square. It's not my fault if the old coot has memory problems and sold them to me for a steal."

Ronan's knuckles cracked. "It's called dementia, and you took advantage of him. You knew what that book set was worth."

Gritting her teeth, Hope took another step forward. "Mr. Allen, I have with me my mother's will stating this copy of *Jane Eyre* was left to me after she died. And I'm prepared to give you the purchase price you gave Ulysses. Fair and square, so you don't lose anything."

Richard picked something from his protruding tooth and rubbed his tongue along it as though to give it a shine. "Look,

I'd love to help you, but I had to remove them from the display because two interested collectors are coming to look at them." He swept his hand toward the cabinet next to the front counter with wood-framed doors and a Rare and Collectible Books sign above it.

"Can I at least see my—I mean, *the*—volumes? I'd like to hold them one last time." Though she still held out hope that Richard would suddenly grow a heart, it wasn't likely.

"Quite sentimental, aren't you?" His lip curled as if showing emotion over a book was distasteful. "Very well."

Richard turned and swept through the curtained doorway behind the counter.

"Hey, guys?" Tate waved them over. He had been enthralled with a display of all things J. R. R. Tolkien. "I think you should come look at this."

Hope and Ronan moved closer to the table with a variety of Middle Earth paraphernalia—books, action figures, trading cards, even a vintage-looking lunch box.

"What is it?" Ronan asked.

Tate held out a copy of *The Hobbit*. "This. It's a fake, and Mr. Sleazeball is trying to sell it as a first edition. I've done my homework."

Ronan tipped his head, an incredulous smile sliding into place.

Tate laughed—the teenager actually laughed. "On Tolkien—I've done my homework on *Tolkien*. All of the first editions, every geeky little detail. Trust me, this isn't it."

"The other kind of homework wouldn't kill you either, you know." Ronan gave Tate a good-natured pat on the back.

Tate rolled his eyes.

"Can I see it?" Hope turned it over and peeked beneath the dust cover. Working with Mags, Ronan and, when his mind cooperated, Ulysses at Dusty Jackets had afforded Hope new insight into the world of collectible books. "Yes, right here. Isn't the board cover supposed to have a picture of a dragon?"

"Impressive." Tate's brows disappeared under his mop of hair. "And the inside says, 'First Edition, 1937' but it should say, 'First published in 1937.' Plus, some of the words look blurry."

Ronan leaned in, sniffing. "Do you smell that?"

Hope and Tate did the same. A musty scent, almost like an old book, but a faint, soured nuttiness too.

"It's walnut oil." Ronan sifted through a couple of pages. "We've seen it at Dusty Jackets when someone's trying to pull a fast one and sell us a counterfeit antiquarian book. They rub walnut oil on the pages to age them and mimic the natural oil left behind over a hundred or so years of people touching the paper."

Hope squinted at the imposter book and then around the shop. "Makes you wonder what else could be fake in here." Richard's fraud didn't surprise her in the least. He was a con man, and she *knew* con men.

Tate pointed at an orc figurine. "I know that's a reproduction too, and he's trying to sell it as the original action figure."

The curtain rustled. Richard walked back to the front counter, carrying what Hope assumed was her three-volume set wrapped in cloth and an archival bag. At least he'd taken good care of them. Probably because they may have been his only *real* first edition.

"Hey, Richard, was it?" Tate grabbed the faux-Tolkien book from her and strode toward the man. Hope and Ronan followed.

Richard grumbled under his breath as if he didn't have time for the boy.

She was torn on whether to stop Tate or not. By Ronan's expression, so was he.

Before they could say anything, Tate held up *The Hobbit* book, his phone in the other hand. Hope spied from the side the video on his phone filming. "These are some great knock-offs you've got here."

Now Richard paid attention, his bloodshot eyes bulging. "Excuse me?"

"Yeah, great job with these replicas. Too bad you're trying to sell them as the real deal and scam people. What's that called again?" Tate motioned with the book.

Ronan folded his arms over his chest. "Fraud."

Tate's smile was downright devious, making Hope glad the kid was on her side. "Oh, right. I'm sure the news, social media and, you know, the police would love to be informed about this. They eat that stuff right up."

Tate tapped his phone. "And I've got pictures on here to prove it."

The color drained from Richard's ruddy face, but then it burned red. "I see what you're doing here. This is blackmail."

"It's better than conning people and cheating Ulysses in the first place." Tate's glare was stony.

Sweat beaded on Richard's shining forehead. Something warred behind his beady eyes. "What do you want?" He addressed the question to Hope.

"Let me buy my book set back." Her hands shook, clenching the strap of her bag.

With mechanical movements, as though an inner storm raged, Richard slid the covered volumes across the counter toward her. She pulled them out of the sleeve to be sure they were hers. There it was—her mom's handwritten name inside the first volume underneath the printed name Currer Bell, Charlotte Brontë's pen name. Even one of her favorite authors had hidden her identity.

Hope slipped the bills from an envelope in her bag and slapped them onto the counter.

She clutched the book parcel to her chest as the trio started toward the door. Tate returned the Tolkien fake first edition to the table, but all three of them were the ultimate book lovers. She couldn't let Richard get away with counterfeiting books. Tate and Ronan must've felt the same.

For now though, she needed to put as much distance as she could between herself, her book and Richard.

"Even if you did turn me in, they'll never find anything," Richard called after them. "I'll make sure of that. And be careful about coming between a man and his business. Watch yourselves." His voice rang out as the door closed behind them.

Once the truck was moving again, Tate drummed the back of Hope's seat in a playful rhythm. "Okay, so you're welcome. I definitely deserve a bellyful of grub after saving the day back there."

"Thank you, Tate." Hope turned in her seat toward him. His face split in an embarrassed but pleased grin. "You were amazing in there."

Ronan held his fist over the back seat for Tate to bump knuckles. "Quick thinking, bud."

Hope ran her fingers over the edge of her books. She now had the first volume of *Little Women* and the three-volume set of *Jane Eyre*. Only *Anne of Green Gables* remained for her to find. So precious. A tether to her mom, to her family. And yet...

Ronan had tried to rush in like the hero as if she were a damsel in distress. The whole thing—the way he'd put himself between her and Richard, the insinuation that they were a couple and Ronan hadn't refuted it, felt constrictive, possessive. Anything that surrounded her like a chain, even if well-intentioned, strangled her. It left her fighting the urge to run as far and as fast as she could. Something about how Ronan handled the interaction surprised, annoyed and scared her.

And any conversation with Richard Allen sent her close to or into a panic attack. In the presence of that guy with enough of the cockiness of her trafficker, King, and the cheap-cigar-and-liquor odor, her wounds split open. Laid bare. Exposed. It unnerved her.

Was it Ronan or was it Richard who left her nauseated with the aftershock of adrenaline? As Ronan drove them closer to the Canal Park area to find a restaurant, she wrestled with the question. Maybe it was both. But the result was the same.

Ronan didn't mind that Hope and Tate took their time at the ice cream stand next to Granny's Café, where they'd shared dinner overlooking Lake Superior.

Since the rainy afternoon had turned into a cool but dry evening, they lingered in Duluth's Canal Park afterward. They strolled the boardwalk on the waterfront. Even with the beauty around them and the victory with Hope's book, unspoken tension hung in the air. She'd been quiet, cold and distant with him. Truthfully, after her initial excitement over the bus he'd given her, she'd acted weird toward him.

Resting his elbows on the cement barrier separating the boardwalk from a drop into the water, he let his senses fill with the nostalgic surroundings. The tangy yet pleasant—at least he'd always thought so—fishy harbor scent. He watched one of the mammoth lakers take its right of way through the narrow canal underneath the Aerial Lift Bridge, churning the water as it belted out its rib-rattling horn. Man, he used to love that sound. The seagulls swooped overhead, checking to see if anyone would share their supper.

Watching those boats pass was like watching his past float by, the man he used to be. But that person was gone. *Lord, the* accident stole more than my leg. *What am I now anyway? Treasure hunter? A desperate person in pursuit of…what exactly? Atonement?*

Ronan had told himself many times that having two legs didn't make someone more of a man any more than owning a stove made someone a chef. It was ridiculous. But like most thoughts tying him to the accident, they were hardwired by now. There wasn't an easy off switch. It wasn't his masculinity alone called into question. Maybe if he'd done things differently, Kyle Gunderson would still be alive.

Kyle. Joyful if not a little careless. Always ready with a joke and a smile. His straw-colored hair, similar to his father's, had stuck up in all directions, making him look like he'd always just rolled out of bed.

If Ronan hadn't been on a ship, hiding away from his grief over his mom, maybe Kyle would be going through the growing pains of a new relationship like Ronan—if he could even categorize what was happening between him and Hope a relationship. Or maybe Kyle—he'd be in his midtwenties now—would be far more successful than Ronan in that department and settling down with a family.

The sun hung rosy gold against the horizon, its twin dancing on the waves. If only he could enjoy this moment with Hope, but every time a tiny bit of the wall between them crumbled, it was as if her defense mechanism took over and added another brick in its place.

Despite the weight still on his shoulders, warmth filled his chest when her laughter carried on the wind. He turned and couldn't help but laugh at the two with their giant ice cream cones. He'd said he didn't need any.

Tate pointed a thumb at Hope as they walked up. "She didn't know that seventeen years passed between Bilbo leaving the ring with Frodo and when he actually starts out on his journey. Amateur. Right?"

"And I thought *I* was the bibliophile." She caught a drip of ice cream before it trickled down her hand.

The golden sunset light caught on her amber eyes. The effect was stunning.

Tate's face scrunched up. "What's that? A bibliophile. Is it even legal?"

This kid was hilarious. "It's someone who loves books and knows a lot about literature."

Hope held up a finger like she had something to say while she slurped another trail of ice cream. It was funny to see her so messy, her hair swirling around her as she tried not to let it fly into her ice cream. She was usually so clean and buttoned-up, as Gramps would say.

"It's also a nice way of saying a book nerd," she said. "But I've never minded that term. I'm a self-described book nerd and proud of it."

Tate kept his eyes on a sailboat passing through the channel under the bridge. "Yeah, well, being a general book nerd is one thing. People usually think you're smart at least. Just being a nerd is another. A Tolkien nerd? Social leper."

Ronan exchanged a look with Hope. Tate used to have one good friend, from what Ronan could gather from the tight-lipped teen. But the family moved away last year.

Hope paused her attempts to catch the melting ice cream. "Don't be afraid to be yourself. Maybe you haven't found your people yet, but you will. Friends who will challenge and accept you for the cool and oddly specific literary buff that you are." She prodded his arm, nearly losing her cone.

Interesting that one of the most alone people he'd ever met would encourage Tate about friends. He was glad she did though. Tate was like any teen boy. He acted tough on the outside, but his pain and insecurities hid under the surface.

Crossing his arms, Ronan leaned on the cement barrier.

"School isn't forever. I know it can feel like it. When people told me stuff like that, it didn't feel helpful right then. But I kept it tucked away and reminded myself later when life got rough. The things you do now *will* affect your future—" he shot Tate a pointed look "—but all of the different groups and cliques? All that stuff won't matter in a few years."

Hope propped an elbow next to Tate. "There's a great big world out there after school, I promise. But, please, don't make choices based on how you feel right now." Her tone suggested a deep connection to the words. Maybe she was thinking of the bullying she'd endured.

"I wish you guys were still in school. We could be nerds together." Tate's gaze never left the water during this admission. He wolfed down the last half of the cone in two bites.

"Who are you calling a nerd anyway?" Ronan squinted at the boy.

Hope, with a sticky voice and equally sticky-looking fingers, said, "Oh, don't let him fool you. He's just as much of a book nerd as I am."

Tate's brows lifted, hiding beneath his mop of hair. "Really?"

Holding a conspiratorial hand around her mouth, Hope leaned in. "I don't know where he's at with Tolkien, but he's read Jane Austen and Charlotte Brontë."

"Whoa, dude. You read that girlie stuff? Like the book Hope got back?"

Ronan straightened, lifting his chin. "Not girlie stuff. Fine literature, *dude*. Now come on, you two." The sun had ducked halfway into the waves.

They walked toward the truck. As they turned the corner, a car alarm blared into the quiet street. It was coming from his truck. The lights blinked on and off and the horn blared. A short-statured person in a hood ran down an alley and out of sight. All three of them jogged to the end of the block where the truck threw its screaming fit. Tate tried to run after the would-be thief, but Ronan called after him to stop.

Ronan fumbled in his pocket for the key and turned off the alarm.

Hope rushed to the passenger door. "My books!"

But she yanked open the door and a sigh gusted from her lungs. A thin metal rod stuck out of the window seam where the hooded person had tried to unlatch it but hadn't managed it before the alarms triggered.

Hope snatched the volumes from the seat and held them to her heaving chest. "Who would try to break into your truck? And why?"

"I mean, people do it all the time. Don't they?" Tate peered inside the truck.

"There's nothing inside to tempt anyone but those books." Ronan hadn't meant it to sound like an accusation, but his tone came out sharp. He traced a scratch in the paint left by the discarded metal rod.

"But who would try to steal them?"

Even as she asked, her shoulders fell, as though her line of thinking matched Ronan's.

"That Richard guy." Tate scowled as only he could. "He wasn't too happy about letting those books go."

The person they'd chased off was too short to be Richard though. Nothing was stolen. Ronan would have to report this to the police to satisfy an insurance claim for the damage to the door, but not much else could be done.

The ride back was quiet. Had he upset Hope? Or was she simply worried someone might try to steal the books she'd fought so hard to get back?

They dropped Tate off at his tiny one-story rambler at the

edge of town. The kid smiled a real smile and thanked them for an "interesting" day.

"I installed the security system at my grandparents'." Ronan drove them toward Dusty Jackets. "Your books will be safe. Even if Richard Allen was behind this, he doesn't know where you are. I mean, he's obviously aware of Dusty Jackets, but he doesn't know you're staying there."

Her "Mmm-hmm" was barely audible above the rumble of the engine.

The air in the truck condensed, thick with unsaid words. The kind of strain he'd always hated as a kid when his parents were about to have it out but didn't want to do it in front of him.

He parked in front of Dusty Jackets. She unbuckled and reached for the door, but he put a hand on her arm to stop her. That was the wrong move. She recoiled as though he'd burned her.

"Stop! Don't touch me!" She jumped, back against the door.

"Whoa! I'm sorry." He put his hands up like the police had shouted, *Freeze! Don't move.*

"I didn't— The other day you hugged me. We've become close, I thought…" Maybe he knew nothing.

"I can't do this." She reached again for the handle, her bag and books clasped to her side.

"Wait. Talk to me. What's the matter?" For whatever reason, even if this woman had caused no end of complications to his life, he was like a drowning man. Grappling for any handhold, any air for his starving lungs at the idea of upsetting her.

Her lips flattened into a straight line. "I'll tell you what's the matter. In that shop, you swooped in like I needed some kind of hero. Or maybe you just needed to *be* one. Well, guess what? If that's the famous Barrick chivalry, it should've stayed in the Middle Ages."

Staring straight ahead, he gripped the steering wheel like it was the life raft he needed. Only she would use something she'd probably learned in a book for a fight. "I'm sorry if that offended you." How could she take offense at *that*? "I was trying to help. I thought if—"

"If I had some big strong man behind me, that guy would listen?" The tense lines of fear that seemed to lessen each day she spent in Wanishin Falls had returned.

He cleared his throat. "Yeah, I mean, no. I don't know. I've dealt with jerks like that before and I see how they act toward women. I didn't want him to treat you like that. I thought I could shield you from him. That's all."

Her eyes narrowed further. "I can take care of myself. I always have."

It was so similar to things he'd told his dad, he almost couldn't argue. Almost.

"But you don't have to."

They stared at one another in silence.

Legs shifting, she growled. "And really? He assumes I'm your 'little woman'? And you just go along with it? Ugh!"

His teeth ground together. "I'm sorry if even pretending to be in a relationship with me is so revolting to you." Oops. He hadn't meant to say that. Why did everything come out wrong around her?

"No, it's not you specifically. But marriage, relationships in general. Maybe. I don't know." She studied the ceiling of the truck, now in almost complete darkness except the streetlamp at the end of the block. "It's the whole thing. I can't do it."

"What whole thing?" His mind was still back on her comment about marriage and relationships in general. A sick feeling rose in his stomach.

"You gave me the bus. I shouldn't have accepted it. And all of your help on the book search? It leaves me feeling like

I… I owe you something." Her body rocked back and forth. "I won't be in a position to owe anyone anything. Ever…"

He caught the unspoken *again.*

What brought that on? What had he missed? Sure, everybody had a backstory. Was hers more…shattered…than he knew? "Hope, you don't owe me anything. I don't expect anything from you. Is it so hard for you to believe I wanted to help?" Because he couldn't touch her, he rapped his thumbs on the steering wheel instead. "And now the books concern us both, remember?"

The real reason—that he cared about her—almost leaked from his mouth, but he'd been rejected enough for one day.

She nodded. Silence followed. Then she said, "Can we pretend today didn't happen, except for finally getting my books back? No pretending or otherwise that we're in a r-relationship?"

It was a spark of positivity, but he didn't miss the implication. Nor the sharp pangs plunging into his chest. "So, can we at least be friends? Just two friends on a treasure rabbit trail together?"

"Yes, that I can manage." Her fingers curled around her books' edges.

He'd tried to build up the nerve for days to tell her he cared about her and wanted her to stay in Wanishin Falls. All the words dissolved on the back of his tongue. How could he fight for a connection she obviously didn't reciprocate? "Okay. We'll erase today with one condition. Keep the bus."

She shook her head, but he kept going. "You'll be doing me a favor. Otherwise, I'll need to pay someone to haul it away. Take it. And let me help you *as a friend* to turn it into your mobile café."

So you can roll right out of my life as quickly and mysteriously as you rolled into it.

The prospect deflated him more than he would have imagined.

She squinted. Finally, a smile returned. It was as if someone opened the window in a stuffy room. The friction in the truck cab calmed. "Okay, deal."

But the sweetness in her voice wrecked him. He didn't want to walk her to the door and see her safely inside with a neutral "Good night."

On the way back to his place after dropping her off, his mind drifted to what it had felt like to finally hold her in his arms. She'd been a perfect fit.

Or so he thought.

Chapter Thirteen

"Hey, Grandma." Ronan's baritone drifted in through the open windows at Dusty Jackets, his uneven but solid gait sounding across the wood-plank wraparound porch while Hope dusted a shelf before returning the books.

Mags returned his hello. She was elbow deep in soil all morning, weeding her flower bed.

The older woman had shared that Ronan had helped her finalize the sale of their small farm plot to the equine therapist Ronan had rehabbed with after the ship accident three years ago. Mags missed digging her hands into the soil, but it had become too much. Ulysses needed her.

Ulysses let out a startled snore from his sunny snoozing spot near Hope, beneath an open window, as Ronan entered.

She stuffed down the absurd joy to see him. So she hadn't scared him away last night... She'd half expected him to renege on his offer to help her and to be her friend. The word *friend* still lodged in her chest like a stone. Cold. Uncomfortable. But what could she do? She'd be gone soon. Besides, she could never be more than that. To anyone. And she wouldn't hurt him like that—let him care and then leave. It was better this way.

He shuffled from his natural leg to his prosthetic. "Hey." He palmed the back of his head.

"Hey." Okay, so a little awkwardness. "What are you up to?"

"I was in the neighborhood doing some street cleanup. I'm taking a break. I was wondering if we could look at your *Jane Eyre* volumes for clues, if there are any. Did you get a chance to inspect them last night?"

She grabbed them from beneath the sales counter. "I did and I've been looking off and on. I haven't found anything specific yet, but I want to show you something."

She spread out her *Jane Eyre* volumes on a little table in the castle room by the window, along with the diary.

He raked his hair off his forehead and she had to keep her hand in a fist to stop herself from brushing a stubborn wavy lock away from his brow. What a notion. She plopped down on the window seat, and he pulled up his grandpa's wingback chair.

"Has Grace said anything about a treasure?" He gestured to the diary.

"Not yet. While I haven't read every word, cover to cover, I've read about half of it and skimmed the rest. Treasure hasn't come up. I kind of doubt, as secretively as she wrote in her diary, that she would've mentioned a treasure, even if it had existed in her era and she knew about our ancestors hiding it."

She bent the pages of the first *Jane Eyre* volume. "See, I thought maybe there would be another clue on the side of the books like there was on the copy of *Little Women*. There's something on the fore edge, but I can't tell what it is."

"Hmm…" He held the book carefully with the pages fringed. Something was there. Now that they knew what to look for, it revealed itself quickly. But the image looked like mere splotches of color, no defined features.

Hope's gaze narrowed. "I can't tell what that is. Can you?"

"No clue." He tried realigning the angle of the pages. Nothing recognizable.

Hope took out the next volume, did the same thing. "This one looks weird too."

Third the same. Her tongue stuck between her lips while she tried every possible slant.

She caught his lopsided grin out of the corner of her eye.

His arms crossed. "Maybe the painting was damaged or faded with time."

"Could be." Her shoulders slumped with an invisible weight. She'd come so far, worked so hard, only to find another dead end.

Hope sat up straighter. "Wait. Do you notice how this blue is running down the middle of each one?"

Boyish excitement lit his icy yet somehow warm blue eyes. He leaned in. "Yes, and the browns and greens are off to the sides."

"What if we were able to hold them all together, all three volumes?"

It took some Twister-level maneuvering, and they had to call Mags in to assist them, but they finally got all three books stacked on top of each other with their paintings revealed. Each book held a cascade of water, ending in a pool at the bottom. Rocks and foliage were the browns and greens to the sides.

Ronan grinned.

"You know where this is, don't you?"

Mags chimed in, "Well, of course he does. That's our town's namesake. Wanishin Falls."

His hand brushed Hope's as they let go of the books. "You up for another adventure?"

"As long as this one doesn't end with me nearly drowning."

"And I don't get knocked in the water." He winked, and she didn't entirely hate the prickle of heat that crept up her neck.

Adjusting the straps on the backpack Ronan had loaned her for the hike to Wanishin Falls, Hope inhaled the damp, earthy air. Ronan slipped a water bottle into his pack's side pocket and zipped up his gear. So concentrated on his efforts was he that she could study his angled profile without him catching her. A longing overtook her, turned down the volume on all of the reasons she told herself not to get too close. Ironic, too, that this followed her informing him they could only ever be friends.

But maybe if she got to know him, understand him, and he in return got to know and understand the real her, it wouldn't be so bad. Terror gripped her chest at the admission to herself. The thing was, wanting something and having the ability to do it were two different things.

Lord, please help me heal.

She'd desired restoration before, but the tender, still-healing surface of her fear and soul-deep injuries were so painful she'd struggled to form the inner words to ask. They poured from her heart now.

I thought I had healed, to the extent that I could, with Dee's and the counselor's help, Lord. I think I'm seeing now that it comes in layers. Like new skin over a wound. Can You help me trust You again? What about Ronan, the Barricks, Kat? Will You help me heal so I can trust them too?

Could she ever be brave enough to allow herself that? Did she even want to let anyone that close? It sounded like the easiest thing in the world. But the pain seemed never-ending, and she might never be ready for that final layer of healing.

"Are you sure you're up for this?" Ronan stood, his brow tilted.

She cleared her throat and with it, her mind. "What? Are you implying my outdoor survivability leaves something to be desired?" Her lips pursed, but she couldn't help the smile breaking through.

"I'm saying that if it comes down to a bear and whatever our ancestors left in that cave, I'm heading in the other direction." He bent to tighten his hiking boots. "Just so you know."

"Bears? No one said anything about bears." She cast a quick glance around the entrance to the nature park as though a bear might hide behind the portable toilet, waiting for the perfect moment to jump out and devour her.

"For the most part, they'll leave you alone if you leave them alone." He grabbed his own pack and locked the truck.

"Great. I feel so much better. *For the most part.*"

It had rained last night after Ronan had stopped by the shop and they found the Wanishin Falls fore-edge painting. She followed as Ronan stepped onto the wet, sloppy trail. She was immediately glad he'd insisted she buy a pair of hiking boots. She'd found a lightly used pair at the thrift store.

Her boot made a *shloop* sound as she pulled it free from a mud pocket between a tree's roots.

"We should probably move quickly," Ronan called over his shoulder. "The weather forecasted only a slight chance for rain today, but with the low-pressure system coming off the lake, I think there's rain or possibly storms headed our way later this afternoon."

"You're moonlighting as a weatherman too? A pirate-weatherman...now, that's an exciting combo."

"And *you* could moonlight as a comedian-librarian." He turned and winked.

She should tell him to stop doing that. It made her stomach do funny little flips.

Streams of late-morning sun filtered through the clouds and made her squint. "I don't know. I think we'll be just fine. Besides, my stomach and I plan to be home in time for the roast and vegetables I put in the Crock-Pot for dinner."

"I'm glad you were in charge of packing our lunch. Usually, if I'm out hiking or fishing, it's beef jerky, sunflower seeds and corn nuts for sustenance. Along with anything I catch, of course."

They walked in companionable silence for a while.

Ronan held back a tree branch for her. She thanked him. "Is Tate almost done with his hours yet?"

He shoved his hands into his jeans pockets while they traversed a flat part of the trail. "He has about forty more to go." There was a regretful undercurrent to his words.

He'd said he'd enjoyed getting to know Tate as much as she had. She'd miss having the young man around. But truthfully, as soon as she found her last book and her two months ended—just over a month to go—there would be lots for her to miss about this place.

"I'm sure he'll show up and hang out once his work at the center's done." She stumbled on a hidden rock beneath a pile of dead pine needles. Ronan reached out and caught her with one arm as if it were second nature.

Righting her without missing a beat, he shrugged. "He said he'll come as long as the activities and food aren't too lame."

"Yeah, that sounds like Tate."

He swatted at a mosquito. Was he avoiding her gaze? "By the way, I've started the bookshelves on the exterior of the bus. It's not too complicated."

The secured bookshelves would have cupboard doors she could lock when she needed to drive the bus and then open them for customers when she parked in a new location. He'd already cut a long rectangular window into the food side of the bus to use as the pay counter. Customers could use the window to order food and pay for books.

"Thank you. I know what I want in my head, but I couldn't do this without your insights and carpentry skills."

His lips angled into a half smile. She'd met a lot of men, and none had ever seemed anything but greedy for acknowledgment. Not Ronan.

"I could never do what you do in the kitchen. And as much as I tease, you are the literary genius. Not me."

He had to take the lead on the trail as it climbed steeper and narrower. The path dropped off on their right to a bubbling stream.

With only the slightest limp, she noted, he picked his way across a tangled web of weather-exposed tree roots.

Sweat trickled down her neck. Beads of perspiration covered Ronan's forehead when he turned his head to indicate two large boulders at the stream's edge. "Let's take a little break."

Grateful, she bent over the stream and splashed the cool water onto her face and neck. When she tipped her chin skyward to sip from her water bottle, the sun no longer streamed into her eyes. Dark clouds had rolled in.

She brushed back wet clumps of hair plastered to her forehead. Her long sleeve fell to her elbow, exposing her pearly round and slash mark scars. King's punishments—cigar burns and knife marks. Hastily, she pushed the sleeve back into place, but the way Ronan's eyes bored into hers told her he'd already noticed.

"How much farther? It looks like your meteorology skills

might be right." She avoided the concern and tenderness in his expression.

"I'd say we're about a fifteen-minute hike away." Like a wilderness explorer, he studied the sky. "I wish we had more time. I'd show you how to fish in this creek. Little Arrow Creek. It's home to some beautiful wild brook trout."

"With fishing poles?" She leaned back on one of the big boulders.

"What else?" Humor colored his words as he sat beside her.

"I thought maybe you were a purist, caught them with your bare hands or something."

"I usually reserve that kind of Davy Crockett display for special occasions, but maybe for you..."

Gesturing back to the trail, he stood. "Okay, we'd better go."

She was grateful for his presence and for his grace in not mentioning her scars. Why did this have to feel so good—here with him, just talking? It shouldn't. She shouldn't let it. But she marveled at how normal their communication had become. Alone with Ronan. In the woods, of all things. Without panic attacks and soul-crushing fear setting in.

"I was thinking, maybe my mom meant for me to have Grace's diary as part of what she left for me. Sort of the unofficial fourth book."

He walked ahead again, leading the way with confident strides. "That could be. It was with Aunt Aggie's things and your copy of *Little Women*. They might have come to Dusty Jackets together. Why would your mom send it?"

"I'm not sure. Maybe to show me a glimpse of the history of this place and the people who lived here. The place where the roots of my family started and where she wanted me to return. Does that sound silly?"

"No, not at all. If she couldn't give you your physical family, it makes sense that your mom would want you to have an emotional connection to the place she and your family came from in some way."

"Exactly. Aggie and I had a special hiding spot in the library. It was way back in this deserted corner, filled with dry, boring textbooks. Like the *History of Concrete* and *How Fast Does Paint Dry?*"

His broad shoulders shook with laughter in front of her.

"When I traveled back to the library after I... I—" whoa, she'd been about to say *escaped* "—learned Aggie had passed, I found a letter from my mom. She said she wanted me to find my family and myself in Wanishin Falls. I now think she wanted me to find not only the books and whatever they led to, but also to find Grace."

"And have you?"

"I've never connected to someone on the page—fiction or nonfiction—as much as I have with Grace. I see myself in her, and I think my mom knew I would."

"What about the other part? Finding yourself?"

She gripped her backpack straps tighter. "I'm not sure yet. How do you recognize yourself, when you don't know who you are?"

His long, mismatched steps stopped. He turned. "I know who you are."

"You do?" *No, you really, really don't.*

"I'm trying to, and I like who you are." He stepped closer. It should've seemed heartwarming, even romantic. But the scent of masculine sweat made her stomach lurch and her heart speed up.

"You're sweet, caring, so funny, a ninja in the kitchen. And I believe you're a person who wants to belong somewhere, but you're too afraid of standing still. You've been hurt, and don't want to risk getting hurt again."

Her throat closed. Her ribs crushed her lungs. "You don't—"

A raindrop plopped onto the end of her nose. Just as well. She didn't know how to end the sentence. Big, wet drops, still warm from the humid late-May day, fell faster and faster, quickly soaking through her thin, long-sleeved top.

She tipped her face to the ominous clouds. "Well, you obviously know more than the weather person. Why did you have to be right, Ronan Barrick?"

"I was hoping I was wrong or that the rain wouldn't come until later. As much as I'd love to bask in that right now, we'd better find shelter. The wind is picking up. This is going to be a nasty one."

She threw her backpack down and dug out the sweatshirt she'd brought and pulled it on, throwing the hood over her head. Ronan, too, slipped on a hooded jacket that looked more waterproof than her choice.

Gales of wind and sheets of water pummeled them as they trekked on as fast as they could in search of temporary shelter.

Ronan grabbed her hand, urging her on as the rain pelted their faces, making it hard to keep their eyes open. "Come on! The falls are right over there."

The sound of the storm had masked the roar of the waterfall. But as they ran over another rise, there it was, a force as strong as the tempest surrounding them. Massive volumes of water gushed between high craggy cliffs as though the earth had split and poured out a never-ending wellspring.

The path narrowed, dropping sharply on her right into the churning water of the pool below the falls.

She pushed her feet to move faster over the knotted roots, rocks and muddy sludge. Her foot caught on a root. She couldn't stop her body from tumbling down the steep bank, nor from plummeting into the freezing water. Everything hushed around her except for the scream ripped from her throat.

★ ★ ★

Ronan's hand reached out of nowhere, gripped tightly around hers. But the rain made it almost impossible for her to hang on to his wet fingers. The water pushed and pulled her legs, determined to whisk her away. It was a lot deeper than she expected. She tried to push her feet off the bottom or a large rock, but there was only more water.

Her fingers slipped in his hands. She yelped. The fear in Ronan's eyes sent a sickening panic coursing through her cold limbs.

"I'm not letting go. Grab this rock with your other hand." His words gritted through his teeth. He pointed with his head, indicating a large rock sticking out of the bank.

As soon as she let go of Ronan with one hand, her other slid to her fingertips in his grasp. He sat on the ground with his heels dug into the wet ground for leverage. He grabbed her arm and shirtsleeve while she held on to the rock. Inch by agonizing inch, he pulled and she squirmed her way up the bank until she could use her feet to push herself up.

They both sat panting for several long moments, no longer worried about the rain falling nor the flashes of lightning. Her lungs burned. Her mouth somehow dry even with the excess of water. He rubbed near the knee, right above where his prosthesis started, a grimace on his face. She reached over, threw an aching arm around his neck and buried her face into his shoulder.

With zero hesitation, his no doubt equally sore arms wrapped around her, enveloping her in their warmth and safety. "It's okay." His breath registered heat against her ear.

"I was almost pulled under." Her words and body shook. The thought of unknown black depths tearing her from his arms sent renewed trills of fear into the pit of her stomach. This time she didn't have a life vest to save her.

But she did have the human equivalent. And he was holding her in a strong, steadfast embrace.

"I wouldn't let you drown. I would come after you, even
if you had slipped out of my grasp."

Overlapping Ronan's voice, muffled into her sopping hair,
were the words King had hissed to her all those years ago.
The ones that had slapped her in the face, telling her no one
cared and no one would come to her rescue.

For the first year, she'd pushed away her trafficker's toxic
claims, believing someone—surely *someone*—would find her.
But as the days turned into years, she'd realized how right
King had been.

The only thing she could do was try to bring something
beautiful to the other girls and women, trapped there just like
her. Sometimes at random houses, motels or hotels, she'd find
abandoned books. She would hide them in her meager pile of
clothing she was allowed to have, then pass them out to the
others during the small pockets of time they were permitted
to sleep. To give them a window into a different life, an escape, if only a pretend one and only for a little while. Somewhere evil never won and good prevailed.

But a girl, Alana, younger than Hope, whom she'd shared
a copy of *A Wrinkle in Time* with, had disappeared one day.
She'd been a sweet girl who still held on to a tenuous faith
she'd find her way back home, just like the children in the
story she loved. The girl had kept the book with her as much
as possible and reread it over and over. Then…she was just
gone and the book left behind. But she was not forgotten. And
Hope was ashamed to say the fight to find beauty, to live, to
escape, left her for a long time.

Ronan's hand made a slow circle on her back. She froze
but inhaled a measured breath instead of tearing herself away.

"It's all right. It's over now. I'm here. You're safe."

He couldn't know that these words washed over the memories of her past and present, carrying away the terror and helplessness.

"Let's get to the cave behind the falls." Ronan helped her to her feet. "With our track record, a lightning strike is next."

They made a careful crossing over the rocks to the waterfall, her hand firmly tucked into his.

"Bears or no bears, I'm going in." Her teeth chattered as they slid behind the curtain of water into the cave behind it. "They're just going to have to share." She had to shout to be heard this close to the water.

The cave was deeper than she'd expected, and they could stand up in it. It appeared vacant of any woodland inhabitants. They moved farther in to separate themselves from the deafening rumble of the water. Even so, she couldn't quite make out the back wall of the cave in the dim light.

Only after they laid their packs on the dry stone floor and she slumped onto a log did she take stock of her battered and bruised body and the sharp pain in her left knee, the memory of its cause lost in the commotion.

She reached down to examine it. A gash, but not severe, peeked through a hole in her jeans. The sleeves on her left arm were torn to shreds where Ronan had pulled her up.

He knelt in front of her, looking as bedraggled as she felt. A focused, determined look lit his eyes. He dug out a first aid kit from his bag. He dabbed at her cut, dried it as best as he could and put a butterfly bandage on it. The cut stung, but it was his gentle hands on her leg that made her draw a sharp breath.

"Sorry." He met her eyes, quite close now.

He kept the same focused expression as he gathered dry wood at the back of the cave. Perhaps some stranded camper had left it there. Fishing around in his pack, Ronan took out a tin of matches. Booms of thunder shook the cave.

He pointed. "Would you check if you have any paper in your pack or see if there's dried moss on that log? Even dry leaves would do in a pinch."

"Sure thing, Mr. Wilderness Man."

"I told you I could survive a good long time out here."

"If someone wasn't constantly trying to drown themselves and/or you." She ventured a little smile.

His chuckle hollowed out. Distracted, perhaps? Or was it the hollow void of the cave?

No moss. She gathered dry leaves. She also removed the brown craft paper she'd wrapped around the now-smushed croissant sandwiches and handed them to Ronan for kindling.

With other bits of tinder Ronan had gathered, he lit the fire in record time. Soon, dancing golden light and warmth filled the cave.

"I have a dry shirt in my bag." Reaching into his Mary-Poppins-if-she-were-a-forest-survivalist bag, he pulled out a dry sweatshirt.

Their hands met when he extended it to her, but he avoided her eyes.

"Ronan, I don't mean to keep getting us into trouble."

He dropped his gaze at the same time he let go of the sweatshirt now in her hand. "I'll rescue you as many times as you need me to."

"I mean, I hope I'm officially retiring the need for a hero for a while. You know how I feel about being a damsel in distress." She bit her lip at his intense expression, at the way his jaw flexed.

"I need to tell you something." His arms straightened at his sides. "You do have a knack for making a guy contemplate his mortality. If the next disaster is our last, I want to make sure you know." Lacing his hands behind his head, he marched to one side of the cave and then back.

"Make sure I know what?"

For a long time, he remained quiet. Perhaps he hadn't heard her over the water and storm.

"I have feelings for you, Hope. There's no one I'd rather rescue, any day of the week. Or go on treasure hunts. Or get knocked into the frigid Lake Superior." He strode to her, steps purposeful. "Any day. Every day. If it means I can spend it with you. I've tried to deny it. You said we could be friends. *Only* friends. You made it clear. But I can't help how I feel about you."

A high-pitched ringing hurt her ears. A croaking sound leaped from the back of her throat.

The squawk made his chin twitch. "I understand you may not feel the same, but I needed to tell you. So, when you make your plans to leave, you have all your options. Nothing left unsaid."

She found her voice. "What do you mean? What options?"

"You don't have to go. You could stay, explore what could be. With me. With everyone who cares about you in Wanishin Falls."

"I can't—"

"You keep saying that, but you *can*." He rubbed his palms together. "If you want to. Unless you don't want to. Maybe all of the signals are crossed and you don't feel the same way at all."

They stood almost chest to chest again. The look in his eyes was heartbreaking, heated, vulnerable. He didn't ask to touch her, but then she didn't wait for him to.

She wrapped her arms around his neck, reaching her fingers into his wet hair. The joy dancing in those blue eyes kept time with the flames. He bent his head, lightly touching his lips to hers as though gauging whether it was okay or not.

Going on tiptoe, she pressed her lips more firmly against

his. The warmth raced from her lips to her toes. His one arm encircled her back. With the other, he traced, featherlight, the line of her chin and cheek, as though memorizing the pattern of her.

His embrace tightened, and unbidden a million horrid memories washed over her. She told herself Ronan wasn't them, but her body didn't believe her. Every bone in her back stiffened as though a hot poker was rammed down her vertebrae. A harsh, foreboding switch flipped inside her mind. Air didn't stay long enough in her lungs. She was suffocating. Her heart hammered against her eardrums.

Ronan stepped back but held her arms. "Hope, what's wrong? I'm sorry. You weren't ready to hear that."

She bent forward, grasping at her throat. She needed oxygen. The cave spun.

"Breathe with me." He let go but stayed close. "It's all right. Let's sit down."

She shook her head and straightened. The panic still clung to her chest, but she needed to get this out. She commanded her brain to work with her lungs. "I have something to tell you too. *You* should probably sit." Her words came out in breathless wisps.

He didn't. Instead, he stood with forehead creased, confusion and worry written into the folds.

"I haven't told you who I truly am. Not really."

His gaze narrowed. "But you told me about your family being from Wanishin. What else is there?"

"A lot. More than I ever wanted to tell you. But then, I was never supposed to care about you or anyone else here. I was supposed to get my books and treasure and leave. I was never meant to let you all in."

If she shared her deepest, darkest secret, would light stream into the locked place in the depths of her soul? Would she finally be free of the invisible chains? Or would unlocking that dark place let out all of her monsters, wreaking havoc on everyone in their path?

Holding her middle, she did the only thing she could and pressed on. She had to be brave. "When I was fifteen, I met an older guy. He was fun, attentive and sweet. Brought me flowers and gifts. It was the first time since my mom died someone said *I love you* and I ate it up like the attention-starved kid I was. Kingston Brasher was his name."

Ronan did sit on the log then, leaning over, elbows on his knees.

"One day, he asked me to run away with him, just me and him. I hated my foster family and school, my life. And I told you about the other kids. So, I met him after school. I was ready to start fresh, a new life. That stupid, immature, desperate decision changed my whole life."

"Can you tell me what happened?" His words thick with compassion.

"It was like a mask suddenly fell off. He was a totally different person. He took me to this run-down house, shoved me inside the basement where there were a bunch of other girls, all tied up. And that was the first day of the hell I lived in for the next ten years of my life. We moved constantly, a couple weeks here, a couple weeks there. Some of us were carted around for years, others..." Her voice choked up as each of their sorrow-filled faces flashed through her mind. The men wouldn't remember them, but she would. How the light slowly drained from their eyes the longer they stayed. Illness, drug use to cope, malnourishment and rough treatment were the typical culprits.

She swallowed then cleared her throat. "Well, they didn't make it. We never knew where we'd end up next but knew what he expected of us."

Ronan's hand covered his mouth. The sadness in his eyes was almost too much, but she forged ahead, bolstered by an unfamiliar courage. Or maybe what propelled her was the long-suppressed need to purge all of the ugly. There was no turning back now.

"It wasn't until after I managed to escape that I heard the term 'trafficked woman.' Someone put words to what no words can adequately describe." She cringed. "It was the polite way of saying these men used me to satisfy their...lust. I wasn't human to them. I was beaten and abused every day for ten years. I, along with many of the girls, was also the scapegoat for petty crimes. We were the check forgers, drug runners, thieves. Whenever King needed something done and he didn't want to get his hands dirty. Now my record shows that I was arrested and processed for these crimes, even if the charges were eventually dropped."

Ronan started rising. She put out a hand to stop him.

He sank back onto the log. "I am not that guy, Hope. I will never be any of those guys. I care about you and want to protect you. That's it."

"I know." She squeezed her eyes shut. "But don't you see? No matter how much I wish it were different, or how many times I try to convince myself otherwise, I can never live a normal life. I can't stay here and pretend a person like me can have real relationships, a real home, a real family. I can't. Not after—"

She raised her arm, letting her scars show. Pulling back the neckline of the shirt, she revealed her deepest shame—the tattooed barcode from King at the base of her neck. "I'm a marked woman, inside and out."

Tears formed in his eyes. Tears. What was she supposed to do with that? She'd caused the tough wilderness man to cry. But maybe that was the biggest tell of all, that he was nothing like any of the men in her past. The pain within her had hurt him too.

Despite her step back, he drew closer. "There's no way to frame trauma like that. I don't know why it happened, Hope. I wish… I wish so much I could take it from you. Every memory, every pain you ever endured."

A few weeks ago, she would have turned on her heels and marched out of the cave at words like that. Not today. She owed him… No. She wanted to give him a full explanation. "No one can take my scars. They are burned soul deep." She managed a wobbling smile. "They're never…coming…off." Her voice cracked, ricocheting off the rocks. Tears streamed down her cheeks now.

He swiped at his own with his sleeve. "That's not true, Hope. There's Someone whose scars can override yours. Jesus."

If anyone understood unmitigated cruelty, it was Him. But… He hadn't saved her from what now permanently marked her. No one had. She'd had to save herself.

"Who would want such a broken person? Not Him, not anyone. Something inside me shattered when…" She let her words trail off.

Ronan tried another step forward. She turned ninety degrees so she didn't have to face him. "I had to shut it off." She buried her face in her hands.

"Shut what off?" A gentle hand rested on her shoulder. She shouldn't have, but she let the comfort of it seep into her skin, trickle toward her heart.

She opened her palms. "For a time, I tried. I really did. I tried to give the other women hope through books I found. But after one of the younger girls I cared about disappeared, I just couldn't find it in me to keep up the beauty in all those ashes. You know? So I turned it all off. My heart. My soul. The ability to let people in and care for them. My humanity,

I guess. To survive all of the…the *hands*." She couldn't say any more. Pushed away their faces. The cruelty. "I had to become this…this—" she gestured to herself "—shell of a person."

What was the catharsis doing to her? She let him wipe the tears from her face.

"Hope, I've never, and I mean never, seen someone more caring and full of concern for others than you. The way you've taken care of my grandparents, the way you've done so much for me. And I'm sure you gave those women a reason to believe there was life after…"

"I didn't do anything. Then or now. Everything I do only leads to more trouble. Look at how you've helped me and bailed me out of sticky situations since I arrived."

He handed her a tissue from his backpack. Was there anything he didn't have? She wiped her face, probably beet red and splotchy by now.

"This—" she gestured between them "—will never work out."

How many gallons of water flowed over the waterfall while she waited for him to respond? Incalculable.

"I can't imagine how hard it is for you to open up and trust again," he eventually said. "But you have to know I won't hurt you. I want to protect your heart, not cause it more pain."

A laugh and hiccupped sob escaped at the same time. "I know. I'm worried *I* could hurt *you*. What could I offer you emotionally, spiritually…*physically*? I mean, do you really want to deal with my PTSD and panic attacks every time we kiss?"

"When you care about someone, you're there through the good times and the bad. You figure it out, together."

"I have a feeling it'll always be more bad than good with me. I don't want that for you. I'm only part of a woman. You deserve a whole person who can love and give of herself freely. I don't think I'll ever be able to do that."

"Why don't you let me decide what I want in my life?" A

stubborn firelight glint flickered in his eyes. "Before you arrived in Wanishin Falls, I felt like I was only part of a man. Between my missing leg and everything that happened on my ship, I was going through the motions every day. You came, and I started to see that I don't need a whole leg to have a whole life."

Something squirmed at the pit of her soul.

He sighed. "Your trafficker stole ten years of your life. All I'm saying is, are you willing to allow him to steal any more of it?"

Crossing her arms, she turned her face away. "It's not that simple."

Her gaze landed on something scrawled on the cave wall. At the very least, it would table this much-too-real conversation for a while. "The rabbit trail continues..." she muttered, pointing to the mysterious message at the back of the cave.

Where no one dares go, it's buried deep below. But beware.

Then another Bible reference underneath: "Matthew 6:21."

Chapter Fourteen

"What do you make of the cave message? It's mysterious again, but the tone seems like it's the same person who painted the words on the arch." She pulled her foot free from another thick patch of mud.

"I agree. This certainly feels like the next clue. But it's not much of one, is it?"

"Not really. Buried below? That could be anywhere." She growled. "If this was our ancestors leaving us clues, how did they ever expect us to find anything with these bare-bones hints?"

No answer. There wasn't one. Ronan held a branch back for her. It showered her with saved raindrops as she passed and he continued forward. They'd waited out the storm for a couple of hours before they could venture out of the cave.

The weight of her soaking boots only added to the heaviness of her every step, burdened by the rock sitting in the hollow of her chest. She'd done what she told herself she never would—shared her story, all of herself.

Where did this leave things between them? It ate at her heart. The way she'd felt in his arms, the way his words put bandages on her wounds. It had terrified her, yes. But underneath, it felt right. Maybe that was the most frightening part of all.

After a steep, slick part of the trail, Ronan cast a glance over his shoulder. "The wall said, 'Matthew 6:21.' Is that the passage about 'where your treasure is, there will your heart be also'?"

When she read the Bible Dee had given her in the early days at the shelter, the four Gospels, Matthew included, had become a quick favorite.

"That sounds right. Play on words by our mystery treasure hunt leaders, I guess."

She made several decisions internally. First, she would labor double time looking for her last book. Second, she'd work on earning back some of the money she'd had to spend buying back her *Jane Eyre* by saving the money she earned at the shop as well as selling a couple more books she could part with. Kat had helped her sell two books online so far. Third, she'd work on her mobile café ASAP. These decisions would get her out of Wanishin Falls without hurting anyone else. Hopefully, Ronan would still help with the bus transformation. If not, she'd figure it out. She always did.

They emerged from the trail into the parking lot. Ronan blasted the truck's heater. She'd changed into his extra sweatshirt in the cave, but she still shivered. Once again, she found herself in his delicious-smelling clothes.

"Can I ask you something? About what you told me?" He glanced over as he pulled onto the road to head back into town.

She mumbled, "Mmm-hmm." Every other cat was out of the semi-truck-sized bag now.

"How did you escape? If it's too hard to talk about, I understand."

"I can talk about it." She rubbed her cracked lips together. "I had given up hope of rescue or escape for a long time after Alana, the young girl, disappeared. It had been almost ten years of captivity. I was being held in a hotel room at one point. When I was alone, which was very rare, I found a Bible in the bedside table drawer. I started reading. It was like someone opened a window into this dark place. I decided I would do whatever it took to get out of there or I would die trying."

His chin dipped, his eyes boring into hers.

"It took some careful planning, but one day, only one of his helpers was standing guard. When he walked down to the pop machine at the end of the hall, I jumped from the third floor. Sprained my ankle but kept running. I felt so guilty about leaving the other girls behind. But half of the women were being transported to the next location, that's why King wasn't there that day. And the other half was spread throughout the hotel so as not to draw suspicion. I didn't even know which rooms." She closed her eyes. The regret still lodged in her throat. Where were those women now? If only she'd been able to take them with her.

She lifted a shoulder. "Whether it was selfishness or survival instincts or the tiny glimmer of hope for freedom, I ran all night, until I was far enough away to ask where I was at a gas station—in Missouri. We were always moving so King wouldn't get caught. I called the cops from there. But, of course, when they arrived at the hotel I described, the girls and the guards had already left. Eventually, people from a church helped me connect with a shelter for women near Chicago."

"Did you ever hear from King again?" The expression on Ronan's face made it look like the word *King* was a loathsome bit of tough gristle he couldn't expel from his mouth fast enough.

"I worried about it for a while. Especially since I ended up back in Chicago, where he originally abducted me. But over time, I realized I was replaceable to him. He probably didn't spend much time looking for me and moved again so that if I told the police, he'd be impossible to find."

Ronan's hands tightened on the steering wheel. "Did you? Go to the police?"

She blew out a breath, trying to force away the remorse with it. "I did, but it was way too late. At first, I was too scared. By the time I mustered the nerve with my mentor Dee's help, they'd vanished. The cops were great. They took all of the information I knew about King, his associates, and how he operated, but they never found him…or the other girls."

"What did you do then?"

"I did what I could to try to build some kind of life. I didn't even know what I liked or was good at. Dee helped me discover my passion for cooking. I did an adult basic education course to get my high school diploma. Got my driver's license, not that I use it much with no vehicle. And I escaped *a lot* into my book worlds. Oh, and I changed my…" *Now or never.* "I changed my name."

"Wait, your name isn't Hope?"

Letting go of her last secret, she imagined herself a bird taking flight for the first time. Both freeing and terrifying. "No. It used to be Emily Carrington." She swallowed, searching for the rest of the words. "It was for safety purposes, but I also wanted a fresh start. The one I never got when I was fifteen. I thought with a new name, I could be anyone I chose to be. So, I picked a name based on something I wanted for myself."

"Both names are beautiful, but Hope suits you." His brows

knitted together. She could tell he wanted to say more. Perhaps a lot more.

"You once said Mackenzie, the woman I was engaged to, was brave." His lips pressed together, his words coming out gruff. "You are so brave, Hope."

He pulled the truck off to the road's shoulder, opening and closing his mouth twice before anything came out. "No matter what you take away from our...friendship—" he averted his eyes but then pierced hers again "—I want you to know, I think you're the bravest woman I've ever met. You're here. You're alive. You don't have to hide, okay? You have nothing to be ashamed of."

A hot tear trickled down her cheek. She turned her face to the window.

"Hey, I mean it. You weren't at fault. They were. Don't forget or doubt that."

Believing those words seemed impossible. Something pressed against her heart, urging her to believe. To reach out for actual truth instead of the things she'd told herself or King had spewed at her. Those were lies. Why had she insisted on using them to build the fortress in which she hid?

"Sometimes—" her voice rasped over the lump in her throat "—I wonder what it would've been like to grow up normal. Like you. Like Kat. To have my mom to talk to during those awkward teen years. Maybe my dad, who I don't remember at all, would've taught me to drive. I never went on a real date, or to prom, or had friends, or sleepovers." Tears streamed in earnest as she clutched her chest. "What would it feel like to not have this brokenness inside? This haunting that tells me I'll never be whole."

He rubbed the scruff on his jaw. "I wish more than anything you could've had a childhood, a life just like that. Simple and pure. Everything you should've had. All I can offer is what I know is true. I care about you. Gramps and Grandma Mags care about you. Kat cares about you. Above all, God loves you. He's your Heavenly Father." He stared at his open palms as if they held the right thing to say. "We support you. We don't judge you or see you as some broken-beyond-repair person. We— *I* see the beautiful person you are. And I'm here for you. Always."

A tingle of anger heated her cheeks at the mention of God, especially as her Father. She pounded her knees with her fists. "But no parent, heavenly or otherwise, should ever abandon a child like He did!" Her words filled the small space.

Her body shook with fury, the pent-up pain. She jumped out of the truck into the damp grass and wildflower-filled ditch. She wanted Ronan to drive away. He should. This was too much. For either of them. Why did she tell him? Regret choked her. But the answer was right there. *Because you didn't want to carry this burden alone anymore.*

Turning her back to the truck, she put her hands on top of her head, threading her fingers into her messy, wet hair.

But he didn't drive away. Instead, the truck door opened. The crunch of boots on asphalt and whisper of steps into the grass told her he was right there with her. Like he'd just promised.

She didn't wait for whatever sympathetic thing he might say. She turned on her heels. "My counselor and Dee told me that God didn't desert me. But they weren't there. You weren't there. Nobody was. I was all alone. God did abandon me."

"Or maybe He gave you the strength and opportunity to escape."

Her frustration built into a growl, and her hands balled into fists.

"That's what you don't get. He *did* leave me." Her voice ran ragged. "He turned His face away. King was right on that count, I guess. No one cared I was gone, and no one came for me." No, that was the years of abuse talking. King wasn't right about anything. She couldn't trust one word he had said. But the fact remained, trust in God or anyone, for that matter, seemed impossible.

Ronan closed his eyes. When they opened, deep pain shone out. "If I could go back and find you…"

"You can't."

"But I can be here for you now. I *am* here now. Standing still. Not going anywhere."

He did what she could not bring herself to do. Be still. Motionless. Solid. Strong. The Psalm she'd come across the other day, opening her Bible for the first time in a long time, came to mind. "Be still, and know that I am God…"

Could she be still? And if so, did God stand beside her, unshakable, like Ronan did now? Did He care about her and the places still unhealed within her?

Didn't He promise to heal the brokenhearted and bind up their wounds?

She let Ronan lead her back to the truck.

"Would you consider staying in Wanishin Falls?" Ronan's words pierced the quiet ride toward Dusty Jackets. Something more significant than the words themselves expanded in the truck cab.

"What would I do with my café *if* I decide to stay?" She honestly had no intention, but more out of irritation than anything, she tossed the question over to him.

"Maybe you could drive it to festivals along Lake Superior in the summers or use it as an outreach to the poor in this area, bringing them food and books."

Okay, so those weren't the worst ideas. "That's great, but food and books aren't free. If I'm only doing the café in the summer or if I'm giving things away, I wouldn't have enough money for supplies and to keep the shelves stocked."

"Let's agree to keep an open mind. I know there are small business grants as well as grants for nonprofit organizations. We applied for quite a few for the youth center. And there's the old-fashioned way, by saving money from working at the bookshop."

She crossed her arms. "What about this? I will consider staying for as long as it takes me to find the last book, finish the bus and get through the two months I committed to Mags. After that, I'll make my final decision."

"You drive a hard bargain, but that'll do for now."

Ronan's concern was for more than her shivering form as he ushered her back to Dusty Jackets. In her kiss, in their conversation, how much she had entrusted to him, he knew she felt something for him. He couldn't make her stay. He couldn't make her admit that she cared about him. But he believed with his whole being that her leaving to wander the country by herself would be the worst thing for her.

That was why, even if she never reciprocated his feelings, he'd needed her to know she was cared for. She was safe and supported here. A plan began to form the moment she admitted she hadn't experienced any of the firsts and pivotal moments of a typical childhood and young adulthood most people, including him, took for granted.

He cranked up the heat another notch. Hope shot him a grateful smile. The smile he lived to see. The smile that stopped his heart dead in its tracks before plowing ahead triple time.

When they arrived back at Dusty Jackets, Grandma Mags took in their disheveled appearance with a frown.

"Did you fall in the water again?" She stepped around the counter.

Hope blew her now-dry fringe of bangs out of her eyes. "Well, I did, but it was different water this time."

Grandma tried to hide her smile behind her hands. "Oh, Ronan, we need to get this girl a life jacket to wear under her clothes for everyday use."

He chuckled. "Don't I know it. It would definitely make my lifeguard job easier."

"I'm steering clear of water for a while." Her nose scrunched. "Unless it's a hot bubble bath, which sounds amazing right now."

Grandma Mags patted Hope's shoulder. "You get the bath started, and I'll bring up a tray of tea in a little bit."

"Where's Ulysses?" Hope asked.

He loved the way she cared so much about his grandpa. It came so naturally. She didn't even seem to realize how much she'd connected herself despite her insistence she couldn't.

"He's taking a nap, dear. I'll get him up for dinner." Grandma pulled a hand across her wrinkled forehead.

Ronan exchanged a look with Hope. Had she heard the exhaustion and worry in his grandma's voice too? Hope's tented brows told him she had.

Grandma Mags held up her forefinger. "Before I forget, I've been in contact with the officer I often called when we had people trying to sell us counterfeit books. I'll need your help and those pictures from Tate to file a report."

He propped himself against the counter, his prosthesis chafing after the water and mud. "That's a hard fight."

"It is." Grandma Mags's lips flattened into a grim line. "But you can rest knowing you did what you could. That Richard seems like a slippery fellow. Might be hard to make something stick."

Hope thanked his grandma for making the calls, her fingers fidgeting at the mention of Richard. Finally, Hope was coaxed upstairs.

Grandma Mags turned toward him. "You still have some extra clothes in the back guest room, Ronan. Maybe you should go change. Would you like some hot coffee?"

"Please."

He grabbed a shirt from the shelf in the guest room closet. A piece of paper fluttered like a leaf to the floor. He picked it up and read his grandpa's messy scrawl: "Check for pirates. The pirates have it."

With his grandpa's mind teetering between worlds these days, a message like that could mean nothing or everything.

He slipped on new jeans and tucked the note into his pocket and finished changing his shirt. He needed to put pirates aside for the moment—not a thought he would have expected to entertain a few months ago. An idea had started to form when Hope told him she'd missed out on so many firsts in her life. Maybe he couldn't turn back the clock for her or erase her past, but he could do something to show he'd listened. But it would require a little bravery on both of their parts.

He wanted to ask her out on her first date. But he'd have to build to it. A look of fight-or-flight had widened her eyes after their talk—flight, most of all—like he'd seen in a rabbit's eyes when caught in a snare. The last thing he wanted was to push her too hard and have her bolt, never to see her again.

Chapter Fifteen

The Founders' Day Festival, the first Saturday of June, arrived in a whirlwind of hustle and bustle. Hope scarcely had time to think about the books she finally had back, let alone the conversation she'd had with Ronan in the cave over a week ago. When she did allow herself a spare moment, she didn't feel the relief she probably should have. Instead, loneliness plagued her. It was like home had started to form, breaking down her inner walls. But when things felt a little off and awkward with Ronan, the warm, homey feeling dissipated.

She'd coped by working extra hard on her bus-almost-turned-food-truck. Being ready to hit the road when the time came seemed to assuage the sense of everything spiraling out of her control. Ronan had been true to his word, at least. He'd helped her cut out the side of the bus for a food counter and window and took out all of the passenger seats. Then they'd repainted it an eye-catching aqua blue. She'd go back later to add Food and Fables Mobile Café & Bookshop to the side.

"Hey, daydreamer." Kat plopped down another tray of Cornish pasties that were already made up but uncooked. Hope had named the meat-and-potato-rutabaga pies Hobbit Traveling Pasties.

"How's it coming over here?"

"Good. I'm just laying out our assembly line and I put the first batch of pasties into the oven."

Tate had taken an interest in the fundraiser and helped her come up with—*what else?*—a Tolkien-themed menu. He'd made signs to go on their tables with not only the menu items and the purpose of the fundraiser, but pictures too. Tate's image he'd drawn of Frodo with the ring stunned her. He'd tied it in with the center name using the heading, "Take a journey to the Refuge Youth Activities Center."

Tate and Matthew grabbed fliers with the menu, prices and a little snippet of the fundraising info from Kat's family's catering van. Tate saluted Hope. "All right, boss. We're ready to hand these babies out and get some green for the youth center." They moved off. Hope's heart swelled to watch Tate befriend Matthew.

Kat checked her watch. "Okay people, T minus thirty minutes until the festival officially opens." Her petite body seemed hardly able to contain her excitement as she bounced on her toes. "I better go check on the café one more time to make sure everything is going smoothly over there. And I'll pick up the soup that's bubbling away. Back in a jiffy."

Their booth was in a prime spot near the entrance to the city park and the buggy-pull arena. A canopy kept them shaded on this sunny June morning. Kat's dad, David, had provided the mobile kitchen equipment they needed. Hope had prepped as much ahead of time as she could at Kat's—the pastry dough, beef and veggie filling for the pasties. She and the café's chefs had created three hundred of the hand pies. She'd also come up with a Sam's Garlic, Mushroom and

Poh-tay-toe Soup as well as Lemon and Lavender Elevenses Doughnut Holes.

Upbeat music blared behind Hope. One of the café's chefs, Sophia, her dark hair braided around her head and kept in place with a rolled bandanna, danced while prepping their doughnut-hole batter. Her husband, beside her, did the same while singing along to the song. Their joy while dancing and cooking together had enlarged the gulf of emptiness growing in the pit of Hope's stomach.

"We're almost set to drop the doughnuts, Hope." Sophia checked the deep fryer's temperature.

They still had a little time. *Breathe.*

Her husband, Abe, wiped his hands on a towel and flung it over his broad shoulder. "So, how are you feeling about your food truck plans now? Did you think about what I advised?" His words rich with his Chilean accent.

Hope rested her hands in the front pockets of her apron. "I agree. I do need to narrow down my menu to the dishes that will appeal to a wider customer base and help me save money in the process. How do I do that? How do I know what everyone is going to like?"

"It's more about what you love cooking because that's what people will respond to." He tipped his head.

"What do you mean?"

He spread his arms out wide, gesturing to the food, the people milling about on the festival grounds and then to his wife, getting her "steps in," as she called it. "This. This is all for love. We make food out of a desire to connect with people. Throughout history, food is what brings people together at the end of the day. They laugh—they share. A meal helps people celebrate or commiserate, as the case may be. Food is community."

This pulled at a loose string in the back of her mind. It unraveled something she'd never consciously thought before, but it made so much sense. She wasn't exactly a social person, and yet here she was basing her dream on something so entangled with human relationships.

Sophia stepped closer. "Hope, we know from experience you can have the perfect menu, the perfect ingredients, all the equipment, but if your creations aren't from your soul and connected to the people you care for..." She pinned Hope with her dark, honest eyes. "Why do you cook?"

A bolt of lightning jolted her core, splitting away the numerous reasons she told herself she loved cooking.

The words she never meant to say out loud tumbled out. "Because I can't get close to people. It's my way of reaching them with a piece of myself." A rogue tear trickled down her cheek. "Cooking is a window into a life I'm not sure I could ever be part of."

Sophia reached for her hand and squeezed it. "But you will. I believe food has tremendous power to heal. Be open to connecting with people and you will cook from your soul. You'll see."

Abe put an arm around his wife. "Use your love of books to help you. The words are read for a brief time, but we remember the way they made us feel for the rest of our lives. The same goes for good food. The taste is for a moment, but the memory forever."

It so echoed a thought she'd had, it made her smile, but her lower lip quivered. "Thank you. You've both been so much help and given me a lot to process."

How could she ever express her gratitude for their ongoing business counsel—sharing their business plan, the vendors they'd used when they'd operated a food truck, even some of their now-unused equipment? They'd abandoned the nomadic food truck life shortly after they discovered their family was growing. It was as if they poured into Hope what they'd once poured into their food truck.

Hope dried her cheek. Ronan, who'd picked up more paper and plastic serving supplies, made his way through the crowd. At least a head taller than anyone else, he was impossible to miss. He wore his hat today with a white T-shirt and jeans. How did he manage to make that look good?

"Wow, this looks awesome, guys." Ronan's fingers grazed one of the coupons she'd made with Kat's help and Mags's permission.

"I thought we could help advertise for the shop while we're raising money for the youth center. Customers get a 'buy one book, get one-half off' coupon with every purchase of food."

"That's great for the shop's business."

Kat returned with the giant slow cooker of soup.

"Mags and Ulysses helped sponsor the food and Kat's Café—" she tipped her head toward Kat "—so we put them on the signs as sponsors for the fundraiser and made coupons for both places."

"Brilliant. What can I do to help?" He shoved his hands in his pockets but they seemed antsy like they needed a more useful occupation.

Hope tucked a stray piece of hair back into the baseball cap she wore—they all had to wear a head covering of some kind. It was part of the health and safety agreement they had to sign to run a booth. She tossed Ronan a pair of gloves.

"You can be my sous chef."

His lips pulled down into a frown. "Did you miss the part where I told you I had the cooking skills to burn a cheese-and-cracker tray?"

Cocking her head to the side, she put a hand to her aproned hip. "Did you miss the part where I told you I like my cheese burned, preferably until it's unrecognizable?"

His chuckle warmed a spot in her aching chest, clearing away some of the unease, at least on her part. This. This felt better. Also, had she just flirted with him? Where had *that* come from?

She pointed to the egg timer. "Make sure we check the pasties every thirty minutes. And then again at forty minutes, basically every five minutes until they're done. Usually, pasties take between forty to forty-five minutes, but I'm not used to these ovens. With two, we'll bake twenty-four at a time. We need to take our first batch out of the ovens now." Which he obediently did, using the oven mitts she handed him.

Hope checked them. They were done and the rich and savory aroma made her mouth water. "Okay, those can go in the warmer. The next batch is right there. Put those in and set the timer. Got all of that?"

"Uh, sure, timer. Forty minutes, no, thirty minutes for each batch. No problem."

"Kat will help some with plating, but she's also in charge of ringing up the customers. Oh, and that oven on the left has been a real temperamental smarty-pants this morning, so watch out."

Kat stepped closer and squeezed Hope's shoulder. "She's amazing at this. Can't you see her rolling around, commanding her own little mobile kitchen?"

Did she imagine the grimace behind his smile?

It wasn't lost on her that this was the first time she would showcase her cooking on a larger scale. She said a silent prayer for the day to go well. She and God were on speaking terms, at least for today. She was trying to connect. Would He do the same?

After her conversation with Abe and Sophia, she wanted to show she could cook from the heart. She reminded herself the heart applied to her care for the youth center, not the man behind it.

Tate and Matthew returned from handing out the pamphlets. They each grabbed a water from the cooler. People streamed in full force now.

After a long pull on his water bottle, Tate's face turned grim. "Let them come."

Only Hope seemed to catch his *Lord of the Rings* film reference until Ronan said in an equally grim tone, "So it begins."

Ronan shrugged at her smirk. "What? So I can't know a little Tolkien too?"

"The nerd scale keeps growing exponentially around here." She pressed her lips together to keep from laughing at his mock-offended expression. "Also, I'm not sure if movie quotes count as *knowing* Tolkien."

Ten years of modern movies had been hard to catch up on after her escape, but Dee had insisted that the *Lord of the Rings* trilogy of movies was a must-see.

Kat crossed her arms. "Humph, you put a whisk in this woman's hands and watch the feisty chef come out." Kat moved behind the table to the mobile register, a lockbox of money and her smartphone with a credit card reader attached. "Battle stations, people."

The morning breezed by with everyone on their team doing their assigned tasks with relatively few hang-ups, other than Hope forgetting about the Lembas bread biscuits she'd made to go with the soup.

"I can run to the café for the biscuits." Ronan, true to his word, had kept up with the ovens, only muttering a few grumbles at the touchy one. He set another baked batch on top of the stove.

Hope checked the time on Kat's watch. "Uh, yeah. Could you? That would be great. I think people are going to want something more than tea, coffee and doughnuts soon."

Ronan tossed his gloves in the trash and dug his keys from his pocket. "Sure. No problem."

Even though it was barely past 10:30 a.m., they started to sell the pasties and soup.

He ducked his head back under the tent. "I'll be right back."

A few people waved at or chatted with Ronan, but a handful whispered and cleared a path around him. How could such a large number of people be so kind in this town and then a resolute few be so unwilling to change their opinion of Ronan or the Barrick family? Was it the supposed Barrick Curse or the ship accident?

Still, it had buoyed her spirits to see townsfolk walking up to the tent throughout the morning thanking Ronan for creating the youth center. From the way it lifted Ronan's shoulders, perhaps he'd sensed the shift as well.

Tate stood beside her, watching Ronan's progress through the parted crowd. "I know what that's like."

"Me too." She sighed.

Tate took over Ronan's station, grabbing a tray from the oven under her close supervision. He rolled his eyes at what he said was her hovering like he was a five-year-old.

When he'd used a spatula to lift the pasties and move them to the warmer, he sent her a covert glance. "So, why did you say 'me too'?"

She ladled up a Styrofoam bowl of soup, put a lid on it and handed it to Kat. "I was a foster kid growing up, and that carried a certain…stigma. Plus, I guess the other foster kids needed someone to take out their frustrations on. That person was me."

"I get it. I'm picked on too. Pretty much since kindergarten."

"Is that why you broke into the school and spray-painted?" She'd never asked him about it.

Tate's jaw tightened as a group of teens walked by, spotted him and started snickering. A tall, athletic-built boy, wearing a jersey with Hamilton and the number 01 on it, called over, "Hey, Morgan! Nice hat. Where's your elf ears to go with it?" Tate had put on a slouchy stocking cap for food prep.

A shorter kid with a nervous laugh pointed at Hope. "Is that your probation officer?"

"No. Is Hamilton your babysitter?"

She couldn't suppress the smirk at Tate's immediate and unwavering reply.

When they left in a trail of twisted laughter, Tate leaned over, fists propped on the table. "That's why. Because I was paying Ryan Hamilton and his little cronies back for making my life miserable."

"What exactly did you do?" She kept her tone light.

"I spray-painted their lockers and left a surprise for them that may or may not have smelled like death run over and rubbed in fish guts."

His matter-of-fact explanation almost did her in. She straightened her apron. "Paying someone back rarely has the outcome you want. It ends up hurting *you* in the long run."

He rolled his eyes, signature move. "Yeah, well, imagining their faces when they opened their lockers was all the reward I needed. Totally worth it."

"What about the punishment? Was that worth it too? All your public service hours?"

"What, are you sick of my company?" He tried flipping back his shaggy hair until his fingers touched his hat. Something vulnerable weighed on his nonchalant shoulders.

"Nah. Who else can I nerd out about books with?"

"You mean, other than Ronan and the Barricks?"

She bumped her shoulder into his. "Yeah, other than them. Besides, no one gets Tolkien like you."

They both boxed up another five pasties for Kat, who handed them to a waiting family. Hope checked the touchy oven, concerned it was cooking too fast, and turned it down.

She let out a long flow of air, trying to expel her own ineptness and sadness over Tate and his situation. How alone he was. She knew the feeling. She wanted to hug him or tell him she cared. Ronan cared. But sometimes the right thing to do or say still wouldn't come out of her, no matter how much she willed it.

Ronan sprinted through the crowd with an alarming sharpness to his expression.

Brows nearly touching in the middle of his forehead, he ducked under the canopy. "Someone tried to break into Dusty Jackets. Did you lock your books in your room?"

"What?" Her ears buzzed. "I, uh…" She replayed the hectic morning getting ready for the festival, but she always locked her door and made sure her books were inside her room when she wasn't there. "Yes, yeah. I locked them in my room. I'm sure of it."

Ronan grabbed the back of his neck. "Who would do this?" His words a snarl.

Kat served a pasty, soup and bottled water to a woman who looked over at Ronan with a curious stare. Abe and Sophia stopped what they were doing.

Kat joined Ronan and Hope, arms folded. "Are your grandparents okay, Ronan? Were they still there?"

Ronan stopped pacing. "Yes, they're okay. They were upstairs, about to head out and come over here, when they heard something in the hall, like someone trying to break into your room." He gestured to Hope.

"But when Grandma Mags came out to check, whoever it

was ran down the stairs too fast for Grandma to get a look. The perp probably thought no one was home."

"Did your grandparents call the police?" Abe asked.

"They're at the house now. But nothing was taken downstairs that we can see. That's why I wanted to know, Hope, if you'd left any of your books downstairs. Whoever tried to get into your room didn't succeed."

Her heart skidded and thumped. What if she'd forgotten one of her books in her favorite window seat reading spots? Or the sitting area in the upstairs hall?

"Do you think it's that Richard guy from the store in Duluth?" Tate kicked a rock and shoved his hands into his pockets.

Scrubbing at the dark shadow of stubble along his jaw, Ronan tipped his head to the side. "I don't see how he'd even find out where Hope was. And would he really go to that trouble?"

"He knows exactly how much those volumes are worth." Hope couldn't fight the rising panic or the guilt. Because of her and her books, Ulysses and Mags were put in danger.

The team remained silent a moment, the festival cacophony—people talking and laughing, children screaming out of anger as well as joy, fiddle music playing somewhere, a man announcing over a loudspeaker that the buggy-pulling contest would soon begin—all fading like a dull hum into the background.

Hope grabbed her purse from beneath the table. "We should go back to Dusty Jackets and check on everyone." And *everything.*

Kat shooed them. "Of course, go. We've got this."

Black smoke poured from the fussy oven. Sophia moved into action, turning it off and removing the pan of pasties. In all the commotion, Hope had forgotten about her timer.

Abe waved her and Ronan off. "Go, you two."

She'd let her first impression as a restaurateur get out of control. Out of *her* control. But she allowed Ronan to lead her away.

They drove the short distance to Dusty Jackets in silence. A police car had parked out front. So had an SUV.

"Is someone seriously trying to shop when a cop is here?" The Barricks were so nice, they'd probably let them.

Something about Ronan's stony expression surprised her.

"That's my dad's vehicle." The words ground out between his teeth.

"Oh" was all she could say.

Ronan's footsteps stomped up the porch steps. His hands tightened into fists as he entered the shop.

She'd always found it strange that his dad, Brock, lived in the same town, and yet he never visited the shop or Ronan. The dad who seemed to place all of the world's problems on Ronan's shoulders. But maybe that was just how Ronan saw it.

"How could you have let this happen?" An older, stonier version of Ronan stood next to the cop, who took notes and spoke in low tones with Mags.

Okay, maybe Ronan hadn't exaggerated.

Ulysses appeared utterly lost and exhausted by the ordeal, slumped in his wingback chair.

But she couldn't stop the flood of relief at seeing them all right. Once again, she surprised herself by how much she cared.

Ronan flexed his fingers, the knuckles popped. "Am I responsible for every negative thing that happens? Tell me how I could've prevented this. You seem to have all the answers."

Brock's piercing gaze, like Ronan's but more cold gray than blue, swung toward Hope. "That. Her. That's how you could've prevented this. She shouldn't be here."

Hope's stomach leaped into her throat. If only there was a hole to crawl into.

"Brock. That's enough." Mags used her no-nonsense voice. The one she reserved for serious situations, including making Ulysses take his medication.

The police officer nodded to them all. "I'm finished here. Let me know if you have any questions or further information for me. We'll be talking to neighbors to see if anyone saw a person or vehicle around that time. We'll do some extra patrols over the next couple of days."

"Don't strain yourself." Brock muttered the words under his breath, while Mags and Ronan thanked the woman. Maybe Ronan hadn't inherited as many manners as he thought from his dad.

When the door clicked shut, Ronan locked it.

His dad didn't even wait for him to turn around. "So, what is this stranger doing here? Other than causing trouble. She obviously has something someone wants."

Ulysses swayed a little, rattled off a jumble of numbers over and over in a slur. Hope ran to his side, sitting him up and holding on to him. She stood next to the chair, arm around Ulysses, letting him lean into her side. He needed to get upstairs to bed.

Brock looked her up and down. "What are you, some kind of drug dealer? You owe somebody money or something?"

She didn't miss how Ronan put himself between her and his dad. This time the gesture filled her with warmth instead of anger. "She is not a stranger." Ronan reached back and touched her shoulder.

"This is Hope Sparrow, and she's the best thing to ever happen to m-m—to us." Ronan's stumble rang as if a book-filled home could echo.

Hope caught Mags's eyes on her. Worry with a hint of joy.

"Oh, really? And did we frequently have problems with vagrants and thieves before Hope arrived?" Brock crossed his muscular arms, so like Ronan's. But his build seemed harder, cut from cold, unforgiving granite.

"How would you know?" Ronan shot back. "Hope's been here for over a month now and this is the first time we've seen you. It seems to me if you cared about what's going on around here and wanted a say in it, you'd be here more."

The raised voices agitated Ulysses further. He murmured the same sequence of numbers a little louder now. Hope rubbed his back in slow, methodical circles the way her mom did when Hope had been upset as a child.

"It's okay," she whispered to Ulysses.

Brock narrowed his eyes at her.

Ronan glanced back with a mixture of pride and something else, the intensity she'd seen that day in the cave.

She cleared her throat. "If *she* may speak for herself…"

Ronan moved to the side so she could see Brock better, but stayed a close step away.

Tightening her grip on Ulysses, she continued, "I'd like to say, I don't know who broke in and I don't know if it was because of me. I hope not. But I would never intentionally put Mags and Ulysses in danger. I… I care very much for them." She bit her lip. An invisible chain fell from her back to admit it out loud.

Mags crossed to Hope and hugged her. "And we care about you too, my dear. Very much."

Ronan swallowed and stayed silent.

Brock nodded, but in a mocking sort of way. "Oh, yeah. I'm sure. I believe you might not *knowingly* put them in danger. But who is Hope Sparrow? And how long before something worse than this happens?"

She didn't like how he said her name, almost as if he knew…

He was ex-navy. Could he know something?

"I should've checked the security system." The anger and hurt vibrated the air around Ronan. "So, if you want to blame someone, blame me, Dad. You usually do."

Brock cast a hand out. "Well, I was driving by and what do I see but cop cars at my parents' shop. I couldn't help being concerned, especially since I find out a strange woman is living down the hall from them."

When this met with silence, Brock grumbled, "Fine, I'll go. My advice isn't wanted here."

Mags clasped her hands together. "It doesn't have to be like this, Brock. Stay."

But he waved her off. "Didn't you know distrust is our family curse? Not only with the town. With each other." With that, he stomped out.

Chapter Sixteen

"So, tell me again why I'd want an oven from someone who loaned us a faulty one that almost burned down our booth?" Hope peeked into the minibus still parked behind the youth center. It was coming along on its makeover. She smiled so Ronan knew she wasn't dead serious.

He lay on his side, hooking up the oven to one wall of the bus's interior, and craned his neck to look at her. "This isn't the smarty-pants one. That one's been retired forever."

"You mean charred to a crisp and in a junkyard?"

"Yup." He wiped his forehead with the back of his hand, leaving a black trail.

The man at the kitchen supply rental place who'd loaned the two ovens to Kat's dad, David, felt so terrible about what had happened with the touchy oven, he gave the commercial oven with a grill top to him. David knew Hope was opening a mobile café so he bequeathed the oven to her.

"There, that should do it." Ronan sat up and wiped his hands on a rag.

"You know I was kidding, right?"

His rugged face scrunched into a confused boyish expression.

"I love it. I can't believe this oven is mine." She took in a slow breath through her nose, clutching her hands over her chest. "Thank you for installing it…and, you know, for everything else."

"No problem. You're welcome." He crouched by his toolbox, cleaning the tools he'd used. She watched the expanse of his back, the muscles through his white T-shirt clenching and releasing as he moved.

He stayed quiet with her. She wouldn't say wary or distrustful like his dad. Contemplative, maybe.

After the run-in with his father, Ronan seemed to grow introspective. He'd worked hard to ensure the shop was protected following the break-in. By his tireless efforts, Hope guessed his dad's blame sank deeper than Ronan let on.

It'd been four days and the police still had no suspects, and since nothing appeared to be missing, they had put the investigation on hold.

Grabbing a bucket of lemon-scented soapy water and a sponge, she hopped into the bus. She stepped around Ronan. It would be a tight space once all of the equipment was in. The same guy who gave David the oven had a lead on a fridge-freezer side-by-side combo she needed. She had set aside her paychecks as much as possible and she'd sold several more volumes from her rare book collection to start her nest egg again after paying for her *Jane Eyre* set. Maybe at the end of their wild-goose chase would be a treasure both she and Ronan could use toward their respective dreams.

Ronan stood from his spot. The six-foot-six-inch bus interior was only a couple of inches above Ronan's head. His height but also his presence filled the space. She hadn't meant to stand nearly chest to chest with him. What would it be like to reach out, without fear, to see what the warmth of his shoulders and chest felt like again?

She tucked a piece of stray hair behind her ear and swallowed. "Sorry. I didn't mean to crowd you."

"You're not." A gentle heat lit in his eyes. She found herself glad she didn't see repulsion or even worse, disinterest, after all she'd shared with him.

Without telling it to, her hand rubbed away the smudge on his forehead. He grew still and covered her hand with his. He pressed his lips to the hollow of her palm but let go.

"I apologize," he muttered, ducking his head.

A throat cleared at the open back door. "Are we seeing how many clowns can fit inside this car?" Kat stood with a hand on her hip and a catlike grin. Oblivious mischief, her calling card. "I wanted to see how this is coming along and to let you know we'll need more paint for the rec area."

Ronan jumped out of the bus. Hope regretted the retreat of his nearness, even if it was a hot, humid day.

"I'll head to the hardware store for paint." Ronan strode to his truck and drove away within thirty seconds.

Kat and her family were inside the building, using the fundraiser money to repaint the recreation side of the open space.

Kat hopped inside and grabbed an extra sponge. She started washing the food prep countertop.

To hide her still-heated cheeks, Hope stooped and opened the oven. In methodical motions, she scrubbed, washed, then repeated to get the oven back to like-new condition. It was gently used but worked great.

"Is everything okay?" Kat used a careful, casual tone. "With you and Ronan?"

Taking her fingernail to an extrastubborn bit of charred remains on the oven door, Hope shook her head. "I don't know what you mean. There is no 'me and Ronan.'"

"Come on. I might be awkwardly unaware sometimes—" so she did know "—but I'm not that dense. You guys were inseparable one day, sort of awkward the next, and then I'm not sure what I walked in on just now. Either you guys are practicing for a spot on a daytime soap opera or you're struggling to figure out where you stand with each other."

Hope closed her eyes and dunked the sponge a little too forcefully into the water, sloshing it over the side and onto her jeans. "Perceptive, Tinker Bell."

Kat laughed at the nickname Hope had taken to calling her. It was no worse than "new girl," which Kat still called Hope. "You don't live in a small town, get this bored and learn to read people this well for nothing."

Sitting back on her knees, Hope tried to wipe the sweat off her brow. A trickle of soapy water dripped from her forehead. "I told him we should stay friends. I mean, I'll be leaving soon. As soon as this—" she threw her hands out to indicate the bus and splashed herself again "—is done and I find the last book, I'll be on the road."

They'd already discussed the idea at length. Kat repeatedly told Hope she should stay. But the road and the safety of anonymity still called to her.

"He told me he has feelings for me when we were stuck in that cave, and I told him about my past. That…that I've had some bad experiences—" what else could she say? "—and I can't return those feelings. And now…" She squeezed the sponge until her hands ached.

"You can cut the tension of the male-female variety with a chain saw?" Kat's arched brows lifted almost to her blond hairline.

"So helpful. But, yes, I guess. I'm sure it's like when you're told you can't have something, you think you want it even more."

Kat's tongue puffed one cheek out as she squinted. "Sure,

sure. And it couldn't possibly be because you do care about him and actually want to stay, right?"

The thing was, Brock had made a lot of sense. Painful and horrible, yes. But he was right. The longer she stayed, the more problems she'd cause for everyone, including herself.

Hope winced. "No. I can't." Even she couldn't lie and say she didn't care. That would be beyond her acting skill level. Because when she allowed herself to think about it, which was next to never, she did care. Very much. About all of them. But good people and good things didn't happen for girls like her.

"Well, whatever is holding you back from staying in one place long enough to make a life for yourself, maybe it's time to let it go." Kat's eyes never strayed from her vigorous scrubbing. "How are you going to grow unless you put down roots?"

Instead of commenting, Hope grabbed the bucket and said she'd refill it with the garden hose near the outbuilding.

A desire to tell the truth rose in Hope's throat. She pictured running back to Kat, spilling everything. Never had the truth sounded so good, smelled of freedom before. But it was quickly squashed. What was the point? Look at how her telling Ronan had turned out. And there was no reason to burden her friend with the horror story of her personal history any more than there had been with Ronan. But she'd needed him to understand, once and for all, why she could never be with him romantically. Why her wounds would only wound him in the end.

Stooping by the outdoor faucet, she tossed out the dirty water and refilled it with clean, cool water. She'd asked God to do that for her once—toss out everything soiled and damaged inside of her and fill her up with the clean and restoring power of His grace. So why did she still feel like such a defective, broken person?

She washed her hands, arms and face before taking her time walking back.

If she ran from Wanishin Falls, what then? How long could she keep it up? She'd forever be a stranger in every town and she'd leave before anyone knew her. A life alone, unknown. At one time, that held a curative appeal and an adventure she craved. Now she wasn't so sure.

The words of her captor rang with laughter through the rafters of her mind. *"No one will care that you're gone. No one knows you or misses you. You're like vapor—"* he'd blown cigar smoke into her face *"—gone."*

He'd been right. Aggie may have looked for a while and probably the police, but Hope doubted anyone else had spared her much thought. Something told her if she left Wanishin Falls though, a few people would care. She found herself hoping they would. She'd certainly miss them. Her pre-Wanishin Falls self would be seriously disappointed in her. Dee, on the other hand, would be proud.

"There you are!" Mrs. Baranski skidded her walker across the parking lot. "I'm so glad you came to visit."

"Hi, Ethel. How are you?" She plastered on what she hoped was a convincing smile.

"Oh, never mind that. You never want to ask someone my age how they are unless you're ready for an earful of medical diagnoses and medications." Her wrinkled lips pursed.

Ronan arrived back. He called a greeting to Ethel.

Ethel motioned for him to join them as though he'd already been part of the conversation. "Come on now, you two. I have something remarkable to show you upstairs."

Ronan raised his brows at Hope as though to ask what was going on. She raised her palms to say, "No idea."

Kat emerged from the bus. "Man, I thought maybe you'd gone down to the lake to get the water or something." She waved to Ethel. "Oh, hey, Mrs. B."

Ethel hardly paused to give a small wave back as she shuffled to the door. The woman was quick when she had a mind to be.

Kat grabbed the paint from the back of Ronan's truck. "I'm going to bring this into the fam. We'll see if we can finish the rec area today."

When she and Ronan walked inside, Ethel waited in the elevator. She tapped her delicate nails against her walker handle. "You'd think as young as you two are, you could have a bit more giddyap in your step."

Hope scratched her upper lip to hide her silent laugh. Ronan's jaw twitched.

With no further explanation, Ethel led the way into the museum and to a back corner with a sign that read Wanishin Falls Legacy. Inside, old photographs, paintings and personal belongings were showcased behind glass with names of the townspeople they belonged to.

Ethel's face, eager now, turned to them. She motioned to the last display. "Here. I told you, Hope, that you reminded me of someone. Look."

As Hope rounded the corner, she gasped. Her hand flew to her chest. Ronan stepped closer to inspect, but her feet stuck to the floor.

A woman's faded sepia-tone picture hung on the partitioned wall. Her dark brown, almost-black hair was piled on top of her head. She wore a late-nineteenth-century lace-and-satin gown, but—without a doubt—it was like someone had superimposed Hope's face on the woman's body. It was uncanny. Startling. Exciting. Unnerving. It felt as though she should know the woman. After all, the half-shy smile the woman wore was her own.

"That's amazing." Ronan rubbed his chin. "Creepy, almost. She looks just like you."

Ethel stood to one side of the framed photograph. "This has been in storage for a long time. That's why I couldn't recall it immediately. Grace Holloway."

"Wait, what?" Hope hadn't meant for her voice to come out so sharp and loud.

Tapping the edge of the frame, Ethel nodded. "Yes, this is Grace Holloway. Her family was integral in starting this town and its economy. Her family helped build the church and had their hand in the shipping and logging industry of the day."

"That's the woman who wrote the diary we found, right?" Ronan crossed his arms, his eyes sweeping between the photo and Hope.

"Yes," Hope whispered.

"If you two aren't related, then you have a doppelgänger." Ronan spoke her thoughts aloud.

She'd always felt a kinship to the woman who shared her thoughts so eloquently in the diary. She related to Grace in so many ways, but never in a million years would she have guessed they were related. What other secrets lay in store for her on this treasure hunt?

Ronan blew out a long whistle. "That's amazing."

Would this entice Hope to stay and perhaps research her roots in Wanishin? Did he even want that? To fall for her a little more each day, prolonging the inevitable until she finally left...?

Hope stood immovable, like one of the wax figures in the museum.

Ethel seemed undaunted by the shock radiating from Hope and waved them over to a display with the label Lake Superior Pirates.

Ethel gestured to a few artist-rendered portraits of rough-looking men and a handful of photographs. "My favorite part is that there have always been rumors about Grace's family's connection to a pirate treasure. You've probably heard of the pirate captain 'Cold Hands' Robert Bartholomew. Grace was said to be the last to see him alive. Then his treasure disappeared and so did he. His ship sank offshore of Wanishin."

Grace's innocent, shy smile reminded him so much of Hope's, it was hard to believe the woman would have had anything to do with a pirate. And yet, even though Hope had finally shared her past with him, she had kept so much hidden behind those amber eyes.

With her fingertips resting on her full lower lip, Hope took a step closer to the picture. "Why was she the last to see him alive?"

Ethel's laugh lines crinkled. "It's just a rumor. Handed down for ages. A bit like playing broken telephone as a child, I suppose. The real truth behind it has been watered down for over a hundred years. Some believe it had something to do with her friendship with Edward Barrick, the lighthouse keeper's son."

It was Ronan's turn to do a double take. "Edward Barrick?"

The older woman's face registered the picture of solemn truth. "Sorry, dear, but there was speculation he wasn't a good influence on this young, naive English girl. You know, of course, about his not lighting the beacon that fateful night."

How could anyone let him forget it?

When he dipped his chin, she continued, "Some speculated perhaps Edward and his family were in league with the pirates, raking in a percentage of their pillaging for allowing them to come through the bay and ransack the merchant boats. Something went awry the night the two ships sank, and somehow Grace got caught up in the middle of it."

He'd heard the stories over the years, similar, but mainly they'd involved his ancestor being some kind of lazy and/or incompetent idiot.

"Rumors, of course. Overactive imaginations." Ethel patted his arm as though she'd referred to him and not his long-dead relative. Did this mean he had to redeem the sins of his own life and his forefathers as well?

Hope studied one of Grace's letters in a display case. If only he could know what she was thinking. She caught his eye with an expression he couldn't read. Wonder or distress? "I've been reading her diary all this time. Now I want to read it with new eyes, you know? See if I catch anything that sounds like..."

She turned away.

"That sounds like she's part of your family?" He stepped beside her. Sure enough, the letter in the case had the same feminine handwriting as the diary.

"I had to show you, dear." Ethel laid a hand over Hope's. "The resemblance is remarkable. Do you think you're related?"

Hope traced the wood frame with her fingers. "I'm not sure. Maybe."

A sharp *clip-clip* on the hard linoleum floor preceded an equally sharp voice. "Mrs. Baranski! Mrs. Lewandowski! I've come to return those articles and research books you loaned me."

Poppy bristled into the exhibit with a stack of file folders and books.

Hope's discomfort in Poppy's presence leaked into the way she shifted, curling her fingers into fists.

Ronan cleared his throat. "This was interesting, Mrs. B. We'll let you know if we find out anything else about Grace. But we'd better head out. We have plans this afternoon."

Hope raised a brow. "We do? I mean, yes, we do. We have that—"

"Project at Dusty Jackets," he supplied, but wasn't lying. It might be time to ask her on that date, even if they went as friends.

They excused themselves under the watchful eye of Poppy along with Ethel's cheerful wave.

Now, he needed to figure out how to ask this woman with walls ten feet high and ten feet deep on a date without scaring her off, *and* what to do with his own invested heart when or if she did leave.

Chapter Seventeen

"I'm giving it a chance. I am… I just… I'm struggling."
Hope gripped her cell phone between shoulder and cheek
and pulled the Bible across the bed toward herself, placing it
over the opened diary.

"I can see that. You've never woken me up before to talk
about God." Dee's voice, though groggy at this early hour,
contained strands of delight. "What is it, dear?"

"For some reason, I agreed to go to church yesterday with
the Barricks and Kat and her family. I was struck by what
the pastor said during the service." She'd stayed up all night
thinking about it. It was seven o'clock. She needed to open
the shop in an hour, but this couldn't wait.

It wasn't that the soft-spoken yet passionate Pastor Rick
had said something wrong, but she'd wanted to run from the
church when the words hit her ears. Every nerve in her body
screamed *Leave!* but she was glued to her seat. Afterward, the
pastor's comments took a back seat, but what he'd read from
the Bible played on repeat in her mind. She couldn't shake it.

Dee stayed quiet, waiting.

"I've found my sticking point, and I'm not sure I can get beyond it. This might be as far as I can go with God."

Hope jumped to her feet, pacing to the other side of her room, disturbing Fitzwilliam, who was still trying to snooze at the end of the bed.

"I can come to terms with God taking my mom. I know she's with Him. And I've started to see His light shining through the dark places in my life. I can *almost* come to terms with His allowing me to endure what I did—though I still have my days. But this?"

"Tell me, what did the pastor say?" Dee's voice carried concern.

"God's perfect love casts out all fear." She pinched the bridge of her nose. "But I'm afraid, Dee."

"Of what, dear? Of someone taking you again or—"

"No, nothing like that." Hope paced to the other side of the room. "I'm afraid of caring, of letting go, of admitting I need people—and not just any people, *these* people, here in Wanishin Falls. It might end up hurting me, or worse, them. And if God's love is so perfect, why am I so afraid He'll leave me when I need Him most?"

A moment passed, a deep breath on the other end. "Do you know what the opposite of fear is?"

"Bravery? Peace?" Dare she say her namesake, hope?

"The true counterpart of fear is faith. It takes faith to walk into the future, the unknown, with confidence. Secure in the love of the One who created you and those around you outweighs any hardship, real or imagined, that lies on the path ahead."

"I want to get there. I do." The wall she'd built to protect herself had instead become her prison. But there, in one corner, the bricks had loosened. A ray of sunshine streamed in.

She sat beside the bed, tugging the Bible onto her lap. "I, uh, was looking through the Bible you gave me. I found this verse in Proverbs. 'Strength and honor are her clothing; and she shall rejoice in time to come.' I want that."

"And I believe with my whole heart, that will be you one day, sweet Hope."

Suddenly, the God of the universe, whom she always assumed was too busy or didn't want to bother with her and whom she'd spent years distrusting, felt a breath away. So near. Tears slipped down her cheeks, snaked into her shirt's neckline.

But what would happen when life got rough or her PTSD triggered? Could she hang on to this glimpse of peace? Life had a funny way of snatching her away from her best intentions.

"Thanks, Dee. I'm not sure if I have it all figured out yet, but I know some things are shifting and I think it's in the right direction."

"Good thing we aren't expected to have it all together or there'd have been no hope for me."

Before they hung up, Dee prayed with her and reiterated what she did every time they spoke—to let the people she'd come to care for in Wanishin Falls inside of her inner wall. Hope agreed and this time, maybe she meant it.

A soft knock sounded at the door.

"Hope?" It was Mags. "Is everything okay?" Hope silently asked for strength before she pushed off the floor and moved to the door. Opening it slowly, she stepped back to let Mags in. Worry was written into every crease of the older woman's face.

"What's going on, dear? I couldn't help but hear you talking, but you sounded upset." Mags sat in one of the chairs in front of the darkened fireplace. Hope sank into the other.

Maybe it was the bolstered hope from her conversation with Dee. Maybe it was the hint of freedom flying through her veins or the bold beat of her heart understanding on a new level for the first time her wall could crumble. And the thought didn't terrify her. Whatever it was, she decided to tell Mags and to do it before she changed her mind.

"There's something I need to tell you. About me, about my past." Hope studied her hands in her lap. "You deserve to know the truth, but more than that, I'm certain I can trust you with it."

She ventured a glance at Mags. Her expression remained open and kind. "Of course, you can tell me anything. Nothing will change how much I care about you."

Hope started slowly, telling Mags about her childhood, much the same way she'd told Ronan. She ended with what she was coming to grips with in her spiritual life and the prayer she'd shared with Dee moments before.

"I'm still trying to figure out how to have a life, never mind a normal one, Mags, after all of this. I'm still not sure if I might be too broken to hope for such a thing."

Mags had stayed quiet, asking the occasional question but letting Hope spill everything out. Now Mags stood and pulled Hope into a tight hug.

"I am so sorry, Hope." Her words were a fierce whisper in Hope's ear. "Who needs normal anyway? None of us are normal, so you fit right in."

When they pulled back from the embrace, both had teary smiles.

Mags kept hold of Hope's shoulders. "It's in our broken places God plants seeds of hope. He will grow something beautiful from ashes. Believe it." She touched Hope's cheek. "You have such a fitting name, my dear."

Her name. One truth bomb at a time...

It reminded Hope of something she'd come across in her Bible during the frantic search during the night—God's promise to bestow a crown of beauty instead of ashes, joy instead of mourning and a garment of praise instead of a spirit of despair for those who grieve. Hope supposed she had been in a state of grief all these years. Over the death of her mom as much as the loss of her childhood and innocence. But maybe it was time for something else—hope.

Mags squeezed Hope's hand. "Thank you for sharing this with me. I hope this can be a new start for you with nothing to hide."

The familiar pull to deflect the comment popped up, but instead, she wiped her eyes and said, "Yeah, me too."

Hope couldn't quite put her finger on how or why, but something was definitely off. Everyone she knew had acted so odd this week, especially today. But she tried to focus on helping Lois Lewandowski from the historical society find a suitable book for her great-niece who was a fan of *Anne of Green Gables*. A pang ran through her heart as she rang up the older woman's purchase of *Anne of Avonlea* and *Anne of the Island*. Hope needed to find her copy of *Anne of Green Gables*. It was the last book still missing, and possibly the key to unlocking the treasure her mother promised and her freedom. Then again, her vision of freedom had started to transform over the last few days.

Hope handed the paper bag to Lois with the books inside. "Let me know how your great-niece liked the books."

"Oh, I will. Thank you, dear, for the recommendation." Lois waved goodbye in a flourish, her flamenco-style vivid blue dress trailing behind her out the door.

Hope wandered to the back of the shop and pushed through the swinging door into the kitchen for a cup of tea as well as to check on Ulysses. The animated, muffled voices of Ronan, Kat and Mags cut off upon her entrance.

They sat around the table, eyeing the other in turn, and casting Hope cautious glances.

Kat fidgeted with her cup. She had never seemed so subdued. "So, what are you up to, Hope? Is it almost time to close up shop?" Kat checked her bare wrist for a watch.

Hope squinted at her. "Not yet."

She heated a cup of water in the microwave and stuck an Earl Grey tea bag into it. Not her preferred method, but it was quick.

She dunked the tea bag, watching for that magical swirl of golden brown, and waited for the three to resume their conversation. They didn't. "I was wondering if someone would mind watching the front while I check on Ulysses."

"Of course, I will." Ronan's foot bounced under the table in a very Kat-like way. Hope had never seen him so jumpy. She narrowed her eyes in his direction.

Mags sat with her lips pressed closed and her gaze fixed on some distant point of interest Hope couldn't see.

Hope backed out of the weird-filled kitchen, mug in hand.

Over the years, she'd been forced to become an expert at reading people. The intentions behind their expressions and words. To know what to expect of them, no matter how gruesome, evil or sincere. Something was up, but this time she couldn't tell what. One thing she knew for sure though was that they'd been talking about her.

What could they be discussing? Now that Ronan and Mags—she hadn't gotten up the courage to tell Kat yet—knew about her past, maybe they felt different about her. Sure, their initial reactions had been more supportive than she could have imagined. But now that they'd had time to process who she'd been, did she disgust them? Maybe they simply felt strange around her and didn't know how to act.

She trudged up the stairs, her steps leaden, her stomach in

knots. Without meaning to, she set her mug on a table beside a reading chair in the hall a little too forcefully.

To make up for the commotion she'd made, she crept to Ulysses and Mags's room in a silent tiptoe. Ulysses was sound asleep. His slow decline weighed heavy on Mags and Ronan. She watched their faces when Ulysses couldn't recall their names or even where he was at times. It weighed on her too. What would their family do? She hated the idea of Ulysses needing a memory care facility and yet, what would happen when Ulysses required more care than they could give?

She stepped forward and pulled his blanket higher. His bushy brows relaxed in sleep. What would happen when she left Wanishin Falls?

Grabbing the empty water glass on his bedside table, she turned to go. He mumbled something. She turned back.

His eyes remained closed in sleep. Must be dreaming. But soon his garbled speech cleared. "Dottie, no. Don't go to Chicago. Wanishin is your home."

His eyelids fluttering, his hands grasped at air.

She took a quiet step toward him. "Ulysses?"

But his fitful dreams had pulled him under again. She left him to rest, grabbed her mug in the hall and headed for the stairs.

Her mind remained at Ulysses's bedside as she descended. Ronan's presence at the bottom of the stairs, like he'd been waiting for her, startled her. The way his body shifted, never settling, one arm behind his back, made her suspect he was nervous. Ronan didn't get nervous. Did he? She stopped on the bottom stair.

Ronan stepped forward. "I know you didn't experience most of the big, important firsts in your life. And I'd like to remedy at least one of those."

She tipped her head. "Oh? Which one?"

He brought his arm from behind his back, holding a beautiful bouquet of wildflowers with sprigs of her favorites, lily of the valley, tucked among the daisies and cornflowers. "Hope, will you go on a date with me?"

The shy yet heated expression while he awaited her answer melted around her heart. "Yes, I will."

He handed her the flowers. "Is Saturday okay? Seven o'clock?"

"Perfect." Had she really just said that?

The wide grin never left his face as he backed out of the room. "Okay, see you then." A date might not erase the ugliness in her past, but maybe it could create new, better memories to overshadow the old ones.

Chapter Eighteen

Hope wrestled another dress over her head. She'd never been one to clothe herself in frills, not that she'd had the money most of the time even if she'd wanted to.

"How's that one?" Kat called from the other side of the boutique dressing room door.

"Just a minute. I'll come out and show you."

The one-on-one time with Kat, shopping for a dress for Hope's first-ever date, filled a soul need. Female friendship. The kind she'd only read about between the March sisters and Anne Shirley and her bosom friend, Diana Barry.

The zipper made it the last inch, and Hope stepped out of the changing room in a long black dress. It was one of the few with the sleeves she required to cover her scars.

Kat's nose wrinkled. "Yeesh. Who died? Or are you going for period clothing? Channeling the melancholy Jane Eyre, are we?" That was one point they could not agree on—Charlotte Brontë's heroine's positive attributes.

Hope grabbed her hip. "Why don't you tell me what you *really* think? Don't hold back or anything."

"Oh, trust me. That *was* me holding back." Kat's smile turned wry.

Kat handed her a deep plum dress with lace long sleeves. "Here, try this." The A-line, knee-length dress was at once vintage inspired yet modern.

Hope took it and moved back into the broom-closet-sized dressing room. "I'm not sure. I've never even touched anything this elegant. I'm not exactly the graceful type. Just ask Ronan."

But when she slipped it on, the dress had nothing to do with the date or Ronan—though she was pretty sure he'd like it. The dress fit perfectly and brought out an inner beauty she didn't know she had. Her chin lifted, her shoulders straightened, her cheeks glowed.

She opened the door. Kat's jaw dropped and she clapped her hands together. "Yes! That's the one, and you don't even look like an 1800s schoolmarm."

Hope cocked her head. "Really? Thanks."

"You look gorgeous, and you're going to have a great time." Kat squeezed Hope's lace-covered shoulders.

Hope smoothed the front of the dress. "I don't know why I'm nervous. It's not like he and I haven't been alone before."

"Then no big deal. Just be the sweet person you always are and have fun."

Hope paid and Kat drove her back to Dusty Jackets. "Thank you for your help. And, well, for the whole day."

"You're welcome. It was so fun." Kat's fingers drummed on the steering wheel. "I'm glad you're here. I hope you stay."

"I, well, I'm not sure—"

"I know." Kat picked at the seam of her jeans, then looked up, her eyes brightened. "You need to make that decision on your own. I just wanted to say that it's nice to have a friend."

"But you're the social butterfly. You must have lots of friends."

"You might assume that because I'm an extrovert. But the truth is, most of the people I grew up with moved away. They got married, had families, started careers. I'm just...here." Her lips pressed flat.

"You're doing incredible things every day. The way you take care of your brother and the café is amazing."

Kat's head bobbed, but she didn't meet Hope's eyes.

Hope tightened her arms around the dress bag. "And for the record, I don't have many friends either—" one, to be exact, and she lived in Chicago "—and this *is* really nice."

With misty eyes, Kat shooed her out of the car to go get ready.

Hope waved to Mags, who was with a customer—likely the last one of the day since it was closing time—as she rushed upstairs. At five o'clock, it was still early to prepare for her date, but she couldn't possibly sit still. So, she breezed through hair and makeup, keeping it simple, and slid into her dress.

When she stepped back into the sitting-room-turned-shop area, there was the clinking of dishes from the kitchen and floorboards creaked in the castle room.

"Ulysses?"

She rounded the corner and found Richard Allen standing there. His face split into an oily grin.

She jumped back. "What are *you* doing here?"

"This is a bookstore, a public place of business, isn't it?" He ran his finger across a shelf ledge, his face pinched, and he rubbed the dust onto his pant leg. "And I confess, I heard a beautiful newcomer to town worked here. I thought I'd visit. See how you're enjoying *your Jane Eyre*."

How naive to think in a small town like this he wouldn't figure out where she was.

He stepped forward, eyes gleaming.

She stood her ground. He wasn't going to intimidate her today. "The store's closed. You need to leave."

"Oh? Where's the old man? Maybe he wants to make another deal with me."

Her hands shook. She curled them into fists. "Please leave or I'll call the police." The words rasped through her constricted throat.

His gaze sharpened. "You've already done that. They've been snooping around my shop. Not that they'll find anything."

She reached for the opening of her purse and the cell phone hiding inside.

"No need, I'll see myself out." He moved around her toward the door.

Hope had to have a talk with Mags. The Barricks kept forgetting to lock the door at closing time.

Turning, Richard pressed a hand to his glossy hair. "By the way, do your friends and the good people of this town know that Hope's not your real name? Looks like I'm not the only one with secrets."

Then he was gone.

She dashed to lock the door behind him.

Hope drew one more cleansing breath to rid herself of the encounter with Richard. She couldn't spoil what Ronan had planned by lingering on the almost tangible odor of Mr. Allen. He'd left without incident. He hadn't managed to do more than startle her. And it was obvious their motley trio of not-so-super-heroes had succeeded in shutting down at least some of his fraudulent activity.

But it would take strength she didn't have to ignore his "your real name" comment. How would he know that? Even though she'd shared her past with Mags and Ronan, that didn't mean she wanted the whole world to find out or have Richard spread the news via the internet or something.

She straightened her posture and turned to Ronan, pushing away the anxiety. They stood together inside the elevator at the youth shelter building. Ronan had picked her up at seven o'clock sharp and said their destination was a surprise. "It's so sweet that your grandpa and grandma are going on a date of their own tonight. Mags said she was inspired to enjoy a night out."

Ronan pressed the button for the top floor. The divot between his brows said he wasn't so sure. "Yeah, I wish they'd done this on a different night when I could be with them. Just in case. You know?"

Ulysses had had a good day. Not fully present, but not agitated either. Mags's joy had been infectious as she'd readied herself for a date too.

"But they're going to Kat's Café, right? And then a little stroll. I'm sure they'll be fine." She reached out in comfort, a gesture she was still attempting to perfect.

"With this Richard hanging around, I—"

"Don't worry." She was just as shocked as anyone that the sight of him hadn't triggered a panic attack. She'd been uncomfortable and mostly angry when Richard spoke about Ulysses that way, but not terrified. "He only wanted to intimidate me. It was kind of pathetic. If he'd intended to hurt me or your grandparents or steal anything, he could've. But he didn't."

"It doesn't mean he won't come back."

What was with his pessimistic attitude? Was his dad in his head again?

"I made sure to lock my books in my room, and we set the security alarm before we left. It's going to be fine."

He seemed to snap out of his worried mood. The veins in his neck slackened, and his mouth pulled into a wide, warm grin as the elevator dinged and opened to the hallway outside the now-quiet museum. "You're right. Come on."

"Where are we going? You still haven't told me what we're doing here."

She and Ronan held take-out bags from a Thai place at the edge of town since he hadn't wanted her to have to cook for their date and he said his cooking for them would end in fire and illness.

"You'll see. Up here."

She followed him through a heavy metal door into a stairwell. "I'm not having dinner in a creepy old attic surrounded by spiders and dusty binding equipment, am I? You might think I love old stuff because of the books I like, but I don't like it *that* much."

His laugh bounced off the bare walls. He kept climbing, leaving her no choice but to follow.

One more flight of stairs. "But I thought this building only had two floors and—"

He opened the door at the top of the stairs and a burst of warm summer air washed over her.

They stood on the roof.

"This is beautiful." She breathed the words, taking in the table for two he'd set up.

A tablecloth, a vase of flowers, flameless candles, his grandpa's record player nearby and even white twinkle lights along the railing. The vast lake and cloud-dotted sky served as their backdrop. If they stayed long enough, this would be a spectacular place to watch the sunset.

He pointed to the twinkle lights. "When I kept bringing this stuff up here, Ethel figured out what was going on. She volunteered her extra stash of white Christmas lights. She's got plenty of them."

He took the food bags from her hands and started dishing up the plates.

They both kept dinner conversation light. With the tingle of heat still on her tongue from the coconut-curry chicken and her stomach full but not stuffed, she moved to the record player.

"Sorry, I forgot to turn it on." Ronan leaned back in his chair.

"That's okay. I thought a little after-dinner music might be nice." She found the album she was looking for.

The first notes of Etta James's "At Last" bloomed from the antique record player. Suddenly nervous again, she held tight to the sides of her dress as she neared the table. "Do you want to dance?" Her words bolder than she felt.

His eyebrows lifted. "As long as you don't mind I'm no Fred Astaire."

"Well, I do have trouble keeping myself from drowning on a regular basis, so…"

She stepped into his open arms. His laugh tickling against her ear.

"Perfect match, then."

Such a light statement, yet it sucked the breath from her lungs. But she didn't push him away. Could he hear her heart thudding between them?

Lord, help me. I don't want to lead him on. I'm not sure if I want to leave anymore. But I don't know if I can stay either.

Ronan rubbed a small circle onto her back with his thumb. She draped her arms around his neck and ventured further, to rest her cheek to his chest. The two of them stayed like that, barely swaying to the romantic melody.

She moved her head from his chest to look into his eyes. His work-roughened hand brushed along her jawline.

"I hope this was an okay first date." His shoulders rumbled under her arms as he spoke.

"Yes. It was amazing. I still can't believe you would do this for me. You're making it hard to consider leaving."

"Good. I'm hoping to make it impossible."

His arms tightened. She had to bite her cheek to keep from squeaking. He must've noticed and loosened his grip.

"Hope, I'm sorry. I know I'm supposed to pretend that being your friend is enough. But I'm not that good of an actor."

His Adam's apple bobbed. "For your sake, I think you need to know my feelings haven't changed since I talked to you in the cave. If anything, they've only grown stronger. I can't help it."

Dipping his head, he hesitated an inch away, the warmth of his breath on her lips. He left her room to pull back. When she didn't, he touched her lips—so gentle—with his. How could such a featherlight touch make every nerve ending in her body zing to life? Just one kiss, then he withdrew to arm's length, searching her face, maybe for her reaction.

A fire blazed in his eyes. He'd never held an expression so intense, so piercing. It thrilled and scared her all at once. He seemed to take in every detail of her face as if memorizing it.

With slow movements, he traced along the scar on her jaw, curved around her chin, brushed against her cheekbones. For the first time since her mom's cuddles and embraces as a child, she savored another person's touch. It held joy instead of pain.

"I… I need to tell you, how I—"

Their words tumbled over each other. "Ronan, I'd like to tell you something—"

Both of their cell phones rang. They exchanged glances.

Both phones at once when everyone they cared about knew they were on their date.

Ronan answered first. "Grandma, slow down...What?... No, we haven't. Where did you see him last?...Hang on. We'll be right there."

His face had paled in the darkening light. "It's Gramps. Grandma Mags can't find him. He must've wandered off. She came back from the bathroom at the restaurant, and he was gone."

In silent agreement, they sprinted for the door.

Hope yanked on the handle. Didn't budge. "It's locked."

"Oh, man!" He smacked his forehead. "I forgot this door automatically locks itself. I had to prop it open when I brought everything up."

"Do you have the key?"

"No, we need to get one made." Panic edged his tone. "We don't have time for this. Who knows where Gramps is. Grandma said he took the car."

Her ears buzzed. Suddenly she recalled a detailed female spy book she'd read. She tugged two bobby pins from her hair, bending the end of one and keeping the other straight.

His feet shuffled behind her as she knelt in front of the lock.

"That only works in the movies, doesn't it?"

"And books." She slipped the bent one into the bottom and slid the straight clip above the other.

"Maybe I should call someone to come let us out."

She waited for the click and turned the bobby pins together clockwise. "No need." Grabbing the handle before it automatically locked again, she threw open the door and gestured for Ronan to go ahead.

Mixed with the fear on his face was amazement. "Save some of that superpower for Gramps."

She clutched her heels into one hand so she could move

faster. They bolted down the steps. She silently prayed. At the bottom, she grasped his hand. "We'll find him."

Ronan's truck squealed into the café parking lot. He and Hope hopped out as if born sprinters. Grandma Mags stood on the sidewalk outside the café, wringing her hands. "I needed a restroom break and told him to stay put. I'd be right back."

Immediate panic and a two-headed blame-monster roared to life inside of his chest. "You should've waited for your date night. I could've gone with you. I should've been there."

He hated how wounded Grandma Mags looked. But he transitioned into survival-logic mode. "Okay, let's spread out. Let's check the back parking lot, the alley and the immediate side streets."

When they jogged around the side of the café, they found Kat with other patrons, searching. A large group joined them, including Abe and Sophia, but each returned without Ulysses.

"Maybe he went home," Hope called to him. It broke him out of his panic-stricken trance.

Ronan waved Grandma Mags over to the truck. Hope jumped in and he broke every driving law racing to Dusty Jackets. "Please be there. Please be there." He chanted the words to himself.

Hope, beside him, gripped the armrest. Grandma Mags sat silent in the small back seat.

He hoped his grandpa would go somewhere familiar and choose to head for home. But what, if anything, registered in his mind as familiar these days?

When they arrived at Dusty Jackets, there was no car, but the front door was open. They jumped out and raced up the front steps. This made no sense. Where was the car?

"Ulysses! Are you here?" Hope called.

No answer.

It took a moment to see that something was seriously wrong—above and beyond Ronan's grandpa gone missing. Shattered glass crunched beneath their feet from a gaping hole in the front door's window. Books were strewed across the floor. Hope caught Ronan's eye and she ran for the stairs.

Grandma Mags flicked the light switch, but nothing happened. He and his grandma systematically checked each room for his grandpa, but a sick feeling rose in his stomach. Someone had broken in.

A shout from upstairs confirmed it.

"Ulysses isn't up here. But they're gone! My books are all gone!" Hope's voice broke on an anguished note.

Ronan ran to meet her in the hall outside her room. The door hung at an odd angle. The wood around the door handle and locking mechanism had been damaged, probably by a crowbar.

He offered the only comfort he could. He held her. "It's okay. We're going to find him and your books. It'll be okay. We need to move quickly though. Let's check outside." He shouted down, "Where's a flashlight?"

"In the little table by that chair in the hall," Grandma Mags called back.

Hope rummaged around in the drawer, pulling out the contents and dropping them on top of the table until she found the flashlight. She clicked it on, then froze.

"What is it? We gotta get moving." Frustration leaked into his tone.

"It's my last book." She picked it up from where the flashlight illuminated it in the table drawer and opened the cover. "He saved it for me."

"'He' who?"

Tears glistened on her cheeks in the dim light. She held the book toward him.

In his grandpa's messy writing, it read, "For Hope."

They stowed the book in her bag and brought it along, not taking any chances. Grandma Mags met them outside. Calling his grandpa's name and shining the light in every dark nook and cranny of the backyard produced nothing.

Obviously, someone wanted those books. He hoped his grandpa hadn't walked in on the robbery. But no car stood in front or the driveway. He probably hadn't come here. Did the thief want the books for the face value though? The bookstore was full of other titles of equal or higher value. He shuddered at the idea that someone might have intended solely to hurt or scare Hope. Or...

No. Ridiculous. Could the thief have been looking for clues to the still-to-be-determined treasure? A certain greasy-haired "antiques" dealer's face came to mind.

But the greater concern now was for his grandfather. "Come on, I have an idea." He waved them over to the truck.

They scrambled inside. He did a U-turn and squealed back down the road toward the lighthouse.

"If Gramps is in the mindset of his younger self like he usually is these days, he might have gone to the lighthouse."

Grandma Mags, in the back, patted his shoulder. "That's a good idea. He has been talking a lot about working the lighthouse lately."

"He wouldn't try to light it, would he?" Hope's voice shook.

Ronan squeezed the steering wheel. "I don't think he could manage all those steps."

Had he remembered to lock his front door that morning? Of course, he always did. That might have been enough deterrent.

What if his grandpa wasn't going for the lighthouse? What if he wandered into the water instead? Ronan didn't dare answer those internal questions.

He skidded into his driveway and they piled out. Sure

enough, his grandparents' car was "parked" in the fence. *In* the fence. A loud, persistent ding came from the open driver's side door. The engine was still running.

The fence usually held Charlotte. As if on cue, Charlotte's bark erupted from the beach below. The rocky pathway to get there was sometimes tricky during the day. It wasn't something he'd let his grandpa walk on, and certainly not at night or alone.

He took the flashlight from Hope and the women followed him down the winding trail hugging the side of the cliff. "Just a little farther."

Charlotte's bark became more insistent, anxious.

Finally, they raced onto the pebbled beach strewed with boulders and driftwood. He shone the light in the direction of the barking. There, dipping under a wave, was the bald top of his grandpa's head.

"Gramps!" He'd never moved so fast over shifting ground— prosthetic leg or not.

He ran into the waves, jumped over a tall one and dived over another's crest, kicking and paddling harder than in any swim meet competition.

Charlotte, smart girl, swam next to him, leading him. The current and crashing waves proved too much for his prosthetic leg. He could feel it loosen with every kick and reached for it just as it fell away from his knee. His shout of frustration was choked by a mouthful of water.

Progress forward was arduous work and a third of the speed with only half a leg on one side. Charlotte barked again. Ahead, his grandpa's head bobbed beneath a wave.

Panic set in. This couldn't be happening. Again.

He dived where his grandpa had slipped under the water, finally feeling sodden cloth, then his grandpa's back.

Ronan scooped an arm around his grandpa's torso and broke the surface.

His grandpa was a limp weight, tugged and tossed by the waves as Ronan made his treacherous way back to shore with only one arm and one leg propelling him. Hope and Grandma Mags helped drag his grandpa's unmoving form up the shore, away from the water's edge. He could do little more than crawl across the beach without his leg. He couldn't think of what he looked like to Hope now.

Ronan started CPR while Hope called 911.

Between chest compressions, he shouted his address into the phone when Hope had explained the situation to the emergency dispatcher. No, this couldn't be happening. He couldn't lose someone else when he should've known better.

"Come on, Gramps. Come on. Fight." He pumped another two chest compressions. "Don't do this." His voice broke.

As Ronan pumped his grandpa's chest, the old bones creaked with the pressure. Ronan kept going, wondering if his own heart would explode from exhaustion. But there was no way he'd stop. Hope and his grandma called their encouragement, telling him not to give up. Even though he could do this for his grandpa, helplessness pulled at him. He had no power over life or death. He'd learned that long ago.

Echoing the women's words, he cried out to the God who did. "Lord, please. Save him."

Ronan's lungs burned, the air wheezed in and out in laborious gasps as the wail of a siren pulled into his driveway above.

The paramedics hustled as fast as they could on the narrow path, carrying the backboard.

They sank down beside Ronan, still pushing on his grandpa's chest.

"You did great. Let us take over. Catch your breath, son."

Without missing a beat, one of the paramedics slipped into Ronan's place.

The other paramedic prepped the straps and neck immobilizer. "We're going to transfer him to the board. We need to get him on a solid surface. Can you help us?" His commanding voice brought Ronan a measure of tentative calm. He could see the same in Hope's and his grandmother's eyes.

Ronan held Grandpa's lower extremities as the male paramedic slid the board underneath him. The female paramedic stopped her compressions only long enough to stabilize Ulysses's neck as they secured him to the board. Then the male paramedic held a bag valve mask over grandpa's nose and mouth to squeeze air into his lungs.

His grandpa was so pale. Deathly white. Hope grabbed Ronan's hand. He had an impulse to throw it off. This was all his fault. He wanted to run down the beach. To unsee this surreal scene unfolding before him. But he couldn't run. He was half a man. His fake leg floated somewhere on Lake Superior or lay on the lake bed under who knew how much water.

Worthless. Helpless. When it really counted, when those who trusted him most needed him, he failed them. His dad was right. Maybe he did carry the Barrick Curse.

The male paramedic had taken over for the female, who huffed and puffed next to Ronan. A rasp and then his grandpa gagged. Both paramedics shouted, "Yes!"

The diligent medical team turned him on his side so he wouldn't aspirate. Water and the contents of his stomach spewed from his mouth onto the beach. His grandpa coughed and retched but eventually looked at Ronan, Hope and Grandma Mags in succession. With recognition.

"Are you okay?" Ronan knelt beside him.

One paramedic took his blood pressure while the other listened to his heart and lungs.

"I just wanted to show you something." Each word like stones grinding together.

His grandpa started to shake. The medical duo wrapped him in a shock blanket.

Grandma Mags bent over and laid her hand on her husband's shoulder. "Don't do that again. You scared me to death. What did you need to show us?"

Unfocused, he blinked. "I've already told you. I've told you all. I was trying to show you. No one will believe me." His arms and legs twitched and flailed.

Hope grabbed his grandpa's hand and he settled. "It's okay, Ulysses. We believe you." Her tone sincere.

Ronan choked back tears.

The paramedics asked them to step back. "We need to get him to a hospital now." They turned toward Ronan, where he was still stuck sitting on the sand, eyeing the stump where a leg should be. "You're okay, right?"

Assured that he was lopsided but okay, the professionals maneuvered the backboard up the steep incline toward the ambulance.

Something nudged his knee. Charlie still thought his prosthetic leg was the best fetch toy. She gripped it between her teeth, a doggy grin stretched wide. He patted her head in thank you. Ronan fastened it back on and tried to dismiss all of the ways this was his fault.

Chapter Nineteen

Roller-coaster. Hope had never been on one, but she didn't need to. The night had been a living roller-coaster of every human emotion she was capable of. So much packed into twelve hours.

A look around the hospital room told her the others felt the exhaustion too. Ronan stood in the corner with arms crossed over his chest, his face creased. Mags slumped in the chair on the other side of Ulysses's hospital bed.

Ulysses, warm and stable now, rested. Every so often, he mumbled the numbers he had the night of the first Dusty Jackets break-in.

The doctor said Ulysses was fortunate the three had gotten there when they did. They even noted Ronan's CPR efforts as the deciding factor for Ulysses's survival. But Ronan didn't seem to hear it. "Those paramedics saved him, not me."

While they all recognized the tireless efforts of the paramedics, if Ronan hadn't reached Ulysses and saved him from the water or started CPR, they would've had a much different ending.

But Ronan had also alluded to God as the hero of the day, not him. Fair enough.

After tests and scans, it appeared Ulysses wouldn't have lasting adverse effects. But his body was already worn-out from dementia's battle in his brain. The doctor wanted him to stay overnight for observation to monitor him for signs of pneumonia, lung infection or heart strain. So far, so good. They'd called Kat and her family as well as Ronan's dad.

She stood, gesturing to the chair. "Ronan, why don't you sit for a while? You must be beat."

He'd done nothing but pace and prop himself in the corner. He looked ready to collapse.

His mouth opened to answer, but another voice cut over it. "Yes, sit down. That's what you do best when you're needed, isn't it?" Brock strode in, steely purpose and bite.

Mags roused from her bedside doze. Ronan pushed off the wall and straightened.

"Dad, it's hardly the time. Gramps is trying to rest."

"Then when is the time? When we're standing over his grave?"

Protective anger rose in her again, like the last time she'd seen his dad. This time she couldn't keep her mouth shut. Stepping closer to Brock, trying not to let his height threaten her—somehow more intimidating than Ronan's—she pointed at Ronan.

"It's because of this man you're *not* at a funeral right now. He saved Ulysses's life."

Brock didn't back off though. Instead, he took another step toward her. Ronan reached for her hand.

The muscles in Brock's jaw flexed. "Or is it because of Ronan that we're here in the first place?"

Mags stood now. "It was my fault if you're determined to blame someone. I shouldn't have left him at the table." Her guilt-laden glance landed on Ronan.

Ronan hugged her. "No, Grandma. It wasn't your fault. I should've never insinuated it was."

Drying her eyes, Mags stepped back. "You know, Brock, you've been a bully, a mostly absent one, but a bully nonetheless, for a long time. You don't want to be around us until something goes wrong. If you care so much about your father, then be here for him. Be careful so you don't wake up one day and realize you missed your chance."

Brock's stony facade cracked, revealing what Hope recognized as hollow grief. "I have to go."

Ronan followed him to the hall. Their voices hushed but still audible.

"Dad, wait. You can't keep doing this. Showing up to point your finger at me. What did I do to deserve this?"

Ronan continued, "There was nothing I could do about Mom passing away. And you can't bring in the ship accident either. That's mine to live with. Mine. Not yours to throw in my face every chance you get. The town has had a hard time forgetting as it is. So, what is it, huh? What did I do to you?"

There was a long pause that made Hope wonder if Brock had walked away.

"You left me to deal with the aftermath alone." Brock's voice was soft but gravelly with emotion.

"What do you mean? Aftermath of what?"

"Of everything. Your mother's heart attack, her passing away, and yes, even the impact the ship accident had on not just you but how people treated me, for being your father. You didn't help with your mother's funeral. You hid away. You went to your grandparents for support instead of me."

"I'm sorry. I am." A deep exhale. "I wasn't hiding. I was

grieving. For Mom, for Kyle, for a life and career I had planned. Can you understand that? It had nothing to do with you."

"Exactly. You didn't think about me at all." Brock cleared his throat. "Maybe that isn't fair, but there it is."

"No, it isn't fair."

Hope could hear anger rising in Ronan's voice.

"It looks an awful lot like you taking out your anger and grief on me for things I couldn't do anything about or change."

Footsteps faded until they disappeared.

Ronan walked back in, devastation dragging on his shoulders.

Hope ran into his arms, holding him tight around the middle, wanting so much to be a source of her name for him— hope.

Mags sat in the chair again, taking Ulysses's hand. The man was blissfully unaware of what transpired.

Not letting go, Ronan laid his cheek on top of her head. "I've let a lot of people down in my life." His words were muffled against her hair. "I won't do that to you, Hope. I'll always be there for you. I promise."

"I know." She desperately wanted— tried—to believe his words. King's invasive speeches played over and over in her mind until it wasn't so much that she didn't believe Ronan would be there for her, but would she always be there for him? Or would she keep running like she usually did? The shame gripped her stomach so tight, she could hardly stay upright.

He deserved someone who could answer without fear, with a resounding, *Yes, I will always be here for you too.*

Monday dawned bright.

She and Ronan stayed all day Sunday in Ulysses's hospital room, but Mags had insisted they find something better than a chair to sleep in last night.

Hope yawned and stretched on her makeshift couch-bed in Kat's one-bedroom apartment. Ronan had informed the police about the break-in at Dusty Jackets from Ulysses's hospital room. The police met them at Dusty Jackets to take their statements. Hope also shared that Richard Allen had been in the shop earlier that day. The officers would check into his whereabouts around the time of the robbery. And an officer in a patrol car sat outside Dusty Jackets monitoring to see if anyone came back. But Hope couldn't stay there and didn't want to.

After Ronan and Hope had told their stories, the officer accompanied Hope to her room so she could pack a bag. He noted every item she collected for the overnight. Her shoulders sagged in relief to find Grace's diary among other books Richard or whoever the thief was hadn't taken. Interesting. The perp had known which books to target. And the person didn't take anything else in the shop, though they'd made a mess of everything. It made her wonder if the thief had insider information that the books might, in theory, lead to a treasure.

Kat's apartment was empty. She'd already left for the café. On her way out, Kat had called over her shoulder, "Take your time getting ready, and you're welcome to anything you find in the kitchen. Like ketchup, salt and possibly expired canned goods."

Even though the small living room contained Kat's eclectic homey touches, it had the air of disuse. With Kat's parents gone often, Kat slept at her parents' to take care of Matthew.

Hope stood and leaned back to massage the muscles in her lower back. Grabbing her toiletries from her bag and a change of clothes, she rushed to the bathroom. She would be ready in case Ronan called and wanted to go back to the hospital. Fifteen minutes later, she emerged with fresh breath, new clothes on and hair brushed.

As if on cue, her cell rang. "Hey, how'd you sleep?" Ronan's voice rumbled as though he'd just woke up.

"Better than in a hospital chair, that's for sure. You?"

"Okay."

That probably meant not at all.

"I'd like to go back to the hospital to check on Gramps and Grandma. You're welcome to come with me. If not, I can drop you off somewhere. Either way, I'll pick you up. Is that okay?"

With Dusty Jackets closed for obvious reasons, she didn't have any responsibilities. "No, there's nowhere I'd rather be. I want to see how they're doing too."

The panic from watching Ulysses lifeless on the beach while Ronan and the paramedics performed CPR kept flashing through her mind. Since her mom's death, this was the closest she'd been to losing someone she cared about.

"All right. Let's get going, then. Visiting hours start at eight. We'll pick up a breakfast to go from the café on the way."

"Good, otherwise, it might be a choice between a dead ficus tree or whatever condiments Kat has in her fridge. We can get something for Mags too then."

She slipped her bag onto her shoulder as well as the backpack with her two remaining precious volumes—the diary and *Anne of Green Gables*. Maybe she could read to Ulysses if he woke up. The loss of her other books started to sink in. It was a devastating setback after they'd worked so hard to find them. And yet, it was nothing compared to almost losing Ulysses. More light-of-day perspective.

They made their stop for egg-and-bacon biscuits and cubed potatoes at Kat's Café. She ordered two teas to go for her and Mags, and Ronan made his a black coffee. Kat hugged her extra tight and told her to give one to Mags for her.

"Tell her I'll stop by later after my cousin comes in. Okay?"

They said their goodbyes and made the quick trip to the small hospital.

Ulysses was awake when they arrived. Mags was folding up the pullout bed the hospital provided. She took the tea from Hope with a grateful smile.

Hope put an arm around her small shoulders. Sometimes Hope forgot how small a woman Mags was because she had such strength inside.

Ronan laid out Mags's food on a tray-sized table. Even though Mags had to be starving, she picked at it.

Ulysses, glancing around at his surroundings with interest, nibbled at the hospital breakfast—Western-style eggs?—on his wheeled tray table.

Ronan answered his cell phone and took it in the hallway.

"How are you feeling, Ulysses?" Hope sat at his side and patted his arm. He seemed a little dazed and didn't answer.

Mags answered instead. "The doctor said his temperature, blood pressure, everything looks fine. Just a little fluid left in the lungs they're going to keep an eye on. But it looks like he'll stay one more day to be on the safe side. If everything still looks good, we can go home tomorrow morning."

Ronan returned, roughing his palm against his jaw. "Well, that was the officer checking into Richard. I guess he's got an alibi and a witness for the time of the break-in. Apparently, he was at another antiques dealer about an hour from here doing some kind of trade. The other business owner already verified his story."

A groan of frustration issued from Hope's throat. "So, either he had this other person lie for him or he really was at this other antiques store but had someone else break in for him or..."

Mags tapped the arm of her chair. "Or he really didn't do

it. But who else would know about the books and where to find them?"

After a moment of silence and no new answers, Hope pulled out her last book, now her only book, *Anne of Green Gables*. She started reading to Ulysses while he ate. He seemed to like it. The more she read, the more he ate until his plate was clean. A relief after his diminished appetite recently.

The story had always put an ache in her heart. A lonely orphan girl without a real home, used and abused by others, finds a family. Not a blood family, but a family of the heart. When she'd read it as a young foster care kid, it made her angry. It was a fairy tale. Not real.

She read the line:

Kindred spirits are not so scarce as I used to think. It's splendid to find out there are so many of them in the world.

Now, as she glanced over the book's edge, watching the people she'd come to care for and who, she believed, genuinely cared for her, maybe it wasn't such a fairy tale after all.

"Have you checked for a painting yet?" Ronan scooted one of the chairs next to hers.

"No. Not with everything that happened. I forgot to look."

Mags wiped her mouth and stood over Hope's shoulder. "Do you mind if I watch? I could use something lovely about now."

"Of course." Hope flipped open the front cover. Inside, her mom had written her name in her swooping, feminine writing before Ulysses had added Hope's name. This one had belonged to her mom.

She took the pages as a whole and moved the outer edge until they slanted down. She whispered, "Yes," when a picture formed. It confirmed the hunt they were already on. With her other books gone now, she could almost talk herself out of the insanity of this pursuit.

She held it for all of them to see. A familiar sight this time. The lighthouse.

Ulysses stuck one finger into the air. "I told you. No one believed me. It's real."

Hope and Ronan exchanged a glance. She'd had a feeling she knew what Ulysses tried to tell them last night, but this time for sure.

Ulysses's near-bald head dipped, a pleased expression spreading across his face. "The pirates have it. But I bought the whole thing."

Chapter Twenty

Mags had shooed Hope and Ronan from the room, telling them to go find this treasure once and for all. None of them could tell if Ulysses truly knew the treasure existed, but too many things kept pushing them along this journey. They had to see where it ended.

"Are you sure? I don't know if we should leave you, with Gramps like this." Ronan stood but hesitated by the door.

"Go. I'm sure. I'll call your cell if anything changes." Mags cast a soft smile Ulysses's way. "I've heard about the lost family treasure for as long as we've been married. Who knows? Maybe it is real. Maybe it was waiting for you two to find it. Together. I can't think of two people who'd use it any more wisely."

Ulysses's words came back to her about their ancestors, who she now knew must be Grace and Edward, keeping it a secret until two people, from each family, could work together to solve the mystery.

Ronan drove them to his lighthouse home in record time. They ignored the standoff situation in the kitchen—Charlotte barking at a fully fluffed out and growling Fitzwilliam, who'd stayed at Ronan's—and ran up the steps. She and Ronan agreed that if anything had been hidden at the lighthouse, the top would be the likeliest place. When they reached the top, where the decommissioned light was housed, they searched for a sign, words, a board out of place, anything Ronan may not have noticed.

He rubbed his forehead. "I redid this whole place but never saw writing like on the arch and in the cave."

Hope did a three-hundred-and-sixty-degree turn. Her eyes landed on the darkened light fixture. The prisms that would've carried light out to the water, into the night. The light that cut through the darkness to warn passing sailors, fishermen and merchants of the dangerous pass between the shore and the island near Arrowhead Bay. Now dark.

The island. The light.

The book alongside a flashlight.

"I'll be right back." She called the words over her shoulder.

She rummaged through the backpack, now sitting by the couch, and found it. The flashlight from the night before. She snatched it up, along with her copy of *Anne of Green Gables*.

Ulysses had meant for her to find them together. The truth of that gripped around her chest and wouldn't let go.

She was out of breath by the time she ran up the stairs again and leaped onto the landing at the top.

Ronan rushed over. "What is it? Did you find something?"

The loud, persistent drumbeat of her heart almost drowned out his words. "What was the only thing you didn't change about this place?"

His brows drew together, then lifted. "The light."

"What if, before Ulysses lost his memory, he left you something there? The one thing he knew you'd never change, history preserver that you are."

They shared a grin and stepped over to inspect the light.

"Since he knew I couldn't turn it on anymore, maybe he made a way to see the clue with another source of light."

Hope nodded, handing him the flashlight.

Ronan shone the light on each prism behind the huge light bulb that originally would've lit up and the mirrors behind it to magnify the intensity. Ronan had explained it had once been a gas-burning light, in Grace and Edward's day. But the light was converted to save money and energy later on.

Which led her to suspect something else. If Grace and Edward had hidden the treasure, had it been someone else, namely Ulysses and possibly her grandma, who'd set up the treasure hunt? The timing, the books, all of it. It made sense that it might have been their generation.

A strange shadow appeared when Ronan held the flashlight to one side of the lantern panes. She and Ronan leaned in to inspect. Someone—likely Ulysses—had painted or maybe used a permanent marker on one side of the bulb. Anyone looking at it casually would see an antique light with dirt or damage.

Ronan lit the flashlight again. Something reflected off the mirror behind it. He gestured to the book. "Hold it open to one of the blank pages. I want to see if it creates a picture when I do this."

She held it open. At first, the image appeared as a blurry blob on the yellowed page. Moving it closer made the edges sharper.

"Is that...the island?" they said together.

To test her theory, Hope revealed the fore-edge painting again on the book's edge. "Yup, that's what the picture was missing. I thought it looked odd." There was no island in the painting beyond the lighthouse.

When the shadow island hit the painting, it looked like an island in the background, behind the lighthouse, with a unique open-maw rock formation in front. Not detailed, but enough that they could tell what it was supposed to be.

Tiny numbers were written backward on the bulb but reflected the right way into the mirror. Of course, they appeared backward again on the page, but that was okay. She read them aloud to Ronan, recognizing them as the numbers Ulysses had recited over and over. Ronan handed her the flashlight and grabbed his phone from his pocket.

Squinting, he muttered to himself, "Those numbers... I wonder... They sound like coordinates."

He typed the numbers into his phone's GPS.

He held it out to show her an aerial map and a tiny dot labeled Lost Lover's Island.

They didn't need to speak to know what to do next.

Ronan bounded down the stairs. "The best and shortest route to the island is from the shore at Dusty Jackets."

He stopped at the bottom so abruptly, she almost ran into him. Turning on his phone's home screen, he gritted his teeth and thrust his phone deep into his pocket. "I'll have to drop you off. You can check in on the shop with the officer and get ready to go."

Why did it seem like he was going to leave her?

"What are you going to do?" She slipped her book and the flashlight into her bag with Grace's diary inside.

"I completely forgot with everything that's going on that today's the day I need to take Tate's community service papers to the city council building. It needs to be dated and notarized before I send it in before 10:00 a.m. today."

Ronan seemed distracted on the way to Dusty Jackets, almost agitated, but his frustration couldn't be with her, could it? Maybe it irritated him that they'd found a clue but was forced to drop everything to take care of paperwork. She told herself not to take it to heart as they pulled up to the shop.

Police Officer Gerard was outside in his squad car, the officer who had taken their statements and checked into Richard's alibi. He rolled down his window, as did Ronan. "Haven't seen anyone. I'll be leaving soon, but I'll check back later."

Ronan put his truck into Park.

A desperate feeling overtook her. As though if he drove away now she'd never see him again. Absurd, of course. But she couldn't help but sense a "now or never" situation before her. "Ronan, I know this could be better timing, but can I talk to you about something?" She'd been about to tell him something on their date, but she'd never finished...

"What is it?" His leg bounced.

"Before we go find this treasure...or not..."

Ronan glanced at his watch. "Hope, I'm so sorry. But I have to get to the city council, for Tate's sake."

"Can I come with you?"

"I'll be back before you know it. Okay? Gotta go."

"All right. Sure." She got out and trudged up the steps. She asked God to help her keep her heart open and willing to trust as Ronan drove away. Something was off and it began to crumble the sense of safety she'd built here.

Building trust on a wounded surface was a little like the man who built his house on the sand instead of on rock. If the house was built on a shaky, unstable surface, it didn't matter how careful the person was or how sure they were it was all going to be okay. The house would collapse. No question. The kind of faith that canceled out fear she'd talked about with Dee seemed far away, unreachable at that moment.

Ronan had been gone for over two hours. Old insecurities nagged at the back of her mind. Okay, the front of her mind. She didn't begrudge his doing his job and taking care of Tate's paperwork. But she knew the city had given him the day off because of Ulysses. And simply filing that paperwork shouldn't take this long, should it?

Maybe he'd had second thoughts about her, maybe even guessed at what she'd almost said the other night on their date—that she wanted to stay in Wanishin Falls. Maybe, despite all of his words to the contrary, the idea suddenly scared him and he decided not to come back to Dusty Jackets at all.

Even a treasure wasn't inducement enough to stick out one more minute with a battle-scarred, slightly neurotic, socially awkward, complicated woman like her. Who would stick around for that? For her? What if she was wrong again? What if she thought she'd found someone who genuinely cared about her, but he'd really been a jerk all along? She pushed every sweet, selfless, patient thing Ronan had done out of her mind. Too much to consider right now. Anxiety took over, her body and mind on autopilot. She was in the back seat, along for the fear-filled ride.

She paced in the front yard.

After a few more pacing laps, the wind picked up. If Ronan didn't want to accompany her on the search, then she would go by herself. How hard could it be? At least now she knew the right way to handle a kayak—or rather, how *not* to handle a kayak. Ulysses and Mags kept a kayak they didn't use under the porch in the back. Mags once told her Ulysses had been an excellent kayaker in his day.

She strapped on a life vest and dragged the boat and a paddle to the water's edge. Grabbing the waterproof backpack Ronan had given her and securing it to her back with her books and flashlight inside, she nudged the boat into the water.

This was the last leg of the journey. Too bad she had to do it alone.

The kayak swayed dangerously when she hopped in. She used her paddle like Ronan taught her and was glad she only had to go straight so far. Steering was its own hazard, but she sort of got the gist of it.

Something kept tapping the back of her mind, a persistent nagging. Why did she assume Ronan would run at the first chance he got? Was she letting her fear and past hurts get in the way again?

When it came time to steer, as she neared the island, the more blood pumped hot in her ears. At one point, she'd pointed the kayak out to the middle of the lake where she'd miss the island altogether. She frantically paddled the wrong way first and then the right way but swayed the boat too much. For a moment, the boat seemed determined to capsize again, but she took deep breaths and moved the paddle with slower, calmer strokes until it settled in the water.

The wind wailed over the island's rocky hollows. Eerie, especially since she was forced to paddle near the jagged, fang-like rock formation. She could see why the townspeople had their superstitions about this place.

Ronan said the best way to get onto the island was on the opposite side, where the cliffs were lower and a small inlet offered a landing spot. It wasn't easy. She had a couple of near misses when she freaked out and steered the wrong way again, almost ramming right into one of the giant rocks sticking out of the water by the cliff face.

But she found the inlet and coasted into its relative safety. The trickiest part was getting out of the kayak without falling out. She kept hold of the tow-line so the boat wouldn't float away and rolled onto the flat rock ledge level with the water—just like Ronan showed her after they'd fallen out.

She dragged the kayak onto the ledge and wrapped the line around a boulder. This was ridiculous. She even laughed aloud while she removed her life jacket and left it in the boat. Why again was she out here by herself?

But that voice, the slippery one who seemed to delight in causing her pain, spoke again: *Because he left you. He doesn't want to be with you. Who would? Everyone ends up leaving you.*

She could let those words break her or let them boost her courage to keep going by herself.

She trudged on, climbing the steep, weather-made stairway to the top of the island, an irregular flattened cliff. Craggy shrubs and trees clung to the rock face, determined to live despite the harsh conditions and lack of soil. She supposed she was like them. She'd survived. Despite lack of love and nurturing. She lived. The question was, now that she'd experienced love and the nurture of a family, could she go back to living in an emotional desert? Alone?

She pushed that aside for the moment, standing on the top of the island, where rocks and trees obscured her view of the shore. All around her the waves thundered against the rocks, fierce gusts of wind swayed her where she stood and water surrounded her as far as she could see, facing into the depths of Lake Superior. Now what? Where should she look? After all this, why hadn't their instructions told them where to find the treasure?

She unzipped Grace's diary from the backpack, but she already knew—the last pages had been ripped out. She'd reached the end of Grace's story and found the woman had never spoken of a treasure, which made Hope both laugh and scream inside. Maybe this really was a fool's hunt. She checked over her *Anne of Green Gables* again too. Nothing she hadn't already seen.

Wait. All of the other books had a fore-edge painting. Even though the diary wasn't technically a book, someone had taken a lot of time and energy to make it for Grace, her ancestor. She fanned the pages. No painting.

What if Grace had written about the treasure but those were the pages ripped out?

The wind whipped her hair into her eyes as she squinted at the gray clouds above as if they held the answer.

Or maybe it was Ulysses and her grandma Dottie who found the entries and wanted to be sure they were good and hidden. The pages could be tucked in one of the two books she held—*Anne* or the diary. She'd read about people making hidden compartments in the lining or spines. Nothing would seem too strange at this point.

She inspected the journal first. On the leather spine, the fine craftsmanship didn't give anything away. But as she opened it, there was something between the leather spine and the pages. A small, thin pocket. Someone could slide folded paper into it. She couldn't see to the bottom of the skinny pocket, so she dug the flashlight out of the bag.

She caught sight of the words on the side of the flashlight:

Behold, I have set the land before you: go in and possess the land…
Deut. 1:8.

Strange words to be etched into the side of a long metal flashlight.

Shining the light into the pocket, she clicked her tongue in disappointment. If there ever had been anything there, it wasn't there anymore.

"Okay, Mom, Grandma, Grace, Ulysses, whoever, what are you trying to tell me?" she groaned to the wind and rocks.

She squeezed her eyes shut for a moment. Suddenly, she wished so much that Ronan was here with her. She'd have loved his support right about now.

Could it be in the copy of *Anne of Green Gables*? Maybe whoever hid the clues hadn't wanted to keep the diary pages with the actual diary. That made sense.

She opened the book and inspected the spine. A pocket, similar to the diary. Slipping a finger into it, she felt folded pages. Carefully, she slid them up and out.

Grace's writing:

I must unburden myself from a grievous incident I fear has altered the course of not only my own life but Edward's as well. I do not know how I will ever live with this secret. But live with it, I must. For I can never tell another living soul. In fact, Edward and I swore an oath to each other that not another living soul will know. Only our ancestors, after we are long buried and with our Creator, will learn the truth of that fateful night...

Grace told of the night she'd made plans to meet a man for whom she cared deeply on the island. It was a secret rendezvous since no one approved of the man, Thomas, who had shown up in the town unannounced, with a disturbing swagger and a disreputable background. But she'd fallen for this dashing, smooth-talking young man, so she agreed to meet him. Edward had warned her against it. He'd told her he didn't trust any man's integrity who'd want to meet her without her parents' permission—customary at the time.

Hope smiled at how much Ronan reminded her of his ancestor.

Grace took a rowboat to the island despite the cautions. Edward had manned the lighthouse that evening and with his handheld telescope spotted a group of rough-looking men waiting on the island, not just her beau, Thomas.

He tried calling out to her from the shore, but a storm had rolled in and she couldn't hear him. Before he could return to the lighthouse, he was accosted by more of Thomas's associates.

The men were part of a Lake Superior pirate crew. They

tied Edward up and shut down the lighthouse beacon to con-
fuse a cargo ship coming through. They planned to run it
aground and steal the goods onboard.

They dragged my poor friend, kicking and shouting,
away from his duties at the lighthouse, a responsibility
he would never neglect. Then they brought Edward out
to the island where they held me captive. I was horrified
and ashamed to learn Thomas's affections were false. Lost
Lover's Island they call it. For good reason...

Thomas's intention for Edward was to hold him for ran-
som or make him an indentured slave, and Grace's fate was
even worse.

Her breakfast started to rise in her throat as she read Grace's
account. Thomas planned to sell her into that century's version of human trafficking. Hope's hands shook, but she forced
herself to keep reading.

Thomas and his three shipmates on the island were to await
their captain's signal. Then they would retrieve their prison-
ers and a treasure they'd stored on the island from previous
ventures and meet the captain aboard their ship.

But their plans went south. The storm raged with full force,
fast and tempestuous. It ran both the cargo and the pirate vessel
under the waves. In the upheaval, Edward managed to over-
power Thomas. His shipmates tried to row out to their ship,
thinking it still had a chance. Thomas jumped in the water
to catch up to them.

All perished.

Edward made me promise to never tell why he didn't
light the beacon. It gnaws away at my heart day and
night. He wishes to live with the shame so I do not have

to. I would be a soiled woman if anyone knew what I had done. To have made plans to meet a man to whom I am not wed, alone, at night...the consequences would be dire. For myself and my family. Sometimes my dear friend Edward shows me what it is to love like our Savior. To bear someone else's shame.

They'd found the treasure abandoned by the pirates, but it would only make things worse between their feuding families. Plus, they'd have to explain where and how they'd obtained it.

All either of us can hope for is for our families, distant and in the future, to find some light out of this darkness. Some beauty out of tragedy. That is why it will remain buried in darkness in the northeast-facing cave and stay there until our two families reunite to bring it back into the light. May they use it well and with wisdom.

Not another cave.

She had no choice now. She folded the pages reverently, tucked them back inside the book and placed both the journal and book in her backpack. Lifting it onto her back again, she retraced the way she'd come. She'd passed a rock ledge cave on the way to the plateau top of the island.

Just as she stepped around a boulder taller than she was, a most surprising figure came into view.

Poppy.

Her bony hand held a gun pointed at Hope.

The expression she wore wasn't the odd gawking bird she usually had. This time she was like a hawk who'd spotted her prey.

Chapter Twenty-One

"Where is it?" Poppy brandished her gun like a sword.

"Where's what?" Hope knew how obsessed the woman seemed with pirate treasure. It wasn't hard to guess what she meant.

Poppy stepped closer, her wiry body taut as if ready to pounce. "You know what. The treasure."

Would continuing to play dumb work? "I don't know what you're talking about."

"I'm sure you're just up here enjoying the view. Right?" Acid spewed from each word.

Poppy circled her. Hope didn't want to turn her back to the woman, so now Poppy stood on the island's plateau, and behind Hope was the steep trail.

"Oh, you know exactly what I'm talking about. Where's the map? I looked all over in your stupid little books and couldn't find it. Tell me now!" She poked the gun near Hope's chest. Hope jumped back and tripped. She slid down the trail several feet.

As Hope picked herself up, with a few new scrapes and bruises, a sinking realization settled into the pit of her stomach.

"It was you." Hope pointed, not as effective without a weapon. "You broke into Dusty Jackets. You were the one who stole my books. Why?"

How could she even know about the family treasure? This was between the Barrick and Holloway-Carrington families.

"All the history pages, the town stories turned to legends, the old wives' tales about where the pirate treasure on Lake Superior is and who's going to claim it, seem to leave out a key ingredient. Me." Poppy jabbed a thumb at her own chest.

"What are you talking about?" Hope inched back on the trail. It was almost vertical and rocky, but maybe if she could move far enough, she could outrun Poppy to the kayak and escape.

Poppy's shrewd eye traveled to Hope's feet. "I already sent your little kayak and life jacket adrift. And you're not much of a swimmer, I've gathered." A merry glint sent a chill through Hope's veins. "And the last I heard, bullets fly faster than a human can run."

Hope craned her head to see down below, the backside of the island. The boat was indeed gone, along with the paddle and life vest. How Poppy got there, she wasn't sure. But wherever Poppy's boat was tied, it wasn't visible from there. "What is this about? What do you want from me? You have my books. You can see that there's no treasure map."

Poppy's curled lip and the theft of Hope's books sparked anger in her. "And even if there was a treasure, it's not yours. It's mine and Ronan's."

That was the wrong thing to say. Poppy shrieked. "No, it's not! Don't you see? Someone is missing from the story." Her face turned earnest like she wanted someone, anyone, to understand.

Since Poppy was the lady with the small but, Hope assumed, real gun, Hope indulged her. "Who?"

"The pirate and his family. *My* ancestors." Poppy's free hand rapped on her chest.

"What pirate?"

"The famous one everyone keeps talking about. The one they have the display dedicated to at the historical society museum—Captain 'Cold Hands' Robert Bartholomew. He was my great-great-great-grandfather."

"Well, I'm sorry to tell you, I don't know anything about his treasure. If you want the truth, Ronan's and my family have a treasure we're looking for. But we haven't found it and it has nothing to do with your pirate ancestor."

"Are you that dense?" Poppy gestured to her own head, unwisely with the gun. "It's one and the same. Your ancestors stole it from mine. If it was first Cold Hands's, then it's mine, not yours."

Hope held up a hand. "He was a *pirate*. Any treasure he had didn't belong to him at all."

"Well, it didn't belong to your ancestors either. But that didn't stop them from hiding it for you to find. Do you even know what happened to the family of Cold Hands? They were shunned and destitute when he didn't return home. Everyone knew who his wife was associated with. Not like she could've changed him anyway. I want to find it for her."

Hope had never considered that the pirate who'd caused the mayhem that night had a family. Never really thought about his side of the story at all. In a twisted kind of way, Poppy wanted to find it for honor's sake.

Poppy took a step toward her. "I've been following you on this rabbit trail." She waved her gun around like she was gesturing with her hands. Unhinged and unconcerned with safety—not a good combo. "I was here researching to finally get this treasure back to its rightful owner when I discovered that your ancestor, Grace Holloway, and Ronan's ancestor, Edward Barrick, were the last to see Cold Hands alive. I knew you both had to be on the hunt for it."

Hope raised her palms. "You don't see it though, do you? No treasure."

"Empty your backpack. I think you had the last clue. That's why you're out here."

Her precious last book and the diary she held so dear could not fall into this woman's hands. "Ronan is going to meet me out here. He'll be here any minute."

"No, he won't." Her sharp chin dipped precisely.

"How do you know?"

"Because I set one fire across town to distract the police and the fire department and then set another fire at the youth center building to keep Ronan distracted. Don't you see the smoke?"

And to think Hope had started to feel a little smidgen of sympathy for the gun-wielding lady. Maybe a little overzealous about finding her family's roots, but trying to restore honor to her family? Not anymore. If she'd set two fires, there was no longer any question whether or not she'd be willing to use that gun.

Hope peered around the tall boulder blocking her view of the shore. Swirls of black-and-gray smoke curled into the sky.

"No, he won't be here for a long time, will he, Hope?"

Touching her fingertips to her lips, she breathed the words, "Oh, no. No." All of Ronan's hard work.

God, please, I know You promise to never leave us or forsake us. Please help me and keep Ronan safe.

"Or should I say, *Emily Carrington*?" Poppy sneered. "I wonder what this sleepy little town would think if they knew who you are, knew you've been lying to them this whole time.

Do they know you're a thief? A check forger? What else are you hiding?"

"How...how did you know?"

A gloating beam lit in Poppy's narrow eyes. "I've been watching you. Suspecting. But it wasn't until I saw the will from your mother in that folder in your bedroom, listing your real name, that I knew for sure."

Questions cycloned through her brain. But people finding out who she was, the books, the treasure, even the fact that Poppy broke into the shop and not Richard Allen who she'd still suspected had a role in it even with his alibi, none of it mattered right now. She needed to get back to Ronan. Why, oh why did she ever believe, even for a second, he'd abandon her?

"You're going to help me find that treasure. Just you and me." Poppy nudged Hope's stomach with the gun, forcing her to stumble farther back on the trail.

The flames licked the exterior of the storage outbuilding. Ronan put an arm in front of his face to shield himself from the heat and smoke. If the fire department, with their one truck, didn't get here soon, the fire could spread to the main youth center building, especially with the turbulent wind gusting off the lake. What were the chances of having two fires at the same time in this small town?

On his way back to Dusty Jackets to meet up with Hope, the fire engine siren screamed past him toward the other side of town. A compulsion to check the youth center had overtaken him so he'd whipped a U-turn. Sure enough, smoke poured out of the storage building. The smoke turned to flames before he could dial 911.

Someone shouted. He turned. No one there. The main building was quiet.

"Help! Help me!"

The panic and the voice, unmistakable. Tate.

"Hold on, I'm coming! Where are you?"

The worst of the fire poured out of the front door. In answer, Tate's hand smacked the glass of the high window toward the back.

It was happening again. Emergency. Out of his control. Nothing registered in his eardrums but the buzz of adrenaline and the gallop of his own heartbeat.

The fire hadn't yet reached the back of the building. Ronan called up to the farthest window. "Tate, see if you can break the glass!"

Banging followed as Ronan turned to find something, anything, he could use to get to the boy.

Help, God!

A long ladder lay on the ground near the building as if it had been put there for this very purpose. Maybe it had.

He seized it and sprinted to the window, the heat and smoke a distant nuisance.

He steadied the ladder against the side of the building and climbed up. Ladders had proven difficult for him with his prosthetic, but not now.

Tate covered his mouth with his T-shirt and waved his other arm frantically. He screamed something into his shirt.

Ronan shook his head. "I can't hear you." He leaned closer.

Pulling his shirt down, Tate cupped his mouth and shouted, "I can't break it!"

"Can you open it?" Ronan pressed his fingers on the panes, trying to slide it open.

Tate's head tossed from side to side to say "no."

Ronan stopped. "Tate, look at me. I'm going to get you out." He had to yell the words over the whoosh and crackle of the fire.

Tate met his eyes, pure terror inside, but managed a weak nod.

Ronan needed to make sure it wasn't an empty promise like he'd made to young Kyle.

"Let's work together, okay? Slide the window. One, two, together." They each gritted their teeth and pulled on the window. The glass was thick. It would be hard to break from this angle. But Ronan would have to try if this didn't work.

Finally, the old window moved. With a stubborn groan, it opened. A cloud of smoke ballooned out and rose into the sky. Ronan reached in and drew strength from God only knew where to pull Tate up and over the windowsill.

Ronan lost balance and they tumbled to the ground. Tate landed hard on Ronan's chest, which knocked the wind out of them both. Tate rolled over, back flat on the gravel. Ronan panted, trying to regain his breath. Tate hacked and gasped.

Ronan sat up and helped Tate back away from the burning building. "You okay?"

Tate coughed again but made a thumbs-up. "Thank you," he croaked.

Holding his T-shirt over his nose and mouth, Ronan ran to the water spigot with the water hose attached near the burning storage building. He turned it on full blast toward the front door where the flames blazed the highest. But over the crackling flames, the fire siren whooped. In their direction. Finally.

While the professionals took over and extinguished the flames, the paramedics examined Tate and placed an oxygen mask over his nose and mouth. Other than a little smoke damage that would heal, he would be okay.

When he was able, Ronan called Dusty Jackets. No answer. Hope's little-used cell phone. No answer. He called the hospital; Gramps was doing fine, and Grandma hadn't seen or heard from Hope.

The firefighters reduced it to a smoking, wet mess in a matter of minutes with their powerful water hose.

Ronan sat next to Tate on the tailgate of his truck. "What happened? How did the fire start and why were you here?" He didn't want to think Tate had started the fire, but he had to know the truth.

Tate leaned over his legs. "I was coming over to steal something. A bike rim I saw in there the other day." His voice was thick with shame and the aftermath of his raw throat.

"Buddy, all you had to do was ask. I would've let you have it."

"My dad says we shouldn't ask for anything. Either you earn it or you take it."

Ronan clasped his hands together, elbows on his knees. "Taking things and destroying other people's property is what landed you with community service in the first place."

"And it's the only reason I stayed sane this summer." Tate's hands balled into fists. "I...I didn't want it to end." The last part came out so fast and jumbled, Ronan almost didn't catch it.

Ronan sat straighter. Understanding dawned. "So, you wanted to do something wrong to extend your community service? But you can come over anytime. You don't need to set a fire and steal from me." He bumped Tate's shoulder with his own.

"I'll own up to my part, but I didn't set the fire."

"Then who did?"

"Poppy. I was in the back of the storage building. I could hear someone around by the front door. Before I could get out, the door slammed and I heard the lock click. I saw Poppy running to her car and squealing out of the parking lot from the window and then the place filled with smoke and flames."

"Did she see you?"

Tate shook his head. "There's no way that cold-hearted crone didn't hear me banging on the window though."

The muscles in Ronan's shoulders tightened. "Did you see anything else that might tell us why she'd do this?"

Black clouds that had nothing to do with the fires in Wanishin had rolled in and with them, a sinking feeling in Ronan's gut.

Tate wiped at his forehead, smearing soot. "I don't— Oh, yeah. Even though, you know, I was about to die, I thought it was weird to see a fishing boat on a trailer behind her little car. I didn't take her for a fisherman, er, woman. She peeled out of the parking lot so fast with it, it almost fell off the trailer."

Something was severely off. A suspicion took hold in his mind.

Ronan gestured to the boy to get up. "I'm sorry to leave like this. But I have to go. The paramedics will want to check on you again before letting you go. And the police will be coming over after talking to witnesses at the other fire. They can take you home." When the boy looked alarmed, Ronan added, "They'll just ask what happened. Tell them about seeing Poppy. You can tell them you were here working."

"But I—"

"It's okay…this time. Be honest next time, okay? And every single time after that."

"All right. Where are you going?"

"I have a bad feeling. I think I'm going out to Lost Lover's Island. I hope I'm wrong. I'll call you later."

Tate seemed satisfied with that. Ronan jumped into the truck's cab and drove toward Dusty Jackets at speeds not even close to legal, praying he was being paranoid, and grateful the police force was occupied at the moment.

His tires screeched to a stop in front of Dusty Jackets and he ran to the back where the neglected boat landing led into the water. There was a silver car backed up to the waterline, Poppy's car, with the boat trailer half in the water, empty.

Like a wild animal had latched itself to his chest, his lungs seized, his heart clambered an irregular beat against his ribs. Okay, he had to calm down.

"Hope!" he called, but already knew she wouldn't answer. He ran from room to room anyway in search of her. Empty. All of them. It all had to be connected. Poppy, the fires, Hope gone.

His grandparents kept a couple of kayaks under the porch. He sprinted to find them. One was gone. Maybe Hope had tried to paddle out to the island alone when he hadn't shown up for her. A few hiccups filing Tate's community service paperwork, and the fire hadn't helped. But his gut twisted anyway. He hadn't been there for her like he'd promised. But he drew strength from the God who'd allowed him to be a part of a rescue that day. Would He be there through one more?

Ronan dragged the kayak and the paddle to the water with as much haste as he could, sloshed into the water and pushed off the rocky shore. He paddled fast and strong. He couldn't imagine Hope doing this on her own, but then, she was more capable than he gave her credit for. She'd escaped her captor after ten years of torture, survived for five years, mostly, on her own. He prayed God would give her whatever wit and strength she needed right now.

Hope's empty kayak, followed closely by a life vest and paddle, floated by him as he neared the island. Not a good sign. His heart sank to the bottom of Lake Superior.

Raised voices echoed ahead. He rounded the island to the other side to the only semisafe landing area. Just down from that spot, Poppy's boat was tied to a rock. Grabbing his towline, he rolled himself onto the rock ledge.

In his determination to get there as quickly as possible, he'd come empty-handed. Flashes of the worst-case scenario zipped through his brain. But again he prayed for help and calm as he removed his life vest.

"Well, look who came to join us." Poppy stood above him on the trail that led up to the top, gun in hand and Hope ahead of her, closer to him.

To his relief, she appeared unharmed, just shocked, like he was.

Hope kept a wary eye on Poppy's gun. "You remember how Ulysses said the pirates had the treasure. Well, I found you a pirate." Her voice shook, but pride filled his chest at how unruffled she seemed.

"Poppy, put the gun down. Let's talk about this." He stepped toward her, hands up to show he intended no harm.

"Stay back!" Poppy waved the gun in the air.

"What's your endgame here?" He gritted his teeth. If that woman gave Hope so much as one scratch…

Like Hope didn't have enough trauma in her life without this. How could he protect her from the emotional toll this would take? This wasn't a "get his hands dirty and fix it" kind of problem.

He stood his ground. "Everyone knows it was you who started the fires by now. I'm guessing you were the one who broke into my grandparents' shop too. What's your plan?"

Hope glanced between them. Poppy's tough act seemed to slip.

But the slow glare slid back onto Poppy's face. "I'm going to get my treasure. Get what I came for. That's my plan."

Poppy turned to Hope. "Now, hand over that book. We're finding this thing." She touched Hope's shoulder with the tip of the gun barrel. It took everything in him not to tackle the small woman. But the gun could accidentally discharge.

How could he get them out of this situation? Distract Poppy

and take her gun? Knock her out? With what? And could he really do that to a woman, even if she *was* out of her mind? Yes. To protect Hope. He could.

Short of taking off his prosthetic leg and brandishing it as a weapon though, what was he supposed to do?

Deep inside, God prodded Ronan to trust Him. He, Ronan, wasn't the God of the universe despite how much he wanted to save everyone and fix every problem. But the real God of the universe had everything under control.

Hope raised her hands in surrender. "Okay, okay." Stooping on the ground, Hope pulled out her *Anne of Green Gables* and slipped several folded handwritten pages from the spine.

After Poppy scanned the pages, her lips curled into a triumphant smile. "The cave. Yes. Let's go get the shovels. Keep your hands on your heads, where I can see them." Poppy's intentions weren't clear, but he hoped the shovels were for the treasure.

One way or another, he was getting Hope off this island unharmed. Poppy nudged Hope down the trail toward her boat.

"Are you okay?" Ronan whispered to Hope while Poppy dug the gun tip into his shoulder blade, forcing him to move to the side of the boat.

"Yeah."

"No funny business." Poppy motioned with her gun.

Poppy grabbed the shovels out of her boat and they walked single file along a rock ledge leading to a cliff and cave. It was precarious navigating, but they made it to the small cave. Poppy could stand inside but Ronan and Hope had to duck their heads.

They dug in two different corners to maximize efforts. This time their ancestors hadn't put any clues, vague messages or a big arrow, which was what he would've liked. But then, their families weren't dumb. They knew stories about pirate treasures would circulate after the shipwrecks. They wouldn't have left any direct evidence.

After both dug in several spots, Hope's shovel clunked against something. He ran over and so did Poppy. He helped Hope dig deeper. An old steamer trunk of some kind, the top made of curved metal. They all seemed to forget the strange circumstances of being in the cave together and bent to wipe away the dirt.

He and Hope shared a glance. Their family treasure. It was real.

He wasn't sure how Poppy factored in, but he was glad to get to the end of this hunt and see it wasn't for nothing. No matter what was inside.

"What are you waiting for? Get it out." Poppy's voice echoed in the small space. She flourished the gun, which had become an extension of her bony arm.

But he saw something Poppy hadn't meant him to—the small firearm didn't have a clip in it. That didn't mean there wasn't a round in the chamber, but if she hadn't loaded a clip, he'd guess not. She'd merely meant to intimidate them.

He'd play it cool for now, but after they opened the treasure, he'd find a way to subdue Poppy and let the police deal with her.

He and Hope lifted and tugged and dug some more around the sides of the trunk to finally free it from the dirt. It was so dark, they fumbled with the latch.

When Hope moved toward her backpack, Poppy pointed the gun at her again.

Hope put her palms up. "I'm getting a flashlight."

His fingers found Hope's arm in the dark for reassurance while she clicked on the flashlight. As they opened the top, it let out a squeak.

Hope shone the light inside and gasped. He was stunned

into silence. Poppy peered over their shoulders and let out an exultant whoop.

Inside sparkled and glittered like a real, live pirate treasure. Just what he imagined one to look like. Gold and silver pieces, paper money, uncut gemstones, strands of pearls, necklaces dripping with diamonds, pocket watches, as well as old bottles of brown liquor. On the inner lid, someone had written:

And the land which I gave Abraham and Isaac, to thee I will give it, and to thy seed after thee will I give the land. Genesis 35:12.

This time a verse alone. No mysterious rhyme or clue. Poppy reached down, running a hand over the treasure. "All mine."

"I don't think so." Ronan had heard enough and dealt with too much because of this nasty little woman. He whacked the empty weapon from her bony hands, and it skidded across the cave floor.

Hope gasped. "What are you doing? That could've gone off!"

"Hope, her gun isn't even loaded." But Poppy chose that moment to bend and grab one of the shovels, her determined expression ghostly in the dim light. She raised it over Hope.

But Hope launched herself forward and knocked the shovel from Poppy's hands. Hope stood her ground, fists at the ready.

Pride swelled in Ronan's chest again. This was the woman he loved.

Poppy growled, trying to get around them to the treasure. "It's mine! Mine!"

He almost laughed, reminded of Tate's favorite Tolkien character, Gollum. Almost. But a commotion of feet scurrying up the rock trail outside drew his attention.

Chapter Twenty-Two

Before Hope could draw a full breath, two police officers slipped into the cave with their own fully loaded guns raised and told Poppy to freeze. Hope backed against the stone wall, trying to shrink into it. Ronan stayed in his position as her shield.

It took some negotiating, but Poppy finally put her hands on top of her head.

As they strapped cuffs on Poppy's wrists, she screamed, "That treasure is mine. Mine, do you hear me?"

The police officer from outside the shop, Officer Gerard, was there and explained that it had been Tate who told them to come out to the island. One officer took Poppy down to their boat. Officer Gerard glanced between the treasure, the two of them and the mouth of the cave, where a screaming Poppy had disappeared.

"Someone want to tell me what's going on?"

Hope smiled to herself. A thought walloped her brain. "Yeah, I can make this simple." Man, she hoped she was right.

She tapped the flashlight and twisted open the top. *Yes!* Clever Ulysses. In the very center were the batteries, around that a protective plastic cylinder, and tucked between the cylinder and the outer metal handle was a slip of paper. She unrolled it to find what she'd hoped was there. The deed to the island with Ulysses's, Brock's and Ronan's names on it.

Ronan's eyes rounded when he skimmed the contents.

She held it up for the officer. "This means he owns everything on and in this island."

The officer read it with the beam of his own flashlight. "Obviously we'll have to have you two come in for statements, check this document with the bank, et cetera. You'll have your Uncle Sam chunk taken out too. But, yeah, you struck oil, man. Metaphorically speaking. Don't spend it all in one place."

Ronan had gone pale. "Yeah. Huh."

The ride back to shore was surreal, she and Ronan with the chest between them on a bench seat in the stern of the police department's speedboat.

A tour guide boat with a crossbones-and-skull flag moved close enough for the passengers to gawk and snap their pictures.

An officer pulled out a megaphone. "Move away from this area immediately, by order of the Wanishin Falls Police Department."

The flustered boat driver turned the watercraft around and zoomed in the other direction.

Ronan stayed quiet after finding the treasure and the deed. He rubbed the scruff on his chin. "How'd you know the deed was in the flashlight?" He kept scanning the shore.

"I saw a verse on the side of the flashlight, and then that verse inside the trunk. Your grandpa and my grandma set some of this search up for us. They'd want no questions about who the treasure belonged to. Plus, your grandpa said something about 'buying the whole thing' when he talked about the pirates having the treasure."

"Hmm…" His lips made a straight line.

She reached over and tapped his shoulder. "We did it. Can you believe it?"

"No, this whole thing is unbelievable. It's over."

She didn't like how he said, "It's over."

They were escorted to the police station, where Poppy made a ruckus in another room and they gave their statements. The treasure would be held at the bank in a safe until the paperwork was processed and the treasure was appraised. There would be taxes to pay on it first before any could be used. They separated her and Ronan for their statements. A formality, they said.

Ronan's distance and pained expression throughout the afternoon wore on her, pulling her out of her panic and into a morose silence.

The itch started slow and began to grow and spread. The itch she'd felt for years after her escape when she'd been too still for too long. When anyone got too close. When things got too uncomfortable or painful. The itch she'd felt almost daily since arriving in Wanishin Falls, only calming in the last couple of weeks. The one Ronan had soothed. The itch to run.

Before the officer who drove them to the station ducked out the front doors to escort them back to Dusty Jackets, he turned back. "Don't be alarmed, but the media has gotten ahold of this and they're kind of losing their minds. A handful of people from a tour boat called in what the news is saying is a *suspicious* situation on Lost Lover's Island. A bunch of reporters were already in town because of the two fires today. They may or may not know about the treasure or what happened with Ms. McGoven, and you don't have to say a thing."

Ronan's eyes darted to the din of the media mob gathered outside the police station. "Hope, I don't think— This isn't good— I mean, you may want to go—"

"What? What do you mean?" Her heart sank to her toes. He wanted her to go?

But he didn't get to answer. The officer pushed the door open and put his arms out to part the crowd. The clamor of shouted questions and flashes of long-lens cameras assaulted them.

Her lungs burned. Air, why wasn't there any air outside? She told herself to breathe slowly.

Her heart beat out of rhythm. An odd tempo to a tuneless song. Cold. She was so cold, even though the back of her neck was slick with sweat.

Confusion, fear, pain and regret swirled a cyclone through her mind.

In her stupor, the police officer taking her arm and moving her through the crowd faded into the background. Ronan yelled something behind her, but she couldn't hear what.

After she'd counted and calmed herself, she sent covert glances to the back seat where Ronan sat while an officer drove them back to Dusty Jackets and Ronan's truck.

She wasn't even worried about the reporters. Not really. It was the noise and commotion that triggered her PTSD. She was more worried about Ronan. Had something changed in all of this between her and Ronan? Maybe he'd started to agree with his dad's assessment—she was more trouble than she was worth.

But they couldn't very well talk with the cop in the car. The officer exited the car first and made the reporters still hanging around the shop leave. Then she and Ronan followed and thanked the officer before he drove away.

And when it was just the two of them, Ronan shifted, staring at the front porch's wood planks under his feet. "I made sure they fixed the lock while we were gone and the security system is up and working again. The officers said they'll be keeping an eye on the place."

"Okay." She fidgeted with a piece of her hair, not sure what else to say. She wanted to run, she wanted to stay, she wanted him to hold her and tell her everything was going to be okay. Most of all, she wanted him to stop acting like she'd done something wrong. But then, maybe she'd done something wrong just by being there. None of this would've happened if not for her and her wild-goose chase.

But he may never have discovered the treasure without her and her books. He should've thanked her, right?

She pressed her lips together until they hurt and didn't say any of that.

Hands in his pockets, he lifted a shoulder. "I'm going to go so I can check on Gramps. Are you going to be okay here? Lock the doors, okay?"

There was no invitation to come along with him. "At least we know the gun-toting pirate is off the streets." She'd tried to keep her voice light, but the words dropped flat instead.

"Kat texted earlier and said she'll stop by to see you after her shift, around six thirty."

"All right."

When he jumped into his truck and closed the door, she said to the quiet shop, "Goodbye."

It felt final. A last note of a song. The final sentence of a book—the thing she always read first to determine if the rest was worth it. This last sentence was bittersweet and the pain of it ran deep. Had all of the good she'd experienced been worth all of the pain writhing within her now? Would she have still read the story if she'd known this ending?

But the urge in her gut persisted. She needed to get out

of there. She'd have to call the police station later about getting her other books back from Poppy, wherever she'd stashed them. And the treasure?

She didn't even want to deal with that at the moment. Maybe eventually she'd call Ronan about her half. She knew he'd give it to her if she asked. For now, she hadn't trusted bank accounts, so she'd hidden the money from her paychecks in the loose floorboard near her bed. She would take what she could carry over to the youth center building, where her semifinished mobile café was parked.

Running up the stairs to her still-torn-apart room, she gathered the possessions she'd arrived with and the few things she'd acquired. For reasons she couldn't explain, she also grabbed one of Ronan's extra plaid shirts from the guest room.

She left the hiking boots she'd used to hike to the cave and the falls, sure she wouldn't need them on the road. The journey to the cave. She should've never told Ronan about her past. With all the drama she'd caused, no wonder he couldn't stand the sight of her now.

It wasn't just about *her* privacy about to be destroyed with finding the treasure—this would probably be on the national news that night. But Ronan had lived his life in a fishbowl for who his family was, the supposed Barrick Curse and for the ship accident. Unfair. But now this whole treasure thing would bring him more attention. Maybe that was why he'd acted so strangely.

Yes. This was the best thing for them both. If she left.

She stuffed her things into her now-too-small suitcase. Grabbing it up along with her shoulder bag/purse, and the backpack Ronan had given her, she sped downstairs.

She breathed in, for the last time, the rich, layered scent of the books, the shop and home she'd come to love. More than that, she'd come to love the people it represented. The desire to hold them all one more time, even Fitzwilliam, who was still staying with Ronan, almost overcame her magnetic pull to leave. Almost.

This is best. She repeated it over and over.

Before leaving, she took out a pen and paper from behind the checkout counter. She wrote:

Thank you for everything. I'll never forget your kindness.

It wasn't enough, but it'd have to do.

She hoofed it to the youth center parking lot, grateful she didn't encounter anyone on the way. No one to recognize her or ask what she was doing.

Ronan had given her a set of keys to the bus a few days ago.

She stowed her stuff in the back in a cabinet Ronan had installed. Lots of little things and a few big things would need to be done to make the food truck operational, but she'd have to take it one issue at a time.

"Okay, this is it. Where to first?" Her voice sounded thin, hollowed out to her own ears.

Maybe she'd start by driving to Duluth. She liked the area despite Richard Allen's presence in the city. There were a lot of food trucks along the canal. She could see if any needed staff, and she could do that until she saved enough to buy the rest of what she needed and fill out the proper permits for the city.

It wasn't a perfect plan, but nothing about this was. She had to get on the road before anyone saw her. So, she drove through town, glad she didn't but half hoping she'd see someone she knew on the way out. Her eyes lingered on Kat's Café, Mrs. Baranski's house, the thrift boutique, Dusty Jackets one last time and the lighthouse in her rearview mirror.

Tears blurred her vision.

She made her foot keep its steady pressure on the gas pedal.

As all signs of Wanishin Falls disappeared from her mirrors, she sobbed. Why was this so hard? This was what she'd planned to do from the moment she'd stepped foot in Wanishin Falls. Before that even. She'd told Ronan she'd consider staying, but never promised.

What she'd been about to tell him before she ventured out to the island alone that morning was she cared about him. She wanted to stay but was scared. Then he'd left her there. And even though it was stupid to feel vulnerable when she hadn't even told him, she had.

Now he'd never know what she'd been about to say or anything else. What kind of person would leave without saying goodbye?

Her. She would.

A stab of guilt pierced through the sadness.

"But I can't. I can't do this. I don't want to care. They're better off without me." Her thoughts tangled with the heartache, and no one would ever know how much it hurt to leave. But God knew. He felt the pain ripping her heart into shreds.

She kept driving, trying to wipe the tears away so she could see, but it was a never-ending downpour.

"Why'd you even bring me here?" She wasn't sure if she was talking to God or her mom. "Huh, why?"

But then the answer hit her.

Because she'd needed to see what it was like to have a family, to love and be loved.

"I don't deserve it. I'm not capable of real love. Giving it or receiving it."

The lie of that statement smacked her between the eyes almost before the words were out of her mouth.

She did love them. The real kind. All of them. Kat, Ulysses, Mags, Tate…and Ronan.

She gasped.

Her hands gripped the wheel, knuckles cracking.

"I love them." Her voice filled with wonder.

So much it scared her. That was what she was running from. Not whatever was going on with Ronan. Not because it was what was best for her or them. In fact, the healthiest she'd been was with them. She was frightened by how much she cared about them and what standing still would mean for her.

She hoped they felt the same about her. Ronan's behavior after finding the treasure wound trepidation around her rib cage, despite his words in the cave and on their date.

Something Dee once told her about relationships popped into her mind. Hope had had a hard time because of her insecurities and trust issues. And Dee said, "If you're not sure how to take someone's actions or words, hold them up next to all of their past dealings with you. Trust and a good handle on someone's feelings about you are built over time. Don't judge based on one conversation or misunderstanding."

Don't judge based on one conversation or misunderstanding. But that was what she'd done. Countless times. She hadn't talked to him about the way he put distance between them after what happened with Ulysses and finding the treasure. Or was it *her* who'd created the distance? A simple conversation. She should have talked to him. And trusted who he'd been over time for her.

Every interaction she'd ever had with Ronan should have led her to believe the best in him and trust his actions weren't rooted in him not caring about her.

Even though the threads of her heart tied to Wanishin pulled taut, ready to snap the farther she drove away, she kept coming back to her biggest emotional roadblock. "But, God, I'm broken. I'm so incredibly broken inside." Her words shattered over each other, ripping at her insides.

"What happened to me...will never be okay. But I'm learning to forgive. To see it as not something *You* did to me, but what evil in the world took from me. I can never get back the pieces that broke away. They're scattered to the wind. I'm like Humpty-Dumpty, and I'm never getting put back together again."

But before an answer could form in her heart, the bus's heat sensor started to rise. The needle jumped to red and smoke poured from under the hood. She swerved to the side of the road and parked on the shoulder, turning off the ignition. Grabbing a towel from the back, she opened the hood to release the heat and smoke.

She groaned. Now what?

Despite finding herself alone on a desolate road, bus broken down and rain starting to sprinkle her cheeks and eyelids, she knew God wasn't done "dealing with her heart," as Dee would say.

How could she reconcile a loving God with the aftermath of who she was now? What could a mangled heart do to return the love so graciously given to her? How could she piece herself back together?

She turned her face skyward, letting the cool rain wash over her. Her eyes popped open, the rain stinging.

That was it, wasn't it? She'd believed she needed to be the one to pick up all of the pieces and make some semblance of a new life. As if her life was a jug of broken pottery and she had to find all of the fitting pieces to glue it back together, but half the pieces were missing.

God was the master potter. He was making something new. In her. Patiently molding her a new story, a new life filled to the brim with goodness and love. He hadn't abandoned her to her own devices, saying, "Here, you're on your own now. Figure it out." And He didn't patch old stuff. He was the Creator of new things.

"Thank you" was the only phrase she could breathe to the sky.

A different sense of urgency overtook her now. She checked the clock on her phone. She'd already been gone for an hour and a half—between packing, retrieving the bus and driving. Three missed calls. Ronan once and Kat twice. Kat had probably gone to Dusty Jackets to check on her and found she wasn't there.

She called Kat back first. She had a plan to surprise Ronan and tell him how she really felt.

"Where in the world are you, new girl?" Kat had answered on the first ring.

Hope told her what had happened. Everything. She floated with her newfound courage, her embarrassment paled.

Kat told her to stay put and she'd be there as quickly as possible.

When Kat arrived, she clutched Hope in a tight hug. "Don't ever do that again. I was so worried about you."

"I won't. I promise." She meant it.

They grabbed her things from the van and jumped into Red Betty.

On the way back, Kat told her Ronan had been summoned to face the council about the fire at the youth center in a special emergency meeting at the town hall.

"They might take it away."

Hope's heart clenched. "But that's not fair. Poppy set the fire."

"Yeah, but Tate was inside and said he'd been working. The council is laying blame on Ronan."

They shared a solemn glance.

"We need to get there fast."

She would do whatever she needed to, to show the council

the man she loved was full of the right integrity and responsibility to run the youth center.

Kat's phone rang on the hands-free cradle on her dashboard. She tapped it to answer. "Hello?"

"Hello?" Mrs. Baranski's voice poured out of the speaker. "Kat, is that you?"

"Hey, Mrs. B. Uh, I'm kind of busy at the moment. Can I call you about the next delivery another—"

"Kat, dear. This is important. Your mom said you might be with Hope. Is she there?"

Hope leaned forward. "Yeah, I'm here."

"Good, listen. I knew there was something else I was missing about your family, Hope. I did some digging in the old town documents. You know they're about to close down the youth center project, right? The historical society might be booted too. And even if we're not, I don't think we'll make it on our own."

Hope squinted at Kat and then the phone. "Okay..."

"Hope, your family, the Holloways, owned the bookbinding building. We found the record. It was a contract for deed sold by your grandma that went unpaid. It defaulted back to your family but eventually ownership was transferred to the city when your family didn't come back to claim it. I know it's a lot to ask, but if you would be willing to put some money behind this documentation of prior ownership, the council may be willing to reinstate the property to you."

She didn't have much on her own; she could only hope the treasure would help in the long run.

"Of course, I'll be there." When Mrs. B. hung up, Kat put out a hand for Hope to high-five.

"Now we need to convince the council, even if I was the property owner, that he's worth trusting with this youth center. He won't get the permits he needs unless they do."

Kat set her jaw. "Let's do this."

Today, she would be the Margaret Hale of her own story and save the day.

"Mr. Barrick." Harold Gunderson's mustache bristled. He glared across the long curved council table at Ronan. "You nearly caused a kid to die on the youth center grounds. How many families need to be hurt by you and your relatives for everyone to realize you're a danger? You can't be trusted."

Every muscle in Ronan's body, even the phantom ones of his lower right leg, tensed.

They knew it had been Poppy who started the fire, but it didn't matter to Harold. Not where it counted.

"Harold, I already told you I wasn't there."

"You're right, you weren't there." Harold drew out every syllable with agonizing precision.

Ronan closed his eyes for a moment. Was this his curse to never be there when he was needed?

No, God had shown him twice in the last couple of days, whatever curse lay on his family didn't extend to him. He'd helped save Tate from the building and was there for Hope on the island, not when he should've been, but even he couldn't be in two places at once.

But he hadn't saved Hope from the reporters. Now, while he was stuck in this emergency council meeting, she was probably a couple of hundred miles away and never looking back.

Kat had called him, worried when she showed up at Dusty Jackets to find it empty. She'd driven over to the youth center to see if Hope was there, but the bus was gone. He hadn't meant to scare her away. It was just that with the book and treasure hunt finally over, fear that she'd leave had paralyzed him. And because of him, she did.

The strength he'd had earlier to find Hope on the island, to keep her safe, was gone.

"What do you have to say for this level of negligence?" Harold tapped the tip of his pen against the tabletop, the sound like a sledgehammer in the quiet but full room.

He opened his mouth to speak, but two other voices spoke first.

"Hey, I have something—"

Ronan turned. Tate had run forward, but his mom clutched his arm. She looked so frail and red-eyed. They'd had quite the day too. Tate spoke to her in urgent, hushed tones. When he didn't continue, Harold shifted his scowl back to Ronan.

"Why was the boy there? Did you know he was there or not?"

The truth required him to out Tate for being there when he wasn't supposed to be.

Another voice spoke. To his shock, it was his dad. "Harold, you can't keep blaming my son for your son's death."

Harold's brows lowered over his eyes, making them almost disappear. "That is neither here nor there, and has nothing to do with this situation."

His dad clapped Ronan on the back and stood next to him, shoulder to shoulder. A thousand questions rocketed into his mind, none of which found their way out of his mouth.

His dad did the talking. "It has everything to do with this. You've always believed in the Barrick Curse, even when we were kids."

It was hard to imagine either austere, stubborn man ever being a kid.

Gesturing to his son, his dad kept going. "None of us can live in the past. Blaming my son, who did everything he could to save your son, will not bring Kyle back. Haven't we all lost enough?"

"Have you? Until you bury a son, don't talk to me about losing." Harold stood now, his face beet red.

Ronan studied his dad's profile. He'd lost a son too, just not to death. "It's not a hierarchy of loss here. We've all had our share of grief. Why hang on to bitterness to lose what life we have left?"

He spoke as much to his dad as to Harold. Understanding for the first time softened his father's face. The stone exterior started to move, change shape. A light shone through his father's eyes Ronan hadn't seen in years.

Harold sat, shoulders slumped, gaze far away like he'd forgotten they were in the middle of a meeting.

Feet shuffled behind him. Tate stepped forward this time. Ronan shook his head. He didn't want the boy to add one more incident to his record. *He* could give him another chance. He wasn't sure the council or a judge would do the same.

Tate raised his hand like a student eager to answer a question. "Mr. Mayor, I have something to tell you. I was at the youth shelter because I intended to steal rims from the storage building. I...I wanted to get my time extended. Ronan didn't know I was there and would never approve of me being there by myself." His words toppled out in a rush.

Harold's bushy brows gathered together. "The judge will hear about this, I—"

Ronan raised a hand. "No, that won't be necessary. I put in my report that Tate's work was exemplary. I do not wish to press charges and he didn't follow through with his intention to take something from the property."

A bang from behind interrupted Tate's confession. The doors in the back burst open so hard they'd slammed into the walls.

Two people pushed their way through the standing-room-only crowd in the back.

Kat…and Hope.

And Mrs. Baranski trailing behind. What was going on?

He hardly knew what to do when Hope stood before him.

She took the lead by grabbing his hand. A flood of relief and love washed through him. No matter what happened, it was going to be okay.

She winked at him. "I've got this. You don't always get to be the hero."

Kat waved at him casually, like he'd sauntered into the café.

Harold blustered. "What is this? You can't just barge up here like that."

Mrs. Baranski held up a piece of paper. "Oh yes, she can, if you're discussing the building that is her birthright."

Harold wasn't the only one to do a double take. Ronan expected Hope to laugh or say it was absurd, but she didn't.

Ethel handed Ronan the paper to inspect. It was the deed to the property under Magnus Holloway, who must've been Grace's dad. Ronan brought it to the front for Harold and then the others along the council table to inspect. Ethel also had a contract for deed with Hope's grandma named as the seller.

Harold lowered his chin, pinning Hope with his gaze. "And you can produce documentation that you're, in fact, related to this Magnus and Dottie?"

Ronan knew what this meant for Hope, to stand here and admit who she was to the whole town.

She swallowed, grasping his hand tighter as though to draw strength. He'd said he didn't have any left, but it had renewed the minute she walked in and he'd willingly give it all to her.

"Yes, that's right." Her voice strong and clear. "I changed my name to Hope Sparrow, and I can prove that my family was one of the first founding families here. Like the Barricks. It may take some time to get all of my paperwork for you, but I will and I am who I say I am. I'm here to make an offer to buy back the land from the city, if you'll accept. Though the payments may be pending the release of Ronan and my recent discovery of inherited family assets."

Harold conversed in low tones with his council members. "Fine. We are willing to consider it. This conversation is suspended until we have your documentation and, of course, proof of your ability to pay."

Ronan assumed she'd just say, "Thank you." Instead, she slid the backpack off her back and pulled out folded yellow sheets of paper. Grace's writing on them.

"I have something I'd like to read to the council and the town since we're gathered here." She caught Ronan's eye.

The crowd murmured, but Harold raised his hand to silence them. "You have the floor, Ms. Sparrow. Or should I call you…?"

"Hope is fine. This entry is from my ancestor Grace Holloway, Magnus's daughter, and she was good friends with Edward Barrick. This is her account of what happened the night of the shipwrecks over a hundred years ago."

She read the entry Poppy had scanned on the island. It told of how Ronan's ancestor Edward had been dragged away from his lighthouse post by the very pirates who'd unintentionally left them their treasure. And how Edward had saved Grace from a terrible fate—probably not too dissimilar from Hope's past.

"Ever since I arrived, I saw how Ronan and the Barrick family name have been dragged through the mud." She held the pages and turned to the crowd. "There is no Barrick Curse except for the one you placed on them."

After an encouraging smile from Ronan, she strode to the front of the crowd. "I've seen them treated terribly in this town, laughed at, belittled, even despised. But the thing is, we all have things we wish we could forget, people who've wronged us or we've hurt, pain and regret. Some of us have whole chapters of our past we would just as soon erase. But the past doesn't tell us who we are, only where we've been."

She turned back to the mayor. "How about a clean slate for the Barrick family? Let's change those local legends and history books to reflect the integrity and honor of this family."

Ronan was surprised by the tears in his dad's eyes.

And he wanted nothing more than an empty room so he could kiss the woman he loved.

Harold and the council nodded their acknowledgment and excused the assembly. Maybe this would change their attitudes or maybe not. But he walked out with Hope, hand in hand, and his town felt more like home than it ever had before. As though a curse truly had been lifted.

Ronan and Hope said they'd catch up with Kat, her family, his dad and Tate later.

Ronan walked her out to the park behind the town hall building, down to the gazebo overlooking the water. The sunset showed a brilliant display of the Creator's hand. Hope's amber eyes reflected the golden light, making his heart thud against his rib cage.

"I have something I want to say—" they both started, then chuckled nervously.

Ronan raised his hand. "Can I go first?" She nodded and he continued, "I'm sorry I acted weird to you today. I thought everything with my grandpa was my fault. That it was my job to save everyone, and then I found something I couldn't protect you from. The public eye. It was killing me. And with the search over, I assumed you'd leave. Then I made you do just that with how I treated you. But I finally realized I need to trust God with everything. Even your staying or going and your safety. Do you forgive me for acting like a jerk?"

She reached for his hand. "Yes, as long as you forgive me for running away like a coward."

"Nothing to forgive. And you're the bravest person I know, remember?" The clamp around his shoulders eased up. "What did you want to tell me?"

Hope clutched the railing of the gazebo. "I want to stay here in Wanishin Falls."

"You do? Just because you like the scenery?" Warmth and joy flooded his chest.

She laughed. It came out jittery. "Well, I like the view from here." Her gaze locked on to his and for once didn't skitter away.

"So, you're staying for the view. What about my family? And Kat?"

"Yeah, them too…"

He brushed a piece of her hair behind her ear. "Is there another reason you'd like to stay?"

If she was going to make this decision, she had to be all-in. She'd told him the truth about what was in her past and he hadn't run. So, she might as well tell him what was in her heart too.

"Because I… I—" her foot bobbed up and down "—love you. I think I love you more than I've ever loved anyone, except my mom." Oh, this wasn't going well. For a woman who'd read as many words as she had, she couldn't seem to make them come out right. "Maybe Mr. Rochester wasn't such an idiot when he said, 'Every atom of your flesh is as dear to me as my own: in pain and sickness it would still be dear. Your mind is my treasure, and if it were broken, it would be my treasure still.'"

She swallowed. "My mind, which overthinks everything, is just now catching up with what my heart, my *soul*, knew early on. I trust you. I feel safe with you. I believe in myself when I'm with you. I love you. All of you. The kind, gentle, book and wilderness-loving man that you are. I've never met someone as patient and compassionate as you are. Because of that, I started to trust God again. At least, I'm trying." Tears fell now, obscuring his expression from her.

She hadn't realized how hard she'd squeezed his hand until he untangled his to wipe the stream of tears on her cheek.

"That is literally the best thing I've ever heard. I love you, too. So, why do you seem so sad about it?"

"Just because that's how I feel and I had to share it with you doesn't mean any of the reality of my situation is gone." She threw her hands in the air. How could she sufficiently warn him? But did she *want* him to fully understand? What if he changed his mind about her and hightailed it away from her?

"What do you mean, your *situation*?"

"I mean, my past will always be the elephant in the room. And not a baby elephant. A giant purple elephant with wings. I don't know if I can ever act normal or not flinch when you try to touch me or not have panic attacks when I'm triggered. Where does that leave us? What kind of future could we have?"

"First of all, I'm thrilled you're even thinking about a future with me in it." He held her shaking hands again. "Second, do you love me because of or in spite of my past and anything that happened to me before we met?"

She sniffed. "I realize that those things are part of what made you who you are. But I love you for you. The past doesn't factor in."

"Exactly." He brought her hand to his lips and kissed the back. "I love you for who you are too. The whole you. Even the parts that are still healing. If I could do one thing in this world, I would take away every pain you went through. But I don't have to work around any of your past or how it affects you in the present in order to love you. I see all of you and that's the person I love and want to protect for the rest of my life. All right?"

"Yes, but I don't think you realize how hard this will be."

"You always assume you have to do everything alone, don't you?" He placed a gentle finger under her chin until she met his gaze. The warmth of his smile traveled to her toes. "We're in this together. We'll figure it out along the way, with lots of help."

Leaning toward her, he brushed a thumb along her jawline. She waited, but he kept himself an inch away. She'd dreamed of his last kiss. She needed another. Trying to be brave, she reached around to run her hand through the back of his hair. The skin on the back of his neck prickled beneath her fingers. Taking a deep breath, she closed the distance and touched her lips to his. Light at first. Then less tentative. Tender yet strong.

They pulled apart, staying close. He ran his hands through her hair, which she'd left loose, and pressed a kiss to her forehead.

She leaned back but kept her hand in his.

"I'd take a kiss like that every day for eternity." Heat crept into her cheeks.

"But?" The boyish grin had disappeared.

"Just make sure you don't want a simpler girl. Okay?"

He rolled his eyes in a way Tate would be proud of. "Stop trying to scare me away. I'm not that easy to get rid of. I don't want simple. I want you."

He leaned down and planted another kiss on her lips.

The fear that accompanied her wherever she went, for years, started to melt away. She understood Grace's words. Ronan's unconditional love mirrored the love of her Savior.

For the first time, she understood why God's word said His perfect love casts out fear. With His love filling her to the brim, there was no room for fear. How could she be afraid when the God of creation and this man in front of her loved all of her? Right down to every broken-but-mending place.

Epilogue

"Blow out the candles, birthday girl. Make a wish." Ronan's whispered words in her ear warmed and tingled her neck.

"I don't do wishes. Besides, I have nothing left to wish for, even if I believed in such a thing."

Their family—and they were now—gathered around the kitchen table at Ulysses and Mags's place. Kat and her family, Abe, Sophia, Ulysses, Mags, Tate, her and Ronan. Even Brock had stopped over for dinner. Their relationship would take time, but it was starting to repair.

Ronan slid his hands around her waist, standing close behind her. "A prayer, then?"

In her new counseling and equine-assisted therapy, she was learning to embrace the safety of their relationship. Things still took her by surprise and triggered her PTSD. Ronan was coming too, to learn what he could do to help her. Especially when she sank into a panic attack. Today, she held his arm firmly in place, reveling in the strength and trust there.

Kat whistled. "Seriously, you two. The cake is going to melt. Blow out the candles already."

She did. Everyone laughed and applauded. Her first birthday party since her mom had died.

Redeemed. Made new. That was how she looked at her life now. What had been taken away was given back tenfold.

Six months since she'd arrived and only four months since she'd decided to stay. And yet it was like looking at someone else's life when she thought about what had come before all of this.

She took the piece of passion fruit, mango and white chocolate sponge cake Kat offered her. Hope had insisted on making her own birthday cake. But it was the only thing they'd let her do for her special day. She watched her family laugh and enjoy themselves. The sparkle and weight of the ring on her left hand was something she was still getting used to. It felt steady, unchanging.

They'd planned a Christmas wedding, and it still took her breath away.

"Oh! I almost forgot. I've waited for the right time to give you this, Kat." Hope ran over to her purse hanging by the back door, found what she was looking for and bounded back to Kat at the kitchen counter.

"It's *your* birthday. Why are you giving me a gift?" Kat wiped at the peach-colored frosting on her lip.

Hope held out the keys to the mobile café-bookstore, now officially finished.

Understanding dawned. "I can't take this. Why are you giving it to me?"

"Like someone wise once told me, I need to put roots down to grow. Well, I'm doing that." She pressed the keys into Kat's open hand. "But other times you have to sprout *wings* to grow."

Kat's eyes misted over.

"Since I won't be needing this, maybe it can help you forge your own path. You told me you thought it would be cool to have a mobile library. Who knows? Maybe you'll come up with something no one's ever done before. A plan all your own."

Kat exchanged a glance with her family. Hope wasn't sure if maybe she'd done the wrong thing. But Kat squeezed her tight and whispered, "Thank you. No one's ever done anything like this for me."

After the birthday festivities died down and people either mingled at the table or in the living room, Hope sneaked away outside. The October wind held a bite so she grabbed her sweater by the door. This place, this view she loved. She could never get enough.

She stood on the back porch with her cardigan wrapped tight around her bare arms. She wore a short-sleeved shirt today, letting her battle scars show. Who would have dreamed that exposure to light would help scars fade?

This wouldn't be called Dusty Jackets much longer. Soon the place would become Hidden Treasures Café and Bookshop. She and Ronan would take over the day-to-day running of Hidden Treasures, though Mags and Ulysses could help or hang out, whatever they wanted. She'd finally found the heart of her cooking like Abe and Sophia said. It was here, cooking for the people she loved.

They'd submitted the compiled proof to show she was the Holloway heir and had finished work on the youth center and aided the historical society. The treasure had been signed over to them sans taxes. But it was a great responsibility. They were trying to be wise and generous with it. Poppy, as misguided as she'd been, had a point that just because their well-intentioned family had hidden it, they shouldn't keep it to themselves.

Last week, a detective with a special human-trafficking task force in Chicago had contacted her with Dee's help. They had tracked down King and his associates and wanted her to testify in court. She was still praying on it, but a peace had fallen over her instead of panic. The thought of putting him away so he couldn't hurt anyone else bolstered her assurance she could do it. That, and Ronan had already said he'd support her no matter what she decided and go with her if she testified. She prayed the other women, now set free, would come to know the peace and healing that was possible after a life of bondage.

She drew a long, cool breath through her nose.

The door creaked behind her, followed by the man she'd soon walk down the aisle toward.

She tipped her head toward the new shop sign leaning against the railing. The one Ronan had made. "A man—you know, the outdoorsy type—said that the best kind of bookshops are like treasure hunts."

"He sounds smart as well as good-looking." Ronan stood next to her and put his arm around her shoulders.

"He is. Quite the catch."

Ronan handed her something from his other hand, his face solemn. "It's from Gramps. I think he might've put this aside before he even knew you'd stay."

Ulysses was generally either in a different era or world now. They'd hired an in-home nurse who came out several hours a day to help care for him. But Hope still relished the time spent reading to him, making his favorite foods or just sitting with him, watching the relentless waves. She would cherish it until the end.

Hope took the book—a beautiful copy of *North and South* with blue mottled calfskin leather and gilded binding. She was learning from Ronan, who was now obsessed with the old binding machines they'd found on her ancestors' property.

"He remembered this is my favorite book." Tears sprang

to her eyes. She would add it to her other beloved books the police returned to her from Poppy's home.

"You mean a lot to him." He stroked her hair.

She opened it and a note fell into her hand.

In Ulysses's shaky writing was scrawled:

My dear Austenite,
Well done. I'm so proud of you, Hope. Your grandma and mother would be proud too. Take it from someone who only has this minute before the fog sets in again— enjoy sitting still. Relish the simple pleasures and the quiet heartbeats God has given you. For we have only the promise of this breath. The memory of this moment. Your grandmother and I brought you and Ronan through this treasure hunt, originally put together by Edward and Grace and then refined by us, in order to show you your ancestors and your heritage but also to help you find yourselves. I hope it has challenged and blessed you. But remember; our ancestors leave us their legacies, not our destinies.
Love,
Ulysses

Tears of bittersweet joy fell, and Ronan held her to his chest. Their two heartbeats became one.

Their destiny did lie before them, sure to have plenty of dead ends, detours and unexpected treasures along the way. The unknown no longer brought her panic. The verse she'd read to Dee whirled back to her. Her new routine had her up in the cobwebby hours of dawn with Fitzwilliam in her lap, a large steaming cup of tea in hand and her Bible open—the way C. S. Lewis had started his day—ready to meet with God in the hushed house.

The Proverbs verse kept coming back to her. Words that were once a distant hope had become quite near. Strength and honor clothed her, the shame stripped away, and she could indeed look to the time to come with rejoicing. Her loving Father and Author of life would write the rest of her story.

★ ★ ★ ★ ★

LOVE INSPIRED

Stories to uplift and inspire

Fall in love with Love Inspired—
inspirational and uplifting stories of faith
and hope. Find strength and comfort in
the bonds of friendship and community.
Revel in the warmth of possibility and the
promise of new beginnings.

Sign up for the Love Inspired newsletter
at **LoveInspired.com** to be the first
to find out about upcoming titles,
special promotions and exclusive content.

CONNECT WITH US AT:

 Facebook.com/LoveInspiredBooks

Twitter.com/LoveInspiredBks

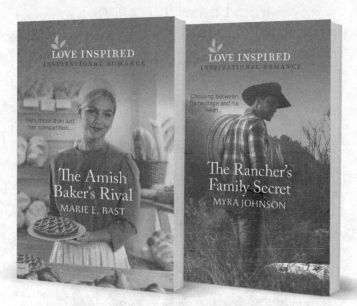

Inspired by true events,
The Secret Society of Salzburg
**is a gripping and heart-wrenching story of two
very different women united to bring light to the
darkest days of World War II.**

Don't miss this thrilling and uplifting page-turner
from bestselling author

RENEE RYAN

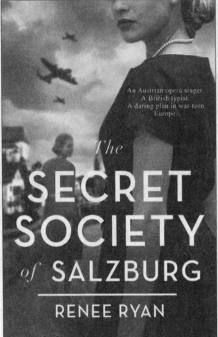

"A gripping, emotional story of courage and strength, filled with
extraordinary characters."
—*New York Times* bestselling author **RaeAnne Thayne**

Available now from Love Inspired!